MOORESTOWN LIBRARY
856-234-0333
W9-CHC-217

Hellcats and Honeygirls

Hellcats
and
Honeygirls

The Collected Collaborative Novels
of Lawrence Block and Donald E. Westlake

SUBTERRANEAN PRESS 2010

First Edition

ISBN
978-1-59606-303-7

Subterranean Press
PO Box 190106
Burton, MI 48519

www.subterraneanpress.com

TABLE OF CONTENTS

INTRODUCTION

IN AUGUST OF 1957 I answered a blind ad, took a test, and landed a job as an assistant editor at Scott Meredith Literary Agency, where I spent my days reading amateur work and writing encouraging rejections. (Encouraging because we wanted the authors to submit more material, accompanied by more reading fees; rejections because the stuff was, by and large, terrible.) It was a great learning experience for a writer-in-training, and by the time I left there the following May I had sold a slew of short stories and articles. The first thing I did when I got home to Buffalo was write a novel, and I wrote a batch more in the months that followed. I was by then back at Antioch College, and was supposed to be writing papers for my professors, but instead I was writing soft-core sex novels for Harry Shorten.

Around this time, Don Westlake answered the same ad, took the same test, and landed the same job. And he too began writing for Harry Shorten at Midwood, and I first became aware of him when I read his first Midwood title, *All My Lovers,* by one Alan Marshall. I remember a scene where the brothers of a slum girl, who's been led astray by a young executive type, go to the rotter's luxurious apartment and beat the crap out of him. Then they leave, and the scene closes with these lines: "They did not take anything. They were not thieves."

I thought that was pretty damn good, and wondered who'd written it.

A few months later Don got his first look at me, although it might have been through a one-way mirror for all I saw of him. I was in New York, on Christmas break, and had gone to the Scott Meredith office, where I was now a client, though not the sort whose picture they put on the wall for all to see. There was a sliding window in the antechamber where they hadn't put my picture, and Henry and I talked through it. And Don was in the bullpen office on the other side of that window, and saw me, although I did not see him.

And this was the conversation he overheard:

"That last book I delivered."

"*A Strange Kind of Love*. What about it?"

"Is it too late to change the dedication?"

"I'm afraid so. Why?"

"I'm not seeing that girl anymore."

Well, I went back to Yellow Springs, and the academic year finally ended, and in June I came back to New York and got a room at the Hotel Rio, on West 47th Street. I turned up at Scott Meredith one afternoon to pick up a check or drop off a manuscript, and I ran into a young fellow on a similar errand. It was Don, of course, who had quit editing and was freelancing, and who lived nearby himself, in a railroad flat on a very nasty block in the West Forties between Ninth and Tenth Avenues.

We introduced ourselves, and walked out of that office and into a friendship that lasted for fifty years. And that is why *A Girl Called Honey*, the first book in this triple volume and itself our initial collaborative effort, bears this dedication: "For Don Westlake and Larry Block, who introduced us."

I had one year to go at Antioch, but it was not to be. Sometime that summer I got a letter from the school saying they'd come to the conclusion that I'd be happier elsewhere. And I knew they were right. I was already doing what I wanted to do, and I figured I'd keep on doing it.

But by the end of the summer I'd decided against doing it in New York, at least for the time being. I moved back to my parents' house in Buffalo, and I went on writing books for Bill Hamling and Harry Shorten, and crime fiction for magazines. Don was doing much the same in New York. He and his wife and infant son were living in an awful block in Hell's

Kitchen when we met, and moved to the upper flat in a two-family house in Canarsie, a ten-minute walk from the Rockaway Parkway stop at the end of the Canarsie Line.

We stayed very much in touch. I don't think it ever occurred to either of us to pick up the phone; long-distance calls were for emergencies, or when somebody died. We wrote letters, and probably put more creativity into that correspondence than into our work.

And somewhere along the way we discussed the possibility of collaborating, and I wrote the first chapter of *A Girl Called Honey*. I sent a carbon copy to Don, and he wrote Chapter Two and sent it to me, and we continued in that vein until the book was done. We never discussed the plot or the characters. At one point I tired of a character he'd introduced, and killed him off, whereupon he retaliated by getting my character arrested for murder.

Damn, that was fun.

The lead's name was Honour Mercy Bane, and Don thought we should call the thing *Piece Without Honour*, and maybe we did. Who knows? We sent it to Henry, who sent it to Harry Shorten, who published it with the title it bears now. We split the money and decided we'd have to do it again sometime.

AND did, before too long. The second book turned out to be *So Willing*, and Shorten published that one, too. I don't know what we'd called it, but it may have been *The Virgin Hunt*, or something like that. This time Don wrote the first chapter, and we tossed it back and forth until we had a book. I may have moved back to New York by then. Or not.

One of Don's chapters began, "Oh well, what the hell, there was always Adele." But when the book appeared some idiot at Midwood changed Adele's name to Della. God knows why. My best guess is that his mother's name was Adele, and he took umbrage.

If he were here, I'd tell him what he could do with his umbrage. And one of the first things that occurred to me when Bill Schafer proposed reprinting these books was that good old Adele could have her name back. She wasn't even my character, it wasn't even my line, but I'll tell you, it's very satisfying to have it the way it was supposed to be.

THE third book was *Sin Hellcat*, and it was brought out by our other mutual publisher, Bill Hamling at Nightstand Books. The first two books were "by Sheldon Lord and Alan Marshall," and that's the byline we tacked on *Hellcat,* but Hamling was having none of it. The book was published as "by Andrew Shaw." I've no idea what our title may have been, but I'm sure it wasn't *Sin Hellcat*—not that there's anything wrong with it…

I blush to admit it, but I'm uncommonly proud of *Sin Hellcat*. If one writer had produced it, it would qualify as a *tour de force*; as the work of two pairs of hands, you could call it a *tour de force majeure*. As you'll see, it's a first-person narrative telling one story in sequential order, with other episodes of the narrator's prior life recounted one per chapter along the way.

What I like most about it is that it's no mean trick to tell which of us wrote a particular chapter. If I flip the book open and start reading, I can't necessarily tell myself. Somehow, without ever talking at all about the book during its writing, we matched our styles to a remarkable degree.

Oh, I could tell you now who wrote which chapters. But then I'd have to kill you.

DON and I never collaborated again after *Sin Hellcat*. Hal Dresner and I wrote a book called *Circle of Sinners,* with a structure inspired by the film *La Ronde*: the viewpoint character in the first chapter has it off with someone, who becomes the viewpoint character in chapter two—and so on. Hamling published the book, by either Andrew Shaw or Don Holliday, Hal's pen name. And I think we may have done a second book as well, but if so I can't recall anything about it.

Somewhere along the way, I collaborated with Bill Coons, a college friend of Don's who moved from Syracuse to New York to write Andrew Shaw novels. (He used my pen name and I vetted the books and took a cut.) At one point I started a book of my own, wrote three chapters, and hated it, so I took it around to Bill. "I can't stand what I've written here," I said, "so would you like to make it a collab? Write three chapters, and then we'll write alternate chapters until we have enough for a book, and we'll split what we get for it."

Bill agreed, and tossed the manuscript on a table and we went out for a drink. When he got home his wife had read the three chapters, the ones I said I couldn't stomach, and assumed logically enough that Bill had written them. "I think you're really getting better," she told him. "This is far and away the best thing you've ever done."

Astonishing, isn't it, that the marriage didn't last?

Years later, Don collaborated with Brian Garfield on *Gangway!,* a comic western. That inspired Don's definition of collaboration as a process consisting of twice the work for half the money.

And then, years after that, some reader turned up at a signing and told me he thought Don and I should collaborate on a Bernie Rhodenbarr-John Dortmunder adventure. Readers are always making suggestions, and I always hate them, but this one struck me as brilliant. Two professional criminals, both featured in lighthearted crime fiction—what could be a more natural combination?

But I could never get Don to go for it. At one point I wrote a first chapter, hoping it would get him into the spirit of things, but it didn't. He wasn't interested.

His initial objection was simple enough. The Bernie Rhodenbarr books were first person, the Dortmunders third. A combination first/third-person novel would read as if it had been designed by a Congressional committee.

I thought it would work just fine, but he wouldn't hear of it. A few years passed, and it struck me that nowhere was it carved in stone that Bernie had to narrate his stories. I could write about him in the third person.

Don allowed as to how that might work, then, and he'd give it some real thought when he had finished his current projects. And he may have meant it, or may have been being polite, but in any case nothing ever came of it. I don't know that the world's any the poorer for the lack of the book we might have written, but I'll bet we'd have had fun with it.

NOW, as I write these lines, Don's been gone a year and a week. And our three joint novels are now available in this handsome hardcover edition. I'm happy about this, and I can only hope that Don would be pleased as well.

I can't be sure of that, as he hasn't had any say in the matter. I do know that, in recent years, he became increasingly open about pseudonymous work that he'd previously kept in the dark. Part of this may have stemmed from a recognition of the inevitability of it all. There are people out there practicing a weird form of scholarship on the crap of which we who wrote it thought so little, and a quick search of the internet can unearth no end of information about our early work, some of which may even be true. The genie, alas, is out of the bottle, and the toothpaste is out of the tube. And, really, what difference does it make?

When Don agreed to have Hard Case Crime reissue some of his early books—crime novels, I should point out, which had nothing to apologize for—a mutual friend asked him why he thought this a good idea. The money didn't amount to much, after all, and the work was not as good as what he'd produced since then, and—

"The difference between being in print and out of print," Don told him, "is the same as the difference between being alive and being dead."

So I don't think it's too great an abuse of our friendship that I'm shepherding these three books back into print.

Lawrence Block
Greenwich Village
January 2010

A Girl Called Honey

this is for
DON WESTLAKE AND LARRY BLOCK
who introduced us

ONE

HER NAME WAS Honour Mercy Bane and she was thoroughly confused.

She was a very beautiful girl. If she had been in New York, sitting at a table at Twenty-One with a whiskey sour at one elbow and a wealthy escort at the other, she would have been a good deal more beautiful, or at the very least a good deal more spectacular. Beauty, despite the histrionics of a handful of hysterical poets, is more than face and figure, more than eyes and lips and even teeth, more than breasts and thighs and buttocks. Beauty consists also in the trappings of the face and figure.

A well-lipsticked mouth is more attractive than an unlipsticked mouth or, god forbid, a sloppily lipsticked mouth. A well-dressed body is more lovely than a poorly dressed body; unfortunately, the bulk of womanhood being shaped the way it is, a well-dressed body is more lovely than a stark naked body. Just as clothes make the man, the proper clothes make the man want to make the woman.

These fundamental tenets seriously militated against the appearance of Honour Mercy Bane.

For one thing, she was not sitting in Twenty-One. She was standing in the Greyhound Bus Terminal in the town of Newport in the state of Kentucky, and that is a far cry indeed from Twenty-One. Instead of a whiskey sour at her elbow she had a ratty cardboard suitcase in her hand.

Instead of a glamorous Schiaparelli original, she wore a man's plaid shirt open at the throat and a pair of faded blue denim trousers patched at the knees and worn at the cuffs. Her mouth had no lipstick to brighten it and her hair, instead of being done up in some exotic style or other, was completely uncoiffed. It just hung there.

But she was still a very beautiful girl, and this is striking testimony to the quality of eyes and lips and teeth, of breasts and thighs and buttocks.

Her hair was chestnut. The adjective is currently used to describe any shade that combines elements of red and brown, but in the case of Honour Mercy Bane it was the proper adjective. It was the color of ripe horse-chestnuts with the husk just removed and the nut still moist on the surface, a glowing red-brown that was alive and vibrant in the long hair that flowed freely over sloping shoulders.

Her face was virtually perfect. White and even teeth. A small nose that had the slightest tendency to turn up at the tip. Full lips that were quite red without lipstick. A complexion that was creamily flawless.

Superlatives could also be applied to the body which the man's plaid shirt failed to conceal and which the tight blue jeans made very obvious. Breasts that were large and firm and that got along without benefit of brassiere—which was fortunate because she was not wearing one. Legs that tapered from swollen thighs to properly anemic ankles. A behind that silently screamed for a pinch.

These, then, were the separate components which, taken together, made up the entity known to herself and the world as Honour Mercy Bane. The total effect was enough to bring words of praise to the lips of a Trappist monk. Not even the stain of a tear on one cheek could spoil the effect.

Seeing her there in the Newport terminal of the Greyhound Bus Lines, a passerby might have wondered who she was, what she was doing, where she was headed. Observing her, with the suitcase dangling from her hand like an umbilical cord after a birth, with a lost look on her face and an incongruous set to her jaw, one well might have asked these questions. The answers are simple.

Who was she? Her name was Honour Mercy Bane. She was eighteen years old, the only child of Prudence and Abraham Bane of Coldwater, Kentucky.

What was she doing? Standing, waiting, planning, thinking. Getting her bearings, really.

Where was she headed? She was headed for a small diner at the corner of Third Street and Schwerner Boulevard, a diner called the Third Street Grill.

She was going to get a job in a whorehouse.

CINCINNATI is a clean town.

This is an expression and little more. It does not mean that Cincinnati does not have garbage blowing around its precious streets, nor does it mean that Cincinnati juveniles do not write dirty words in lavatories. It means, in the coy jargon of twentieth-century America, that Cincinnati lacks prostitutes, gambling dens, dope parlors, and similar appurtenances of modern living.

The citizens of Cincinnati are no more virtuous than their brothers in Galveston or New York or Cicero or Weehawken or Klamath Falls. They are, on the contrary, as sinful and lowdown and sneaky and sex-crazed and vile as any other collection of people. But, fortunately for them, they have no need for prostitutes or gambling dens or dope parlors. Not in their home town.

They have Newport.

Newport is located directly across the Ohio River from Cincy. A streamlined bridge connects the two cities and makes it possible for Cincinnatians to get from Cincinnati to Newport in very little time. They don't even have to pay a toll.

And Newport, fair city that it is, has everything that Cincinnati lacks. Cathouses by the dozen. Gambling dens by the score, a pusher on every corner, and bootleg whiskey sold over the counter in every drugstore.

Residential Newport is as pleasant a little town as anyone could want to live in. The schools are relatively good. The streets are wide and lined with trees. The cost of living is low; the gambling and whoring and drinking keep down taxes.

Commercial Newport is the living end. No loose women walk the streets—this is strictly forbidden to eliminate amateur competition which would harass houses that charge five to twenty dollars for a quick roll. Dice games can never be found in darkened alleyways; a Cleveland syndicate runs gambling in Newport and runs it with an iron hand. If a person were stupid enough, he could walk the streets from dawn to dusk and from dusk to dawn without seeing anything out of the ordinary. But if he so much as mumbled his wishes to a cabby, he could enjoy any form of gambling, according to Hoyle, or any form of sexual activity, according to Krafft-Ebing.

Newport is a going town.

Madge liked it that way.

She sat at the counter, her big body perched precariously on a stool, her fingers curled around a cup of very light coffee. There was an ashtray next to the cup of coffee and a filter-tip cigarette was burning in the ashtray. A thin column of smoke rose from the cigarette to the ceiling in one long and unbroken line. Madge glanced at the cigarette from time to time but let it burn without touching it. She smoked between two and three packs of cigarettes a day but rarely took more than two puffs from each one.

Madge finished her coffee in a single swallow, then waggled a plump finger at the woman behind the counter. The woman was a beanpole in her forties with stringy washed-out black hair and protruding teeth. Her name was Clara and she had come to Newport years ago to be a whore, failed at it and became a waitress instead. Now she filled the cup half-full of coffee and half-full of milk and gave it back to Madge.

Madge sipped the coffee. She looked as unlike Clara as was humanly possible. Her hair was bleached a raucous blonde, her body as plump as Clara's was thin. She carried a tremendous amount of weight without being genuinely fat, and even though she was pushing fifty she remained sexually desirable, with a pretty kewpie-doll face and breasts that were still mildly appealing although they had lost their pep. Beautiful she wasn't, but she thought contentedly that she could still have a man when the urge hit her without paying some young jerko to satisfy her. If only she could lose about thirty-five pounds....

But that, she realized, was out of the question. When you were a junkie who was no longer using junk, you ate. You had to eat or you would get nervous, and it wasn't good to be nervous. Especially when you were a madam. A nervous madam made things hectic for the girls and set the customers on edge, and as a result the customers were occasionally impotent or at the very least enjoyed their turn in the saddle less than they would have otherwise. So you ate—it was better for your health and better for business, and at forty-eight you didn't have to be a beauty queen anyway, so the hell with it.

A Girl Called Honey

Madge was a junkie. She hadn't had a shot or a sniff in close to seven years, hadn't touched the stuff since they let her out of the federal hospital at Lexington and told her she was cured. But she was still a junkie and she knew she would be a junkie until she was dead, at which time she would become a dead junkie. She didn't call herself an ex-addict any more than members of Alcoholics Anonymous call themselves ex-alcoholics. She was well aware that at any time she might break down, might take a needle and load it up and pop it into a vein. The physical dependence was mercifully gone but the urge remained. It wasn't a constant thing—for that she thanked God, because if it had been she would never have lasted almost seven years. But there were times when the craving for heroin came to her, times when all she could remember was how good she felt when the white powder had been cooked in a spoon and shot home into her bloodstream.

At those times she had to remind herself of the bad part of it, the times when she couldn't score, the one abortive attempt at cold turkey when she locked herself in a cellar and clawed her own breasts raw when the full force of withdrawal symptoms hit her. And each time she mastered the craving, and now the cravings were fewer and further apart.

Now she was an inactive junkie. She didn't run around anymore, didn't turn a quick trick when the money had run out and she needed a fix, didn't have bad times like when she and Bill and Lucas had broken into that drugstore outside of Xenia up in Ohio to steal morphine, and the cops chased them for ten miles and they threw the stuff out of the windows of the car, and finally the fuzz caught them and she stood on her head in Lexington for a goddamned year....

No, now things were a hell of a lot better. Now she had a business of her own, and running a whorehouse was a damned good business to have in a town like Newport. You paid a certain amount every week to the right people, kept a lunch counter in the front of the house so that you didn't look bad from the street, took good care of your girls, talked friendly with your customers, and generally ran a decent establishment. If a girl got sick she went out on her ear. If a girl got knocked up you saw to it that she got rid of her excess baggage in the office of a cooperative and enterprising physician. You made a good living, not enough to get rich on, but enough so that you'd be able to retire before too long, enough so that you ate too much and kept a nice apartment and dressed as well as you wanted to dress.

There were footsteps coming from the rear and Madge turned around slowly. A tall thin man in a tan wind-breaker and Levi's was on his way out and she smiled at him automatically. He didn't smile back and he had a guilty look on his face. Madge wondered idly who he was cheating on—his wife or his girl or his religion.

"Come back and see us," she cooed.

He didn't answer and the screen door banged after he had gone. "Surly son of a bitch," she mumbled to herself, drinking more coffee and motioning to Clara for a hunk of Danish pastry.

Yes, she decided, it was a good life. The house was open from noon to four in the morning, seven days a week, and the girls worked eight-hour shifts. Long hours for whores, she thought, but there was plenty of time when they just sat around on their fannies with nothing to do. Made good money at it, too—half of every trick they turned, as much as they could get anywhere else. But they were worth it, damn it. A girl had to be a Grade-A hustler to get work at the Third Street Grill.

And they were damned good girls. Take the ones she had on the night shift now—Dee and Terri and Joan. She was one girl short ever since that tramp Lottie had run out on her, and the three of them were working like troupers to handle all the trade.

Take Dee, for instance. Dolores was her name, but that was too long a handle to be bothered with. Besides somebody had said that it meant sadness in Spanish and that was a hell of a name for a whore. Now Dee had been with her—she calculated quickly—God, Dee had been working there for a good four years, closer to five maybe. A hustler had to be one hell of a champion to last that long at one place, but as far as Madge was concerned Dee could work there forever.

Dee was tall, close to six feet tall, and she had the build to carry her height. High firm breasts that were about mouth-high for most of the customers. Legs and hips that were damn well muscled from good honest work. Thick black curly hair and a mouth that had a fine-looking smile on it even when she was working away for the fifth guy in an hour. And the men had told her how good Dee was, how she would do anything and do it perfectly. Dee was a jewel.

Not only that but the girl was good company. She wasn't so god-awful dumb like the rest of them. Why, the pair of them could sit down and talk over coffee, talk about real interesting things. Dee had been to college for a year; she was no dumbhead like the rest.

Take Terri, now. Now Terri was stupid, so stupid she didn't know her ass from her elbow. Fortunately there was another part of her anatomy which she was able to distinguish from her elbow, and which she used with remarkable skill. And Terri was easy to look at, damned easy to look at.

The bell rang and Madge eased herself off the stool and walked to the door. The man outside was a runt—a sawed-off little pipsqueak with a bald spot on the top of his dumb little head and a nose that was three sizes too big for him. He looked frightened.

"The counter's closed just now," she said breezily. "Would you like to go back and see a girl?"

He nodded quickly and she opened the door. He followed her lead and found his way to the parlor in the back where Dee and Terri were sitting. Joan was upstairs with one of her regulars. The sawed-off jerko picked Dee, just like all the little guys always headed for the biggest gal, and the two of them went upstairs.

Madge sat down again, bit off a hunk of Danish and washed it down with coffee. Let's see, where was she? Terri—that was it. Terri was short and blonde, a little on the chunky side but not so's anybody would mind it. The special thing about Terri was that she made a guy feel as though he was the greatest man in the world. Everybody who had Terri was firmly convinced that he had given her the thrill of a lifetime. This not only made the customers happy, but it brought them back for another go with the little blonde girl.

Joan was newer than the others and Madge hadn't yet decided what was so special about her. She wasn't hard on the eyes, but the little brunette wasn't beautiful by any means. Nothing really special about her, all in all—but she was good at her work and easy to get along with. A good man, according to the song, is hard to find; a good hustler is harder to get hold of.

The man who had been with Joan left smiling. A truck driver who stopped there whenever he had a haul through Newport came in and took Terri upstairs.

Time passed.

Madge was working on a slab of chocolate cake when the bell rang again. She swore under her breath and got up to answer it.

"The counter's closed," she began, the suddenly stopped in amazement.

The person standing at the door was not the general run of customer.

It was a girl with chestnut hair.

HONOUR Mercy Bane sat with her hands in her lap and looked at her nails. There was bright red polish on them, and she had never had nail polish on before. For that matter, never before had she been wearing such a pretty dress as the red-and-blue frock she had on now, never before had her lips been lipsticked and her cheeks rouged, and never before had she sat in the parlor of a whorehouse at eight-thirty in the evening waiting for a customer.

It hadn't been difficult getting the job. Madge needed a girl, needed one quite desperately with the weekend coming up and the rush sure to be literally backbreaking for Dee and Terri and Joan. Madge's experienced eye quickly knew what Honour Mercy Bane would look like in a dress and what she would look like out of a dress.

Madge had been a little put off at the girl's lack of experience. The madam preferred to hire a girl who had worked at a house before, or at least one who had done a little hustling. This was not the case with Honour Mercy Bane. She had had one and only one lover and that was hardly enough.

But she was beautiful, which made a big difference.

"Crap," Madge had said. "Fust thing we'll have to do is change your name. Can't have a whore named Honour and Mercy. It'd keep the customers from feeling right about the whole thing. Hell, you look too much like a virgin as it is. How do you go for the name Honey?"

Honey was all right with Honour Mercy Bane.

"Straight's ten bucks, half-and-half is fifteen, French is twenty," Madge informed her. "Anything special, you make your own price. You want to cut your rate it's your business, but you pay me half of the asking price, no matter how much you get. And don't think you can hold out on me. You might try to give me ten bucks for a French where you collected twenty and tell me you turned a straight trick. You'll get away with it for a while, but the minute I catch on you go out on your fanny."

"I wouldn't cheat you," said Honour Mercy Bane. And she was telling the truth because she never cheated anyone.

"You'll live in the Casterbridge Hotel down the street," Madge told her. "Gil Gluck runs it and he gives all my girls a straight deal. Ten bucks a week for a private room with private bath and it's a good clean place."

Honour nodded in agreement. She really didn't care where she lived.

"I'm trying you on the night shift this week," Madge went on. "It's probably a mistake, what with you so inexperienced, but I rotate the girls every two weeks and I don't want to mess up the schedule." Honour nodded again.

"Dee's just finishing up," Madge said. "She's been up there with a little pipsqueak of a guy for better'n fifteen minutes. Any second now she'll be down and she'll show you what's what and get some clothes for you and all."

A minute or two later a small man with a bald spot on the top of his head appeared with a huge smile on his face. In another minute a tall girl appeared with a smile on her own face and Madge introduced them. And up the stairs they went.

Dee taught her the ropes. The lesson was a time-consuming one but Dee didn't seem to mind. She taught Honour how to dress, how to undress, how to make up her face, how much perfume to use and where to put it, what to say to the customers, what they would want her to do and how to do it, how to make them want special things and how to do the special things, how to excite an impotent man, and how to make a man get through fast.

Important things.

How to clean herself so that she wouldn't get sick or pregnant. How to freshen up after finishing with one customer so that she would be ready for the next in a matter of seconds. How to be bright and friendly, how to look sexually desirable always.

Honour listened carefully. The tall brunette never had to repeat a word, and Honour remembered every word she was told. She concentrated and learned very quickly.

When the house closed, she went with Dee to the Casterbridge Hotel, a block away on Schwerner Boulevard and Fourth Street. There she was assigned a room on the second floor with a private bathroom and a comfortable bed and a nice rug on the floor. She took a restful bath, unpacked her ratty cardboard suitcase, and went to bed. She fell asleep at once.

The next morning she was awake by ten. It was Friday and she would start work that evening at eight o'clock. She had breakfast at a little restaurant on Fourth Street—Madge had advanced her fifty dollars against future earnings—and then went shopping. She followed Dee's elaborate instructions and bought what clothing she would need for the job, plus what cosmetics and supplies would be necessary.

Now it was 8:30. Dee and Terri and Joan were all upstairs with their first customers of the evening; soon it would be her turn. She sat alone in a lounge chair in the parlor, waiting for her first customer, her hands in her lap and her whole body in perfect repose.

Perhaps you are wondering what she was doing there, getting ready to play the whore in a room above the Third Street Grill in Newport. This was precisely what she was thinking about just then....

FIFTEEN hundred people live in Coldwater, Kentucky. Abraham and Prudence Bane lived in a small white frame house on the outskirts of town. Abraham Bane was a foreman at a distillery which was the town's sole industry; Prudence Bane was a housewife. They were good God-fearing Baptists, both of them, and their household was run according to the tenets of a frightening brand of Puritanism that started with Wycliffe and ran downhill via Cromwell and Cotton Mather until it lay half-buried in the Kentucky foothills.

Abraham and Prudence Bane lived by the Bible. Although Abraham Bane worked at the Kelmscott Sour Mash Distillery and served that distillery with a loyalty second only to the loyalty he bore to his strange and fearful God, not a drop of bourbon had ever passed his lips. He and his wife lived the clean life, the good life, and while their idea of an exciting evening was a hot game of checkers in front of the fireplace, the promise of heaven more than compensated for the relative boredom of their existence.

With this in mind, you may readily understand their violent reaction when they discovered their daughter, Honour Mercy Bane, with a man.

They were appalled.

The man who occupied the place of honor with Honour was a schoolteacher in the Coldwater high school, a thin and nervous man named Lester Balcolm. He had made love to Honour Mercy Bane many times before the two of them had been discovered in the act. He had told her that he loved her, and while she did not believe him, she did know several things. She knew the way her mouth tingled when he kissed her, the way her tongue felt deliciously alive when his tongue touched it and caressed it. And, finally, she knew what it was like to accept his manliness, to move with him and move with her own passion until it happened for both of them and they were bathed in the sweet sweat of love.

But they were discovered. Lester Balcolm left Coldwater with the marks of Abraham Bane's belt on his thin back and the warning that he would be killed if he was ever found in Coldwater again. Honour Mercy Bane left Coldwater with a ratty cardboard suitcase in her hand and the advice never to return ringing in her ears.

"You're no good," they told her. "You're not our daughter any longer.

And so she left.

"Go to Newport," they told her. "Be a bad woman there. You're not our daughter." And so she did.

THE man was huge. He had a shock of red hair that stood straight up on his cannonball head and eyes that looked like those of a recently slaughtered hog. He grinned at Honour Mercy Bane and she led him up the winding flight of stairs to the room that was hers for the evening.

They entered the room and she closed the door. She smiled as she had been taught to smile and the man grinned as he had grinned before.

"My name's Honey," she said.

"Good," the man said.

Her smile widened. "How do you want it?"

"What's on the menu?"

She told him the three standard varieties and the price of each. Then he smiled, reached out a hand and gave her breast a pinch. He didn't hurt her but she realized that with his muscles he could probably rip her breast right off her.

"I got a better idea," he said. "I got something special the two of us can do."

TWO

A MAN AWOL is a man running scared. Richie Parsons was a man AWOL, and he was scared out of his mind. A boy AWOL, really, for Richie Parsons had crept into his eighteenth year only a scant four months ago.

Richie Parsons was running scared. He was used to being scared, he'd been scared of one thing or another as long as he could remember, but he wasn't used to running. He'd never run before in his life, he'd always crept or sidled or tiptoed. His grammar school teachers had talked about him as "the shy, quiet little boy, the one who always edges along the wall, as though afraid to be seen." His high school teachers had mentioned him as "the loner, the boy who doesn't belong to the group, but only creeps around the fringes, watching and silent." His Tactical Instructor in Air Force boot training had complained about him as "the little sneak with two left feet." His contemporaries, in grammar school and high school and the Air Force, at all times and all ages, had spoken of him as "the gutless wonder."

Richie Parsons, eighteen years old, five foot seven-and-one-half inches tall, weighing one hundred thirty-five pounds, with watery eyes of a washed-out blue and Kansas drought blond hair, was everything everyone had ever said about him. He was silent, solitary, sneaky and gutless. And, at the present moment, he was also running and scared.

He'd hated the Air Force. He'd hated it from the minute he'd walked into the recruiting center for his physical and his qualification tests. He'd been one of a group of about fifty young men, thrown into close proximity with them all, and he'd hated that. When he'd tried to move back against the wall, away from the milling jumble, a uniformed sergeant had hollered at him to get back with the group.

They had all been herded into a long, cold, linoleum-floored room, and they had all had to strip, down to their shoes. Then they were fifty chunks of ill-assorted, poorly developed, goose-bump-covered flesh, forming a long line and shambling on by the bored and annoyed doctors, whose examination might have been funny if it hadn't been so pathetic.

Richie had hoped he would fail the physical. He knew he was weak, he knew he was underweight, and his eyes, without his plastic-rimmed glasses, were almost useless. But every doctor had passed him, even though he had fainted when they took the blood sample from his arm. He had fainted, calling attention to himself, and when he came back to consciousness, lying on the Army cot near the busily stabbing doctor, the rough Army blanket itchy against his nakedness, the whole line was looking at him. Frightened, embarrassed, so nervous he could hardly stand. He had crept back into the line, hoping they would all forget him, look at somebody else for a change, hoping somebody else would faint and draw the crowd's attention away from him.

He had passed the physical. But he still believed there was a chance he would fail the mental tests, the qualification exams. Until he took them, that is, he believed he might stand a chance of failing them. After all, he had never done very well in school. He had spent seven years getting through the first six grades of grammar school, and four years getting through the three grades of junior high school. He had only gone to senior high school one year, had flunked half the courses, and quit school at seventeen to join the Air Force.

But Mama hadn't wanted him to join the Air Force. Mama hadn't wanted Richie to do anything not suited to a boy of ten. So Richie had to wait until his eighteenth birthday, when he could enlist without Mama's consent.

And already, even before actually enlisting, he hated it, and he hoped he would fail the qualification tests, because he would never have the courage to just turn around and walk out. He would be doing something different, calling attention to himself, and he just couldn't do it.

Nor could he fail the qualification tests. High score was one hundred. Passing score was ten. If Richie Parsons had been imported just that day from the jungles of the upper Amazon, speaking only Ubu-Ubu and unable to read or write, he still could have passed the Armed Forces Qualification Test. In fact, there were three Puerto Ricans among the fifty enlistees, three Puerto Ricans who spoke only Spanish, and *they* passed the test.

The test went like this: On the left is a picture of a screwdriver. On the right are four pictures, a wrench, a hammer, a screwdriver, and a pair of pliers. You have to match the picture on the left with the similar picture on the right. If you make a mistake, one of the recruiters will come to you and "explain the instructions" to you again, to make sure you do it right.

Richie tried to fail. He tried his darnedest to fail, and he got a score of forty-eight. He passed with drooping colors.

In his four-month Air Force career, the only thing Richie really came close to flunking was basic training. Left and right were totally mysterious concepts to him. It took him a month to understand that spitting on a shoe doesn't make it dirty; when done right, spitting on a shoe makes the shoe shinier than ever. During familiarization with the carbine (in which there is no failing score), he plugged virtually every target on the field except his own. He was always at the wrong end of the formation when his group had KP, and he always wound up either in the garbage room or the grease trap. There were seventy-two trainees in his basic training flight, and his Tactical Instructor assured him he was by far the worst of the lot. When they all went to the indoor swimming pool to learn the proper way to jump off a torpedoed ship, in case they ever were onboard a ship and it happened to be torpedoed, Richie Parsons was the only one of the seventy-two basic trainees who had to be dragged, half-drowned, out of the pool.

There is always petty thievery in a barracks containing seventy-two young men. There was petty thievery in Richie Parsons' barracks, too. The petty thief is usually never discovered. Richie Parsons was never discovered either.

Richie Parsons had never once been discovered, in a lifetime of petty thievery. It had begun with Mama's purse, from which an occasional nickel or dime filched wasn't noticed. It had moved on to the grammar school cloakroom, where candy bars and coins, even if their absence were noted, could certainly never be traced. The junior high school locker-room had been next, and the magazine rack at the neighborhood candy store. And in the Air Force it was his barracks-mates' wall- and foot-lockers.

He was never discovered. He was never even suspected. His perfect record of perfect crime was not the result of any brilliant planning on his part at all. He didn't plan a thing. His perfect record was caused by equal parts of his own personality and dumb luck. His own personality, because he was such an *obvious* sneak. No one in the world skulked quite as obviously as Richie Parsons. No one in the world was as obviously incompetent in absolutely everything. A guy who is completely obvious in his sneaking, and completely incompetent in his actions, could never possibly get away with petty thievery. The idea never even occurred to anybody. During the eleven weeks of basic training, almost everybody in the flight was suspected at one time or another, but no one ever suspected clumsy, obvious Richie Parsons.

During the last couple of weeks of basic training, Richie and his fellow-trainees were classified. That is, they were tested, inspected, and assigned their particular Air Force careers, usually on the round-peg-square-hole method. Richie was given an IQ test, and amazed everybody, including himself, by coming up with a score of 134. Apparently, hidden down beneath the layers of confusion and cowardice and inferiority feelings, way down deep inside Richie Parsons, where it was never used, was a mind.

On the basis of this IQ score, and because it was one of the few careers open that week, Richie Parsons was assigned to Personnel Technical School, at Scott Air Force Base, near St. Louis, Missouri. He was given a seven-day leave at home after basic training, where Mama slobbered over him at every opportunity, and he edged along walls more furtively than ever, and then he took the bus and reported to the school squadron at Scott Air Force Base.

The Personnel Technical School was ten weeks long, but Richie Parsons only lasted the first three weeks. Then, all at once, he was AWOL and running scared.

It was the petty thievery again. There were only fifty-six young men in the barracks with Richie at Scott, and the barracks had been given interior partitions, forming cubicles, in each of which slept four men. There were no doors on the cubicles, no way to seal them off from the outside world.

As usual, in an open or semi-open barracks, there was petty thievery. As usual, no one suspected bumbling Richie Parsons, who was having such a terrible time in school, and who still didn't know his left from his right. No one paid much attention to the fact that most of the thievery was done on weekends, when everybody else was in East St. Louis, and Richie Parsons was practically alone in the squadron area.

Richie Parsons went to St. Louis twice, and East St. Louis once. St. Louis and East St. Louis have virtually the same relationship as Cincinnati and Newport. St. Louis is a clean town, where *all* the bars close at midnight, and the local churches have free Sunday breakfasts for the soldier boys from the air base and the Army camps that ring that city. East St. Louis is a hell-hole, where the bars never close, the cathouses have everything but neon signs, and the soldier boys work up their appetites for Sunday morning breakfast across the river.

The first time Richie Parsons went to St. Louis, he attended a major league baseball game, which was free to men in uniform. He'd never seen a major league baseball game, and it disappointed him. The second time, he went to the concert at Kiel Auditorium, which was also free to men in uniform. He'd never been to a concert either, and that bored him stiff.

The one time he went to East St. Louis, he was brought along by a few other guys and he was scared out of his wits. While the other guys trooped into the whorehouse, Richie stayed out on the sidewalk, furtive and scared and lonely, the gutless wonder to the end, incapable of either going inside to lose his virginity or going back to the base to save it. A dark-haired, evil-grinning girl in a ground-floor window of the whorehouse kept talking to him, saying, "Wanna make it with me, airman? We go round the world for fifteen, boy. Come on, live a little. Wanna see what I got for you? Hot stuff, airman. I do anything you want, boy, all you has to do is ask."

Richie made believe he didn't hear the woman, cooing at him from the window. He walked jerkily back and forth in front of the building, head down, staring hopelessly at the sidewalk and wishing he'd stayed at the base or gone to the USO in St. Louis. But all you could do at the USO was dance with high school girls, and he knew he'd be too afraid to ask a strange girl to dance with him. Besides, he was a terrible dancer; he danced the way he walked, furtively, sneaking and shuffling, round-shouldered.

Nobody noticed that the stealing didn't happen when Richie Parsons was in town. But everybody noticed the stealing, and people began to get mad about it. The Captain, the commander of the squadron, heard about it, and he called a special formation of that barracks, because there was more filching than usual going on there. "I want you men to find the sneak-thief in your midst," he told them, passing the buck. "You know the other men in your barracks with you. I want you to find him, and I want you to drag him to my office by the heels. And I won't raise a fuss if you kick his ass before you bring him to me."

Everybody liked that. The Captain was all right. Everybody watched everybody else, and nobody trusted anybody.

But still nobody noticed Richie Parsons.

Until that last Saturday night. A six-foot fullback named Tom Greery decided to find out who the hell the dirty crook was. He didn't go to town that Saturday night, though he would have loved to spend another ten on that red-haired Bobbi in the cathouse on Fourth Street. He stayed in the barracks, lying on the floor under his bed, looking down the row of cubicles at the shoes and bed-legs. The partitions didn't reach all the way to the floor, and he had a clear view all the way to the end of the barracks.

He spent four hours under the bed, impatiently waiting for something to happen. He kept thinking about redheaded Bobbi, with the pneumatic drill hips, and he kept getting madder and more impatient by the minute.

And finally he saw movement. Way down at the other end of the row of cubicles, a pair of feet came into view. They moved around in that cubicle for a minute, and Greery wondered whether he should make his move yet not. But this might not be the sneak-thief. It might be guy who bunked in that cubicle, and Greery didn't want his presence to be known too early. Not until the lousy bastard son-of-a-bitch of a thief showed up.

The feet, moving very softly, left that first cubicle, and reappeared in the second. Greery watched, growing more and more sure of his quarry. When the feet moved on to the third cubicle, Greery was positive he had his man. Awkwardly, trying to be absolutely silent, he crawled out from under his bed and tiptoed down the center corridor, past the empty and defenseless cubicles, to the one where his man was waiting. He got to the doorway, looked in, and saw Richie Parsons with both hands in Hank Bassler's foot-locker.

"All right, you son-of-a-bitch," said Greery, and Richie leaped around, terror and confusion distorting his face. "Now," said Greery, "I'm going to kick the hell out of you."

"Please," said Richie, but that was all he said. Because Greery was as good as his word. He kicked the hell out of Richie Parsons, and then he dragged him, with a painful grip on Richie's elbow, out of the barracks and down the row to the Squadron Headquarters building.

But the Captain, too, was in East St. Louis, working up an appetite for Sunday morning. There was no one in HQ but the Charge of Quarters, an unhappy airman given the duty of sitting around the orderly room all Saturday night, in case the phone rang.

Greery shook Richie Parsons by the elbow, and announced to the Charge of Quarters, "I got the bastard. The lousy sneak-thief."

"This one?" asked the CQ in surprise.

"Caught him red-handed," said Greery. He spoke in capitals. "Caught Him In The Act!"

"You want me to call the AP's?" asked the CQ.

"No," said Greery, considering. "The Captain will want to see this little son-of-a-bitch." He shook Richie again, and glowered at him. "You hear me, you bastard?" he said. "You are going to go on back to the barracks, and you are going to hit the rack, and you are going to stay there until Monday morning. You hear me?" Richie nodded, quivering.

"Eight o'clock Monday morning," said Greery, "we are going to go in and see the Captain. You better show up, too. If you don't, you're AWOL. You've got your ass in a sling as it is, so don't add AWOL to everything else."

Richie shook his head, mute and terrified.

Greery dragged the sneak-thief back to the barracks, booted him through the doorway, and went off to town to see the redhead, Bobbi.

Ninety-nine out of a hundred people in Richie Parsons' position would have stayed and taken their punishment. Richie had only been in the Air Force four months, and he had been well-indoctrinated, as all recruits are, in the horrors of going AWOL. It was, all things considered, a much more serious crime than thievery.

Besides, ninety-nine out of a hundred in Richie Parsons' position would have realized they could beat the rap without half trying. Monday morning, you go to see the Captain. You're all bruised up, because Greery kicked the hell out of you. You look scared and remorseful and hangdog. You throw yourself on the Captain's mercy. You tell him this is the first time you've ever done anything like this, and you don't know what made you think you could get away with it. You mention—not as an excuse, because you know and admit there isn't any excuse for your terrible behavior, but just in passing—you mention the fifty-dollar allotment (out of your eighty-four-dollar a month pay) that you are sending home to your widowed mother. The Captain looks at your Service Record and sees that you do have a fifty-dollar allotment made out to Mama, and that your father is dead. He sees how contrite and terrified you are, and he sees that you've had the crap kicked out of you. So he gives you a stern chewing-out, and lets you go, with the warning that next time you'll be court-martialed. You go back to the barracks, where everybody joins in to kick the crap out of you again, and it's all over and forgotten. And you don't do any more stealing until you've been reassigned somewhere where nobody knows you.

Ninety-nine out of a hundred people could have figured that out, and acted accordingly. Richie Parsons never did go along with the group, not in anything.

Richie Parsons went AWOL.

He packed a small suitcase, stuffing some uniforms and underwear into it, put on civilian slacks and shirt and jacket, and took the base bus to the front gate. East St. Louis was down the road to the left, to the west. Richie headed to the right, to the east.

The only sensible thing he did was bring along a complete uniform. They'd told him in basic training what the difference was between AWOL and Desertion. When you were AWOL, you figured to come back some day. When you Deserted, you planned to never come back. And the evidence that counted was your uniforms. If you threw your uniforms away, or sold them, or pawned them, then you weren't planning to come back. You were a Deserter. If you held on to your uniforms, you were planning to come back. You were only AWOL. The difference being that Deserter gets a Dishonorable Discharge, and somebody who's AWOL gets thirty days in the stockade.

Richie Parsons wasn't planning on coming back to Air Force, not ever. But he remembered the ground rules of the game, so he brought along a complete uniform, just in case he was caught.

He headed east across Illinois, hitchhiking, terrified of cops and Air Police and just about every adult he male saw. He got a few rides, across Illinois and southern Indiana and into Kentucky, and up through the tobacco fields of Kentucky toward the Ohio border and Cincinnati. And one ride he got left him in Newport, Kentucky, at nine o'clock on Monday evening. The old farmer who'd given him the ride pointed out the direction to the bridge for Cincinnati, wished him luck, and putted away down a side street. Richie started walking, lugging his suitcase.

He was running, and he was scared. He didn't know where to go, he didn't know what to do. He knew only that he couldn't go home, to Albany,

New York. He knew the Air Police would first look for him there, and they would watch his house. He couldn't go home.

And he didn't know anyone at all anywhere else in the world. Billions and billions of people in the world, and he knew only a handful of them. A few relatives and schoolmates in Albany. A few guys who hated him at Scott Air Force Base. He didn't know anybody at all anywhere else in the whole wide world.

He had about sixty dollars left. He'd gone through the barracks like a vacuum cleaner before he left, grabbing bills, change, rings, watches, electric razors, everything he found that could possibly be turned into cash. He'd had to carry the stuff on him all weekend, but today, Monday, he had pawned his way across Kentucky, leaving one or two pieces of stolen property in every pawnshop he saw. All he had left now were a watch and a high-school ring, and the pawnshops were closed at that hour. They would go tomorrow.

He was hungry. He hadn't eaten since ten o'clock this morning. He decided to find a diner or something here in Newport, before walking to Cincinnati and hitchhiking farther on to wherever it was he was going.

He was on Third Street, with Schwerner Boulevard just ahead. Down at the corner was a diner, with a modest red neon sign saying, "Third Street Grill."

He walked faster, feeling the hunger pangs inside him. He got to the diner and pushed on the door, but nothing happened. He looked through, and saw that the diner was all lit up. A skinny, stringy woman in a soiled white apron was behind the counter, and a plump, well-girdled, incredibly blonde woman was sitting on one of the stools, drinking coffee and eating Danish pastry.

The place was open. That was obvious. But the door was locked, or stuck, or something. Richie looked at the door, trying to figure out how to open it, and saw the bell-button on the right. He'd never been in Newport before. He'd never been much of anywhere before. As far as he knew, you had to ring the bell to get into all diners in Newport. Maybe that was the way they worked it.

He pushed the button.

The plump woman eased herself off the stool and padded to the door, looking heavy and ominous and much too mother-image. Even before she opened the door, Richie Parsons was terrified, his mind a daze.

The woman opened the door, and grinned at him. "The counter's closed just now," she said, speaking rapidly in an obviously-routine pattern. "Would you like to go back and see a girl?"

Richie was a blank. The woman had asked him a question, something that had sailed on over his head. He was afraid she suspected him, that she would turn any second and call the police: "We've got a Deserter here for you!"

He nodded, jerkily, hoping it was the right answer, hoping his face wasn't giving him away, hoping he'd get out of this all right, and be able to hurry on out of Newport.

It was the right answer. The woman's smile broadened, and she stepped back from the doorway, motioning to Richie to come in. He did, and followed her through a door to the right of the counter. She motioned for him to go on back, patted him chummily on the arm, and went away to the front again.

Richie, not knowing what else to do, barely knowing his own name at this point, kept on down the hall, and found himself in a dim-lit parlor, where a girl with reddish-brown hair and a smiling mouth was looking at him from where she sat in an over-stuffed chair near a doorway and a flight of stairs leading up.

The girl got to her feet and walked toward him, smiling, her eyes fastened on his, her body undulating gently as she moved. "Hi," she murmured. "My name's Honey."

And Richie Parsons, numbly gripping the handle of the suitcase, finally realized he was in a whorehouse.

FOR Honour Mercy Bane, the last two weeks had been busy (though happily, not fruitful) ones. There'd been so much to learn, much more than she'd expected. It was, in many ways, more difficult to be a bad woman than to be a good woman. No good woman ever had to douche herself twenty times a day. No good woman had to keep smiling when her insides felt as though they'd been scraped with sandpaper; and here comes another one. No good woman had to try to be glamorous and desirable while doing the most unglamorous things in the world. Such as accepting money, and even sometimes (how silly could men get?) having to make change. Such as checking a man for external evidence of disease. Such as squatting over an enamel basin.

No good woman had to learn as much about the act of love, and its variations, as a bad woman did. And no good woman was exposed to quite so many variations all in one day.

Not that Honour Mercy Bane was unhappy in her chosen profession. Far from it. There were any number of things she enjoyed about it. First and foremost, of course, she enjoyed men. By the end of an eight-hour stint on her back, her enjoyment was usually on the wane, but she always snapped right back with it the next day, just as fresh and eager as ever.

And she liked the other girls, her coworkers. The other three girls on the night-shift with her were the ones she knew best, of course: Dee and Terri and Joan. Dee was a little difficult to understand, sometimes, with that big vocabulary of hers, but she was really friendly, and gave Honour Mercy a lot of good advice. Dee was a real pro, a girl who'd been working here for almost five years and knew just about everything there was to know about the business. Madge didn't know it, but Dee was saving up to start a house of her own. She talked with Madge a lot, finding out what it took to become a madam, who had to be paid off, the ins and outs of the trade. And Dee had promised that Honour Mercy could come with her when she set up her own place.

Joan was kind of strange, in a way. She never talked much, never seemed to care to go to the movies in the afternoon with the other girls or do anything, never seemed to care about anything but her eight hours a day at the Third Street Grill. She was friendly, but reserved, saving her smiles for her customers.

Terri was Honour Mercy's best friend of the bunch. Terri and she enjoyed the same things, loved to go to the matinees at the movie down the block from the hotel, loved to go window-shopping. They could talk together for hours without getting bored. Terri had come from the same kind of town and family as Honour Mercy, and for pretty much the same reason, and that made a bond of understanding between them.

As for Madge, Honour Mercy didn't see much difference between Madge and her parents back in Coldwater. They both had strict sets of rules and regulations, ironbound values, and absolutely insisted on complete obedience. Madge's set of rules and values was, of course, quite different from Honour Mercy's parents', and a lot easier to conform to, but the similarity was still there.

This was now her second Monday night, and her last night shift for two weeks. Starting tomorrow, she'd be on the noon-to-eight shift, which meant a little less money, but that was all right, because her period of forced inaction would come during that time. It would be better than being inactive while on the night shift, which was what kept happening to Terri.

In the last two weeks, she had come to learn that every man is different, and every man is the same. Every man is different in the preliminaries, and every man is the same in thinking that he is different in the act itself. At least twice a night, someone would come in with a brand-new variation he'd just thought up, and these variations were never brand new at all. Of course, Honour Mercy wouldn't tell the poor guy he wasn't as original as he thought he was. After all, it was extra money for extra service, and special tricks rated as extra service.

She had been worried that the other girls would get all the business, because they knew more, but it turned out that she got all the business she could handle. There was something naturally fresh and unspoiled and virginal about her, and a lot of men were attracted to that, liked to have the impression that they were the very first, though of course they had to know better, since she was working here and all. But still, they liked the impression, and she was making darn good money at it.

Of all the men who had come to see her in the last two weeks, this pop-eyed boy with the suitcase was by far the most different and most same one of them all. The fear and indecision and doubt that were, she knew, hidden deep in every man that paid his way here, was right out in the open on this boy's face. Sameness and difference. It was strange that a thing could be the same and different all at once.

She spoke to him, and he simply looked more pop-eyed than ever. Dee had told her, when a man got stage-fright in the parlor, bring him immediately upstairs. Seeing the bed will snap him out of it, one way or the other. Otherwise, you could waste half an hour with a man who might change his mind at the last minute and run off without paying a cent or doing a thing.

So Honour Mercy took the pop-eyed boy by the elbow, and gently led him upstairs. He followed obediently enough, but he didn't look any less terrified, no matter how much she smiled at him, or how gently she talked to him.

She led him to her room, empty except for the sheet-covered bed and the stand and the chair and the enamel basin and the sink. And, upon seeing the bed, he froze solid.

"Come on, now, honey," she said soothingly. "It isn't as bad as all that. Why, some men even think it's fun. Specially when I do it with them. You come on, now."

He stayed frozen.

This was the first time a man had done this, but Honour Mercy was ready for it. Dee had warned her it might happen, and told her the antidote was nudity. She should take off her clothes, in front of him, as provocatively as possible.

She did. She crooned to him, telling him how much fun it would be, and she slipped out of her dress, wriggling her hips to make the dress slide down away from her body. Beneath the dress she wore only bra and panties. A slip was a waste of time, and a girdle would be a horror to remove.

She kicked off her shoes and walked over in front of the boy. "Unsnap me, will you?" she asked him, and turned her back.

She was afraid he'd stay frozen. If he didn't unsnap her, she didn't know exactly what she could do next. She waited, her back to him, holding her breath, and all at once she felt his fingers fumbling at the bra strap.

"That's a good boy, honey," she said. She turned to face him again, still smiling, and said, "Slip the old bra off me, will you, honey?"

His face was still frozen, but his arms seemed capable of movement. He reached up, gingerly, just barely touching her skin, and slid the bra straps down her arms, releasing the fullness of her breasts.

She cupped her hands under her breasts. "Do you like me?" she asked him. "Am I all right?"

He spoke for the first time, with something more like a frog-croak than a voice. "You're beautiful," he croaked, and his face turned red.

"Thank you," she murmured, and leaned forward to kiss his cheek, rubbing her body against him as she did. He stiffened again, and she swirled away, afraid of rushing him. She slid out of her panties, and walked, hip-rolling, toward him, her arms out to him. "Come on now," she crooned. "Come on now, honey, come on now."

His head was shaking back and forth. "I didn't know—" he started. "I thought—I didn't know—"

"Come on now, honey," she whispered, her outstretched arms almost reaching him.

"I can't!" he cried suddenly, and collapsed at her feet, sitting on the floor and covering his face with his hands.

She stared at him, amazed, and suddenly realized he was crying. A man, and he was crying. It was the strangest thing that ever happened.

She knelt on the floor beside him and put a protective arm around his shoulders. "That's all right, honey," she whispered. "That's all right."

"I can't," he said again, his voice muffled by his hands. "I can't, I can't, I can't. I've never done it, I've never, never done it. I don't know how, I can't—"

It seemed as though he'd go on that way forever. Honour Mercy interrupted him, saying, "If you never did, honey, how do you know you can't? There's a first time for everybody, you know. There was a first time for me."

Something—her voice, her words, her arm around his shoulder, she wasn't sure what had done it—something managed to calm him, and he looked at her with the most pathetic and wistful expression she had ever seen. Like a lost puppy, he was.

"I can show you how," she whispered. "It'll be all right, you'll see."

"I don't think I can," he said hopelessly.

"We'll try," she told him. "Here, I'll help you with your clothes."

Normally, she discouraged a man from undressing completely. It meant more time spent afterward, waiting for him to dress. But this, she knew, was a special case. This was the pop-eyed boy's first time, and she felt that it was her job to make it as good for him as she possibly could. She didn't stop to think that she was feeling this way solely because the boy was the first person she'd met in the last two weeks who was even less experienced than she.

She helped him undress, even to his socks, and they both looked at his body. "You see," he said mournfully. "I can't."

"Yes, you can," she said. "Come on to bed, and we'll take care of that."

Obediently, he crawled onto the bed with her, and they lay side by side. She touched him, holding him with one soft hand, and smiled at him. "I'll make you ready," she promised him. "Don't you worry."

"I want to," he said. "I really do, you're beautiful and I wish I could. But I just don't think I can."

"Yes, you can. Now, when you go downstairs, if Madge—that's the heavy woman out front—if she asks you what you had, you tell her it was just a straight trick. That's ten dollars. You've got ten dollars, haven't you?"

He nodded vigorously.

"All right. You tell her it was just a straight trick." She smiled again, and squeezed him. "But it's going to be a lot more than that," she told him. Dee had told her how to get a man ready, all the different ways, and she did them all. At first, he lay awkwardly on his back, his brow furrowed with doubt and alarm, but gradually he relaxed to the soothing strokes of her voice and hands and lips. And all at once he was ready, and finished. It had happened like that, so fast, and he looked mournful all over again. But she whispered to him, fondled him, assured him would be all right, and soon he was ready again, and this time it lasted. She didn't have to fake passion this time. Then he was finished again, completely finished this time, and they went through the mechanical aftermaths without losing any of the glow. He paid her the ten dollars, and she took him back downstairs, where she squeezed his hand and said, "You come back again, now, d'you hear?"

"I will," he said. "I sure will."

THREE

WHEN SHE AWOKE she was not alone and for this she was very grateful. The monotonous walls of the hotel room were painted a dull gray that was no color at all and the made her feel trapped sometimes. A few pictures here and there might liven up the walls, and several times she had told herself to tear a picture or two from a magazine and get some scotch tape at Mr. Harris's drugstore on the corner, but she never remembered and the walls remained as depressing as ever. When she woke up they seemed to hem her in, and when she went to sleep they appeared to be watching her.

But now, now that she was no longer alone upon awakening, the walls were not nearly so hard to bear. Now that there was another warm body beside her own warm body, another human being sharing her bed, now everything was much more pleasant and it was a genuine joy to open her eyes and face the day.

She yawned a luxurious yawn with all her muscles participating. She stretched and yawned again. She closed her eyes and snuggled her face against the pillow that was warm with the cozy warmth of her own body heat.

When she opened her eyes again Richie was still in bed and still had not moved. She put her head on his chest and listened to his heart beating, listened to the rhythm of his breathing and smiled a slow and secret smile to herself. She put out a hand and touched his chest right over his heart, touched him once and just for a moment, and then removed her hand. He didn't move, didn't wake up, but he made a small sound through closed lips and he seemed to be smiling in his sleep.

He's just a little boy, she thought contentedly, and she put her head back on her warm pillow and closed her eyes again and thought about him, her little boy. She was glad that he was the way he was, that he was like a little boy and all afraid of everything and never quite sure what to do. He needed to be taken care of, needed her to hold him and cuddle him and watch him sleep, and for this she was thankful.

She remembered that time, the first time with him, and she remembered how he had been waiting for her when she left the house that night after work was finished. It was 4:30 in the morning by the time she got out of the house and the sun was getting ready to think about rising. The sky was light. The first birds were already out after the first worms and the ground was moist with dew.

She left the house and headed toward Schwerner Boulevard. She had walked maybe thirty yards when she heard a voice, a voice calling "Honey!" It was a few seconds before she realized that the voice was calling her because Honey was only her name during working hours, and that only with customers. Madge and Dee and Joan called her Honour. Terri, who seemed to think her full name was humorous, called her Honour Mercy, sometimes Honour Mercy Bane. She would drawl it out southern-fashion until even Honour Mercy, who thought her name a perfectly sensible one, would find herself laughing.

But now a voice was calling "Honey!" and the Honey it referred to was quite obviously herself. She turned around and got scared for a minute because he was just a foot or two away from her, his eyes very intense, his mouth half-open and scared.

"Oh," she said. "It's you."

He seemed frightened by something, but after she took his arm he wasn't frightened any more. He told her that he had just come to town, that he didn't know where to go and that he didn't have any place to stay. She nodded thoughtfully, liking him and feeling sorry for him, and the two of them began walking toward Schwerner Boulevard. She was taking him to her hotel, although she did not know it at the time, and would have been surprised if someone had suggested it to her.

On the way he talked, talked about himself, and from the tone of his voice she got the feeling that he was telling her things he had never told anybody before, telling them to her without knowing why. Her customers often talked to her, sometimes before but more often afterward, but now it was not as if it was a customer talking to her. When the customers spoke she would nod her head and say "Uh-huh" without really hearing a word they spoke, but now she listened to everything he said. It was more like talking with one of the girls in the house but it wasn't quite like that either.

He told her that he was supposed to be with the Air Force at Scott Air Force Base near St. Louis. He told her that he was AWOL, that he had left without permission and would be punished if they caught him. He did not explain why he had left the base, not that night, although he did tell her several days later, but she knew then that he had done something wrong and that was why he had left.

She was glad to hear his confession. When he told her, she felt a kinship with him—they both had done something wrong and had been forced to run away. Neither of them could go back where they had come from. She was very glad, and when he told her she understood the similarity between them and she hugged his arm tighter.

At the entrance to the Casterbridge Hotel they stood awkwardly for a moment and he shifted from one foot to the other. Then she told him that he could stay with her for the night—or morning, more accurately—because it was no hour to go looking for a hotel room and because the police might arrest him if they found him out on the streets at that hour. He accepted gratefully and they went into the hotel and up the stairs and down the corridor to her little room.

In the room they got undressed and ready for bed and it was very funny to her. They undressed and they were not unaware of each other or embarrassed by each other. They were two human beings undressing and getting ready for bed and it was an extremely natural thing.

She turned out the light and they got into the little bed. It was a small bed and they were very close together and each was very conscious of the presence of the other. At first she lay down with her back toward him, but then she rolled over and let him take her in his arms. He kissed her and he did it very awkwardly because he did not know anything about kissing. It was the one thing she had not shown him that night, and he did it badly as a result, but she didn't mind because she thought it was cute the way his nose pressed against hers and the way his hands on her back moved shakily and nervously.

Then she showed him how to kiss, how to make his mouth behave the way his mind wanted it to behave, and they lay very still holding each other and kissing each other, lips gentle and tongues explorative. His hands examined her body with a combination of wonder and admiration and he murmured "Honey, Honey, Honey!" into her chestnut hair.

She told him her name was really Honour Mercy, and after that he never called her Honey again but always called her Honour Mercy. He always used both names, but when he said it it never sounded funny the way it did when Terri said it.

They did not make love that night. That is, they did not take possession of one another. In a larger sense they made love much more certainly than two strangers who copulated. They held each other close all night through, and while both of them were far too tired for intercourse, then simple presence together was a full and satisfying act of love.

She had been the first woman for him and she was glad, glad that it had been she who taught him how to love. Other women are generally grateful for a man's experience rather than for the lack of it, but for her it was the other way around. She had already decided that experience wasn't particularly important, that one man was quite like another in bed, that the ones who had done the most and bragged the loudest were usually the most disappointing. Men seemed to think that their prowess hinged upon the length of time they could sustain intercourse, and the variations with which they were acquainted.

Other things were more important: the joy Richie took in her body and in his own, the happiness she was able to bring him, the shy smile on his young face and the mistiness in the corners of his eyes, the way he held her hand. Another man, while he knew seventeen variations on the old theme and could sustain the act almost indefinitely, never could make her feel the way Richie did.

And so she was glad she had been the first for him. In another way he was the first for her.

He was the first man she ever slept with.

When she went to work the next day at noon, he took her work for granted just as she took it for granted that he would be there when she returned. The two of them moved into another room on the same floor of the Casterbridge Hotel, a larger room with a double bed, and that night he unpacked his suitcase and hung his Air Force uniform on a hanger in the closet.

They never talked about her work. It was her job, a well-paying job and a job she enjoyed, and in his mind as well as hers it was completely divorced from their life together. He accepted it so completely that it was unnecessary to talk about it. In turn she accepted the fact that he had to stay in the hotel room as much of the time as possible, that he couldn't get a job or spend much time out of doors because the Air Police might be looking for him. She put in eight hours a day at the house, and during those eight hours he read the paperback novels and detective magazines that she bought for him at the drugstore. She thought now that she would have to remember to get him some more magazines on her way home from work, and reminded herself that she ought to pick up a roll of scotch tape at the same time and put some pictures up to make the room nicer.

She ran her hand over his chest, stroked his stomach, felt him wake up ready for her and wanting her. His eyes never opened but he didn't have to have his eyes open to reach for her, to hold her and whisper her name and move with her and against her, and love her.

It was over quickly but not too quickly. It was the way it should be, with him still drugged with sleep and her still not fully awake, and when it was over he kept his eyes closed and his heart was beating rapidly and his chest heaving. Then, his eyes still shut, he rolled free of her and lay on his own pillow, face downward this time. Seconds later he was asleep once more.

She looked at him for several minutes, her eyes filled with the love of him and the need for him, her body thoroughly satisfied and her mind happy. She was smiling now without realizing it and the smile remained on her face as she slipped out from under the thin blanket and tiptoed to the bathroom. She showered and stepped out of the shower and dried herself on one of the hotel's towels, which were too small and not absorbent enough, and reminded herself that she really ought to buy some good towels on sale for 49¢ and it would be worth it to have a towel that really got you dry.

She dressed quickly but carefully. She put on a pair of panties and a bra and a frilly green dress that went well with her hair. The dress was cut low and the bra showed so she slipped out of the dress, shed the bra and put the dress on again. She checked herself in the mirror—her breasts showed a little but not too much and it made her sexy without looking cheap. Madge was very firm on that point. She said that when a man paid ten dollars or more he deserved a girl who looked classy.

When she was fully dressed she looked at the little alarm clock on the night-table. It was 11:45 and she had to hurry. It was time for her to go to work.

IF Richie Parsons had one regret it was that he couldn't sleep fifteen hours a day.

He slept with Honour Mercy. When she came back to the hotel room, at 4:30 in the morning if she was working nights, and at 8:30 in the evening if she was working the early shift, they were together talking and eating and just plain being together until it was time for her to sleep. If she worked the early shift, they went to sleep around three in the morning; when she worked nights, they went to sleep between five and six. When he was asleep it was good because she was in the bed with him, and when they were together it was good simply because it was always good when they were together. But for eight hours every day—and closer to nine hours, what with her leaving a little early and staying at the house a little late—he was alone by himself in the hotel room, alone with some paperback novels and detective magazines.

Richie never cared too much for reading. The only reason he read the paperback novels and the detective magazines was that there was very little else to do when you were cooped up in a hotel room for eight hours. So he read the novels and magazines and played solitaire. Honour Mercy had brought him a deck of playing cards once, a fancy deck that one of her customers had given her for a joke with a different pornographic illustration on the back of each of the fifty-two cards, and for a time he played solitaire constantly when she was gone. He even made a running game out of it, keeping careful score of how many games he played and how many he won on a scrap of paper, but after a while it became far more monotonous than the paperback novels or the detective magazines. He only knew one game of solitaire and it wasn't a particularly complex one, so after a week or so he stopped playing.

The pictures on the backs of the cards, which had been a source of interest and amusement for a time, were now too familiar to arouse his attention. The playing cards alone would have driven him insane with desire before he met Honour Mercy, but now that he had a completely satisfactory sexual relationship the pictures were not exciting in the least. He didn't need pictures any more.

It was twelve-thirty before he got up that afternoon and he wished he could have remained unconscious until half-past-eight when Honour Mercy would come back to the room. But finally he couldn't sleep any longer and he got out of bed, rubbed the sleep from his eyes and went to the bathroom to shave and shower and brush his teeth. He put on a worn flannel shirt and a pair of dungarees and went downstairs for breakfast.

Gil Gluck, who owned the Casterbridge Hotel, also owned a luncheonette around the corner where Richie Parsons had his breakfast each day. If there was one characteristic that distinguished the lunch counter from any other in Newport, it was the fact that Gil Gluck conducted no other *sub rosa* business there. There were no rooms behind the lunch counter where harlots entertained men, no rooms where men wore green eyeshades and dealt cards around tables, no rooms where bootleg moonshine was sold or white powder peddled. The Canarsie Grille, endowed the name of Gil Gluck's beloved hometown and spelled "grille" because the sign-painter Gil Gluck had hired was an incurable romantic, dealt solely in such eminently respectable commodities as eggs, wheat cakes, coffee, hamburgers, home fries, coca-cola and the like.

The fact that the Canarsie Grille was plain and simple, a luncheonette, the fact that there was nothing at all illegal in Gil Gluck's operations either in the luncheonette or in the hotel, was a source of tremendous consternation to the police force of Newport. Time and time again they had pulled surprise raids on first the hotel and then the Canarsie Grille; time and again they had found nothing more incriminating than a roach in a closet or a dirty spoon in a drawer.

Since the roach in the closet was a bewildered cockroach and not the butt of a marijuana cigarette, since no heroin had been cooked in the spoon, there was nothing the police could do. Gil Gluck paid the police nothing, and this bothered them. While metropolitan police, a far more sophisticated breed, would have found a way to squeeze money out of Gil Gluck, come hell or high water, no matter how honest he was, the Newport police cursed softly under their collective breath and let him alone. They also drank coffee there, since Gil was the only man in town who made a really good cup of coffee.

Richie Parsons drank coffee at the Canarsie Grille. He drank it with two spoonfuls of sugar and enough cream to kill the taste of Gil's good coffee. This bothered Gil, who was justly proud of his coffee. But the fact that

Richie always ordered wheat cakes, and licked his lips appreciatively after the first bite, endeared him to Gil.

The fact that Gil was a regular customer of Honour Mercy's might not have endeared the little bald man to Richie, but it was a fact that Gil Gluck sagely refrained from mentioning to the boy.

Richie finished the last of the wheat cakes and poured the rest of the coffee down his throat. He put the cup back in the saucer, then raised it a few inches to indicate that he wanted another cup. Gil took his cup, rinsed it out in the sink and filled it with coffee. He brought it to Richie, who in turn polluted it with cream and sugar and sipped at it. It tasted good and he took a cigarette from his pocket and lit it to go with the coffee.

When the cop came in and sat down next to him, Richie was suddenly scared stiff.

The cop was a big man. Richie didn't dare to look at him but he could see the cop's face out of the corner of his eye. It was composed primarily of chin. Richie could also see the cop's holster out of the corner of his eye, the black leather holster with the .38 police positive in it. The gun, to Richie at least, was composed primarily of bullets, bullets which could splatter Richie to hell.

Richie sat there on his stool, the cup of coffee frozen halfway between saucer and mouth, the cigarette clutched so tightly between his fingers that it was a wonder it didn't snap in two. Richie sat there terrified, waiting for something to happen.

Gil Gluck came over and stood in front of the cop.

Gil Gluck said: "What'll you have?"

"Coffee," said the cop.

Gil brought the coffee. The cop, who liked coffee and who appreciated good coffee, drank the coffee black and without sugar. He smacked his lips over the coffee and Gil Gluck glowed.

"Nice day," said the cop.

"If it don't rain," said Gil, who had absorbed the subtleties of Kentucky conversation.

"You sure ought to open up a game in that back room of yours," said the cop, for perhaps the eightieth time. "Be a natural."

Gil let it ride. "How's business?"

The cop shrugged. "Usual."

"Anybody get killed?"

The cop laughed, thinking that Gil sure had a sense of humor. "Usual," he repeated. "Hold-up over on Grant Street but the jackass who stuck the place up ran out of the store and smack into a cop. He didn't get ten yards out of the store before he had handcuffs on him."

"What kind of store?"

"Liquor store," said the cop. "Grobers package store. Up near Tenth Street on the downtown side. Know the place?"

"Sure."

"Well, that's all we had. Oh, there was a jailbreak down in Louisville and we got a few wanted posters on it. And an out-of-state air force base sent down a picture of a deserter they figure headed this way, but that's just the ordinary stuff. Nothing much is happening in Newport."

Richie Parsons went numb.

What Richie Parsons did not know, although any jackass ought to have been able to figure it out, was that the out-of-state air force base the cop was referring to was Wright-Patterson Air Force Base in Dayton, Ohio. Scott Air Force Base would hardly bother sending wanted notices as far as Newport. But to Richie Parsons, who had been born scared, any mention of a deserter was sufficient cause to crawl under the nearest rotting log and await Armageddon.

The deserter that the Wright-Patterson people were looking for was not at all similar to Richie Parsons. His name was Warren Michael Stults, he was twenty-three years old, six foot three and built like a Sherman tank. He was being searched for not only because he had gone over the hill but also because, as a prelude to desertion, he had kicked the hell out of his commanding officer. The commanding officer, bemoaning the loss of three front teeth and a goodly amount of self-respect, wanted to get hold of Warren Michael Stults as soon as possible.

But Richie Parsons did not know this angle.

And Richie Parsons was scared green.

He put money on the Formica top of the counter for his breakfast and edged out of the Canarsie Grille. The familiar skulk was back in his step and the familiar look of barely restrained terror was back on his face. The door stuck when he tried to open it and he almost fainted dead away on the spot. But he got through the door without attracting any attention and scurried around to the hotel.

The cop had noticed him, however. "What's with him?" the cop wondered aloud after Richie was gone.

"Him?"

"The little guy," the cop said. "The one who just scurried out of here with his tail between his legs."

"Oh," said Gil.

"He new around here?"

"He lives up at the hotel," Gil said. "Been here about a month."

"What's he do for a living?"

"Lives with one of the whores," Gil said.

"He pimp for her?"

"Must," said Gil, who couldn't imagine a man living with a whore and not pimping for her.

"Good for him," the cop said. "At least he's making an honest living. It's guys like you who give this town a lousy reputation."

Gil smiled—an infinitely patient smile—and filled the cop's cup with more black coffee.

THE hell of it was that he had read all of the books and magazines in the room.

That's what made it so impossible. Seven hours in an empty hotel room is a bore, whatever way you look at it, but it would have been a lot easier to bear if he had a book or magazine to read. As it was, the room was full of books and magazines but he had read every last one of them.

He couldn't go out of the room. That much was obvious. He couldn't go out, not even to the drugstore to buy himself something to read, not even down to the Canarsie Grille later on for another cup of coffee. There were candy bars at the hotel desk, but he was too petrified to chance going downstairs again, so he did nothing but sit in his room in the hotel, going quietly out of his mind.

Newport was not safe anymore. In his mind he saw every policeman in the town studying his picture with interest and devoting every minute of his time to a careful search for *Richie Parsons, Deserter.* Just as it never entered his mind that the deserter could be anyone but him, it never occurred to him that the Newport police couldn't care less about an out-of-state deserter, that they got a notice like that every day of every week, and that the cop had mentioned it solely to show what a bore the day was.

Richie knew only that he was a hunted man.

The fact that he remained for seven-and-a-half terror-stricken hours in room 26 of the Hotel Casterbridge is striking testimony to the hold Honour Mercy Bane had upon him. If it were not for her, he would have been on the first bus or train out of Newport. No, that's not right—he wouldn't have chanced recognition at the bus or train station, fearing that the police would be watching such areas of escape. He would have hiked clear to the city limits of Cincinnati and then hitched a ride.

But not now. Now he had to wait for Honour Mercy because he could not possibly leave without her.

He got the deck of cards, shuffled them and began to deal out a hand of solitaire. He had to cheat once or twice, but he won three games straight before it became so boring that he couldn't stand it. Then he ran through the deck and observed the positions of the men and women on the back of each card, trying to take some vicarious interest in their obvious celluloid joy, but they left him cold.

He put the cards down and sat in a chair facing the door. At any moment he expected a knock, but after a half-hour his fear changed its manifestation from nervousness to a strange calm. Instead of fidgeting, he sat stiff as a board and waited for time to pass, waited for it to be eight-thirty and for Honour Mercy to come home so that they could get the hell out of the town of Newport.

He barely moved at all. Periodically he lit a cigarette, periodically he ducked ashes on the rug, periodically he dropped the cigarette to the floor and stepped on it.

And periodically he wiped the cold sweat from his forehead.

HONOUR Mercy Bane was tired.

She was tired because, for an early shift, there had been one hell of a lot of action. It had been a back-breaking day which had culminated in a thirty-five-dollar trick at five minutes to eight, and now that she was out of the place she felt she would be happy never to see the inside of a house again.

She was hungry but she didn't stop for a bite to eat, preferring to wait and have supper with Richie. She didn't forget to buy magazines and books for him, but she was in such a hurry to get home that she remembered the books and magazines and passed the drugstore anyhow, figuring that she could get them later.

She had to get back to the hotel room in a hurry. She didn't know why, but she had a strange feeling that the faster she saw Richie, the better.

When she opened the door of the room he straightened up in the chair and his eyes were wide. Before she could say anything, he stood up and motioned for her to shut the door. She did so, puzzled.

"We have to leave," he said.

She looked at him.

"They're looking for me," he said, "and we've got to get out of town."

She nodded. She thought that Madge would be disappointed when she didn't show up at the house the following day, that Terri would miss her and that some of her steadies would grumble when they discovered she was literally nowhere to be had. But the thought of remaining in Newport never entered her mind.

"Better start packing."

She got her ratty cardboard suitcase from the closet and spread it on the bed and began filling it with clothes. At the same time, he packed his own suitcase, and the first thing he put into it was his uniform.

She had, fortunately, quite a lot of money. There was good money to be made at a Newport whorehouse and she had been making it. Neither she nor Richie could be classed as a big spender and she had over four hundred dollars in her purse. That, she thought, ought to be enough to last them quite a time.

She packed up her dresses and they were much nicer than the clothing she had carried with her from Clearwater. She didn't have room for everything in the little suitcase and had to leave some of the dresses behind, but she managed to take along the ones she liked best.

They packed in a hurry. It didn't take them more than fifteen minutes all told before both suitcases were jammed and lay ready to go. Then she went to Richie and he took her in his arms and held her very close and kissed her several times, his arms holding her firmly and tenderly. When he held her like that, and kissed her like that, he didn't seem scared at all.

And when he did that, the memory of that last thirty-five-dollar trick was washed out of her system. She completely forgot about it.

Then he let go of her. There would be time later to make love, plenty of time when they were out of Newport and out of Kentucky and away someplace safe. She picked up her suitcase and he picked up his suitcase and they walked out of the room and down the stairs and out of the hotel. If Richie skulked as he walked, his thin body hugging the sides of the buildings they passed, Honour Mercy Bane didn't notice it.

He would not hitchhike, not with her along, and they were walking to the bus station. She wondered what it would be like where they were going. She had not asked him where they were headed and did not have the slightest idea whether he was taking her north or south or east or west.

She was like Ruth in the Bible that Prudence and Abraham Bane read from every day of their lives. Wherever he took her she would go.

FOUR

IT WAS WELL after midnight, and the bus, mumbling to itself, rolled steadily northward, toward Cleveland, leaving Cincinnati far to the south behind it. Ohio is built something like a grandfather clock. At the top is Cleveland, the clock-face, and at the bottom is Cincinnati, the pendulum-weight, and in between there isn't very much of anything. In the middle of the night, there's even less.

Most of the people on the bus were asleep. Honour Mercy was asleep, her head, in a mute declaration of alliance, resting comfortably against Richie Parsons' shoulder. Only three people in the whole bus were awake. One of them, fortunately, was the driver, up front there. The second was a soft guitar-player, sitting way in back and singing quietly to himself: "You will eat, you will eat, by and by; In that glorious land in the sky, way up high; Work and pray, live on hay; You'll get pie in the sky when you die. That's a lie."

It was a soothingly quiet guitar, and a soothingly quiet voice, and it helped, with the vibration of the bus, in putting everybody asleep. But it didn't soothe Richie Parsons. He was wide awake, and the song sounded ominous to him. At that point, any song would have sounded ominous to him.

He was thinking of the fiasco he had made of buying the ticket. The thing was, he didn't *plan*. He just stumbled ahead, willy-nilly, hoping for the best, and every once in a while a chasm opened up in front of him.

A chasm had opened at the ticket window in Newport. The thing was, Richie just wasn't a world traveler. His entire traveling history had been similar to the traveling of a yo-yo. He traveled *from* home *to* someplace else, or *from* someplace else *to* home.

Besides which, he hadn't thought about a destination. He had thought only about leaving Newport, not at all about going somewhere else.

So when he stood in front of the ticket window at the bus depot, he said it automatically, without stopping to think about it at all. "Two tickets to Albany," he said, and the chasm opened up as big as life and twice as deep.

He couldn't go to Albany! That was where he lived, for the love of Pete, he couldn't go there!

But he'd already said it, and he was now too petrified to say anything else, to change the already announced destination. To be a draft-age young man on the way to Albany was suspicious enough. To be a draft-age young man who changed his mind and decided not to go to Albany after all wasn't suspicious, it was an absolute admission of identity.

While teetering on the brink of the chasm, he heard the calm (not suspicious!) voice of the ticket agent say, "One way or round trip?"

With the impulsive cunning of a treed raccoon, he said, "Round trip." There, that would allay the ticket agent's suspicions.

Two round-trip tickets to Albany cost him a hundred dollars and change. It was a pretty expensive way to allay suspicions, all things considered, depleting their finances by one-quarter.

He was too embarrassed and ashamed to tell Honour Mercy what he'd done. Happily, she didn't ask him where they were going, and the public address system, in announcing their bus, mentioned so many other cities (Cleveland, Pittsburg, Harrisburg, Philadelphia) that his blunder was lost in the crowd.

So here he was on the bus, well after midnight, surrounded by gently snoring (innocent, untroubled) passengers, being serenaded with songs about death, and hurtling toward doom and destruction and Albany.

What to do? He considered leaving the bus at one of the cities before Albany, and rejected it. The driver, who kept a head-count, would notice that two passengers were missing, and would delay the bus for them, for a few minutes, thereby calling attention to their absence. The Authorities would somehow get into the act, and Richie could visualize the scene in which the driver described the runaways to these Authorities, who wouldn't take long to realize that the absent male was none other than the deserter from Scott Air Force Base, Richie Parsons.

He couldn't stay on the bus all the way to Albany, and he couldn't leave it beforehand. The problem was too much for him. He stared gloomily at the night-shrouded empty flatness outside the window, and the guitarist in the back seat switched to a new song: "Hang down your head, Tom Dooley; Hang down your head and cry; Hang down your head, Tom Dooley; Poor boy, you're bound to die."

It was a long night.

They had breakfast in Cleveland, where Richie was too nervous to operate the silverware, and Honour Mercy finally asked him what was wrong. It was obvious he hadn't slept all night.

So he admitted his mistake, shame-facedly, and out-lined the horns of the dilemma. And Honour Mercy, the practical one, immediately gave him the solution. "We change buses in New York," she said. "We just won't change, that's all. People do it all the time. Get later buses and things."

Richie smiled with sudden relief. "Sure," he said. "Sure!" And when they got back on the bus, he fell immediately to sleep.

He woke up to discover that the bus was inside a building, with a lot of other buses, and the confining walls and roof made the sound of all those engines a tremendous racket.

He didn't know where he was, or where in the world he possibly could be, and the panic that always rode just beneath his surface popped out again, and he stared around in absolute terror.

Fortunately for Richie Parsons, Honour Mercy Bane was a girl loaded to the gunwales with maternal instinct. She now put a soothing hand on his arm, and told him, quietly, that they were in New York City and this was the bus depot. "I didn't know whether I should wake you up to see everything when we came into the city or not," she added. "But you looked so peaceful, sleeping there, I thought I should let you alone."

"You can just disappear in New York," Richie told her. "It's so big." He'd read that someplace, and firmly believed it.

People were getting off the bus. Richie blocked the aisle for a minute, getting the two suitcases down from the overhead rack, and then he and Honour Mercy followed the other passengers into the brightly-lit main waiting room of the Port Authority bus terminal. Honour Mercy, this last part of the trip, had been thinking again about finances. Four hundred dollars—now three hundred dollars—seemed like an awful lot when your chief expenses were magazines and paperback books and other items from the drugstore, and meals. But three hundred dollars seemed like an awfully small drop an awfully big bucket when it was all you had to live on in New York City. Somebody had told her that living New York was more expensive than anyplace else in the world, and she believed that as firmly as Richie believed that it was possible to just disappear in New York.

They had an awful lot of money tied up in two tickets from Albany to Newport, two cities neither of them expected to be going to for some time. It seemed wasteful, and Honour Mercy, if she retained nothing else from Abraham and Prudence Bane, her begetters, retained a rock-like sense of thrift.

In the middle of the waiting room, she made her decision. "Give me the return tickets, Richie," she said. "I'll go see if I can turn them in."

Richie considered for a second. The Air Police weren't looking for a girl. "Okay," he said. He handed her the tickets, and she went off to find the right window.

That wasn't too easy. She'd never known so many bus companies were in existence, and every window was for another group of them. But she finally found the right one, and turned the tickets in, explaining that she wasn't going back to Newport after all. The man at the window had her fill out a slip of paper, to which she affixed a false name, and ungrumblingly gave her almost forty dollars.

She returned to Richie to find him quaking in his boots. Two young men in uniform, one an Air Policeman and the other an Army Military Policeman, were strolling slowly around the waiting room, like casual friends on a promenade.

Honour Mercy took Richie's trembling arm. "Act natural," she whispered, which only made him look more terrified than ever, and she led him past the Authorities and out the door to New York's Eighth Avenue.

It was five p.m. and the rush hour. They stood on the sidewalk on Eighth Avenue, between 40th and 41st Streets, and watched the mobs of people rushing by in both directions, bumping into one another and rushing on with neither apology nor annoyance. It was obvious a Martian in a flying saucer could disappear in a crowd like that. Certainly Richie Parsons, who was practically invisible to begin with, could disappear in that multidirectional stream with no trouble at all.

They turned left, because the choice was between left and right and one was just as good as another, and joined the herd. They crossed 42nd Street, and kept on going northward, purposeless at the moment, following the momentum of the crowd and waiting for something to happen.

The crowd thinned out above 42nd Street, and they could walk more easily, without a lot of shoulder-bumping and dodging around. Honour Mercy was keeping an eye out for a hotel, which was their first concern, and saw a huge block-square hotel between 44th and 45th Streets, with a uniformed doorman and a curb lined with late-model cars. That wasn't exactly the kind of hotel she had in mind. They kept on walking.

At 47th Street, they saw a hotel sign down to their left, toward Ninth Avenue. This was the kind of hotel she had in mind. It was made up of three tenement buildings, five stories high, combined into one building, with the same ancient coat of gray paint on the faces of all three. The entrances of the flanking buildings had been removed, replaced by windows indicating that additional rooms had been set up where the entranceways had been, leaving the front door of the middle building as the only remaining entrance to the hotel. A square sign, white on black, stuck out over the street, saying simply, "HOTEL," not even gracing the place with a name.

"Down this way," she told Richie, and gently steered him around the corner. He saw the hotel sign then, and homed on it gratefully, anxious to have once more the sanctuary of four peeling walls around him.

The hotel didn't have a lobby, all it had was a first-floor hall, with stairs leading upward, a few dim light bulbs ineffectually battling the interior darkness, and frayed maroon carpeting on the floor and staircase. Just to the right of the entrance was a door to what had probably been the front apartment, when this building had been a separate entity and not yet a hotel. There was only the bottom half of a door there now, with a board about ten inches wide across the top of this half-door, and a grizzled, grimy old man leaning on the board, his elbows between the registry book and the telephone.

Honour Mercy, knowing Richie would be unable to effectively go through the process of renting a room, did the talking. The old man didn't bother to ask if they were married, and didn't bother to look at the false names Honour Mercy wrote in his registry book. He asked for fourteen dollars for a week's rent, gave Honour Mercy a receipt and two keys, told her room 26 was on the third floor, off to the right, and that was that.

They climbed the creaking stairs to the third floor, and turned right. The hall, narrow and dim-lit, passed through an amateurishly breached wall into the next building over, and at the end of it, left side, was room 26. Honour Mercy unlocked the door, and they walked into their new home.

It was a step down from the Casterbridge Hotel, back in Newport. The walls were almost precisely the same color, which didn't help, and the one window looked out on the back of a building on the next block. The dresser was ancient and scarred and sagging, the closet had no door on it, and the ceiling was peeling, as though it had a gray-white sunburn. There was a double-bed in the room, which would perhaps be a bit more comfortable than the single bed they'd shared at the Casterbridge, but that was the only good thing in sight.

They unpacked, trying to get some of their own individuality into the room just as rapidly as possible, and a couple of brown bugs dashed away down the wall when Honour Mercy opened the dresser drawers. Before she could get at them with a shoe heel, they'd disappeared under the molding. The Casterbridge Hotel hadn't had bugs, and no one had prepared her for the fact that New York City was infested from top to bottom with cockroaches, nasty little brown bugs with lots of legs and hard shell-like backs, who took one generation to build up immunity to virtually any poison used against them, which made their extermination more wishful thinking than practical reality.

The sight of the bugs made Honour Mercy want to get out of there for a while. They could come back when it was dark. She had a childish faith in the power of electric light to keep bugs from venturing out of their crannies in the walls.

Richie was torn between the desire to just sit down in the middle of the room and breathe easily for a day or two and a hunger that had been building since Cleveland. The hunger, aided by Honour Mercy's prodding, won out, and they left the hotel to find a place to eat.

They had dinner at a luncheonette on the corner of 46th and Eighth, and then went back to the hotel. It was dark now, and Honour Mercy hopefully turned on the bare bulb in a ceiling fixture which was their only light source. The bulb, in an economy move on the part of the management, was forty watts, and gave a smoky light not quite good enough to read by.

They sat around on the bed, digesting and talking lazily together about their successful flight from Newport. After a while, Honour Mercy spread their money out on the blanket and counted it, finding they still had a little over three hundred dollars. At fourteen dollars a week for the hotel room, and the cost of food, and movies or whatever to fill their time, it wouldn't take long for that three hundred dollars to be all gone.

There was only one sensible thing to do. She should go back to work right now, while they still had some money ahead, rather than wait until they were broke. The idea of having money ahead, in case of emergencies of one sort or another, appealed to Honour Mercy both as a child of thrifty parents and a girl in a risky line of work.

A little after ten, she gave Richie two dollars and told him to go to a movie for a while. They'd seen a whole line of movie marquees on 42nd Street, on their way to the hotel, and Honour Mercy was sure she'd heard or read somewhere that 42nd Street movies in New York City were open all night long. And if she were going to go back to work, she would need a room with a bed in it. She was pretty sure this was the kind of hotel where she could carry on her trade unquestioned.

Richie was reluctant to leave the room. In the first place, the outside world was heavily patrolled by policemen of all kinds; city police, state troopers, Air Police, FBI agents, Shore Patrol, Military Police, and the Lord knew what else. In the second place, the idea of Honour Mercy bringing work home served only to force the nature of her work—which was supporting him—right out into the open, where he had to look at it. Back in Newport, Honour Mercy was "away at work" eight or nine hours a day, and he could more or less ignore the facts of the work. Here, *he* was going to have to be away, while Honour Mercy worked here, right on this bed. It made a difference.

"Don't be silly," she told him. "You certainly can't get a job, at least not yet, not until you've been gone long enough for everybody to have forgotten all about you. And there's only one way I can earn enough money for both of us to live on. And besides that, I really don't mind it. It isn't the same as with us, you know that, it's just what I do, that's all."

It took her half an hour to soothe his newly-risen male pride and hurt self-respect, but finally he admitted that she was the practical one and he would follow her lead, and he went off to the movies, skulking along next to walls.

Honour Mercy's next problem was one of location. Back in Newport, there'd been no problem about where to go to find work. One just went downtown, that was all. But New York was a different matter. To the new arrival, New York seemed to be one giant downtown, extending for miles in all directions. Now where, in all of that, was the section where Honour Mercy's trade was plied?

Honour Mercy didn't know it yet, but she was lucky as to location. Eighth Avenue, in the Forties, is one of New York's centers of ambulatory whoredom. Just a block away, on 46th Street, there were a couple of bars, interspersed with legitimate taverns and restaurants, which specialized in receiving telephone calls for predominantly feminine clientele. The building in back which she could look at from her window was jam-packed with whores, most of whom were at the moment making exactly the same preparations Honour Mercy was making in the communal bathroom down the hall from room 26.

So Honour Mercy wasn't going to have to walk very far.

She left the hotel a little after eleven, and started retracing her steps toward 42nd Street, which had looked more downtowny than anything else she'd seen so far in New York, and which therefore seemed like the best place from which to start her search for Whore Row.

She found it sooner than that. The corner of 46th and Eighth was a poor man's Hollywood and Vine. Girls were going by in all directions, singly and in pairs, and their faces and clothing told Honour Mercy immediately that she had found the right place.

That was nice, she thought. It was handy to the hotel.

She walked around a bit, looking at things. It was still pretty early, and the middle of the week besides, and there wasn't much doing just yet. So she just looked at everything, wanting to familiarize herself with the local and local methods just as soon as possible.

Then a woman holding up a wall on 46th Street called to her, and motioned her to come over for a talk. Honour Mercy, wondering what this was all about, complied.

The woman, without preamble, said, "You just get into town?" She looked to be in her late twenties, with frizzy black hair that stuck out in wire-like waves from her head, and much too much makeup on her eyes.

Honour Mercy nodded.

"Who you working with?" asked the woman.

"Nobody," admitted Honour Mercy. "I just got here." Remembering that Newport hadn't liked the girl who hustled on her own, without the blessing of one of the established houses, and assuming that New York would probably be much the same, she added, "I've been looking around for somebody to show me what to do. I just go here today, and I don't know New York at all."

"You found me," said the woman. She left the wall, which didn't topple over, and took Honour Mercy's arm. "And it's a good thing you did," she said, leading Honour Mercy down 46th Street, away from Eighth Avenue. "The cops would've picked you up in no time. They got to make some arrests, you know, so they're always on the lookout for strays."

"I didn't know," said Honour Mercy humbly, showing her willingness to learn and to adapt.

The woman took her into the building Honour Mercy could see from her hotel window, and up the stairs to room on the second floor. The room was severely functional. It contained a bed and a kitchen chair, and that was all.

"My name's Marie," said the woman, sitting down on the bed.

"Honey," said Honour Mercy.

"Glad to know you. I'll introduce you to a couple people after a while. They'll explain the set-up to you. Good-looking girl like you, they'll probably put you on the phone."

"Thanks," said Honour Mercy.

"Of course," said Marie, grinning a little, "I can't just recommend you out of hand. You know what I mean: I got to be sure you're okay. I tell you what, you take off your clothes. Let's see what you got to offer."

Honour Mercy's reaction to that was complex, and it would be impossible to give the succession of her thoughts as rapidly as she thought them. Within a second, her thoughts passed from recognition through memory to decision, and with hardly a pause at all, she acted on the decision.

Here were the thoughts: Recognition. Marie was a Lesbian. Honour Mercy knew it as surely as she knew anything in the world. The unnecessarily tight grip on her arm as they came up the stairs together. The unnecessary demand that she take off her clothes. Marie was a Lesbian, and the price of her introducing Honour Mercy to the people who could give the unofficial blessing to her working in her occupation here in New York was that Honour Mercy be Lesbian with her for a few minutes.

Memory. The girls in Newport had talked about Lesbians more than once. It was a problem girls in their trade had to think about. In the first place, a surprisingly large percentage of prostitutes became Lesbian, at one point or another. Since they got from men only sex without love, they tried to get sex *with* love from other women. In the second place, Madge had been one hundred percent opposed to hiring Lesbians, on the grounds that dykes couldn't give a man as good a time as a normal woman could.

Decision. Sex was Honour Mercy's stock in trade. It was the way she made her living. With the help of Richie Parsons, she had successfully severed sex from love, without severing love from sex. She gave her body to men so she could have money to support herself and Richie. It wasn't really such a large step farther to give her body to a woman so she could have the right to work.

She took off her clothes. The woman kept grinning at her, and said, "You know what I have in mind, Honey?"

"Sure," said Honour Mercy. She said it as casually as possible, not wanting this Marie to get the idea that Honour Mercy thought the whole thing repugnant. That might spoil everything.

Marie's grin now turned into an honest smile, and she joined Honour Mercy in the disrobing. They lay down together on the bed, and out of the corner of her eye Honour Mercy saw one of the brown bugs run out of a crack in the wall and diagonally down to the molding, where he disappeared again. She closed her eyes, struggling to keep her face expressionless, and Marie leaned over to kiss her on the mouth.

Having sex with a woman, Honour Mercy decided later, wasn't having sex at all. It was just having a lot of preliminaries, all jumbled up together, and then stopping just when things were getting interesting.

Marie got a lot more excited than Honour Mercy did. She squirmed and writhed around, and somehow she managed to build herself up to a climax. Honour Mercy, thinking it was expected of her, made believe she had one, too; and then Marie, as satisfied as any of Honour Mercy's satisfied customers, crawled off and started to dress.

Honour Mercy wanted to wash, very badly, but she thought it would give the wrong impression to mention it, so she didn't say anything. She just dressed again, and waited for Marie to tell her what was next.

"That was fun, huh, Honey?" said Marie, and she patted Honour Mercy on the behind. Her hand lingered, and Honour Mercy unobtrusively moved out of reach.

"We'll have to see each other some more," said Marie. She came closer and took Honour Mercy's arm, again with the unnecessary tightness, and said, "Now let's go see a man about a whore."

FIVE

WHEN JOSHUA CRAWFORD was a little boy his name was not Joshua Crawford. The Joshua part had been with him all his life, but the Crawford part had become his when he made out his diploma a few days before graduation from PS 105 on Hester Street.

The teacher, a sad-faced man with fallen arches and red-rimmed eyes, went through the traditional pre-diploma rites of New York's lower East side. "You may now, for probably the last time, change your names without the formality of a court order," he intoned. "This is the last chance for all Isaacs to become Irving, for all Moshes to become Morris, for all Samuels to become Sidney." And all the Isaacs and Moshes and Samuels were quick to take advantage of the opportunity, the last chance, never quite realizing that all they were accomplishing was the strange metamorphosis of Irving and Morris and Sidney from English to Jewish names.

Joshua Cohen liked his first name. It was his—his father and mother had given it to him and he wanted to keep it. But he had no such feelings toward his surname, which was properly neither his nor his father's. When his father had migrated from Russia the Immigration Officer had stood, pen poised, and asked him what his last name was.

"Schmutschkevitsch," said Joshua's father.

The Immigration Officer didn't make the mistake of attempting to find out or guess how Schmutschkevitsch might be spelled. He asked, instead, where Joshua's father had been born. It was convenient to use the place of birth as a last name, far more convenient than worrying over the possible spelling of Schmutschkevitsch.

"Byessovetrovsk," said Joshua's father. The Immigration Officer, who sincerely wished that all these Russian Jews had had the good sense to be born in Moscow or Kiev or Odessa or something simple like that, closed his eyes for a moment and wiped perspiration from his forehead.

"Your name's Cohen," he declared. "Next!"

When Josh Crawford walked off the little stage in the small auditorium on Hester Street with his diploma in his hand, he felt thoroughly comfortable with his new name. Some of his classmates tried to make him a little less comfortable—it was all well and good to change Isaac to Irving, but the boy who changed Cohen to Crawford was taking a pretty big step. Josh ignored them, and in the fall he registered at Stuyvesant High School as Joshua Crawford and nobody saw anything wrong in the new name.

Even before the graduation ceremonies at PS 105, Joshua Crawford's life was mapped out and set on its course. He would go to Stuyvesant and graduate at or near the top of his class. From there he would move on to City College where Ivy League educations were dispensed at no cost to the recipient.

Meanwhile he would work—afternoons after school, evenings, and Saturdays. His mother would not approve of his working on the Sabbath but this could not be helped, for law school was not tuition-free and he had already decided that he would go to law school immediately upon graduation from CCNY. In order to do this he would have to have money saved up, and in order to save up money he would have to work, and if Sabbath observance had to suffer that was just one of those things. Even at the age of nineteen, Josh Crawford had come to the profound realization that the only way to hold your head up and enjoy life in America was to have as much money as possible. America was filled to overflowing with money and he was out to get his.

He got it. It was not easy and it was not accomplished without work and sacrifice, but Josh was a born worker and a willing sacrificer. He was by no means the smartest boy at Stuyvesant but he finished far ahead of most of the brighter boys. Many of them were dreamers while he was a planner and this made a big difference. He studied what had to be studied and worked over what had to be worked over and his marks were always very high.

He worked afternoons pushing a garment truck on Seventh Avenue for a dress manufacturer who had lived on Essex Street just a block or two away from where Josh was born. The work was hard and the pay was small, but while he did not earn much money he spent hardly any at all. He worked Saturdays wrapping parcels at Gimbel's, and he saved that money, too.

When he went to City as a pre-law major his studies were correspondingly harder and he had to give up the afternoon job. But it didn't matter—by the time he had completed three years at City, he had enough money and enough academic credits to enter law school at New York University.

Law school, clerkship, bar exams, flunkey work. Junior partner, member of the firm.

Hester Street, 14th Street, Central Park West, New Rochelle, Dobbs Ferry.

$15-a-week, $145-a-week, $350-a-month, $9550-a-year, $35,000-a-year.

His life was a series of triumphs, triumphs represented by titles and addresses and numbers. The setbacks, such as they were, were negative rather than positive disappointments. He never failed at anything he set out to do, not in the long run, and his few setbacks were in point of time. If it took him a year longer to become a junior partner, an extra few years to become a member of the firm, if his salary (or, when he was a member of Taylor, Lazarus and Crawford, his average annual income) moved along more slowly than he wished, this was unfortunate but something swiftly corrected.

The apartment on 14th Street was more private and more comfortable than the flat he had shared with his parents on the Lower East Side. The apartment on Central Park West was still more comfortable, as were in turn the house in New Rochelle and the larger and more desirable house in Dobbs Ferry.

Somewhere along the line he got married. Marriage never figured prominently in his plans. After a time it became professionally desirable, and when that happened a marriage broker in the old neighborhood went to work and came up with a wife for him.

The girl, Selma Kaplan, was neither homely nor attractive. Her reasons for marrying Josh paralleled his reasons for marrying her. She was at the perilous age where an unmarried girl was well on her way to becoming an old maid, an altogether unappealing prospect. Joshua Crawford was a young man with all the earmarks of success, a definite "good catch," and as his wife she would have security, respect, and a small place in the sun.

They were married between 14th Street and Central Park West, and a month or so before the junior partnership Selma Crawford was deflowered at a good midtown hotel and broken to saddle during a two-week honeymoon at a run-down resort in the Poconos. She was neither the best nor the worst woman Josh had slept with, just as she was neither the first nor the last, and her general lack of enthusiasm for sexual relations was cancelled out by her lack of distaste for the sex act.

She was a good cook, a good housekeeper, an adequate mother for Lewis and Sybil Crawford. The family's living quarters were never untidy, the cupboard was never bare, and the children grew up without displaying any of the more obvious neuroses that Selma read about periodically in the books that were periodically being read on Central Park West.

Her life was her home, her children, and her female friends who lived lives much the same as her own. Her husband's life was his work, his own advancement in the world, his business acquaintances. If you had asked Selma Crawford whether or not she loved her husband, she would have answered at once that she did; in private she might have puzzled over your question, might have been a bit disturbed by it. If you asked the same question of Josh Crawford he would probably answer in much the same way. He, however, would not puzzle over the question—it would be answered automatically and forgotten just as automatically the minute he had answered it.

Love, all things considered, had nothing to do with it. Joshua and Selma Crawford lived together, brought up children together, worked separately and together to achieve the Great American Dream. They enjoyed what any onlooker would have described as the perfect marriage.

That is, until Josh Crawford did a very strange thing, a thing which he himself was hard put to explain to himself. He might have blamed it on his age—he was forty-six—or on the fact that his professional advancement had more or less leveled off to an even keel. But wherever you place the blame, the action itself stands.

Joshua Crawford fell in love with a young prostitute named Honour Mercy Bane.

"ACCREDITED Paper Goods," said a female voice.

"This is Joshua Crawford."

A pause. A name was checked in a file of 3 x 5 index cards. Then: "Good afternoon, Mr. Crawford. What can we do for you?"

"I'd like a shipment early this evening, if possible."

"Certainly, Mr. Crawford. We've got a fresh shipment of 50-weight stock that just arrived at the warehouse a week ago. Good material in a red-and-white wrapping."

"Fine," Crawford said.

"You'll want delivery at the usual address?"

"That's right."

"We can have the order to you by nine o'clock," the voice said. "Will that be all right?"

"Fine," said Crawford.

Crawford rang off, then called Selma in Dobbs Ferry and told her he'd be working late at the office. The call completed, he leaned back in his chair and lit a cigarette. The phone call to "Accredited Paper Goods" wasn't particularly subtle, he thought. Fifty-weight stock in a red-and-white wrapping meant a fifty-dollar call girl with red hair and white skin, and by no stretch of the imagination could it have anything in the world to do with paper.

But the subterfuge did have a certain amount of value. It kept any law enforcement personnel from gathering anything other than circumstantial evidence over the phone, and it kept undesirable clients from getting through to the girls. Besides, he thought cynically, the cloak-and-dagger aspect of it all lent a certain air of excitement to the whole routine.

Crawford finished the cigarette and put it out. He was looking forward to the arrival of the shipment. It had been almost two months since he'd had any woman other than his wife and that was a long time, especially in view of the fact that it was a rare night indeed when he and Selma shared the same bed. He wasn't a chaser the way so many of his friends were, didn't want a young thing to make him feel young again, didn't make a habit of seducing his friends' wives or chasing down the young flesh that worked around the office.

He was a man who believed in buying what he wanted, and when he wanted a woman he bought one. The fifty dollars or so that it set him back for a woman was inconsequential to him and, in the long run, far cheaper than wining and dining a girl for the doubtful joy of seducing her free of charge. This way seemed far cleaner to him—you dialed a number, said some crap about a shipment of paper goods, had a good dinner at a good restaurant, and then went to your apartment on East 38th Street.

The apartment, which cost him a little under two hundred dollars a month, was something which he had to have, anyway. There were enough nights when he had to work late legitimately, sometimes until two or three or even four in the morning before an important case, and at that hour it was a headache to look around for a hotel room and a pain in the ass to drive home to Dobbs Ferry. He'd had the apartment for better than five years now and it was a pleasure to have it, a pleasure to be able to run over there for a nap in the middle of the day if he was tired, and a pleasure to be able to have a girl there every once in a while.

He knocked off work a few minutes before five, had a pair of martinis in the bar across the street with Sid Lazarus, and had a good blood-rare steak and an after-dinner cigar at the steakhouse on the corner of 36th and Madison. One of the junior partners had recently managed to become a father and the cigar was the result of the occasion; it was a damned fine Havana and Crawford smoked it slowly and thoughtfully. He took a long time over dinner and a longer time with the cigar, and it was almost eight-thirty when he took the elevator to the third floor of the apartment house on East 38th Street.

The girl who arrived on the stroke of nine was young and lovely with chestnut hair and a full figure. They had a drink together and then they went to the bedroom where they took off their clothes and slipped into the comfortable double bed and made love all night long.

IT had been better in Newport.

The thought was a disloyal one and Honour Mercy took a long look around her own apartment to get the thought out of her head. She and Richie had been sharing the apartment for almost two weeks now and it was a pleasure to look at it. It was easily the nicest place she had ever lived in her life.

Shortly after she and Marie had "gone to see a man about a whore," Honour Mercy had learned that it was unnecessary to live in a rat-trap like the hotel on 47th Street where they had taken a room. The man Marie had taken her to see had decided that Honour Mercy was too damned good-looking to waste her time streetwalking and had put her on call. Since she didn't have to take men to her apartment but went either to theirs, or to a hotel room rented for the occasion, she didn't have to live in the type of hotel that would let her earn her living on the premises. She could live wherever she could afford to live, and after a few days on the job she saw that she could afford to live a good deal better than she was living.

She earned roughly two hundred dollars the first week on the job and close to three hundred the second. If a man wanted her for the afternoon or evening it cost him fifty dollars, if he wanted her for a quickee it cost twenty-five, and half of what she was paid was hers to keep. The organization which employed her took care of everything—she had a phone at the apartment and they called her periodically, telling her just where to go and exactly what to do.

One day she had seven quickees in the course of the afternoon and evening. Another day she was paid to entertain an out-of-town buyer from noon until the following morning, accompanying him and another couple to dinner and a night club. That time she was paid an even hundred dollars. Then, too, there were days when she earned nothing at all, but with her half of the take, plus whatever tip a client wanted to give her, her take-home pay added up to a healthy sum.

As a result, there was no reason in the world for her and Richie to be living on West 47th Street. It took her two days to decide this and a few more days to find the right apartment, but now she was settled in a first-floor three-room apartment in the West Eighties just a few doors from Central Park West. It might be pointed out irrelevantly that her apartment was right around the corner from the apartment in which Joshua and Selma Crawford had first set up housekeeping eighteen years ago.

And it was very nice apartment, she thought. Wall-to-wall carpeting on the floors, good furniture, a tile bathroom, a good-sized kitchen—all in all, it was a fine place to live.

Much better than the Casterbridge Hotel.

She shook her head angrily. Then why in the world did the thought keep creeping into her head that things were a lot better in Newport? It didn't make sense, not with the nicer place she was living in and the nicer money she was earning.

The trouble was, things were so all-fired complicated. In Newport, things couldn't be simpler. You got up and went to Madge's house and went to work. You turned a certain amount of tricks and went home to Richie. You sat around, or maybe went to a movie or spent some time talking to Terri, and then you went to bed with Richie. In the morning you woke up and went to work, or in the evening you woke up and went to work, and either way it was the same every day, with the same place and the same people and the same thoughts in your head.

But not anymore. Now she was working in a different place every day, taking cabs to hotel rooms and apartments, working all different hours. And Richie wasn't at the apartment all the time the way he was always at the hotel room in Newport. You'd think that with a nice apartment to stay in he'd be home all the time, but not Richie. She wondered where he was now, where he'd been spending all his time.

"You got a pimp?" Marie had asked her once. She had told her that she hadn't, and then another time she had mentioned Richie.

"This the guy who's your pimp?"

"No," she said. "I told you I don't have a pimp. He just lives with me."

"He got a job?"

"No."

"He lives on what you make?"

"That's right."

Marie laughed. "Honey," she said, "I don't know where the hell you're from, or what the hell they call it in Newport, but you got a pimp, whether you know it or not."

This sort of talk didn't exactly bolster her morale. Honour Mercy knew what a pimp was, certainly. She knew that almost all the girls in the business had one. But she had never thought of Richie in just those terms. Oh, he fit the definition well enough. She supported him and he didn't do any work at all, didn't even look for work.

But....

Well, he *couldn't* work. That was what she told herself, but it was harder to believe it in New York than it had been in Newport. He was about as safe in New York as a needle in a haystack, and no Air Police all the way from Scott Air Force Base were going to chase clear through to New York for him. But he still didn't try to get a job.

She shook her head. No, she had to admit it was more that he didn't want to work. Whenever she brought the subject up, he went into how it wasn't safe, how they had his fingerprints on file and he couldn't make a move without them getting on his trail. Each time he explained it to her, but each time the explanation became just that much less convincing. Why, he could get a job without getting his fingerprints taken. And he could surely be as safe on a job as he could walking all over the city and heaven-knows-what.

She paced around the apartment for a while, sat down, got up and paced some more. A good friend would help, she thought. Somebody like Terri, for instance. For a while she had thought that Marie would take Terri's place, but with Marie being a Lesbian, things just didn't work out that way. Whenever she was with Marie, the older woman would want to do things that Honour Mercy didn't want to do, and the situation was strained on both sides. Now she hadn't seen Marie in days and didn't much care if she never saw her again.

She paced some more, sat some more, and started pacing again.

She kept walking and sitting until the phone rang and she was in business again.

WHILE the cab carried her to 171 East 38th Street, she wondered what kind of a man Mr. Crawford was that he wanted her again so soon. He was a very nice man—he tipped her ten dollars both of the times she had visited him at his apartment and never asked her to do anything that she didn't like to do. He was good, too, and when she was with a man all night she had a chance to enjoy it if he was good. Sometimes this made her feel a little disloyal to Richie, but then she would tell herself that this was her work and it was no crime to enjoy your work.

But the thing about Mr. Crawford that she especially liked was that he didn't make her feel bad. And that, when you came right down to it, was what made New York worse than Newport. In Newport you were just with a man for a few minutes and he didn't have a chance to make you feel bad, but in New York you were with a man sometimes for the whole night—and with the out-of-town buyer about twenty hours—and when you were with a man that long, you usually felt bad by the time it was over.

Not from anything the men did. Not from anything they did or said, but from the way they felt toward you and the way you felt toward yourself when you were with them. When you were with a man that long, you couldn't have sex *all* the time, and when you weren't having sex you felt uncomfortable. It was hard to explain but it was there.

That was the good thing about Mr. Crawford. She never had felt uncomfortable with him, not either of those times. The second night she had been so at ease that, when they made love, she just closed her eyes and pretended to herself that she and Mr. Crawford were married. It was funny, and very weird, and afterward she felt guilty, but while they were doing it, it was very good for her, and it was even good afterward when they lay side by side in silence and he looked at her with his eyes gentle and his mouth smiling.

He was waiting for her when she got to the apartment. He opened the door for her, closed it behind her and took her coat. He led her to a chair, handed her a drink, and took a seat in a chair across the room from her.

"It's good to see you," he said. "How have you been, Honey?"

"All right."

"I haven't," he said. "I just lost an important case."

"Oh," she said. "I'm sorry."

"So am I, but I expected it. Damn fool of a client didn't have a leg to stand on, but he insisted on going to court. Some of them are so damned stupid they ought to be shot. They get the idea of suing for a few hundred thousand and the numbers get them intoxicated. They smell money they haven't got a chance in the world of collecting, and the money-smell goes to their heads. I told the damn fool he couldn't collect, but he was determined to go to court. What the hell—I figured we might as well get the fee as some shysters. But it's a pain in the neck, Honey."

"I can imagine."

His face had been very serious and now it relaxed. "By the way," he said, "do you call yourself anything besides Honey? It's a hell of a name."

She told him her name.

"Honour Mercy," he echoed. "I like that. Has a good sound to it. You mind if I call you that instead of Honey?"

"Whatever you want, Mr. Crawford."

He laughed, and after she realized how funny it was to be calling him Mr. Crawford, she laughed too. "My friends call me Josh," he said. "Josh belongs in the same class with Honey as far as I'm concerned. Why don't you try Joshua?"

"Joshua," she said to herself, testing the name.

"The guy who fit the battle of Jericho."

"And the walls came tumbling down."

He nodded. "You know, there's a rational explanation for that whole episode. If you find the right note for a certain object, the right vibration, and sound it long enough, the object'll fall or crack or whatever the hell it does."

She didn't understand, so he went over the explanation in more detail, which wasn't easy because he wasn't too clear on just what he was saying. But they talked about the battle of Jericho, and the Bible in general, and Honour Mercy started suddenly when she realized that she hadn't been thinking of the conversation as part of turning a trick. It was just two people talking, two friendly people in a pleasant apartment, and the real purpose of the visit had gotten lost in the shuffle.

When he had finished talking about vibrations and wave lengths and other sundry physical phenomena, there was a moment of silence and Honour Mercy realized that he couldn't turn the conversation or the mood to sex now, that he was probably a little embarrassed and that it was up to her. She got halfway out of her chair, intending to go to him and embrace him and kiss him, but before she was on her feet he shook his head and she sank back into the chair.

"Let's just talk, Honour Mercy."

She nodded agreeably.

"I mean it," he said. "I just want you to sit here and talk with me. For the moment, anyway."

Normally she would have gone along with him. That was automatic—if a customer was paying for your time and just wanted to talk or watch a floor show or listen to music, that was his business. Marie had told her that quite frequently homosexuals engaged girls for the evening to kill rumors about themselves, that other men actually wanted no more than an evening's companionship exclusive of sex. Already she had met men who liked to build themselves up by talking for hours before getting down to business.

But this time—perhaps the closeness she was beginning to feel for Crawford—made her ask: "Is that what you called me over for? To talk?"

"I don't know."

She looked at him.

"I really don't know," he said. "As a matter of fact, I didn't have anything in mind one way or the other when I called the agency. Neither sex nor conversation. I felt a little disappointed about the case I had been working on and a bit annoyed over things in general and I simply wanted to see you."

"All right."

"I wanted somebody," he said. "Do you have any idea what it's like to want somebody—not anybody specifically, but just somebody to relax with? I wanted to talk to somebody. Who could I talk to? My wife? I haven't talked to her in years, just the usual where-did-you-go-what-did-you-do crap. My partners? With them I could talk law. That's all we have in common—law. My kids? They're good kids, fine kids. I don't know 'em, but they're good kids. If something happened to them it would kill me. I love them. But how in hell could I possibly talk to them? We wouldn't have anything to talk about." She didn't say anything.

"Forty-six years," he said. "Forty-six years and I've done fine not talking to anybody. Forty-six years and I haven't missed it. So this afternoon I felt like talking for maybe the first time in forty-six years, and there wasn't a soul I could talk to. It's a hell of a thing."

He lapsed into silence. She waited a minute and then said: "What do you want to talk about?"

"You talk. I've talked too damned much already."

"What should I talk about?"

"I don't really give a damn," he said. "Talk about whatever the hell you want to talk about. Tell me what you eat for breakfast, or where you get your hair done, or who you like in the fifth at Tropical. I'll just listen."

She wondered what he was driving at. She thought that he was probably making some sort of a pitch, a private speech, a summation to a private jury. But he was a nice man and she liked him and so she started to talk.

She started with her childhood—perhaps because that's an easy place to start, perhaps because coming of age in Coldwater is hardly a controversial topic of conversation. She started there, and before she knew what was happening she was giving him a short history of her life. She talked about Lester Balcom and Madge and Terri and Dee, about Richie and Marie, about the way she felt when she was home alone and the way she felt riding in a cab to an assignation. She needed to talk at least as much as he did and the words poured out of her, and as they did they had a somewhat therapeutic effect upon both of them. Any priest will tell you that confession is good for the soul even if there has been no sin, that the urge to share experience with another human being is a powerful urge that demands satisfaction.

Neither of them kept any track of the time. Finally she had run out of words and the two of them sat quietly and stared thoughtfully at each other. Honour Mercy sipped at her drink and discovered that her glass was empty. Perhaps she had finished it or perhaps it had evaporated; she had no memory of anything but a continual monologue.

Crawford stood up, walked over to her and looked down at her. He reached into his pocket and took out two bills, a fifty and a ten. He handed them to her.

"Go on home," he told her.

She handed the money back to him. "You can't pay me until I earn it."

"You've earned it. More than earned it."

"Joshua—"

He smiled when she said his name. "I mean it," he said. "I don't want to...sleep with you. Not now."

"Because you're paying for it?"

He didn't say anything.

"You listen to me now," she said. "You're going to take this money and put it back in your pocket. Then you and me are going back in that bedroom and we're going to bed together. And when we're done you're not giving me any money because I'm not going to let you. You understand?"

"Don't be silly."

"I'm not being silly."

"Look—"

She stood up and looked straight into his eyes. He had very dark brown eyes that were almost black in the artificial light of the room. "You wanted me to talk to you," she said. "I liked you and so I talked to you. I told you a lot of things I never told to anybody else."

"I know."

"I told you because I like you. And now I want you to go to bed with me. Don't you like me enough to do that?"

He didn't say anything.

"Take my arm, Joshua."

He took her arm.

"Now...now lead me to the bedroom. And afterwards don't you dare to try to give me money or I'll hate you. Maybe I won't hate you but I'll be mad. I mean it."

He took her into the bedroom and put on the small lamp and closed the door. He stood motionless by the side of the bed until she had removed her dress; then he too started to disrobe.

When they were both nude they turned to look at each other. He looked at full thighs and a narrow waist and firm breasts; she looked at a body that was still youthful, at a chest matted with dark curly hair.

He didn't move. She stepped close to him and her arms went around his body.

She said: "Please kiss me, Joshua."

SIX

THE BARTENDER, STANDING down at the end of the bar, looked at Richie and obviously didn't much care for what he saw. Richie was impaled by the look; he squirmed on it, his face got red, his eyes dropped. He knew what was coming.

With an exaggerated air of Job-like long-suffering, the bartender pushed himself off his elbow and came dirty-aproned strolling down the length of the bar. Stopping in front of Richie, he said, in a weary voice, "How old are you, kid?"

Richie met the barman's eyes for just a second. In Richie's eyes were pleading, in the barman's implacability. Without a word, Richie slid off the stool and skulked, round-shouldered, back to the cold and sunlit street. He turned left, aimlessly, and walked along with his hands in his pockets, imagining himself, after an extensive course in judo, coming back and drop-kicking that bartender through his back-mirror.

The hell of it was, Richie was eighteen. And eighteen was legal drinking age in New York State.

But he just didn't look eighteen. He was short and skinny to begin with, and that didn't help. His face was weak and watery, and that didn't help. And he'd been living soft. He'd put on over twenty pounds, and he'd spouted acne instead of whiskers, and *that* didn't help. The twenty pounds didn't make him look less skinny. It just made him look like a skinny sixteen-year-old with baby fat on his cheeks.

Nine chances out of ten, he could have shown his Air Force ID card (being on active duty, he had no draft card) and been served without question. But he was terrified to show that card anywhere, just as he was honestly terrified to try to get a job or to open a bank account (assuming he had money to put in it) or get to know anybody besides Honour Mercy. Richie Parsons' concept of Authority was basically the same as George Orwell's in *1984*. Authority was a Big Brother, mysteriously everywhere, all-knowing and all-seeing, waiting to pounce upon Richie Parsons the second he made a mistake, and bear him whimpering back to Scott Air Force Base, where the whole squadron would line up to kick the shit out of him, and then he'd probably go to Leavenworth or something.

The days, for Richie Parsons, were long and empty. And the nights were even longer. Staying in the apartment all the time, waiting for a Knock On The Door, was too much for his nerves to stand. And Honour Mercy was practically never at home. Her work now took her away, usually, in the early evening, and she was never back before two or three in the morning, and sometimes she wasn't back until long after sun-up. She'd even been away over a whole weekend once, off on somebody's yacht, she and a number of her coworkers, with a group of rich college boys and a photographer from a men's magazine. That was only two weeks ago, and Honour Mercy was already haunting the newsstands, wondering if they'd used a picture of her. "They probably won't, though," she kept saying. "The only picture he took of me was one I don't think they could use."

The point was that Richie was most of the time alone. Honour Mercy was the only one he knew that he could freely associate with, and she was usually either working or sleeping.

Besides that, Honour Mercy seemed to be changing. Her attitude toward Richie was undergoing a very uncomfortable transformation. She was talking more and more frequently, lately, about the fact that Richie wasn't working. She was even beginning to nag a little about it, as though he could safely go off and get a job somewhere, when he knew without question that it was too dangerous to even think about.

Honour Mercy was changing in other ways, too. Sometimes, her customers would take her out to dinner or a show or something first, and Honour Mercy had by now seen most of the Broadway shows and been to a lot of the midtown nightclubs. She was learning to dress like the ads in the fashion magazines (though nothing in the world could shrink her bust to fashionable boyishness), and a faint southern-ness in her speech was rapidly disappearing. She was, in a word, becoming sophisticated, and she and Richie no longer had quite so much in common.

It was a problem, and Richie gnawed worriedly at it as he wandered down the street from the bar where he hadn't been served. Life had been comparatively sweet for him the last couple of months. With neither the cloying demands of his mother or the harsh demands of the Air Force to contend with, he could live at his own slow pace. He had no duties, no responsibilities. But now, with Honour Mercy on the one hand growing away from him, and on the other hand becoming more insistent that he should find a job, life was getting complicated again, and Richie, as usual, didn't have the foggiest idea what to do about it.

He was walking east on 77th Street, toward the park. Central Park West was straight ahead, at the end of a row of brownstones. When he got to the corner, he hesitated, wondering where to go next. The park was loaded with frantic, round-eyed boys who kept trying to pick him up, and that made him nervous. To the right was midtown, where he could probably find a bar that would serve him if he looked long enough and hard enough. To the left was home, eight blocks away, but this was Thursday afternoon and Honour Mercy would be at the hairdresser's.

He wanted something to drink, but he didn't feel like braving the histrionic weariness of any more bartenders. On the other hand, he could buy a six-pack of beer in any grocery store, take it home, and wait for Honour Mercy to come back.

All right, that's what he'd do. He walked uptown, on the side away from the park, and turned left at 85th Street. The apartment was in the middle of the block, and a tiny grocery store was two doors farther down. He walked slowly, having nothing in the world to hurry for, and when someone said his name as he was passing his building, he almost fainted.

He froze. He stood still, staring down the empty sidewalk toward Columbus Avenue, and the voice ran round and round inside his head. "Richie Parsons?" A strange voice, one he'd never heard before, and there had been a questioning lilt on the last syllable.

It was Authority. It had to be, nobody knew him here, nobody wanted to know him. He froze, and wished desperately to disappear.

The voice repeated his name, still with the rising inflection, and Richie forced himself to turn and look at the Authority that had descended upon him.

But it didn't seem to be Authority after all. There was a black Lincoln parked at the curb in front of the building, and there was a man in the driver's seat, looking out at Richie. He was middle-aged, black-haired, with dark and deep-set eyes, a thin-lipped wide mouth and a heavily lined face. He seemed Stern and he seemed Successful and he was obviously Rich, but he didn't look like Authority.

He didn't look like Authority because his expression was one of polite curiosity, the expression of a man who has asked a not-too-important question and is waiting for the not-too-important answer. Such was not the expression of Authority.

Richie hesitated, wondering what to answer. Should he deny the name, go on down to the corner, go to a movie, wait until this man had given up and gone away? Or should he admit that he was, in fact and in essence, Richie Parsons?

The man had called him by name. He could have gotten the name only from one of two sources: Honour Mercy or Authority. The latter, despite his expression, seemed the most likely. Authority, in a Chinese-eyed Lincoln?

The man broke into his hesitation by smiling and saying, "Don't worry, Richie. I'm not the law. I'm a friend of Honour Mercy's."

"Honour Mercy?" he echoed. He was at a complete loss.

"Hop in," said the man. "I want to talk to you."

"Talk to me?" When Richie was confused, more than usually confused, he was in the habit of repeating what was said to him, turning it into a question.

"Don't worry," said the man. "I'm not going to turn you over to the Air Force."

Richie stared at him, and fought down the urge to say, "Air Force?" Instead, he said, "How do you know about it?"

"Honour Mercy told me. Come on, hop in. I'll explain the whole thing."

Richie couldn't think of anything else to do, so he hopped in. He walked around the Mandarin front of the Lincoln, opened the shiny black door, and sat tentatively on the maroon upholstery.

The man immediately started the engine, which purred at the lowest threshold of audibility, and the Lincoln pulled smoothly away from the curb.

For the first part of the ride, the man was silent, and Richie followed his example. They went directly across town first, and up a ramp to the Henry Hudson Parkway, where the speedometer needle moved up to fifty and hovered, while the city rolled by to the left, and the Hudson became the ocean to the right. They dipped into the Brooklyn Battery tunnel, emerged on the Brooklyn side, and headed almost due east.

Brooklyn was, as usual, snarled with traffic. Their ride was hyphenated by red lights, and the man began to talk. "My name is Joshua Crawford," he said. "I'm forty-six years of age, I've got two children, both of them older than you, I'm a well-to-do lawyer, and I've believed in the straight-forward approach all of my life. I want you to know this about me, I want you to know anything you want about me. For two reasons. First, I know at least as much about you. Second, I want you to have the full facts in the case before you make your decision."

"My decision?" Richie was confused again.

"Just hear me out," said Joshua Crawford. "I've known Honour Mercy now for about two months. You might say we were business acquaintances. Her business, not mine. Something—I'm not sure what—made me think of Honour in an unbusiness-like way. Don't get me wrong; I don't make a habit of befriending whores. This time, something is different. I can't define it any closer than that."

A traffic light ahead of them switched from green through orange to red, and the purring Lincoln stopped. Joshua Crawford looked over at Richie Parsons. "Has Honour Mercy mentioned me at all?" he asked.

"No," said Richie. "She doesn't tell me much about her—about her work."

"Good," said Crawford. "That's just another example of how she's different. Practically any whore, if she gets a steady customer, and she and the customer are friends, she'll go around boasting about it. Honour Mercy's different. She isn't a whore by nature. She shouldn't be in such a business."

His words hung in the air between them, the light switched back to green, and the Lincoln nosed forward again.

"I want to help Honour Mercy," said Crawford after a minute. "I want to put her into what might be called semi-retirement."

"Your mistress," said Richie, beginning to understand at last what this was all about.

Crawford nodded without taking his eyes away from the traffic-filled street. "My mistress," he said. "I have plans for Honour Mercy. A good apartment—better than where she is now. Money of her own, charge accounts at a couple of the better stores. She would, in every sense but the legal, be my wife. There's a woman out in Dobbs Ferry who is my wife in the legal sense, and that's all."

While Richie waited for what he knew was coming next, Crawford spun the wheel and the Lincoln made a right turn. They were on a wider street now, with less traffic, and the speedometer needle inched upward again.

"I have plans for Honour Mercy," repeated Crawford. "But you don't fit into those plans. You were apparently willing to share the girl with all takers. I'm not willing to share her with anybody."

Richie nodded, and a lost and helpless feeling was beginning to spread over him, and he wondered, with a vague fear, what Joshua Crawford's plans were for Richie Parsons.

"We're in competition, you and I," continued Crawford. "Ridiculous, but true. And I think you'll have to agree with me that there's no contest."

The silence lengthened again, and Richie realized he was expected to make some sort of answer. At last he mumbled, "I suppose so."

"The easy thing for me to do," said Crawford, "was let the police know where you were. Easy. But also cruel and unnecessary. I'm not a cruel man, Richie, and I don't do the unnecessary. So I'm giving you your choice."

"What choice?" asked Richie miserably. He could see no choice.

Crawford took one hand from the steering wheel long enough to reach within the jacket of his tailored suit and withdraw a business-size envelope. He dropped the envelope on the seat between them. "It's getting cold in New York," he said. "Winter is on the way, and you're going to have to start shifting for yourself. There's a one-way plane ticket to Miami in that envelope, plus five hundred dollars in ten-dollar bills. Enough to keep you alive until you find a place for yourself down there. You can take the ticket and the money and go to Miami, and that's the end of it. Or you can decide to stay."

Richie knew that he was now supposed to ask what would happen if he were to decide to stay, and he also knew what the answer would be. But he was supposed to ask, and he did. "What if I don't go?"

"I call the police," said Crawford, "and you go back to Scott Air Force Base."

Richie looked gloomily out the window. He saw a street sign, and saw that they were now traveling on Rockaway Parkway, and it seemed to him that it shouldn't be "Parkaway, we'll rock away together."

He parked his thoughts back where they belonged. Joshua Crawford was driving him to the airport, that was clear enough. He had to decide, he had to make up his mind what to do.

But what decision was there? Take the ticket and the money, take the plane, go away to Miami and see what would happen next. Or stay here and be taken by the police. What choice was that?

A sudden thought came to him, and he voiced it. "What does Honour Mercy say?"

"I haven't said anything to her yet," said Crawford. "I want you out of the way first."

"How do you know she'll become your mistress?"

"She will," said Crawford. "If you aren't around. And you won't be around, one way or the other."

Richie leaned against the door on his side and gnawed on his lower lip, sinking easily into depression and self-pity. He compared himself with Joshua Crawford, and he found himself coming in a very distant second. Joshua was rich, he was successful, he was assured, he was strong. He was driving this car, he could give Honour Mercy anything she wanted. Richie Parsons was young, he was poor and uncertain and weak and afraid. He could give Honour Mercy nothing but himself, and that was a poor gift indeed.

"What's your choice?" Crawford asked him.

Wordlessly, Richie reached out and picked up the envelope.

"You understand," said Crawford, "that this is permanent. If you try to get in touch with either Honour Mercy or myself, I'll have to turn you in. You understand that?"

"Yes," whispered Richie.

Somewhere, they crossed the line separating Brooklyn from Queens, and wound up on a divided highway, and the speedometer needle moved up to sixty. Then they turned off the highway to another highway and signs said that they were entering New York International Airport, known as Idlewild.

Idlewild was as big as Scott Air Force Base, which meant it was larger than any airport should be. There was a four-lane divided highway within the airport grounds, and sprawling low buildings far off the highway on either side bore huge signs giving the names of various airlines.

The temporary terminal was miles away from the main entrance, but finally they got to it and the Lincoln slowed to a stop. "Here we are," said

Crawford. He looked at Richie and his expression was now sympathetic. "I'm sorry," he said. "But I think this is the best way to do it. For everybody concerned."

Richie mumbled something and got out of the car. Then, all at once, he remembered his uniform, still packed away in the AWOL bag and in the closet at the apartment he'd been sharing with Honour Mercy. "My—my clothes," he said. He was poised half-in and half-out of the car. "I've got to get my clothes."

"Buy some more," said Crawford. His hand dipped down, came up with a wallet, six twenty-dollar bills were suddenly in Richie's hand. "Buy some more," Crawford repeated. "Your plane is leaving at six, and it's after four now."

"But I need—" He couldn't come out and say it, about the uniform.

Crawford was impatient now. He'd obviously thought the whole distasteful thing was over with. "Is there something special you need?"

"Yes."

"What?"

"My—my uniform."

Crawford looked puzzled, and then surprised, and then he smiled. "You're smarter than I gave you credit for," he said. "My apologies. The old deserter dodge, is that it?"

Richie was humiliated and defeated. He mumbled and nodded his head.

"I'll mail it to you," he said. "General Post Office, Miami. You'll have it within the week."

"I need it," said Richie desperately.

"Don't worry; I'll send it to you."

There was nothing Richie could say, nothing he could do. He stepped out onto the concrete, and the door swung shut behind him. He turned to say something—goodbye, something—but the Lincoln was already purring away. He watched it pull out to the main airport road and swing away, back to the city again.

The envelope was cold and crisp in his hand. Holding it tightly, he went into the terminal building and searched for the men's room. Finding it, he invested a coin in privacy, and, once within the stall, opened the envelope. It contained the ticket, one-way, and some ten-dollar bills, fifty of them. With the money Crawford had just handed him, he now had six hundred and twenty dollars. And the ticket.

He'd been bought out, paid off, patted on the head and sent on his way. Never before in his life had he felt quite as weak and puny as he did this minute. He was the ninety-seven-pound weakling from the ads; but in his case the condition was worse. He wasn't merely weak physically. He was weak in every way. He had no force, no stamina, no courage. He could stand up to no one. Crawford had bought him, paid him off—

A sudden thought came to him. Crawford had paid him off. *Why?* Crawford had waited until he was out of the way before approaching Honour Mercy. *Why?* Crawford hadn't taken the easy and simple and inexpensive method of turning Richie over to the Authorities. *Why not?*

There was only one possible reason. Richie was more competition for Crawford than he had supposed, or than Crawford had admitted. There was no other explanation for Crawford's actions.

He thought about the relationship between himself and Honour Mercy, of their meeting in Newport, of her unquestioning acceptance of him, of her no-strings-attached sharing of his lot with him. He remembered how readily she had left Newport with him, willing to go anywhere with him, to leave a steady income and a comparably good life because *he* was in trouble.

Lately, she'd been growing away from him, she'd been talking as though only laziness was keeping him from working and supporting himself. But still they lived together, still they shared the same bed and gave him freely of her money. Still, when they were in bed together, they made love and enjoyed each other as much as ever.

What if Crawford had gone straight to Honour Mercy and given her the choice? Which way would she have gone? Richie had supposed, for a few traitorous moments, that she would naturally go to the stronger and abler and richer man, the man who could offer her the most. But now, when he stopped to think about it, it was obvious that Crawford didn't think that way. Crawford saw little Richie Parsons as a serious threat. And Crawford might be absolutely right.

That was why Crawford had taken this expensive and roundabout method of getting rid of Richie Parsons. If he had reported Richie to the Authorities, and Honour Mercy had found out who had turned Richie in, she would probably have had nothing at all to do with Crawford.

Of course. Crawford himself had said that he did nothing unnecessary, and only if Richie was a strong competitor for the affections of Honour Mercy was this expense of time and money necessary.

Having gone that far, Richie was stopped again. Because there was nothing he could do about it.

If he didn't take the plane, if he went back to Honour Mercy, Crawford would turn him in. There wasn't any doubt of that. If he went back to Honour Mercy, and Honour Mercy chose him over Crawford, Crawford could lose nothing by reporting Richie. But he could gain quite bit. He could gain revenge against Riche for having double-crossed the line.

So there still wasn't any choice. He still had to take that plane at six o'clock.

Richie felt miserable. This was the story of his life. The strong came along and took from him whatever they wanted for themselves, and there was nothing he could do about it. He could sneak around and take bits and pieces from others, coins and watches and wallets left carelessly where he could get his hands on them, but it wasn't the same thing. He couldn't go boldly up to anybody and take what he wanted. Yet other people could do that to him whenever they wanted. They could do it, and they did.

If only he didn't have to be afraid all the time. If only he *could* go out and get a job, any job, just so he wouldn't have to be living on Honour Mercy all the time. If only he could live without being terrified of Authority.

He had to think about it, he had to think this out carefully. He sat in the stall in the men's room at the temporary terminal, Idlewild, Queens, New York City, fifteen miles from Honour Mercy Bane, and he tried to think of something to make the inevitability of her loss less inevitable.

If he had some sort of phony identification card—But still, his fingerprints were on file in Washington. If his fingerprints were ever taken—

For what? Why would anybody take his fingerprints? They don't take your fingerprints when you just get a simple job somewhere. All he'd need would be false identification of some sort.

If he could steal a wallet—No, that wouldn't be any good, he'd have to steal a wallet from somebody his age and his size and his hair-color and everything else. He needed identification that was clearly *his*. Besides, stolen identification would be just as bad as real identification.

There was a place where he might be able to get a fake identification card. Fake draft card, Social Security card, driver's license, everything. It was a place he'd heard about when he was in high school, a bar you went to and the bartender, if you looked all right, he would pass you on to the guy who could give you the identification. The only trouble was, the place was in Albany, where Richie's home was, and where the police would be most on the lookout for him.

Still, if he wanted to keep Honour Mercy, he had to have fake identification, he had to be able to work, he had to get free of this fear of Authority. If he wanted Honour Mercy badly enough, he would go to Albany and get the fake identification.

But, by the time he came back, Honour Mercy would have gone off with Crawford already, and he wouldn't know where to look for her. Besides, false identification cost a lot of money.

He had a lot of money. He had six hundred and twenty dollars. He had a ticket to Miami, and he could turn that in for more money. And he didn't have to come back for Honour Mercy; he could bring her along with him.

Of course. That would be a lot safer, anyway. The Albany police would be looking for Richie Parsons, but they wouldn't be looking for him with a girl. They'd be looking for him alone.

And if he took Honour Mercy away with him, then Crawford couldn't get her.

He hurried from the men's room, searching for a phone booth, finally found one, and dialed home. It was quarter-past-four, according to the clock high on the terminal wall. Crawford had started back only fifteen minutes ago, and it would take him an hour at least to get to the apartment. If Honour Mercy were home—

She was. "It's me," Richie said, when she answered the phone. "It's me. Richie."

"Where are you?" she asked. "You sound as though you've been running."

He was on the verge of telling her the whole story, but instinctive caution stopped him. Crawford thought Richie was dangerous competition. Richie was inclined to agree with him. But something told him not to chance putting it to the test. Instead of telling her the truth, therefore, he said, "Something's happened. We've got to get out of New York."

"Right now?"

"Right away. We can go to Albany. I can get some phony identification cards there, and then we'll be all right."

"I thought you didn't want to go to Albany."

She was right. He didn't. The idea of it made him weak. But if he wanted Honour Mercy, he had to do it. And he wanted Honour Mercy. "I'll explain when I see you," he said. "Pack everything right away. I'll meet you at Grand Central Station. By the—by the Information booth. Get two tickets to Albany. I'll be there as soon as I can. An hour, maybe less."

"What happened, Richie?"

"I'll explain when I get there," he said, and hung up before she could ask any more.

It took five long minutes to turn the ticket in for cash, filling out some silly form about why he wasn't going after all, and then he ran out of the terminal and to the nearest taxi-stand. He climbed into the back seat of the cab and said, breathlessly, "Grand Central Station."

The driver looked at him doubtfully. "That's going to cost quite a bit, buddy."

He had six hundred and twenty dollars. He had forty dollars and ninety-two cents for the ticket to Miami. And he was going to stay with Honour Mercy. "I've got the money," he said, and the expansive smile was a new expression on his face. "Don't you worry about it."

SEVEN

JOSHUA CRAWFORD WAS sitting with a phone in his hand. The line was dead but he had not yet replaced the receiver. He was staring at a spot on the far wall and his fingers were clenched tight around the receiver.

After a moment he finally did hang up. But he remained in the same position, propped up in front of his desk by his elbows, his eyes still focused absently on the spot on the far wall.

He thought about the conversation. It had been an interesting conversation, to say the least. Almost a fascinating conversation.

It had gone something like this:

"Joshua, this is Honour Mercy. I'm afraid I won't be able to see you tonight."

"Really? What's the matter?"

"I just got a call from Richie."

Guardedly: "Oh?"

"We have to leave town right away. We're catching a train for Albany."

"I see. How come?"

A moment's pause. Then: "He wouldn't tell me. He said something about getting false identification there. I don't know. I think he's afraid the Air Force is after him."

"Is he with you now?"

"No, I'm supposed to meet him right away at Grand Central Station. I have to go now, Joshua. I wanted to call you, though, so you wouldn't worry when I didn't come tonight."

"Well. Thanks for calling."

And that had been that.

The question, Joshua Crawford thought, was just where you went from here. His first reaction, one of cold fury for the little pipsqueak who had the colossal nerve to take his money and use it against him, changed to somewhat renewed respect crossed with determination. The little punk had guts, albeit his own brand of guts. He was putting up a fight, and whether or not that fight consisted of sticking a knife into an obliging back didn't appear to be too relevant.

Whatever way you looked at it, Joshua Crawford was damned lucky. Because this fool Parsons hadn't had the brains to tell her not to, Honour Mercy had given him a more or less complete run-down on their plans. Evidently, Parsons wasn't sure enough of himself to let Honour Mercy know just what was coming off, and this was just fine with Joshua Crawford. The ball had been handed to him; now it was up to him to decide where to throw it.

He toyed with the idea of tipping off the Air Police. The Air Police were, he knew, a most efficient group of gentlemen. In addition to catching Richie as soon as they heard about him, they were almost certain to kick the crap out of him before turning him in. Which, when Joshua Crawford gave the matter a little thought, was just what the little son-of-a-bitch had coming to him. A fast arrest, and a good beating, and as long a sentence in the stockade as they were handing out these days, and Richie Parsons would disappear from his life like a pesty fly stuck on a ribbon of flypaper.

Crawford hadn't even thought about it before, about what to do if Richie crossed him. The possibility hadn't even occurred to him. Richie, a skulking sneak, a cowardly clod, would take the cash and run like the devil. Period. But things weren't that simple.

Crawford thought about calling the Air Police, thought about Honour Mercy's instant and obvious and inevitable interpretation of such a move, and tried to put himself in her place. If *he* were Honour Mercy, and if some son-of-a-bitch hollered copper on *his* own true love, he would be somewhat annoyed.

It stood to reason that Honour Mercy would react along similar lines.

This more or less ruled out the Air Police. Crawford sat at his desk, thinking, growing even more annoyed. He was beginning to realize that he had blundered, had perhaps done a seriously stupid thing. Everything had been going his way: Honour Mercy and Joshua Crawford were growing more and more together, Honour Mercy and Richie Parsons were sliding further and further apart. In time, with Honour Mercy seeing him constantly and discovering how much more enjoyable his companionship was than Richie's, the battle would have been won.

But he had been too impatient, and in this case impatience and stupidity were identical. He couldn't leave well enough alone—he was like a lawyer with a safe case who tries to bribe the judge for a dismissal instead of waiting for the jury to exonerate his client legally. By rushing things, by being a stupid man, he had forced Honour Mercy and Richie closer together.

Now, he realized, the question had been put. If Richie had a source of false identification papers in Albany, then he no longer had to fear Joshua Crawford, no longer had to be quite so much of a sneak. He would be in a position to offer serious competition to Crawford. It was, all in all, one hell of a mess.

Crawford sat and thought and smoked. The ashtray overflowed and he was developing a callous on his rear from sitting and doing nothing.

There wasn't one hell of a lot he could do. That was the sad part, and it was very sad, but the fact remained that there wasn't a hell of a lot he could do.

He could forget Honour Mercy Bane.

Sure, that's what he could do. He could forget all about her, forget what she was like in bed, what she was like walking and talking and sitting and simply doing nothing but look beautiful. He could forget how he felt alive when he was with her and dead when he was without her.

He could forget her, just as he could forget his name, just as he could remember that he was married to a slob named Selma, just as he could forget that he was alive.

Or, damn it to deep hell, he could get rid of Richie Parsons.

Get rid of him. Get rid of him because he was in the way, because he was an infernal fool who did not fit in with Joshua Crawford's plans. Get rid of him, squash him like the insect he was, use him up and throw him away like a discarded sanitary napkin. The image, he had to admit, was a damned good one.

Get rid of him. Who would miss Richie Parsons? Who could feel anything for him other than a mixture of compassion and contempt?

Joshua Crawford thought some more, then opened his desk drawer and hunted around for a small book of telephone numbers. Acme Paper Goods was listed in that book, as was Honour Mercy's home phone and a good many other numbers that didn't belong in the official business telephone book. The number Joshua Crawford was looking for was the number of a man named Vincent Canelli. He found the number and dialed it, remembering who Canelli was and what Canelli had said.

Canelli had come to him once, years ago. Canelli did something, God knew what, and Canelli had some sort of mob connection. Along with whatever illegitimate racket the man ran, he also had a dry-cleaning route business that was having hearty tax problems. Crawford had saved the day for him, partly by legal means, partly by reaching people whom Canelli could not have reached on his own.

Canelli had paid a fat fee, which was fitting and proper, but Canelli had also said something else in parting. "Josh," he had said, "you're a right guy. Anything has to be done sometime, you let me know. The way I figure it you got a favor coming. You want a man killed, you just let me know."

The phone was answered on the second ring. Joshua asked for Canelli.

"Who wants him?"

"Joshua Crawford," he told the man, wondering whether Canelli would remember him. Canelli, as it turned out, remembered him perfectly.

He asked if the offer was still good.

"Your phone clear?" Canelli wanted to know. "This line's safe. You sure yours ain't tapped?"

"It's okay, Vince."

"Right. We still better keep it sort of up in the air. Even the telephones have ears. I make it you want to order a hit. Right?"

"Right."

"Here in town?"

Crawford thought for a minute. "No," he said. "Upstate. Albany."

Canelli whistled. "I know people in Albany," he said. "Not too many, but enough. You got somebody to finger the mark?"

The conversation was a little too far up in the air and Crawford had to ask for a translation of the question. "Somebody to point out the prospect so that we make sure we contact the right man," was how it came out the second time around.

"Oh," Crawford said. "Well, no."

"You got his address?"

Crawford thought again. He did not know where Richie would be staying, and he did not know what name Richie would be using, and all in all he did not know one hell of a lot. He considered giving Vince a description, having him meet the train, but he realized that if there was one distinguishing characteristic about Richie Parsons, the insect, it was the utter impossibility of describing him.

"Vince," he said finally, "I guess it won't work. I can't give you enough."

"It's rough without a finger, Josh."

"Yes," Crawford said. "I can understand that."

"If he makes it back to the city—"

"Right," Crawford finished. "I can always call you. In the meantime forget I ever did, okay?"

A low laugh came over the wire. "Josh," Canelli was saying, "I ain't seen you or heard from you in...hell, it must be three years."

"Fine," Crawford said. And, as an afterthought. "How's business?"

"Legit," Canelli told him. "Mostly."

IT is no particular problem to get from New York to Albany. The state capital is located approximately one hundred miles due north of the only worthwhile city in the state, and train service between the two points is frequent and excellent. There are a whole host of milk trains departing every few minutes from Grand Central, as well as a bevy of long-haul passenger trains that make Albany the first hitch of a journey that starts from New York and ends up anywhere from Saint Louis to Detroit.

Richie Parsons and Honour Mercy Bane took the Ohio State Limited. The train's ultimate destination was Cincinnati, and it planned on getting there via the indirect route which included Dayton, Springfield, Cincinnati, Buffalo, and, happily, Albany.

Richie and Honour Mercy were on the train when it pulled out of Grand Central at a quarter to six. They were also on the train when it pulled into the Albany terminal at 7:30. The hour and forty-five minutes of monotony which they spent on the train was uneventful, which was just as well as far as Honour Mercy and Richie were concerned. Excitement was the last thing they craved at this point.

"A guy asked me for my draft card," Richie had explained. "He gave me a funny look when I said I left it in my other pants. If he was a cop it would of been all over."

Honour Mercy had nodded sympathetically, but Richie had the feeling that the lie needed a certain amount of embellishing. "So I kept walking," he elaborated. "And I get a few blocks away and I take a quick look over my shoulder, sort of casual-like, and I see the guy. He was trying to be real cool about it but I could tell he was following me."

The additional trappings were obviously just what the lie had needed. Honour Mercy caught her breath and looked worried. Richie had to think for a minute to be sure that it really was a lie, that there hadn't been anybody following him, that no one had asked for his draft card.

"I lost him," he went on. "Leastwise I think I lost him, but maybe he just passed me on to somebody else. I read about how they do it. When one of them gets spotted he signals another one and the other one takes out after you. I looked hard but I couldn't see any other one following me so I guess I got clear."

"It's good you called me," Honour Mercy said. "We have to stay out of town until you have some identification." She was about to tell him that she had called Crawford but she decided not to. He might be jealous, and she didn't want that to happen. It was all perfectly natural discussing Richie with Crawford—he was the kind of man who could listen calmly to anything she said. He understood things. But for some reason it was not perfectly natural to discuss Crawford with Richie.

The private compartment on the train had been Richie's idea. It cost a little more but it was worth it for two reasons. First of all, it was a safety measure—there was no telling when somebody would recognize him, somebody who had known him before. Secondly, it made it look as though he was really worried about being discovered. By this time it was his own private conviction that a visit from the Air Police was about as pressing a danger as an atomic attack on south-central Kansas, but there was no point in letting Honour Mercy in on the fact.

The private compartment, however, accomplished something else. It left Honour Mercy and Richie thoroughly alone with each other, more alone than they had been in quite some time. There they were, the two of them, and with the compartment all closed up they were alone. The togetherness and the aloneness, combined with the marvelous feeling of security that was bound up in the whole idea of false identification papers and the false new identity they would bring, made Richie suddenly very strong, very much the dominant personality. He took Honour Mercy on his lap, and he held Honour Mercy close to him and kissed her, and after he had kissed her several times and touched her breasts, he wished fervently that the trip was over already and they were in a hotel room in Albany.

Which, before too long, is where they were.

From the terminal they taxied to the Conning Towers on State Street. The Conning Towers was, and had been for more years than Richie had been alive, Albany's finest hotel. He had never so much as stepped into the lobby before. It was hardly the most inconspicuous place in town, but Richie reasoned this way: the better the place they stayed in, and the nicer the restaurants they ate in, and the more exclusive neighborhood they roamed around in, the less chance he stood of running into anybody who had known him before.

He figured this out, and he had explained it to Honour Mercy on the train. Even so, he had a tough time telling the cab driver where he wanted to go, and a tougher time actually squaring his shoulders and walking into the lobby. Once inside it was even worse. The high ceilings and the thick carpet made him more nervous, and his voice squeaked when he asked the thin gray clerk for a double room.

The clerk nodded and handed him the register and a ballpoint pen. Richie got enough control over his fingers to get a tentative grip on the pen and leaned over the register to sign his name.

He almost wrote RICHIE PARSONS. The pen was actually touching the paper, ready to make the first stroke of the "R," when it occurred to him that he was no longer Richie Parsons, not if he wanted to stay alive and free. His hand shook and the pen dribbled from his grasp and bounced onto the floor. He reached over to pick it up, hating himself, hating the thin gray clerk, hating everything, and suddenly incapable of thinking up a name for himself.

Then, the pen recovered and poised once more, he remembered the author of a book he had been reading the day before and signed the register ANDREW SHAW. The clerk nodded, attempted a smile, and rang for a bellhop. The bellhop picked up the suitcase that Honour Mercy had packed and led them up an impressively winding staircase to their room on the first floor. The bellhop opened the door, ushered them inside, took an idiotically long time opening the window and checking for soap and towels, and finally accepted the quarter that Richie barely remembered to hand him. Then, mercifully, the bellhop left and closed the door after him.

Only then did Richie relax. He relaxed quite visibly, throwing himself down on the big double bed and letting out his breath all at once.

"Well," Honour Mercy said, "I guess we got here all right."

"I almost ruined everything down there. Signing the book, I mean."

"That's all right," she told him.

"He must figure it's not my name, the way I had so much trouble getting it written."

"Sure," she said, smiling. "He probably thinks you signed another name because we aren't married and you're embarrassed. It's better that way. Surest way in the world to hide something is to pretend you're hiding something else."

Richie thought about that. It made a lot of sense, especially in view of the fact that he had adopted much the same tactics in getting Honour Mercy and himself the hell out of New York. The only difference was that he had hidden what he was running from by pretending to be running from something else, but it worked out to about the same.

"Andrew Shaw," he said aloud, testing the name. "Sounds okay to me. Maybe you ought to practice calling me Andy."

She said *Andy* twice, then laughed. "Sounds funny," she complained. "Can't I call you Richie any more?"

"Not in public. Not when we're out where people can hear and get suspicious."

"How about in private?"

"That's different," he said. He watched her, moving about and unpacking things and putting them away, and he thought that it was time for him to get out of the hotel and get in touch with the man who could fix up the phony identification for him. He watched her some more, watched the way her body moved and studied the way it was formed, and he decided that although it was definitely time to get in touch with the man, the man would be around for a few more hours.

"In bed," he said. "In bed you can call me Richie. When you're in bed with me."

She turned and looked at him. "You want me now?"

He nodded.

"Now?"

"Now."

She started to come toward the bed and he stood up to take her into his arms. When he kissed her he sensed something that he couldn't pin down, some uncertainty or anxiety, but he didn't care to spend any time analyzing it. Anyway, it was gone when he kissed her a second time, and during the third kiss when they were lying together on top of the big bed he forgot that the uncertainty or anxiety had ever existed at all. He needed her very urgently and he could not wait this time, could not wait and do things nice and slow the way she usually liked to do things. He was in a hurry.

"Honey, you'll rip my dress!"

"I'll buy you a new one."

The voice did not even sound like his own. And the hands that hurried with her clothing were much stronger, much more certain of themselves than his hands. The hands, the clever and hungry hands that touched that perfect body all over, they were not his hands at all.

He took her and it was good, very good. It was hard and tough and fast and the blood pounded against his brain. It was an affirmation, a declaration, and when it was over he felt not exhausted but reinvigorated, as if he had taken a vitamin pill instead of a woman.

Usually, after they had made love, he would lie limp and weak in the shelter of her arms. This time, however, he rolled away from her as soon as the initial glow had passed from him. He lay on his side, not facing her, and for some reason he did not want to look at her just then.

A moment later he was on his feet, drawing the covers over her nude body and heading for the bathroom. "I want to take a shower," he called over his shoulder. "Then I'll go see about the papers. You stay right here until I come back."

He turned on the shower and stepped into the tub. From the bed Honour Mercy could hear the water pounding down in steady torrent. Then, above the roar of the shower, she heard another sound, one she had never heard before.

He was singing.

AFTER the abortive phone call to Canelli, Joshua Crawford had sat at his desk for perhaps twenty-five seconds. Then, all at once, he sprang to his feet and hurried out of the office without saying goodbye to anybody. He hailed a cab and left it at the corner of Third Avenue and 24th Street in front of an establishment known only as HOCK SHOP. That was what the black letters on the dingy yellow clapboard proclaimed and that was what the three golden balls were there to signify. That was enough.

The owner, a round-shouldered man with thick glasses who looked like all pawnbrokers everywhere, was speedily persuaded to sell a .38-caliber police positive revolver to one John Brown for the sum of two hundred dollars. The pawnbroker, who had bought the gun from a sneak thief for ten dollars, was pleased with the transaction. Joshua Crawford, who didn't give much of a damn what the gun cost him, was equally pleased. He put the gun in his briefcase, tucked the case under his arm, and strode out of the store.

He called Selma from a pay station in a candy store two doors down the street. "I'm working late," he told her, hardly caring whether or not she believed him. "I'll see you tomorrow."

Another cab took him to Grand Central. He bought a ticket on the Empire State, boarded the train and collapsed into a coach seat. The train seemed to crawl and the briefcase on his lap weighed a ton but he lived through the trip without knowing just how he managed it. It was a few minutes to nine when he was on his way out of the Albany terminal with the briefcase once again under his arm.

Finding them, he knew, was going to be a problem. He had to nose them out all on his own, and he had to do it without attracting any undue attention, and this was not going to be the easiest thing in the world. Then, when he did find them, he had to get to Richie without Honour Mercy seeing him. Then, and only then, he had to put a bullet into Richie, a bullet that would forever eliminate Richie as any sort of competition whatsoever.

Then he had to get away. If nobody saw him and if he got clear of the scene of the crime, then he ought to be safe all the way. There was no connection between him and Richie other than Honour Mercy, and it was extremely unlikely that she would have any suspicion at all that he had killed Richie. The gun was untraceable. The anonymity of a coach seat on the Empire was complete.

But the big thing went beyond guns and witnesses. It was simply that the police would never suspect him, and unless they started investigating him, they would have to leave the crime forever unsolved. If they had any idea it was him, they would get him in no time, no matter how much trouble he took in covering his trail. That was why murderers got caught—because they had motives for their murders. If a man had no motive, or if his motive was sufficiently obscure, getting away with murder was a lot easier than it sounded.

But first he had to find them. And before that he had to eat—there was no point in killing a man on an empty stomach. He went to Keeler's, on State Street, because it was supposed to be the best restaurant in Albany. The steak they brought him was tender and juicy and the baked potato was powdery with a crisp skin. The coffee fit the three traditional tests—it was black as hell, strong as death, and sweet as love. He had three cups of it and felt one hell of a lot better when the caffeine got to work on his system.

It was almost ten when he left the restaurant. The night was cold and clear, the streets virtually empty. He started walking downtown on State Street, wondering just how he was going to find that idiot Parsons, when, impossibly, he saw him.

At first he did not believe it. For one thing, the guy a block ahead of him wasn't walking like Richie had walked. His head was held high and his shoulders were back; there was even a certain amount of spring to his step. That didn't jibe with the picture Crawford had of him.

But it *was* Richie. Crawford got a look at his face when he stopped to study a window display at a sporting goods store, and there was no longer any question in his mind. It was Richie, and Richie was just standing there waiting to be killed, and now all he had to do was catch up with him and take the revolver from the briefcase and blow a hole in Richie Parsons' head.

Which would be a pleasure.

But how?

He kept following Richie, staying about a block behind him, hoping he would leave the main street and find himself a nice quiet alley to get shot in. That would be the best way, the easiest way all around. Shooting him dead on State Street would be a pretty tricky proposition, especially since the damned gun didn't have a silencer. He had tried to buy a silencer, but that ass of a pawnbroker hadn't had one to sell him. When the gun went off, it was going to sound like a cannon, and State Street was hardly the place to shoot off a cannon.

When Richie went into the Conning Towers Hotel, Crawford felt like crying. But there wasn't a hell of a lot he could do about it. He had missed his chance for the night, but there was always a chance that he would get a crack at Richie in the morning, or later on if the two of them didn't go back to New York the next day. The identification Richie had come for might take a while to prepare, in which case Richie Parsons would never leave Albany alive. If Crawford never got another chance at him, then Canelli could have the job in the city and Crawford would do the fingering. That would be safer in the long run, anyhow, even though there was a certain personal satisfaction in doing the job on his own.

Joshua Crawford decided to have a cup of coffee in the beanery across the street from the Conning Towers. The coffee was not at all good and he almost left after the first sip. But for some reason he stayed, sipping at it from time to time and smoking constantly, his eyes flashing from the glowing end of his cigarette to the impressive entrance of the Conning Towers.

If he had not lingered over the coffee, he would not have been there to see Richie Parsons emerge alone from the hotel about a half-hour after entering it. When he did, a jolt of excitement went through him and he dropped a dime on the counter and left the diner in a hurry. He waited until Richie was half a block ahead and then began to follow him.

This time Richie didn't stay on State Street. This time he walked into just the sort of neighborhood Crawford would have selected—a warehouse district, empty of people and homes and apartment buildings. An ideal setting for a quick and quiet murder.

Crawford began walking faster. Without breaking stride he opened the briefcase, got the gun in his right hand and closed the briefcase again. He kept walking faster and in no time at all he was just a few feet behind Richie.

The gun was already pointed at Richie when he turned around. He stared and his eyes took in first Crawford and then the gun, and then both Crawford and the gun at once. For the shadow of an instant he stared and his face was a study.

Then there was a hole in it.

EIGHT

THERE WAS A full-length mirror on the back of the bathroom door and Honour Mercy, emerging from her shower, toweled the steam from the surface of the mirror and looked at herself, trying to find comfort in the appearance of her body.

But there was no comfort there, there or anywhere else. "He's going to leave me," she told the girl in the mirror. "He doesn't need me anymore, and he's going to leave me."

She wondered if Richie himself knew yet that he would be leaving her soon, and she thought that he was probably beginning to suspect it. The difference in his attitude, the way he had sung in the shower, the fact that he was now out of the hotel somewhere; they all gave indication of the change in Richie Parsons that was making her unnecessary to him.

A month ago, Richie wouldn't have dared set foot it Albany. Once in Albany, he wouldn't have dreamed of registering at the city's most expensive hotel. Having rented a hotel room, no power on earth would have moved him from that hotel room, to roam the streets of his home town late at night.

She understood some of the causes of the change. She was a major cause. When he had been at his most bewildered, his most frightened, she had given him refuge and friendship. More than that, she had given him an appreciative sexual partner, without which he would never have emerged from his cringing, cowering shell. She had built up his ego, supported him, comforted him, protected him, and his personality had developed character.

There were other factors, too. The longer he had successfully avoided capture by the authorities, the less the authorities were a menace in his mind. And with that threat waning, he gradually had less reason to cover, less reason to be afraid.

The decision to come to Albany was the final step in the change. He had made no decisions at all since he had run away from the Air Force; Honour Mercy had made all the decisions for both of them. Now, at last, he had made a decision of his own. And his decision had been to brave his terror where it would be the fiercest. In his own home town.

As she thought about it, it occurred to her that there was a step missing in the chain. Richie was a different person today—had been a different person when she met him at Grand Central—from the Richie of yesterday. Something had happened that had forced him to make the decision; and then he had made the decision, and the change had been complete. But what had forced the decision?

The man who had asked him for his draft card? She considered that, and rejected it. No, it would have had to be more than that. An incident like that would simply have sent Richie running for shelter to their apartment, and he wouldn't have ventured out on the street again for days. There had been something else; something more than what he had told her.

For the first time, Richie had kept something from her, had lied to her. And that knowledge only confirmed the idea that Richie was going to leave her.

She dried herself hurriedly, taking no enjoyment from it. Usually, she luxuriated in the shower, and in the drying after that, with a huge soft towel like this, rubbing her skin until it tingled and shone. Tonight, she couldn't think about such things. She patted herself dry as quickly as possible and went out to the other room to look at the clock-radio on the nightstand.

Richie had said he was going to be out for an hour at the most. He had gone out for a walk a little before ten—proving to himself his new independence and fearlessness—and then he had gone out at eleven o'clock exactly. This time, to talk to the man he knew who might be able to arrange false identification for him. And he had promised he would be back within the hour; he would be back by midnight for sure.

The clock-radio said that it was now quarter to one.

A Girl Called Honey

"He isn't coming back," she said. She said it aloud, without realizing she was going to, and then she listened to the echo of the words, and wondered if she'd been right.

Would he do it this way? He couldn't, that would be too cruel, too unfair. To leave her stranded here, in a city she didn't know, in this expensive hotel room, with no money, with nothing—that would be too terribly cruel.

But it would be the easiest way out, for him, and Honour Mercy knew her Richie well. Richie would always take the easiest way out.

If he isn't home by one o'clock, she told herself, I'll know he's left me.

Fifteen minutes later, she said to herself: If he isn't home by one-thirty, I'll know for sure that he's left me.

When the big hand was on the six and the little hand was on the one, she started to cry.

When the big hand was on the eight and the little hand had edged over toward the two, she finished crying.

By the time the big hand had reached the nine and the little hand hadn't done much of anything, she was dressed and lipsticked, and ready to go.

Honour Mercy Bane was a pragmatist. "Go to Newport and be a bad woman," her parents told her, and she went. "We've got to pack up and get out of Newport," Richie said, and she packed. "Talk to me," said Joshua Crawford, and she talked.

And now, now she was alone and penniless in a strange city, with a huge hotel bill that would be hers alone to pay, and once again she was a pragmatist. It was quarter to two in the morning, and time for Honour Mercy to go to work.

Honour Mercy had learned a lot, changed a lot, grown a lot since Newport, too. Six months ago, in this situation, she would have been at a loss. She would have tried to hustle on one of the wrong streets and spent the night in jail. Now, she knew better. She left the room, pressed the button for the elevator, and said to the operator on the way down, "Where can a girl find some work in this town, do you know?" Because elevator operators in hotels always did know.

He looked at her blankly, either not yet understanding or playing dumb for reasons of his own. "Lots of Civil Service jobs with the state around here," he said.

"That isn't exactly what I was thinking."

He studied her, and chewed his cud, and finally made up his mind. "Management don't allow hustling in the hotel," he said.

"Don't tell me where I can't," she told him. "Tell me where I can."

"I get off duty here at six o'clock," he said.

She understood at once, and forced a smile for his benefit. "I imagine I'll be back by then."

He nodded. "When you go outside," he said, "walk down the hill to Green Street. Turn right."

She waited for more directions, but there were no more forthcoming, so she said, "Thanks."

"Don't mention it," he said.

The elevator reached the main floor, and she walked through the empty lobby to the street, and started down the State Street hill.

SIX blocks south and one block west of the Conning Towers, Joshua Crawford sat in a chair beside the CID man's desk and said, "I just don't remember a thing. It's all a blank."

"Lawyer Crawford," said the CID man, with heavy emphasis on the first word, "I hope you aren't going to try for a temporary insanity plea. You had the gun on you. We can prove premeditation with no trouble at all."

Crawford rubbed a damp palm across his face. "I *must* have been crazy," he whispered, meaning it sincerely. "I *must* have been crazy." He looked pleadingly at the CID man. "My wife," he said. "This is going to be hell for my wife."

The CID man waited.

"In many ways," said Crawford seriously, "my wife is an excellent woman." His hand came up to his face again.

The CID man waited. He was bored. He had nothing to do but wait now. They always cried before confessing.

THE first two blocks of Green Street were dark and narrow and lifeless, except for an occasional derelict asleep beside an empty bottle in a doorway. The third block was just as narrow, but brightly lit from a double row of bars, and people were constantly on the move. Cars were parked on both sides of the street, leaving only one narrow lane open in the middle for the one-way traffic, of which there was practically none. The derelicts who were still shakily on their feet were all over this block, mingling with short, slender, bright-eyed homosexuals, hard-looking hustlers, strange-uniformed sailors—since Albany is also a port city, shipping grain and manufactured goods to the European markets—and clusters of skinny, black-jacketed teenagers. It didn't look good to Honour Mercy; it was lower and harder and more primitive than anything she'd ever run into before, and so she kept on walking.

The fourth block was half-bright and half-dark. Bars were scattered here and there on both sides of the street, but crammed in with them were dark, empty-windowed tenements. And in the doorways and ground-floor windows of the tenements were women, watching the street. This was closer to the world Honour Mercy knew, and so she stopped at the first dark doorway on her side of the street and looked at the Negro woman standing there, "I just got to town," she said.

"Come in here off the street!" hissed the woman.

Honour Mercy, surprised, did as she was told, and the woman said, "What you want?"

"I just got here," repeated Honour Mercy. "I don't know what things are like."

"They ain't good," said the woman. "The goddam police is on the rampage." She laughed harshly at Honour Mercy's blank look. "No, they ain't honest," she said. "They just greedy. They want all the bread they can get. The only way to make a dime in this town is hustle on your own and take your chances on being picked up." She looked out at the street and ducked back, clutching Honour Mercy's arm. "Get back in here!"

Honour Mercy, not understanding what was going on, cowered with the woman in the darkest corner of the entranceway. Outside, a three-year-old Buick drove slowly by, two men in the front seat. The car was painted black, with small gray letters on the front door reading, "POLICE," and a red light, now off, attached to the top of the right fender.

The car slid by, slow and silent, and the hand gripping Honour Mercy's arm slowly relaxed. Honour Mercy, impressed by it all, whispered, "Who was that?"

"The King," said the woman, and the way she said it, it wasn't as funny as it should have been. "He runs this section. He's the only cop in the city dares walk down this street alone. He goes into a bar—crowded, jumpin'—and he picks out the man he's after, and he says, 'You come with me.' And he walks out, with the guy at his heels, and nobody stops him. Any other cop in this town try that, he'd get his badge shoved down his throat."

"How can *he* do it?"

The woman shrugged. "He breaks heads," she said. "And he's straight. He don't take a penny, and he don't make a phony rap. Get rid of him, you get somebody bad down here to take his place."

When Honour Mercy left the hotel, it had seemed simple enough. She would go to work. Now, it didn't seem so simple any more. This city had a set-up unlike anything she'd ever seen before.

"You got a pad?" the woman asked suddenly.

Honour Mercy shook her head.

"No good," said the woman. "You stuck to guys with cars. That means you got to stay on the sidewalk, where they can see you. And where the law can see you. You ought to wait till you get a pad."

"I need money tonight," said Honour Mercy. It wasn't strictly true. The hotel wouldn't start asking for money for a day or two at least. What Honour Mercy needed tonight was to work, to be doing something that would take her mind off the defection of Richie Parsons.

The woman shrugged again. "Then you got to hit the pavement. Look out for one-tone cars, specially Buicks and Oldsmobiles. That's the law, whether it says so on the car or not."

"Thanks a lot," said Honour Mercy. "I appreciate it."

"We all in the same racket," said the woman.

"What—what are the prices around here?"

The woman looked her over. "You're white," she said. "And you're young. You could get away with charging ten."

Ten. That was low pay indeed, low, low pay after New York. Honour Mercy decided right there to get enough money together to get back to New York as quickly as possible. Back to New York, where the organization was so much smoother, the prices so much higher, the clientele so much better. Back to New York, and, come to think of it, back to Joshua Crawford.

Joshua was going to ask her to be his mistress. She knew that, but she'd avoided acknowledging it before this, because it would have brought up the problem of Richie. But now that Richie had left her, there was no problem.

She would get the money quickly, get back to New York, and she would become Joshua Crawford's mistress. It would be a good life.

"Thanks again," she said to the woman, and left the darkness of the doorway.

She walked for twenty minutes before she got a customer. Single-color Buicks and Oldsmobiles had driven by, slowly, the drivers watching the sidewalks, but she hadn't even glanced at them as they passed her. She had walked purposefully, as though to a set destination, when cars like that passed her, and she hadn't been stopped.

The customer—or customers—arrived in a late-forties Ford, amateurishly painted gold and black. There were four teenagers in the car, and the driver slowed to a crawl, matching Honour Mercy's speed, and they went half a block that way before he murmured. "Hey. You lookin' for somebody?"

She turned and gave him the big smile. "Nobody in particular," she said.

He stopped the car completely. "Come on over here."

She went, studying the driver's face. He was about seventeen, sharp-nosed and dissatisfied-looking, with a crewcut. The other three were all in the shadows within the car, but she knew they would look very much like the driver.

When she got to the car, the driver said, "How much?"

"I charge ten dollars—" she noticed the change of expression in time "—but with a group like this, of course, it's cheaper."

"How much?" he repeated, more warily.

She thought rapidly. Seventeen-year-old boys, she knew from past experience, had a habit of not lasting very long. She could probably go through all four of them in fifteen minutes, including time lost changing partners. If they didn't have to drive very far to find a place where they could park in privacy, and if they didn't waste too much getting down to business once they'd parked, she might even be able to get back in time for one more trick tonight. Thinking of this, and judging, as best she could, the amount of money the boy and his friends would be able and willing to spend, she came, almost without a pause in the conversation, to a number.

"Twenty-five dollars."

She waited through the whispered consultation. Once they'd figured out that that was only six dollars and twenty-five cents apiece, the consultation was rapidly over. The door to the rear seat opened, a tall blond-haired boy stepped out, and the driver said, "Okay. Climb aboard."

To her left was the blond boy. To her right was a short, black-haired, large-nosed boy, who looked terribly nervous. Up front, the boy beside the driver was black-haired and spectacled. She gave each of them a mental tag, to keep them straight. There was the Blond, the Driver, the Glasses, and the Nervous.

The car turned left at the next intersection and drove through dark and twisting streets. The Blond put his hand on her knee and squeezed experimentally. Remembering that she wanted them to be in condition to make short work of it, she smiled at him and squeezed back. He grinned and slid his hand up her leg, under the skirt, then murmured, "Why don't you get the panties off right now? Save some time."

"All right."

It took a lot of squirming, in the crowded back seat, to get them off, and she made sure she did a lot of the squirming against Nervous, to her right. She wanted to get him in the mood, too, and she was afraid that would take some doing.

The squirming did the trick. When she was settled again, the Blond's hand was once more up under her skirt, and the Nervous had a hand inside her blouse. He tugged at the bra and whispered, betraying the fact that he was still nervous, "Take that off, too."

More squirming this time, complicated by the fact that the Blond's hand was doing distracting things beneath the skirt, and finally her blouse was open and her bra off and lying on the ledge behind the seat. The Nervous bent forward and kissed her breast, and the Blond's hand was still moving beneath her skirt. She closed her eyes and stopped thinking.

The car was on a main street for a while, and then off that, and there were occasional glimpses of the river off to the left. They passed warehouses and trucking concerns and bakeries, all closed and dark and silent now. They passed the spot where Richie Parsons had stopped living three hours before, but there was no longer any sign that there had been violence here tonight. This was also the spot where the cruising prowl car had so unexpectedly caught Joshua Crawford, open-faced and panting, the gun still in his hand, in the hard bright beams of its headlights, but the spot bore no witness of him, either. The car drove by, and farther on it turned left again, toward the river, and then right, and stopped.

Honour Mercy was ready. She wouldn't have to fake her responses with these boys. But she still retained enough presence of mind to say, "Money in advance, boys. That's standard."

The four of them got out of the car, leaving Honour Mercy in the back seat, and consulted together outside. The Driver came back, finally, with the money. A five-dollar bill, a bunch of wrinkled singles, and two dollars in change. Honour Mercy stashed it all in her purse, stashed the purse on the window ledge with her bra, and smiled at the Driver. "Are you first?"

"You bet I am," he said.

She'd given him the right nickname. He came at her fast and brutal, crushing her down in the cramped back seat, driving her down and back, half-smothering her. But his very force betrayed him. He was finished before he was barely started, leaving Honour Mercy moving alone. But he seemed satisfied as he crawled out of the car again, and walked over to the waiting group.

The Blond was second, and he had read books on the subject. He tried to come at her slow and gradually, full of technique. Under normal circumstances, she would have followed his lead, because she enjoyed the niceties of technique, no matter how academic. But there had been the hands and lips all over her on the ride, and the Driver had just finished with her, and she was in no mood to be gradual. She sunk her teeth into his shoulder and her nails into his buttocks and he forgot the textbooks.

They stopped together, rigid and straining and open-mouthed, and when he left, the inside of the car was beginning to be heavy with the acrid perfume of love.

Glasses came next, and he had a variety of ideas. There were other things he wanted done first, some of them very difficult in the back seat of a late-forties Ford, and she had a chance to cool down a bit and to begin to think again.

Glasses had her spend too much time with the preliminaries, and all at once the main event was canceled. But he smiled and shrugged and said, "That's the way it goes." And she knew that that was the way he had wanted it all along, and she wondered if he understood yet that he was homosexual.

Nervous came last, and Nervous wasn't even ready. She realized, with a sinking feeling, that this was Nervous's first time. The backseat was cramped, the air in the car was now too heavy for comfort, and she knew that she was a sweat-stained, disheveled and panting mess, stimulating to a man, perhaps, but not to a boy coming to sex for the first time.

She did what she could for him, smiling at him, talking gently with him, telling him that lots of men needed help in getting ready. She gave him the help he needed, half-afraid that it just wasn't going to work out, and slowly she felt the interest growing within him. And when he was ready, she didn't try to rush it, she tried to make it last, because she understood how important it was to him, this first time.

But nothing could have made him last. He was here and gone again in two shakes of his nervous tail, and then it was all over and she was alone in the back seat of the car and slipping back into her clothes.

They waited outside until she was ready. When she was dressed, she climbed out of the car, needing fresh air and a bit of walking to revive her completely.

The four of them were clustered around the front of the car, and she glanced at them, and all of a sudden she realized what was going to happen. She panicked, standing frozen beside the car, not knowing what to do.

The money, that was the important thing. The purse was still on the window ledge, and she tried to be casual in her movements as she opened the rear door again and got the purse.

But when she got back out of the car, they were bunched around her, and the Driver was standing directly in front of her, grinning bitterly and saying, "Where you going, Sweetheart?"

"Please," she said. "I need the money. I need it."

"Don't we all," he said.

Nervous, a step back of the rest, piped up, "Let her have the money, Danny. We can afford it."

The Driver—Danny—whirled and snapped, "Shut up, you clown. Now she knows my name."

"Let her keep the money," Nervous insisted, but it was weak insistence, and Honour Mercy knew he was a poor, albeit willing, ally.

If she was going to get out of this, she'd have to get out by herself. While they were all distracted by Nervous, she might just be able to—

She got two steps, and the Driver had her by the arm and was spinning her around, shoving her back against the side of the car. "Where do you think you're going, Sweetheart?" he asked again, and hit her solidly in the stomach.

The punch knocked the wind out of her, and she sagged against the car, clutching her stomach, her mouth open as she gasped for air. And the shrill voice of Nervous was sounding again, but she knew it was no use, and the sound stopped when the Driver snarled, "Shut that idiot up."

She could do no more than stand, weakly, leaning against the car, trying for breath. When the purse was ripped out of her hands, she could do nothing to stop it. And when she heard the Driver say, "I think I'm going to teach this little bitch a lesson," she could do nothing to protect herself or to get away.

One of the others—Glasses?—said, "What the hell, Danny, leave her alone. We got the money."

"She wants a lesson," insisted Danny. And he backhanded her across the side of the face.

She would have fallen, but he caught her and shoved her back against the side of the car again, and held her with one hand cruelly gripping her breast while he slapped her, openhanded, back and forth across the face. She cried out, finally having breath, and he switched at once, punching her twice, hard, in the stomach. As she doubled, he punched her twice more, on the point of each breast.

She screamed with the searing pain of it and fell to her knees. He slapped her—forehand, backhand, forehand, backhand—and dragged her to her feet once more, shoving her back against the car, and as he did so he kneed her, and ground the knuckles of his right hand into her side, just under the ribcage.

He wouldn't let her fall. He held her with a clutching, twisting hand on her breast, and his other hand beat at her, face and breast and stomach and side, open-hand and closed fist.

The Blond and Glasses pulled him away from her finally, and she collapsed onto the dank, weed-choked ground, unable to move or make a sound, capable only of breathing and feeling the pain stabbing through her body from every place that he had hit.

After a moment, she heard the car start, and she was terrified that now he was going to drive over her, but the sound of the motor receded to silence, and she knew they had gone away.

She lay for half an hour unmoving, until the worst pain subsided, and then she struggled to a sitting position, and had to stop again, because movement brought the pain back, hard and tight, and she was afraid she would faint. And then she hoped she would faint.

But she didn't faint, and after another while she managed to get to her feet. Behind her was the street that would lead her back to the downtown section. Ahead of her was the faint rustle of the river. To either side of her were the dark hulks of commercial buildings.

She knew she must look horrible, and with the lessening of the pain she could think about that. If she showed herself on the street looking like this, the police would pick her up right away. And even if she managed to avoid the police, she would never get through the hotel lobby.

Moving painfully, she made her way toward the sound of the river. There was a narrow, steep incline between two buildings which overhung the river's edge, and old wooden pilings to lean against on the way down. The water was brackish and foul-smelling, filled with sewage and industrial waste, the filthy pollution of a river beside which industrial cities had been built. But it was water.

She knelt gingerly, and pushed her hands into the water. It was cold, and she waited, unmoving, letting the chill move up her arms to her torso, reviving her, restoring her, and then she lay prone and splashed the fouled water over her face, washing away the smudges and stains of her beating.

She almost went to sleep, and her head would have fallen forward and her face would have been underwater. She caught herself in time, and backed hastily away from the edge, terrified at the nearness of death.

She used her panties to towel her face and hands and arms, then threw the sodden garment into the water, and turned toward the street.

Midway, she found her purse, lying on the ground. She carried it out to the street, where a streetlight across the way gave her enough light to check its contents.

There was no money in it, but nothing else had been touched. Her hand mirror was there, and she inspected her face critically, seeing that the signs of the beating were still there. And her hair was a mass of tangled knots, damp and filthy.

She had a comb and lipstick and powder. She repaired the damage as best she could, and when she was finished, she looked presentable enough, if she didn't get too close to anybody. She smoothed and adjusted her clothing, rubbing out some of the stains, and started off for the hotel.

She was still weak. Every once in a while, she had to stop and lean against a building for a moment, to catch her breath and wait for the dizziness to go away. And when she came to the bottom of the State Street hill, she looked up at the hotel, so high above her, and she thought she would never be able to get up that long steep hill.

But she made it, finally, and entered the hotel lobby softly, circling away from the desk, where the night-clerk was busy with file cards, and getting to the elevator without being stopped.

The operator looked at her with surprise. "What happened to you?"

She, shook her head. "Nothing. Never mind."

"Listen," he said. "There's cops in your room."

She stared at him.

The weakness was coming in again, and she thought that this time she would faint for sure, but the operator was still talking, and what he said next drove the weakness away and left her pale and trembling, but only too conscious.

"Yep," he said, nodding, chewing his cud, happy to be the news-bearer. "Some crazy queer shot him. Right between the eyes. Signed a confession and everything, and then jumped right out a window." He shook his head, grinning. "Them coppers are sure mad," he said. "It don't look good when a prisoner manages to kill himself that way. Hey! Where you going?"

But she didn't answer him, because she didn't know.

She didn't know until she was at the foot of State Street once more, and looking at the signs on a telephone pole. The top sign was shield-shaped, and said, "U.S. Route 9." The bottom sign was rectangular and said, "NEW YORK," with an arrow underneath.

New York. She nodded, and noticed she'd dropped the purse somewhere. She was empty-handed. Not that it mattered.

New York. She would be Joshua's mistress.

She started walking in the direction the arrow indicated. A chill breeze snaked up under her skirt, and she was no longer wearing panties, but she didn't notice. She just walked, and when false dawn was streaking the sky to her left, Albany was behind her.

NINE

TIRES SCREECHED AND kicked gravel as the big car pulled off the road and squealed to a stop on the shoulder. The driver leaned across the seat, opened the door and stuck his head out.

"Want a lift?"

She ran to the car. In the back of her mind she heard her mother cautioning her not to accept rides with strange men. But then there had been many things that her mother had told her. It was no time to start listening to those things.

"Where you headed?"

"New York."

"Hop in."

She hopped in. The car was a new Buick and it was big. So was the driver. A shock of straw-colored hair topped his big boulder of a head. His hands were huge and they held the steering wheel as if it might fall apart unless he personally held it together. When she had closed the door, he let out the clutch and put the accelerator pedal on the floor. The car responded as though it was scared of him.

"Nice car you got."

The man nodded, agreeing. "She'll do a hundred easy," he told her. "One-twenty if I push her a little. The mileage isn't much, but if I wanted to worry about mileage I'd get myself a bicycle. I want a car that'll move when I want her to move."

He had what he wanted, in that case. When Honour Mercy looked at the speedometer she noticed that the little red needle was pointing at sixty-five and edging over toward seventy.

"That's why I travel this road," he went on. "Thruway takes you from Albany down to New York just the same, but those troopers watch the Thruway pretty close. Limit's sixty and when you go much over sixty-five they stop you and hit you with a ticket. That's no fun. Costs a guy twenty, thirty bucks for the ticket plus a few bucks in tolls. No fun at all."

The needle was pointing at seventy-five.

"You come from Albany?"

She nodded.

"Figure on hitching? Reason I ask is I didn't see you standing with your thumb out. Just walking. Looked like you were trying to walk clear to New York."

This was precisely what she had been doing, but she didn't think the man would accept it as a logical explanation. "I was having trouble getting a ride," she said. "So I just started walking for a few minutes. I thought maybe I'd have more luck if I went on down to the first intersection."

He nodded and she decided that she had picked the right reply. "I'm not from Albany myself," the man was saying. "Pass through there a lot, though. I live up in Rome; got a business up there. You know where that is?"

She didn't.

"Yes," she said.

"Have to run down to New York a lot," he went on. "On business. So I come through Albany. Don't stop there too often, but this time I made a breakfast stop on the outskirts. I like a cup of coffee now and then when I drive. Keeps my mind on what I'm doing."

The needle pointed at eighty.

"Quite a thing up there last night, wasn't there? I had a look at the paper while I was eating; just had time to skim over the front page. Quite a thing. Double killing and all. You hear about it?"

She shook her head. Richie had evidently made the papers, she thought. Maybe if she just let this man run off at the mouth about it she could learn a little more about what had happened.

"Quite a thing," he said. "Quite a thing. Young kid checked into a hotel with a girl, went out for a walk and a guy came up behind him and blew his head off. Shot him smack dab in the face and there wasn't a hell of a lot of his face left afterwards. Least that's what the paper said. They seem to build these things up."

She shuddered. He looked at her and misinterpreted the shudder as normal female revulsion and patted her knee to soothe her. When he touched her she wondered how long it would take him to make a pass at her. She knew he was going to; knew that was why he had picked her up in the first place. He would make a pass at her and she would let him do whatever he wanted to do with her. He was going to New York and he would take her there, and in exchange he had a right to the temporary use of her body. That was fundamental.

"Who did it?" she managed. "Did they catch the man who did it?"

"Sure did," the big man said. His hand was still on her knee, not to calm her, not now, and the speedometer needle was moving toward ninety. She hoped they would live to get back to New York. Because that was all that mattered—getting to New York and becoming Joshua's mistress. That was what she had to do and the man with his big hand on her knee was just another means to the end.

"Caught him in the act," the man said. "Just about in the act. Red-handed, the way they say it. Paper said he was standing there with the smoking gun still in his hand when the police took hold of him. Didn't make a fuss or anything."

He lapsed into temporary silence, becoming preoccupied with her knee, and she had to prompt him. "You said double killing. Who else did he kill?"

"Didn't kill nobody else. Killed himself. Police had him up at the station house and he took a dive through the window. Fell a couple stories and that was the end of him."

She shuddered again, as memory tried to intrude, then regretted it because it only got the hand more interested in her knee. Now who in the world would want to kill Richie? It didn't make the slightest bit of sense to her, and she decided that it must have been a case of mistaken identity.

"Do they know why the man did it?"

"Nope," the driver said. "Don't know a thing. All they know is his name and the name of the guy he killed. The young fellow's name was Shaw, Anthony or Andy or something of the sort."

For the merest shadow of a second her heart jumped at the thought that Richie hadn't been killed after all, that the dead boy was somebody else. Then she remembered that Shaw was the name Richie had picked out for himself. That was the way he'd signed the register at the hotel.

"Can't remember the other one's name," the driver continued. "It's on the tip of my tongue but I'll be damned if I remember it. Just took a quick look through the paper before it was time to hit the road again."

The "quick look" had nearly committed the whole story to his memory. Honour Mercy could picture him, gulping down his coffee and reading the grisly article with his eyes bugging out of his head.

"Seems I ought to be able to remember the name," the driver said. "But I can't."

"Was he a...gangster?"

The man shook his head. "Nope," he said. "Wasn't even from Albany. Came from New York. One of them New York lawyers. I've met some of those fellows and I wouldn't put anything past them. Sharp ones, them."

A warning bell sounded inside the back of Honour Mercy's head. It wasn't possible, she told herself. It was a coincidence, that was all. It couldn't be, just plain couldn't be.

But she was afraid. Memory was crouched, ready to spring. She looked out the window at the ground that was passing by very swiftly, then looked at the speedometer needle that told how fast the ground was passing by, and then looked at the hand on her knee.

Not Joshua. She was going to Joshua, that was the important thing. It hadn't been him.

"His name," she said, slowly. "Funny thing you can't remember it."

"Hardly makes a difference."

"I mean," she said, "the way you remembered the other one, the boy who got shot. Just seems funny that you couldn't remember the name of the one who shot him."

"Yes, funny," the man said. "Right on the tip of my tongue, too. Paper must of mentioned it a dozen times, if they mentioned it once. And I'm usually pretty good when it comes to remembering."

Think, she thought. Say it wasn't Joshua.

"Damned if it isn't coming back to me now," the man said, excited at the prospect of demonstrating just how good he was at remembering things. "Some sort of a Bible name, now that I think about it."

She couldn't breathe.

"Sure," the man said. A vein was throbbing on his broad forehead. "Sure, that's what it was. It's coming now. Who was it fought that battle at Jericho? The one they got that song about?"

"Joshua," she whispered.

"Yep," the man said, happy now. "Joshua. Last name was something like "Crawfish," but that ain't it. It'll probably come to me in another minute if I think about it awhile."

She wanted to tell him not to waste his time but she couldn't because she knew that if she opened her mouth she would scream.

SHE was in her apartment off Central Park West, alone, and she ached all over. Her body ached, first from the four boys, and then from the big man who had driven her to New York, and whom she had obligingly permitted to lead her into the privacy of a motel room en route.

And her lower lip ached from biting it, and her head ached because her brain was spinning around. But the worst ache of all was somewhere inside.

She was alone.

That was it. She was alone, completely alone, and she had not been alone since that time when she stood with a ratty cardboard suitcase in her hand in Newport's Greyhound station.

Alone.

There was no one with her, because Richie was dead, and there was no one to call, because Joshua was dead. And, because Richie and Joshua had been the only two people in her world, this left her, according to the inexorable laws of mathematics, alone.

Alone.

And, incidentally, penniless.

That was silly, because she had quite a bit of money in the bank. But it was after three and the bank was closed, so for the moment the money in the bank was quite useless. Actually she could do without money until the bank opened for business again in the morning; the refrigerator was filled with food and all she had to do was cook it and eat it. And even if the refrigerator had been empty, she could easily last until morning without eating. The big man had bought her a meal which she had forced herself to eat. She wouldn't starve.

But if she stayed in the apartment she might go out of her mind. That's what would happen—she would go crazy. She would look at the walls and look at the ceiling until the walls closed in and the ceiling fell on her, and she would go crazy.

Because she was so damned alone.

For a long time there had been no problem. She was with Richie and the two of them shared an apartment and a bed and a way of life. There was a pattern and she lived within the pattern.

Then there wasn't Richie, all of a sudden, but there was still a pattern. The pattern centered around Joshua. She would go back to New York and let Joshua ask her to be his mistress, and then she would live with him, sharing his apartment and his bed.

Another pattern.

And then, out of the blue, there wasn't Joshua any more. And there wasn't any pattern. There was simply Honour Mercy Bane alone by herself, all alone, terribly alone, with nothing to do and no place to go. In a day, two patterns had been shattered, in twenty-four hours or so, Richie had gone and Joshua had gone, and they had both left her alone.

And now?

Now there was no pattern. Nothing fit together. There were any number of things she could do, but nothing added up to a pattern, nothing gave her a life that got rid of the aloneness.

She would stay in the apartment, have something to eat and go to sleep. In the morning they would call her and tell her what tricks were lined up for her, and she would go out and handle her tricks and take home her money. She would live alone in her apartment and save her money and turn her tricks, and that would be her life.

And the walls would close in and the ceiling would fall, and one day would follow the other without shape or pattern, and she would go mad.

She would stay in the apartment, have something to eat and go to sleep. In the morning she would go to the bank and draw out all her money and buy a ticket to Newport. When she got to Newport she would find Madge and get her old job back, or get Madge to line her up a job at one of the other houses.

And she would live by herself in an empty room at the Casterbridge Hotel, and she would eat Gil Gluck's tasteless food and walk up and down a flight of stairs for eight hours every day, and one day would follow the other without shape or pattern, and she would go mad.

She would stay in the apartment, have something to eat and go to sleep. In the morning she would go to the bank and draw out all her money and buy a ticket to Coldwater. When she got to Coldwater she would find her parents and fall on her knees and beg forgiveness, and Prudence and Abraham Bane would forgive her and take her back and she would get a job and live at home with her parents.

And she would eat grits and ribs and fatback, and she would read the Bible every day and go to sleep by ten, and people would stare after her when she passed them on the street, and one day would follow the other without shape or pattern, and she would go mad.

Alone.

And empty.

She got up from the bed, and that helped a little. She had a bite to eat, a pair of scrambled eggs with some cheddar cheese melted in them, and that helped. She took a bath and washed away the odor of the man who had driven her from Albany to New York, and that helped.

She left the apartment. That also helped. She walked halfway to the subway stop before she remembered that she had no money and consequently couldn't buy a token for the train. She thought that she could stop someone on the street and ask for a token, or go to the man at the turnstile and talk him into letting her crawl under free. But she decided instead that she might as well walk, that where she was going was only a little over a mile and that the walk would do her good.

She headed downtown.

EIGHTH Avenue, which is what Central Park West turns into when Central Park is no longer to the east of it, was still Whore Row in the blocks of the Forties. And Honour Mercy, although she was wearing a sixty-dollar dress, and although her behind did not wiggle when she walked, still half-belonged there. She had not realized this, not consciously, but the men seemed to recognize the fact.

"Girlie!" one of them whispered from a doorway, his eyes hungry. She ignored him and went on walking. Another one mocked with his eyes; his lips curled, and he said. "How much, sister?"

She swept past him.

The one who took her arm was more difficult. But she got rid of him, too, and she kept walking. She walked a block or two more until she was at Eighth and 44th, and here she stopped walking. She stood in front of a drugstore and pretended to interest herself in a display of ancient pharmaceutical instruments, but the mortars and pestles, symbolic of her work as they might be, were not nearly so fascinating as she made out.

Why had she stopped there?

In a vague way, it seemed to her that she might find a friend here, someone to talk to. She was a whore, of course, and Whore Row seemed the proper place for a whore to look for friends. She certainly didn't want to turn a trick, a cheap ten-buck trick when she had all that money in the bank. So, obviously, she had come to Whore Row to see a friend.

The hell of it was that she didn't have any friends. Not on Whore Row or anyplace else.

But that was silly. She hadn't come there just to stand around like a lamppost. The whole thing didn't make any sense at all.

She turned around slowly, feeling lost and more alone than ever with all of these strangers wandering busily back and forth around her. She told herself that somewhere there was a pattern and it was only a question of discovering it for herself, of locating the pattern and pinning it down and studying it closely.

Whatever it was.

Then there was a woman coming toward her, a woman with frizzy black hair and pale skin and too much makeup on her mouth and cheeks and eyes. At first Honour Mercy looked at her, thought *whore* and looked away. Then she looked again, and this time she recognized the woman and her eyes went wide and her mouth dropped open.

It was Marie.

Marie, the prostitute who had been her first contact in New York. Marie, who had also happened to be a Lesbian, the first and last with whom Honour Mercy had come into mildly distasteful contact. When she left Marie she would have been perfectly content not to see the woman ever again, but now, because she was alone and fresh out of patterns, she discovered that she was glad to see her, glad to have the woman take her arm, glad at last to have someone, anyone, to talk to.

"Honey! Well, I'll be damned!"

"Hello," she said. "Hello, Marie."

"Well, I'll be damned!" Marie repeated. Her smile was somehow awkward and her eyes seemed out of focus, a little glassy.

"A long time," Marie was saying. "Little Honey landed on the phone and high-hatted her old friends. Where you been, baby?"

Marie's words were sleepy, coming through a filter. Her eyes were half-closed now and she barely moved her lips when she spoke.

"I've been living uptown," Honour Mercy said. She had to say something.

"Uptown? One of those post pads off the park. That sounds nice. Post pads off the park. All those 'p' sounds. Goes together real nice with a swing to it."

Honour Mercy opened her mouth, then closed it, then opened it again. "You're different," she said.

"Different? Just because I like girls? That's not all that's different, baby. It's my scene. You've got to be tolerant of another person's scene, baby. It's the only way."

"I don't mean that."

"NO?"

"Your eyes," Honour Mercy said. "And the way you talk and everything."

Marie giggled. "I didn't know it showed that much. I must be carrying a heavy load."

Honour Mercy didn't understand.

"C'mon out of the light, baby. Around the corner where the bugs don't chase you. Light is evil."

She let Marie take her around the corner to 44th Street. They walked a ways and then the older woman led her into a doorway.

"You tumbled quick," Marie said. "You hipped yourself fast. Or are you making the same scene?"

Honour Mercy was lost. Then Marie lifted her own skirt all the way, and when Honour Mercy's face screwed up in puzzlement she pointed to her legs.

There were marks running up and down the insides of her thighs.

And Honour Mercy understood.

"JUNK," Marie said. "H, horse, junk. Sweet little powder that makes happy dreams. You put the needle in and everything gets pretty."

"You ever make horse? Ever put the needle in and take it out empty?"

"No."

"Ever make pot? Ever break a stick with a buddy? Ever smoke up and dream?"

She shook her head.

"Ever sniff? Ever skin-pop and smile all night at the ceiling?"

"No."

Marie smiled. "A virgin," she said reverently. "A little virgin with bells on. You better let me take your cherry, Honey. Better let Marie turn you on to the world, the pink world. You come with me."

Marie took her arm again, but Honour Mercy stayed where she was.

"Aren't you coming?"

"I don't know."

"You want to come, baby. You want to see what's wrong and what's right. You see the way I am now?"

She nodded.

"High," Marie said. "High in the sky with a pocket full of rye. Four-and-twenty spade birds baking in pie in the sky. Come fly with me."

"I…what does it do?"

"Makes the world good," Marie said. "Makes everything fit where it should. Makes a whore a queen. And a cat can look at a queen. Right?"

She hesitated.

"Come *on*," Marie told her. "No charge, no cost. Sample day, every ride a nickel at Coney Island. Ever ride the comet, baby? Or the caterpillar?"

"I—"

"You will, baby. You'll lie down and ride them all, every one of them. This time it'll be you riding instead of some man riding you. You just come on and ride, baby. You just come with me."

MARIE had the same room as before. Honour Mercy sat on the edge of the bed, remembering the other time they had been together in Marie's room, remembering what they had done. She wondered what they were going to do now, what it would be like.

Marie was holding a match under a teaspoon. A small white capsule rested in the spoon, and the heat from the match melted it. When it was all liquid, she pushed in the plunger of a hypodermic needle, then sucked up the liquid with it.

"Your leg," Marie said. "Don't want it in your arm or the mark'll show. Want it in your leg, so pull up your dress for me. That's right. And we're not going to turn you on in the vein because you don't need it, not yet. Just a skin-fix, that ought to be enough. Ought to put you up so high you'll fly all over God's little acre. That's right, that's the way."

Marie sank the needle into the fleshy part of Honour Mercy's thigh. Honour Mercy sat, watching the needle go in, watching Marie depress the plunger and send the heroin into her thigh. And she waited for something to happen.

And nothing happened. For a moment or two nothing at all happened and she wanted to tell Marie to stop teasing her.

Then something happened.

And she stretched out on the bed and closed her eyes and stared at heaven through the top of her skull.

TEN

IT WAS A big metal room full of women. High on the back wall was a barred window, above the woman-crowded metal bench. That bench, running the full width of the back wall, was the only furniture in the big square metal room. A dozen women sat hip-crowded on the metal bench, dressed in shapeless gray bags of dresses. Another dozen women sat on the scuffed black metal floor. A few more leaned against the gray metal walls, trying to talk. But it was tough to talk, because of the screaming.

Up front, draped against the metal bars like an old newspaper flung there by the wind, Honour Mercy Bane hung screaming. Honey Bane now, Honey Bane now and forever more.

Honey Bane was a mess. Her chestnut hair lay tangled, dull and streaming, stuck to her head like a fright wig. Her face was white, the white of the underbelly of a fish, except for the gray around her staring eyes and the dark red gaping wound of her screaming mouth.

She'd been screaming for a long while, and her voice was getting hoarse. They'd brought her in at three in the morning, two rough-handed cops, and tossed her in the female detention tank with the rest of the dregs scooped from the murky bottom of the city that night, and at first she'd stood hunch-shouldered in a corner, leaning against the wall, chain-smoking and glaring at the hollow-eyed broads who'd tried to talk to her.

At four, she started to pace back and forth across the metal floor and around the perimeter of the walls, pacing and shaking her head and rubbing her upper arms with trembling fingers, as though she were cold. Some of the women, knowing the signs, watched her in silence, like beasts of prey. The rest ignored her.

At five, she began to tremble and stretch and rub her cheeks with hard fingers, and the watching women licked dry lips. At five-fifteen, she fell, rolled, struggled up and lunged into the bars. She hung there, quivering, and at five-twenty-five, she started to scream.

With the first scream, three of the women had darted forward. The first one to reach her jabbed into the pocket of Honey Bane's prison dress and pulled out the crumpled remains of her cigarettes, then ducked away form the angry, envious clutching of the other two. And Honour Mercy screamed for the second time, neither knowing nor caring that her cigarettes had been stolen. It wasn't cigarettes she wanted.

Now it was seven o'clock, and she was still screaming, though her voice was getting hoarse. One or two guards had tried to stop her, telling her the doc would come at seven, but she neither heard nor understood. One or two of the other women, unnerved by the screaming, had tried to stop her, to pull her away from the bars, but she had clung and shrieked and they had given up.

And now it was eight o'clock, and the metal door down at the end of the long gray metal hall clanged open. Two guards came through, followed by an annoyed young man in a business suit. They came down the hall, their shoes ringing on the black metal floor, and the annoyed young man waited while the guards unlocked the detention tank door. The three of them came in, and the guards efficiently peeled Honey Bane from the bars and held her rigid, still screaming, her back against the wall.

The annoyed young man put down his black bag and slapped Honey Bane twice across the face, forehand, backhand. "Stop that," he said, and his voice was emotionless and cold. "I'm going to give you something now."

The silence itself was like a scream, coming so abruptly. Honey Bane blinked rapidly, her eyes tearing, trying to focus on the annoyed young man. "Give—give—give me—"

"Got to get you ready for the judge," said one of the guards. He grinned, holding her arm with one hand, rolling the gray sleeve up with the other. "Can't have you all shook up in front of the judge," he said.

A Girl Called Honey

Honey Bane fought the two realities, the hot hurtful hating reality within, the cold cruel killing reality without, and slowly she forced her attention away from the reality within and saw and heard and smelled and felt the reality without.

She looked upon the real world. In the background, a mob scene from the Inferno, women in shapeless gray, milling and staring, scratching their sores, grimacing their lips. In the foreground, the annoyed young man, down on one knee and crouched over his now open black bag, preparing a hypodermic.

A hypodermic. The needle glinted in the light from the unshaded bulbs high up against the metal ceiling. The needle glinted and gleamed, drawing her eyes, drawing her attention, drawing her soul.

Her mouth opened, working. "You'll—give—me—something?"

"Sure thing," said the guard. "Got to make you pretty for the judge," he cackled, showing yellowed teeth.

The world was coming back, stronger and stronger. To either side there was a man, holding her. Men in uniform, guards, and the annoyed young man was rising up with the golden gleaming needle, and the one guard had rolled up her right sleeve.

With sudden violence, she shook her head, pulling away, her mouth distorted wide. One thing she knew in all the world, one thing and one thing only, and she screamed it at them. *"Not the arm!"*

"Hold her still," said the annoyed young man. He was petulant, unjustifiably detained, left standing there with the cotton swab in one hand and the golden gleaming needle in the other.

"Not the arm!" shrieked Honey Bane. "The leg, the leg, not the arm!"

The two guards held her, crowded her close against the wall, and the annoyed young man came forward, the cotton swab moving with practiced indifference on her upper arm. "Where you're going," he told her coldly, "it won't make any difference." And the golden gleaming needle jabbed in.

When they let her go, she slumped back, sliding down the wall, her legs crumpled beneath her, her knees sticking up and out, the gray shapeless skirt falling away to her hips. The prison dress was all she was wearing.

The two guards looked at her, grinning, but the annoyed young man curled his lip and pointedly looked the other way. The guards unlocked the tank door, and they and the annoyed young man stepped through to the hall. The door was relocked, and three men walked back down the echoing hall and through the door at the far end.

Now that there was silence, more of the women got into conversations, and some of them lay down on the floor to try to get a little sleep before appearing in court. A few of them, new and curious and uncertain, watched Honey Bane with wondering eyes.

But she didn't notice the looks or hear the conversations or know that her skirt was piled high about her hips. The outside reality had faded away once again, and the reality within had taken over. Slowly, quiveringly, painfully, far down within the crumpled huddled body that was and wasn't Honey Bane, she was beginning to live again. Slowly, she was being reborn, she was returning from the dead. High hot color began to glow in her face. Her hands, which had been trembling and shaking so badly just a few moments before, grew still and languid. Her whole body relaxed, as tension drained away, leaving her limp and unmoving. Her eyes were distant and high-seeing, gleaming with a pale life of their own.

She stood, with slow and languid movements, and waited unmoving, her arms hanging still at her sides, her eyes almost blank-looking, staring far off at the reality within.

She had returned from the dead. On the island of Haiti, they would have called her undead, the zombie. On Manhattan Island, where the magic phrases were different, they called her junkie, the snowbird.

It took a while for the first high keening to wear off, and for Honey Bane to gradually circle down from that high-flying cloud and descend close enough to make out the details of the reality without. Finally, though, she did come down, and saw and realized where she was.

And this time, she realized, they'd picked her up just before she was due for a needle. And she was carrying the stuff on her when she'd been grabbed. So now they had her on a user rap.

That was bad—very bad. A simple charge of soliciting wasn't anything to worry about all by itself—she'd been through that she didn't know how many times, and she'd never gotten more than a suspended sentence out of it for disorderly behavior—but a user rap was something else again. It would mean six months at Lexington, taking the cure. It would mean getting dragged in by the cops every time there was a general narcotics pick-up. It would mean having cops banging on the door all the time, breaking in and looking for more of the stuff.

That's the way it had been with Marie. Twice she'd been grabbed and convicted on user raps. The first time, she got the six-month taper-off cure at Lexington. The second time, she got the cold-turkey cure at a state hospital out on Long Island.

The third time they hadn't wasted time with a user charge. She'd taken a fall for possession, and was now in the woman's prison upstate, on a seven-to-ten. And Marie wasn't the type to get time off for good behavior. Whatever years she had left when she could make a dime hustling, she'd be spending behind bars. By the time she got out, she'd be through. Too old to make it on Whore Row; too beat up to make it anywhere else. And she'd be back on the big H in forty-eight hours, with no way to raise the cash to feed the monkey on her back.

That was no way to go. Honey Bane was now starting down the same three steps Marie had taken, and she knew she couldn't afford to go down more than just the first step. She'd have to make sure she fell no farther.

It never occurred to her to keep away from the stuff once she'd had the cure and been freed. No, that wasn't a solution, not conceivably a solution. She would simply have to be more careful in the future, that was all. She'd have to find some absolutely safe hiding place for the stuff.

There was Roxanne. Since Marie had been sent up on the possession charge, Honey had found herself a new lover. Roxanne, a young kid from South Dakota somewhere, a short, fiery brunette, now working Whore Row. Roxanne wasn't a user, and she'd never even been pulled in by the cops on a soliciting charge. Her place would be as safe as a convent. The stuff could be left there, and Honey could stop by every time she needed a fix. That would work out, all right, that would work out fine.

As for Lexington, there was nothing to worry about there. As a matter of fact, it would be a nice little vacation. No hustling, no crazy hours or eating greasy meals in Eighth Avenue luncheonettes, no dodging the cops all the time.

And the best part of it was that they believed in the slow cure at Lexington. That meant she'd be getting free H for the next few months, and that was heaven. The amount would gradually taper off, and eventually they'd stop feeding it to her completely, but that was way off in the future somewhere, and she didn't have to worry about it. Free H. It was the goddam answer to a maiden's prayer that's what it was.

And when she came back, she'd stash the stuff with Roxanne. No problems.

One problem, maybe. Roxanne was young, damn good-looking. She was just liable to get switched to the phone business. That would be a good break for her, of course; she'd make damn good money, have a nice apartment uptown and go out with the better class of customers. But it would also mean the end of her relationship with Honey Bane. Honey knew how that worked. She'd been on the phone herself, and she knew that the girls who worked the phone didn't hang around with the girls who worked the street.

She nodded, smiling to herself, lost in her memories. She'd been on the phone herself, she had, and she'd had a great little apartment uptown. Until that one lousy customer had seen the marks on the insides of her legs and bitched that he hadn't paid to get mixed up with a junkie. Then all of a sudden she hadn't been working the phone anymore. She'd been back to working the street.

But maybe it wouldn't happen. Maybe Marie—no, Roxanne—maybe Roxanne wouldn't get switched over to the phone. There was no sense worrying about it, anyway. No sense worrying about anything.

At eight o'clock, a matron came, a stocky, sour-faced woman in an unattractive uniform, and took Honey Bane away, holding her with a too-tight grip on the elbow. Honey went willingly, not worrying about anything, not caring about anything, and the matron led her to a small room where her clothes were waiting, and she changed from the prison dress back to her own clothes, and the matron turned her over to a guard to be taken up to the court.

The courtroom was up on the next floor. The guard led the way to the stairwell, and stood aside for Honey to go first up the stairs. She did so, and the guard slid his hand up her leg, beneath the skirt, grabbing her.

Her voice flat, she said, "I hope you get syphilis of the hand."

He jerked his hand away, and growled, "You're a tough one, huh?"

She didn't bother to answer.

He reached up and grasped her elbow, pinching it with his fingers, saying, "Not so fast, girlie. There's no rush."

She allowed herself to be led up the rest of the way and into the courtroom. Then she had to wait for fifteen minutes, sitting in the front row while the judge worked with people ahead of her.

This was Judge McBee. He smiled and told jokes, and called the defendants by their first names. He could skin you, slowly, with a hot knife, but he'd smile and joke and make friendly chatter all the while. Everybody along Whore Row knew Judge McBee. They hated his guts.

She sat, not listening, not caring, in a soft and pleasant haze. After the first hard jolt and the crystal clarity of thought, she had sunk slowly into a soft cottony mist, and she would be there now for most of the day. She sat, not listening, not thinking about where she was or what was happening to her, and they had to call her name twice before she realized it was her turn before the bar of justice.

She got to her feet, and a guard walked her forward, placed her in front of the judge's high bench. She looked up at him, the round cheerful face framed with gray-white hair, and he beamed down at her, nodding and saying, "Well, now, Honey, I thought I wasn't going to be seeing you anymore."

She smiled a little in return. "Me, too," she said.

"Looks like things are a lot more serious this time," said the judge happily. He pawed among the official documents on his desk, and the young man to his right reached over his shoulder and plucked out the particular paper he wanted. The young man was Edward McBee, the judge's nephew, a law student up in Connecticut. He'd asked Judge McBee to let him sit in at court, behind the judge's bench, to see the proceedings from the judge's angle of vision.

Judge McBee now took the paper from his nephew, beaming and nodding his thanks, and slowly read the document. Finished at last, he peered at Honey Bane and said, "It says here you were found with heroin on your person, Honey. You using that stuff now?"

"Yes," she said.

Edward McBee strained forward, his eager face inches from his uncle's black-clothed shoulder, and stared at Honey Bane, as though trying to see Honour Mercy, lurking somewhere far beneath.

"That's terrible stuff, Honey," said the judge. "You want to get off that, you hear me?"

Some answer was expected of her. She felt a moment of panic, until she realized she could answer the last part of the question. Yes, she did hear him. "Yes," she said.

"Now," said Judge McBee, "I'm going to have you sent to Lexington. Have you heard of Lexington?"

"That's where they have the slow cure," she said.

"That's right." He beamed paternally at her, pleased with the right answer. "I'll have you sent there, for six months. And when you come back, I want you to stay away from narcotics. Completely." He looked down at his papers again, and smiled suddenly. "I'm going to help you, Honey," he said. "I'm going to help you stay away from narcotics. You have also been charged with disorderly conduct, you know. Soliciting again. The last time you were here, you promised me you wouldn't be doing that anymore."

She hung her head, hating him. There was nothing she could say.

"When you come back, then," he said cheerfully, "you can begin a ninety-day sentence in the city jail for disorderly conduct. That's to begin the day you are released from Lexington." Uncapping a silver fountain pen, he wrote hastily, and looked up once again, smiling. "I won't be seeing you for a while, Honey," he said. "Not for nine months. You be a good girl in Lexington, now."

"Yes," she said.

"And I'll see you in nine months."

"Yes."

He shook his head, smiling sadly. "Yes," he said. "I'll see you here again in nine months. You won't be changing, will you? All right, Honey, that's all. Go on with the matron."

Another hand was gripping Honey Bane's elbow, too hard, and she let herself be taken away, through the door to the left of the judge's bench, as Edward McBee stared after her, his forehead creased in the lines of a puzzled frown.

Nine months. She hated that bastard. In nine months, Roxanne would be God knew where. She'd have to find somebody else to hold the stuff.

COURT was finished for the day, and Judge McBee sat with his nephew in his office, smoking his first cigarette of the day. "Well, Edward," he said. "How did it look from my side of the bench?"

"Frightening," said Edward McBee earnestly. "Sitting back in the spectator's seats, you don't see the expressions on their faces. That girl—"

Judge McBee raised a humorous eyebrow. "Girl?"

"The one you called Honey. Charged with using heroin."

"Oh, yes." Judge McBee nodded, smiling. "She's an old friend," he said. "In once or twice a month, for playing the prostitute. Been around for years."

"How old is she?"

"Oh, I don't know. Twenty-four, I suppose, maybe twenty-five."

"She looked thirty or more."

"They get that look," said the judge wisely. "It's the kind of life they lead."

"How does a girl like that get involved in such a life?" his nephew asked him.

"A girl like what?"

The nephew blinked in embarrassment at his uncle's amusement. "There was something about that girl—" He stopped in confusion.

"Now don't go romanticizing a common whore," said the judge sternly. "That's all the girl is, a common whore."

"But how did she get that way, that's what I want know. How did she get that way?"

"They're *born* that way," the judge told him. "It's simple as that. They're born that way, and nothing can change them." He heaved to his feet. "Now, let's get some lunch," he said. "I'm starving."

So Willing

ONE

VINCE PARKED HIS father's car in front of Betty's house, checked in the glove compartment to be sure he hadn't forgotten the "necessary equipment," smoothed his hair on the left side, where the wind coming in the window had mussed it, and stepped out of the car.

Betty's father was sitting on the porch in his undershirt. It was seven-thirty of an evening late in June, and just twilight. Betty's father was an indistinct figure seen from the street, an expanse of white undershirt and a glowing cigarette, that was all.

Vince frowned. Betty'd told him her parents were going to be out tonight, and he'd planned to bring her back here after the movies. A bed had it all over a backseat any day, particularly with a virgin. Well, the hell with it. The backseat would have to do.

Erasing the frown and replacing it with an easy, deferential smile, Vince walked around the car, across the sidewalk and up the walk. "Hi, Mister Baxter," he said, as he went up the stoop.

"Good evening, Vince."

"Betty ready yet?"

"I don't suppose so. You know how women are."

Mister Baxter chuckled. He had an asinine habit of trying to get on a pals relationship with Betty's dates. It made Vince uncomfortable, but he managed not to show it. If you wanted to get anywhere with a girl you had to get along with her parents. That was rule number one.

Mister Baxter motioned at the screen door. "You might just go on in and see," he said.

"Thanks, Mister Baxter," Vince said. It hadn't taken long with the Baxters, not long at all. He'd taken Betty out three times, and already he was at the stage with her parents where he could just walk into the house. The fact that Mister Baxter worked so damn hard to make everybody like him had helped, of course. Mister Baxter was a sales manager for Modnoc Products, the local plastic company. He'd started as a commission salesman and learned to treat everybody like a long-lost buddy. He still had the habit, combined with an obsession to get along with the younger generation just to prove he wasn't old yet. So Vince hadn't had to work hard to make Mister Baxter like him at all. He'd just shown up that first evening, three weeks ago, smiling politely, a conservatively dressed, good-looking young man of seventeen, and Mister Baxter had fallen all over himself to be chums.

As for Mrs. Baxter, it didn't matter a bit what she thought. Mrs. Baxter was the closest thing to being invisible of anyone Vince had ever met. Not physically invisible—she was about five foot four and weighed nearly two hundred pounds, topped by stringy tight-curled, gray hair and a simpering fat face—but her personality was invisible. Her voice was so faint it was almost non-existent, and if she had any opinions or beliefs or thoughts about anything, she kept them to herself. She inevitably stood around in the background somewhere, smiling her please-don't-hurt-me smile and fumbling with her faded apron. Vince had given her about thirty seconds worth of charm the first time he'd come to the house, and had ignored her ever since.

He ignored her now. He opened the screen door and stepped into the foyer of the house. The stairs to the second floor bedrooms were straight ahead, the living room off to the left. Mrs. Baxter was in the living room, watching some stupid television program, and when she heard the screen door close she looked over, smiling as usual, and in her faded voice said, "Good evening, Vince."

"Hi, Mrs. Baxter," Vince said. He returned her smile for a tenth of a second, and then went forward to the foot of the stairs. "Hey, Betty!" he shouted.

"In a minute!" came the answering shout.

"Sure," Vince said, under his breath. Betty, in her own sweet way, was as bad as her parents.

Mrs. Baxter leaned forward in her chair to say, "Why don't you come in and watch television with me while you wait, Vince?"

The prospect sickened. Vince thought it over for a second. If he went back out on the porch, Mister Baxter, who was convinced that everybody in the whole United States of America was as psycho about baseball as he was, would start jabbering about who did what on the ballfield this afternoon, and Vince couldn't have named three major league ballplayers if his life depended on it. He might even have had trouble naming three major league teams. At least there wouldn't be any conversation with invisible Mrs. Baxter.

"Sure," he said politely. "Thanks a lot."

He went into the living room and sat down facing the television set. His eyes were aimed at the set, but he didn't pay any attention to the blue-gray shadows flitting back and forth across the screen. He spent his time thinking about Betty, who was sixteen and good-looking and well-built and a virgin. His first virgin, by God!

Vince had been fifteen when he had first discovered how easy it was for him to get a girl to go the limit with him. He'd made another discovery at the same time. He discovered why it was that people spent so much of their time thinking about sex and talking about sex and planning for sex and having sex and chasing after sex. It was because sex was the greatest thing since rings with secret compartments. Girls, he had discovered, had secret compartments, too, and they contained a map to paradise. It was farewell Captain Marvel, a new marvel has been found.

Sex was great. Sex was great before, when you were leading up to it, working around like the coolest strategist who ever lived, like a band of Indians sneaking up on the fort, ready to crash through the wall the minute they were close enough. And it was great during, which went without saying. And it was great after, when the girl would look at you like you were God and you knew she'd give anything to have you do it to her again. And it was great even later, when you got together with the other guys, and everybody has sex on the mind, trying to figure out how to get some for themselves, and you could tell them you've had it, and this is what it was like.

For some guys it was tough to get some. For Vince it was the easiest thing in the world. You just had to have the right attitude for it, that was all. You had to see it as a kind of war, with the girl and her parents and adults everywhere as the enemy. First, you had to play sheepdog and break the girl loose from the pack, get her off by herself. Then you had to play the strategist, and that was where Vince had a natural talent.

The thing was, every girl had a Dream Man. Usually, he was some movie star, or maybe a combination of movie stars, or singers, or something like that. You found out who the Dream Man was, what his qualities were, what he was like—and the girl never got tired of talking about her Dream Man, once you got her started—and then you simply showed her you had the exact same qualities the Dream Man had, plus one more quality: You were flesh and blood, and available. And she'd be on her back before you could say, "Unzip."

For two years now, Vince had been sharpening his form, going with girl after girl, and he hadn't grown bored with the game yet. Nor did he think he ever would grow bored with it. But tonight was the first time with a virgin. Every other girl he'd ever had had come to him at least second. And a girl who already knew what sex was all about would naturally be more eager than a girl who'd never had any at all.

He'd tried a couple of virgins, two years ago, shortly after losing his own virginity, and had gotten nowhere. So he'd given up virgins as being more trouble than they were worth, and this was the first time he'd purposely gone after a virgin since.

A virgin, by God, a certified virgin. He'd noticed Betty in school, and had talked with a few guys who had taken her out. According to them, it was impossible to get anywhere at all with Betty. You couldn't even cop a feel without her getting all upset and mad.

She was the one. He knew her casually, from school, and two days before he was due to graduate, he asked her for a date. She'd accepted, as he knew she would, and that first date he'd been as sexless as a spayed cat. They'd gone to the movies, and they'd talked, and they'd had hamburgers, and they'd driven around for a while, and then he'd taken her home, being sure to get her home fifteen minutes before the one o'clock deadline her parents had set. Get along with the parents and you'll get the girl.

The second date had run pretty much like the first, except that they'd parked for a while up at High Point, and necked. He'd kissed her, but he'd kept his hands to himself, and he got her home ahead of schedule again, with a chaste goodnight kiss on her front porch.

The third date, they'd necked at the movies, and she'd responded nicely. By now, he knew a lot about Betty's Dream Man. He was polite and gentlemanly, but he was also the outdoorsy type, the kind who goes off to the woods and lives in a tent, hunting and fishing, every once in a while. And he was frank, outspoken, and sincere

So that's the way Vince played it. He necked with her in the theater, and then they went back to High Point again and necked some more, and he could feel her getting excited, and at just the right moment he'd pulled away from her and said, "I think we ought to go for a walk and cool off, Betty. I'm having trouble keeping my hands to myself." And he'd gotten out of the car before she could answer and walked around to open the door on her side.

Theirs was the only car at High Point that night, and so they had strolled around for a while, hand in hand, looking down at the scattered lights of the town below them. Vince had talked about the cabin his family owned at a lake in the mountains, upstate, and he had played it as outdoorsy as he possibly could. He had also talked about the trouble he was having keeping his hands off her, and he was very honest and sincere—and flattering—about it. By the time they got back into the car, she knew he was her Dream Man, and she knew he wanted her.

He didn't even have to make the first move. When he kissed her, she reached out and took his hand and laid it against her breast, and whispered, "It's all right, Vince, it really is."

Maybe he could have had her that night. He didn't know. He wasn't sure, and he hadn't tried. He had the program set up, and he was following it. That night, he had gotten her blouse open and her bra off. He had touched her breasts—lovely full breasts for a sixteen-year-old, pink-tipped and firm—and kissed them. He had slid his hand up the inside of her leg and touched her with slow, lingering fingers, and she had closed her eyes and sighed, and her hands had been taut on his back.

But he'd stopped. He'd played it sincere and gentlemanly, he'd been the original Square Shooter, and he had shot not. And he even got her home by curfew time. The goodnight kiss on the front porch that night had been combined with two busy hands, and he had left her to go to bed with the hot memory of his left hand on her breast and his right hand up under her skirt.

And tonight was the night the program culminated. Tonight, Vince was going to get himself a certified virgin. Already he had gone farther with her than anyone he knew—and the guys he knew weren't reticent about their conquests or near-conquests—and tonight he would finish the job. He was leaving for the cabin by the lake soon, and this would be just about the last chance.

Betty had told him that her parents were going to be out tonight, and he'd planned on coming back to the house early. He'd checked the TV listings and found out what movie was going to be on the Midnight Show, and he would have told her how much he had been looking forward to seeing this movie. It was some old World War Two movie about counterspies and Gestapo agents and all that jazz, which he wanted to see like he wanted to fall down a manhole, but he didn't plan on watching much of it.

Now, there was Mister Baxter out on the front porch, in his undershirt, and there was Mrs. Baxter, sitting across the living room in her flower-print dress and faded apron, and it seemed pretty clear that neither of them was intending to go anywhere at all. Which meant it was going to have to be the backseat of the car, or maybe on a blanket if he could find someplace secluded enough. And he had been looking forward to making his first virgin in her own bed.

And here came the virgin now, down the stairs, her blonde hair pulled back in a ponytail, her full breasts jutting out against an electric blue sweater, the center of interest wrapped in a hip-tight gray skirt. Vince got up, smiling at her, and she smiled back, saying something about being sorry for her lateness.

The goodbyes were over with quickly. Mrs. Baxter had said, "Have a good time," and Betty had answered, "You have a good time, too," and they had gone out to the porch, where Betty had the exact same exchange with her father, and then they went down to the car, a '57 Dodge, cream and green, with beige fins. Vince, the perfect gentleman, held the right-hand door open while Betty slid into the seat, clutching her skirt down at her knees. He closed the door once she was settled, and went around to his own side. He glanced back at the house just before getting into the car. Mister Baxter was still sitting on the porch in his undershirt, and Mrs. Baxter was standing in the doorway, her nose not quite touching the screen, her round shape framed by the living room lights behind her. Simultaneously, as though some director off in the bushes on the next-door lawn had given them a signal, they both raised their right hands and waved. Vince waved back, and got into the car.

In that quick glance, he had also noticed again the wooden fire-escape on the side of the house. This was a residential district, all two-story one-family houses, but after a trio of bad fires in houses of this type, a town ordinance had been passed making it compulsory to have an outside stairway in any house where people lived on more than one floor. The wooden fire-escape, Vince had learned after gentle questioning, led to Betty's bedroom. Since learning that, he had entertained idle daydreams about crawling up that fire escape and spending a few quiet hours in Betty's bedroom and in Betty's bed. But that was strictly day-dreaming. That wasn't the way to get her, sneaking through windows at three o'clock in the morning. The way to get her was to make her want to be gotten.

Vince started the car and drove down to the comer, then turned left toward downtown. "I thought your parents were going out tonight," he said, as casually as he could.

"They are," she answered.

"Wearing undershirt and apron?"

"Oh, they don't have to leave the house till nine o'clock. And it's only a little after seven-thirty now. They've got ages."

"Where they going?"

"A surprise party for my Uncle George up in Votzburg. The party doesn't start till eleven. My Aunt Edna is keeping him out of the house till then."

"Votzburg is forty miles away from here," he said, surprised that Betty's parents would be going, of their own free will, more than ten feet from the house.

"I know," she said disinterestedly. She couldn't care less what her parents did.

Vince calculated rapidly. The party was going to start at eleven o'clock. It would have to run a couple of hours anyway, until around one, maybe two. Betty's old man would have half a bag on by the time he left the party, and the road from Votzburg was narrow, winding, hilly and two lanes wide. Forty miles of that road, at two or three o'clock in the morning, with half a bag on. They wouldn't be home before four a.m. at the earliest.

He smiled. "You know," he said, "I was looking at the paper tonight, at the TV listings." He forced enthusiasm into his voice. "And do you know what's playing—?"

They got back to the house at a quarter to twelve. In the movie, he had spent the first half of the double feature with his arm around Betty's shoulders, occasionally leaning over to kiss her, his free hand clasping hers. The second half, he'd progressed. The arm around her shoulder had drawn in tighter, so the hand dangled down over her breast, just barely brushing the tip of it at first and then gradually touching it more insistently, holding it and stroking it and squeezing it. Their kisses had become longer and fiercer, his tongue searching and probing deeply within her mouth, and her breathing was faster, her eyes bright in the dimness of the movie theater. His other hand had touched her knee, slid under the hem of her skirt, stroked slowly up the inside of her thigh, and she squirmed in the seat, whispering, "Oh. Oh."

In the car, he had driven one-handed. His other arm was around her, the hand reaching around to massage her breast, as he had done in the theater. She sat close to him, her breath hot and fast in his ear, and she had begun to grow bold herself. Her hand had rested on his leg, and he knew that she wanted to touch him as he had touched her. And he also knew she was going to get the opportunity very soon.

They got to the house at a quarter to twelve, and Vince immediately sat down on the sofa, expecting Betty to come sit beside him. But she said something about coffee and went out to the kitchen. He followed her out, saying, "Who wants coffee?"

"I do," she told him.

He stood in the kitchen doorway. "Betty," he said.

She stopped her fussing with cups and saucers. Her back was to him, and slowly she turned to face him. Her eyes were bright, as they had been in the movie, but they showed wariness, too.

"Come into the living room, Betty," he said. "Come sit with me in the living room."

"I was—going to make coffee," she said hesitantly.

"Never mind the coffee. Come on in the living room."

She hesitated a moment longer, and then smiled and said, "All right."

They went back to the living room, and this time she sat down on the sofa beside him, but almost immediately moved to get up again, saying, "You didn't turn the TV set on."

He grabbed her arm, pulling her back down on the sofa. "We've got fifteen minutes yet," he said. "All that's on now is news and weather. Who cares about news and weather?"

She was half-turned, facing him, and she smiled again, her eyes brighter than ever. "Nobody does," she said. And when he reached for her, she came soft and eager into his arms.

But it wasn't as easy as he'd thought. She let him French kiss her, she let him fondle her breasts and slide his hand up the inside of her leg, she let him push the sweater up and open her bra, she let him touch the bare breasts, pinching the hard tips gently between his fingers, kissing her breasts, but when his hand, beneath her skirt, slid up to grab the waist of her panties and slide them down, she pulled away from him at once, pushing the offending hand away, whispering, "No, Vince. We can't go that far. No."

He was obedient, that time. He let his hand slide down again across her silk-covered belly, and pulled her close to kiss her again, to touch her breasts with fingers and lips and tongue.

He waited. Stroking her, kissing her, caressing her, nipping her flesh with his teeth. He waited until her eyes were closed and her mouth was open and her breath was loud and short and ragged, her arms limp and weak around him, her hips writhing and revolving on the sofa. Then he made the move again, and this time she didn't stop him, and her panties slid away to the floor. And when he touched her, she groaned and clutched him tight to her.

He undressed her there in the living room, piece by piece. The sweater went and the bra, and finally the skirt. And when she was nude and pliant in his arms, he whispered, "Let's go upstairs." And she nodded, whispering, "Yes, Vince, yes."

She led the way up the stairs and he followed, pulling off his shirt and undershirt on the way. She walked ahead of him, her firm round buttocks moving as she climbed the stairs, and he stroked their roundness, wanting to bite them.

Up on the second floor, he started into the first bedroom he came to, but she said, "No, that's my sister's room. My room is down here."

"Your sister." He hadn't known there was a sister. He suddenly felt cold. What if the sister were to come in while he was in the bedroom with Betty? There'd be hell to pay.

His thoughts must have shown on his face, for she laughed and said, "Don't worry. She doesn't live here anymore. She got married two years ago and moved to Denver."

"Oh." Weak with relief, he hurried after Betty to her bedroom.

He had his clothes half off, holding them in one hand. When they reached the bedroom he whipped the rest off right away. He knew the danger in letting the emotion of the moment be washed away by too much time spent on the mechanics of the thing, on the moving to the proper room or from the front seat to the backseat of the car, or getting the clothes off. The mechanics had to be gotten over and done with fast, before they could spoil the mood.

Her room was large and airy and girl-styled, but he didn't notice a thing in it except the three-quarter bed. The covers were turned neatly back, the sheets were crisp and clean, and already he could visualize Betty atop the bed and himself atop Betty.

She sat down on the edge of the bed and raised her arms to him, smiling. He came into her arms, sat beside her, kissed her and stroked her, slowly laid her back and down onto the bed.

"I won't hurt you," he whispered, reassuring her. "You don't have to worry, I won't hurt you."

They were lying crosswise on the bed and gradually they shifted position until they were lying the right way, she on her back and he on his side next to her, still stroking her and kissing her and very gradually rolling forward onto her.

"I've never done this before, Vince," she whispered suddenly.

He was terrified that she would suddenly stop him at the last second, that she would realize she was about to become an ex-virgin, and wouldn't go through with it. "I know," he whispered. "But don't worry, Betty, wonderful wonderful Betty, don't worry."

"You've got to promise," she whispered, and her hands were suddenly firm against him, not pushing him away but not letting him get any closer either. "You've got to promise," she repeated, "not to ever tell anybody. Not anybody."

"I never will," he promised fervently. "I'd never do a thing like that."

"This is the first time," she whispered.

"I know."

"My sister," she explained, whispering in his ear, "always told me to never do it with a boy from my own school or my own town, because that way I'd get a bad reputation. She said I should only go for boys from other towns. I've never done it before. You're the first boy from our school I've ever done this with."

The full import didn't hit him for a couple of seconds, and then he practically yelped. She wasn't a virgin! She wasn't a virgin, after all! He almost said it aloud, as an incredulous, shocked, screamed question: "You're not a virgin!?" But he stifled it just in time, because that question would have ruined the whole thing. He would never been able to explain why it was so important to him that she be a virgin without destroying the mood, and without destroying his chances with her forever.

She was still whispering to him, earnestly and matter-of-factly, and he knew at last that this girl was far from being a virgin. "So you've got to promise never to tell anybody. I don't want to get a bad reputation."

He swallowed, forced himself to answer her. "I won't tell, Betty. Believe me, I won't."

She kissed him and smiled. "The first night we went out," she told him, "I knew I had to have you. No matter what my sister said."

And who, he wondered, had been stalking whom? He felt suddenly young and inexperienced.

"Well, come on," she whispered. "What are you waiting for?"

She was no virgin. There wasn't a virgin in the world who could move like that. She was no virgin, and after thirty seconds it no longer mattered a tinker's dam that she wasn't a virgin. Because she was the most tremendous bed-partner he'd ever held in his arms.

She tore him apart. She was a wild thing, grabbing him with a violence he'd never known before, squeezing him dry like a grape and flinging him away again. And it was over before it was barely begun, and he was lying beside her in the narrow bed, panting, the sweat cooling and drying on his belly and chest, as she leaned over him, kissing him, licking his face, stroking his chest.

He regained his wind slowly, and finally started, "You—you—"

Once again, she understood what he was trying to say. "There's nothing to worry about," she told him, smiling. "I checked on the calendar this afternoon. This is the safe time."

THERE were voices downstairs!

"It's my parents!" Her whisper in his ear was terrified.

He crawled off the bed and to his feet. He took one step toward the door, but he could hear them coming upstairs.

"They'll look in here," she was whispering. "They always look in to see if I'm asleep."

His wildly searching eye fell on the luminous dial of her bedside clock. It was almost four-thirty in the morning. He should have been out of here long ago, instead of falling asleep like a dope.

"Down the fire escape," she whispered urgently. "Hurry!"

"My clothes!"

"I'll throw them down to you. Hurry, Vince, hurry!"

He had one leg over the windowsill before he realized he was stark naked. Then he remembered the car, still parked out in front of the house. "The car," he whispered.

He saw the shock on her face, and thought fast. "Tell them," he said, "tell them something went wrong with the starter, and I took a bus home, and I said I'd come back in the morning and fix it."

She nodded. "All right. Now, hurry." And she ran around the room, gathering up his clothes.

He went out the fire escape and down the wooden steps, rough against his bare feet. At the bottom step, he carefully lowered himself, until he was hanging by his outstretched hands, facing the street.

Clip-clop. A horse went by, pulling a milk wagon. The milkman stared at Vince, swinging back and forth, his toes three feet from the ground, completely nude. Vince stared at the milkman, and the horse calmly clip-clopped by, and Vince's clothes went sailing down past his face.

He dropped to the ground, fumbled around until he had his clothes in a jumbled bundle in his arms, and ran for the backyard.

There was a shade tree in the backyard. Hidden by it, he hurriedly dressed, then climbed over the fence to the yard of the house on the next street, out to the street, and headed for the nearest bus stop.

"A week from now," he grumbled to himself, as he walked along with his shoelaces flapping, "I'll think this was funny as hell."

TWO

EVERYTHING, AS A matter of fact, stank. Everything stank out loud, and in spades. And with everything stinking so thoroughly it was no wonder that he wasn't laughing himself silly.

In a sense, you could blame everything on Betty. There she was, all pure virginal, and there he was, all ready and willing, the experienced hunter tracking down the soft-eyed doe, when all of a sudden his whole frame of reference was shattered. Betty the virgin had suddenly metamorphosed into Betty the old hand.

That got things going to a fine start.

When the family left two days later for the cabin on the lake he was not at all sorry to say a fond goodbye to the little town of Modnoc. He'd sprawled alone in the backseat of the car while his mother and father said stupid things to each other in the front seat, and he'd looked back at the town out of the rear window, thinking unpleasant thoughts about it.

As the sun goes out to sea, he thought, *and as our boat sinks slowly in the west, we bid a fond adieu to the sleepy town of Modnoc, with its friendly huts and its rudely plastered natives.*

The cruddy little cabin by the cruddy little lake looked a good deal better to him than it really was. The idea of staying in the same town with Betty made him feel little weak in the knees. Of course there was no reason for him to be ashamed of himself. As far as she was concerned, he was the conqueror, the only boy from Modnoc who had managed to get in her pants. From his point of view it was a little more complex. He'd been loaded for bear, and when you're loaded for bear you can't get too excited over blowing the tail off a squirrel.

So the cruddy little cabin by the cruddy little lake represented two things—an escape from Betty and a chance at new fields to conquer. There would certainly be girls at the lake, plenty of them, and girls away for the summer were girls removed from the soppy security of the parental abode. If a girl was ever going to take the plunge, she was going to take it on summer vacation.

And if anybody was ready to do the plunging for them, Vince was.

He felt like the Great White Hunter, and he was so pleased with the picture that the discomforts of the safari failed to bother him. He didn't mind the lousy roads, or the creative stupidity of his father who insisted on driving a steady thirty-five every inch of the way. He didn't mind the stomach-churning food at the hot dog stands where they stopped en route, he didn't mind the senseless patter issuing from the front seat. He was the Great White Hunter on the trail of a pack of virgins. The little hardships of the chase didn't bother him a bit.

When they finally got to the cabin it looked much better to him than it really was. A kitchen, furnished with colonial implements and quietly disintegrating. A bedroom for his parents. Another bedroom, incredibly small, for Vince. A living room that no one in his right mind would attempt to live in. The cabin was looking around for a president to be born in it, and anyone born there could certainly boast of humble origins.

But Vince didn't care. He didn't figure he'd be spending much time there. He'd be with girls, around girls, near girls, by the side of girls.

And, eventually, in girls.

BUT things weren't working according to plan. Right now, for example, the afternoon was in the process of becoming evening. It was cool, with a breeze coming from the lake that was just a little too brisk to be perfect. The sun was gone and the moon was starting to rise. It was perfect weather for girl-hunting, and what was he doing?

He was sitting. Sitting quite alone by the side of the lake with nothing doing, nothing at all.

So Willing

All because of that bitch, Rhonda.

The trouble with Rhonda was double trouble. She was impossible to touch and impossible to stay away from. The first day he saw her, which was the second day at the cabin, he knew she was going to be the one. She just had to be. She was perfect.

For one thing, she was different from any of the Modnoc girls. She was from New York City, and this made a big difference. Not just the way she talked, but the way she looked and the way she acted. She was far more mature, far more sophisticated.

And far more attractive.

Of course, if Vince himself had come from New York, he would have thought that Rhonda looked exactly like everyone else. She had dark hair and she wore it long, and the ponytail that hung to her waist looked just like the ponytail of every other girl who went to Bronx Science or Walden or Elizabeth Irwin or Music & Art or New Lincoln High School. She also wore sandals and dark-colored Bermuda shorts and very plain white blouses. She was in uniform, but of course Vince did not know this.

Vince thought she was beautiful. The purple eye shadow was beautiful, too, and the pale lipstick. But most of all, the girl underneath all the garbage was beautiful.

And obviously a virgin.

She was the only one he wanted. There were other girls at the lake, but next to Rhonda they seemed pretty pallid and dull. They could have been easy, some of them. A few gave him come-on glances that meant he could have them flat on their pretty backsides just by saying the word. But he didn't feel like saying the word, not to them.

But Rhonda, damn her to hell, didn't want to hear the word.

All she wanted to do was talk, and walk around in the woods, and go out rowing on the lake, and look at the stars, and think very deep thoughts. This fooled him at first. He dated her about five minutes after he first set eyes on her, and when he asked her what she wanted to do that night she told him she wanted to go rowing on the lake.

Which pleased Vince no end.

Because, as everybody knew, a girl who wants to go rowing on the lake is a girl who wants to do other things. And if the girl herself suggests the rowing expedition it is an odds-on bet that the rowboat is going to get one hell of a workout.

That wasn't exactly the way it turned out. When Rhonda said she wanted to go rowing on the lake, that was precisely what she meant. She wanted to sit in her end of the boat and look up at the stars and think profound thoughts. That was all she wanted to do.

Fortunately, he figured this out before he made the mistake of making a pass. Otherwise everything would have been shot to hell right at the start. But he played things very cool, very cool indeed, staying on his side of the boat and helping her stare at the stars. In between staring at the stars and leaning on the oars he did some supplementary staring at Rhonda's breasts. The blouse she wore was trying to hide the fact that she had any breasts, but Vince had a good eye for that sort of thing. He could tell that she was built very well, soft and firm and very nice to look at, and undoubtedly still nicer to hold onto.

She was, he decided, worth waiting for. So what if she wasn't going to fall into his arms on the first date? Maybe things worked differently in New York.

And, following this line of reasoning, he didn't try to kiss her goodnight. He just stopped her at the door to her cabin, took her chin in his hand, and looked deeply into her eyes. Her eyes were brown and very soft.

"Tomorrow night," he said. She hesitated, then nodded, and he turned on his heel and walked off into the night. He had it made, he knew, because he had suddenly figured out Rhonda's Dream Man. Her Dream Man was sort of a cross between Tony Perkins and Cary Grant, if such a combination was possible. Shy and deep like Perkins, polished and assured like Grant. All he had to do was play that role properly and the prize was his.

Maybe.

THE next night was a disappointment. They took a walk to the woods, another type of scene which with any other girl would have been an obvious prelude to a more advanced form of entertainment. Not with Rhonda, however. They walked through the woods and she rambled on and on about how wonderful nature was while he half-listened and half-contemplated how wonderful nature really was.

When he tried to kiss her goodnight she pulled away from him, her eyes very sad. "Don't, Vince." He didn't say anything.

"I like you, Vince. But it's so...so physical, kissing and all that. I'd like us just to be friends, to share things with each other."

He felt like telling her something she had that she really ought to share with him. But that of course would have ruined it for good, so he played his role and hung his head and told her that he was sorry, that of course she was right, and that it was his fault that he had permitted himself to get carried away by animalistic desires.

When he got home he took a cold hip bath, as recommended in that corny Boy Scout Manual. It didn't help.

And if that was bad, the next few nights were worse. Bit by bit he managed to convince her that an experience couldn't be meaningful unless bodies as well as souls merged. While he told her this he kept his hands to himself, speaking slowly and soulfully. And she agreed, more or less.

More or less. Oh, she wasn't one to minimize the importance of physical love. She knew how wonderful a thing physical love could be, when two people shared everything there was to share. There was just one little catch. She herself, she explained sadly, was a cold woman. She couldn't feel anything that way, couldn't get excited or interested. It just didn't do anything for her.

"I'll help you, Rhonda," he told her. "Let me kiss you. Let me make you feel our love."

She was willing to be kissed. So he kissed her, first gently and then not so gently. But kissing her wasn't nearly as pleasant as it should have been. She didn't struggle or pull away. She didn't respond, either. She just stood there like a window dummy and let him do the kissing.

It was about as stimulating as kissing a dead fish.

He kept trying. When the kisses didn't do anything he tried touching her and, although his hands had been itching to get hold of her body, the act itself didn't live up to his expectations.

The body did. He didn't undress her, just ran his hands over her clothing. It was enough to convince him that all that was there belonged to little Rhonda. And little Rhonda was not little at all. She had as nice a body as anyone he had ever came across.

Her breasts were better than Betty's—a little larger and quite a bit firmer. Her legs were perfect.

But all she did was submit to his touches. She didn't quiver or breathe hard or clutch at him or anything. She just acquiesced, and her body as a result was not the body of a warm girl but the body of a very well-formed statue. Perfect and flawless, but no more responsive than a slab of marble.

And somehow this took all the fun out of it. At first it was a challenge, trying to find some way to coax a response out of her. Then, as he kept meeting the challenge and failing wretchedly, it began to become a bit of a bore. Especially because of the way she talked.

They would kiss (or rather he would kiss her) and they would pet (or rather he would pet her) and every few minutes she would pull her head to one side and start telling him how miserable she felt over the fact that she didn't feel a thing. It was bad enough knowing that she didn't feel a thing without hearing about it all the goddamned time. That made things just so much worse.

It was a week now, a week of frustration that didn't seem to be getting him anywhere in particular. And the fact that there was so much other stuff available didn't help matters. He would see girls down by the lake and know damned well that they'd spread their pretty selves for him the minute he said the word.

And here he was with Rhonda.

Who wouldn't.

He had a date with her in half an hour, but somehow he didn't even feel like going. To hell with her. Let her sit in her cabin and play with herself or something. There wasn't any sense wasting his time with her. And it was sure as hell a waste of time. Maybe some of the guys would be all excited at the prospect of playing doctor with a pretty girl, but he'd been around long enough to want more.

To hell with her. He could go out now and find himself something within five minutes, something that would come across on the first date and be all ready and willing any time he wanted. That made one hell of a lot more sense than wasting his time on a hunk of ice from the big bad city of New York.

He hung his head in disgust. The Great White Hunter was out of his class, that was the trouble. He just wasn't good enough to drag down this particular prey.

And then, suddenly, he stopped hanging his head and began to shake it resolutely. Dammit, he wasn't giving up! And he wasn't going to play games any more, either. He was going to win.

He got up, went back to the cabin, got the keys to the car from his father and drove into town. The man at the liquor store was decent enough not to ask to see his draft card. He bought a gallon jug of red wine, knowing that wine was the only drink that had a chance of working on her. Beer was too vulgar and liquor was too strong. Wine would appeal to the romantic side of her, and that was what he wanted.

It didn't seem fair, somehow. But it was no time to worry about fairness. He was going to use the wine, and the wine was going to get her drunk as a skunk, and then he was going to have Rhonda and get her out of his system so that he could concentrate on other girls. This virgin bit was a pain in the neck. Maybe once he got his first virgin out of the way he'd be able to concentrate on bigger and better things.

Although, when you stopped to think about it, it wasn't easy to imagine any bigger and better things than the two big and good things under her blouse.

He hopped back in the car, put the jug of red wine in the backseat and broke some speeding laws on the way to her cabin, which was no mean trick in his father's car. She was waiting for him, and, happily, her parents weren't around. Coming on strong for the parents was a big thing with him, and it was sort of annoying that it was so useless with Rhonda's parents. They didn't really care who she went out with and she didn't care what her parents thought about him, so talking to them was a total waste of time.

"Come with me," he told her mysteriously. "Tonight is our night."

He led her to the car and drove off to the lake. "We're having a picnic," he explained. "A special place that I've never taken you to before. It's sort of a private place of mine."

The place, he went on to explain, was an island in the middle of the lake. What he didn't bother explaining was that he usually avoided the island because it was the dullest spot in the world.

He led her to the rowboat, carrying the jug of wine in one hand. She asked him what the wine was for and he told her a picnic was just not a picnic without a jug of wine. She seemed to accept the explanation.

Rowing across the lake was a real pain in the neck, but he was so fired up at the prospect of finally getting at Rhonda that the rowing didn't bother him as much as it usually did. It was, he reflected, a nice night for seducing a virgin. Dark, quiet, just a moon in the sky with no stars out.

"The wine will be good," he explained. "You see, there's been something wrong with our relationship."

Relationship was one of her favorite words.

"I know," she said. "I know, Vince."

"The wine will help," he told her. "It will relax you, which is the important thing. You'll be able to escape from your inhibitions."

Inhibitions was another of her favorite words.

"I suppose so," she said.

"And after all," he went on, determined to fit her two favorite words into the same sentence, "inhibitions can damage a relationship."

"You're right, Vince," she said. "You're right."

They beached the boat and climbed out onto the crummy little island. Instantly she started going into orbit over what a beautiful private place it was and how glad she was that he liked her enough to share it with her. While she talked on and on he managed to pull the cork out of the wine jug with his teeth.

"Come with me," he said. "Sit by my side."

She sat with him.

"Here," he said. "Drink some of the wine."

She took the jug and tilted it, taking a healthy swallow. He waited for her to choke on it but she didn't. Instead she passed him the jug, her eyes shining.

"It's good wine, Vince."

He tried a sip and decided that either she was off her nut or that he just plain didn't like wine. But it didn't much matter. The important thing was getting the wine into her. He didn't have to drink anything himself.

So he passed the jug back to her.

She took another swig and this time her eyes were very dreamy. When she spoke, her voice was husky.

"I think you're right, Vince. I think maybe the wine is a good idea. It might relax me. It might push my inhibitions to one side so that the real person can shine through."

"Sure," he said.

"I want the real person to shine through, Vince. I don't want to be inhibited forever. You know that, don't you, Vince?"

"Sure," he said. He handed the wine back to her and she took another drink. Then she kicked off her sandals and stretched out on the ground.

"Makes me sleepy," she said. "I have to lie down, Vince."

His heart jumped. It was working. Evidently she wasn't used to drinking. Hell, she was young. Maybe this was the first time anybody'd ever given her anything stronger to drink than a glass of chocolate milk. Whatever it was, he knew he'd picked the right way to do it. If it was cheating to get a girl drunk, well, that was just too bad. If it was cheating; he was a cheat. It was working, and that was all he cared about.

"Vince—"

"What it it, Rhonda?"

"Come lie down next to me."

She didn't have to ask him a second time. It was the first time she'd ever wanted him near her—other times she'd merely accepted him. So he stretched out beside her and took her in his arms.

At first he thought it was going to be different. When he kissed her her lips pressed hard against his and her arms went around him, holding him tight. For a second, just a second, he thought the wine had done its work.

Then she relaxed completely. She was a statue again, a hunk of plaster.

He went on kissing her, forcing his tongue between her parted lips, running his hands over her body. But it wasn't doing him a bit of good. He was getting excited, but that wasn't important. The important thing was to get her excited.

"It's no use, Vince."

"Don't worry." Trying desperately to sound tender instead of obeying the impulse and snarling at her. "Everything's going to be all right, Rhonda. There's nothing for you to worry about."

"But it's not fair. I want to like it, Vince. I want to feel it."

"I know you do."

"But I just can't."

"Of course you can," he said automatically. "Of course you can, dear."

"I can't."

He sat up, reaching for the wine, and he told her that of course she could, that for a moment she had started to respond.

"I felt you getting...excited," he said. He had almost said hot.

"For a second, but—"

"That's a beginning," he went on. "Have a little more wine. That should do it for you."

She took the wine from him and he sighed with relief when she started to raise it to her lips. Then suddenly, she lowered it. Her eyes were troubled.

"Vince," she said, "what will happen after I drink enough of the wine?"

"I'll kiss you."

"I know that. I mean—we won't go all the way, will we?"

"Of course not."

"That's good," she said. "I...I can't help being worried. I know you wouldn't try to do anything...wrong, but I can't help worrying."

"You don't have to worry with me," he said.

"I know it, Vince."

"I'm not that kind of a person."

"Oh, I know, Vince."

"I wouldn't try to take advantage of somebody like you, Rhonda."

"I know."

"I'm just doing this for you. That's why I bought the wine—so that you'll learn to relax. It hurts me to see you so tense all the time."

He felt like telling her where it hurt.

"I know, Vince."

"And for us," he went on, wondering if Hollywood would give him a job if they heard him. "I'm doing it for us, so that we can be closer together."

"I know, Vince."

"Drink some wine."

She drank some wine.

"Have another drink, Rhonda. I think it'll do you good."

"Do you really think so?"

He nodded, and she had another drink. This time when she put the jug down he could see how flushed her cheeks were.

He knew just how to play it. After each swig of wine he would kiss her and stroke her as long as she went on responding, and the minute she stopped he would stop also. Then he'd get some more wine into her stomach and start in where he left off.

It was time to begin.

He stretched out beside her and reached for her. This time the kiss was good all the way—her mouth was hot and eager and her tongue matched his own tongue in passion. He hadn't been prepared for that strong a response and for a minute he thought somebody had sneaked up and switched girls on him. But no, nobody else had a body like the one pressed up against him.

He worked expertly, kissing her, stroking the nape of her neck with the fingers of one hand and fondling her breast with the other hand. He kept waiting for the wine to wear off and for the responses to cease, but the responses just got stronger.

He began unbuttoning her blouse. Now, he thought, she was going to stop him.

But she didn't.

He unbuttoned all the buttons and managed to lift her up so that he could get the blouse off. While he had her that way, he got up the nerve to unsnap her bra and get that off, and once he got rid of the bra and there was nothing between him and those breasts, it was no longer a question of nerve. There was just no stopping, not for him.

"Don't, Vince. We don't want to lose control. We have to be careful, Vince."

He wanted to pick up a rock and crack her skull with it. Somehow he forced himself to remain patient. "There's nothing to worry about," he told her. "I can control myself, Rhonda. I just want to touch you. You like it when I touch you, don't you?"

Her answer was a kittenish purr.

And then they were both naked and their bodies were touching and she was more excited than any girl he had ever been with in his life. He knew that she was ready, ready for him, and he was certainly ready for her. More than ready. He couldn't wait any longer.

It began, and he was surprised that she didn't feel any pain. There was supposed to be pain with a virgin. That was what everybody said. But everybody was evidently wrong, because Rhonda was taking to it like a duck to water. She was having a ball.

When it was over she started to cry. He calmed her, reassured her, told her everything was all right.

"I didn't want it to happen," she said. "I was afraid it would happen. And it did."

"We couldn't help ourselves," he told her. It was a good line for this sort of situation.

"You liked it," he said. "Didn't you?"

She nodded.

"Well," he said, "that's the important thing. You got rid of your inhibitions."

"Of course," she said. "I always do when I drink." He just looked at her.

"Every single time," she said. "But only when I drink. With Norman and with Phil and with Johnny and with Dave and Allen and Robert. Every time I drink it's all right and I like it, but I like it so much that I can't stop. That's the bad part. I always go all the way when I drink. I just can't help it."

He couldn't believe it. He knew instinctively that it was true, all true, but he just plain didn't want to believe it.

"It's very strange," she said, her voice almost clinical. "I suppose it's a reaction formation. I'm all repressed and inhibited, and then when I lose my inhibitions I lose all control and I just have to go all the way."

She looked sad, then grinned. He had never seen her grin that way.

"But it's worth it," she said. "Pass me the wine, Vince. I'll have a little more wine and then we can do it again."

THREE

OH WELL, WHAT the hell, there was always Adele. Once Vince had managed to unload Rhonda, he'd checked the available quail, and decided that Adele was next.

Not that it was all that easy to unload Rhonda. When Rhonda lost her inhibitions, she had a hell of a time finding them again. After that first night, out at the island, she'd been ready for wining and twining on a steady basis, and Vince was to be the lucky guy.

They had a relationship now, that was the thing. That was the way Rhonda saw it, anyway. They had a relationship, and so now her inhibitions and complexes and mental blocks were all soothed and quieted, as far as Vince was concerned. But not as far as any other guy was concerned. Vince was the only one she could feel really free with. That was the way she expressed it. He was the only one she could feel really free with.

And did she want to feel really free! She wanted it as much as she could get it.

So it wasn't too easy to unload Rhonda. Every time he turned around, there she was, the old gleam in her eye and a bottle of wine in her hand. Vince finally had to resort to psychological double-talk himself.

"I think our relationship is strained," he told her. He knew something was strained, or would be if they kept on like this. "It's because," he told her, "you still need the wine. I can't feel as though it's really me you want. Do you understand?"

Of course she did. She understood completely, and it was a very natural reaction. But she also had the solution. They'd go out to the island without any wine, and they'd see what would happen.

"I bet I don't really need any wine," she said, and rubbed against him a little bit.

He was pretty sure she was right. But he hadn't gotten over his disappointment that the little bitch hadn't been a virgin after all. All he wanted between Rhonda and himself anymore was distance. And lots of it.

He told her he thought they ought to part for a while, that it was time to test their relationship and see if it was really strong. And the only way to do that was to not see each other for a while. Then, when they met again, if the relationship, if the feeling between them—"simpatico" she murmured at that point, nodding—if the feeling between them was still strong, they'd know they really had a solid and lasting relationship on their hands.

She agreed, finally, though with reluctance. And off she went, preceded by her chest, and Vince mopped his brow and went swimming.

Then he lolled around for a couple of days, trying to talk himself into calling off the virgin-hunt.

He gave himself lots of good reasons. He lay around out on the strip of sand between the cabin and the water, soaking up sun and counting off the reasons on his fingers.

The reasons: In the first place, it was by now obvious to him that you could never tell for sure whether a girl was a virgin or not. Her own statements on the subject were worse than useless, of course, and even her actions didn't mean much. Nor did her reputation. Nor did her appearance.

In the second place, virgin-hunting was one of the most frustrating and annoying projects in the world. Vince had been in a lousy mood for a couple of weeks now, and all because of the virgin-hunt. If it weren't for that, he'd be enjoying himself up here at the lake.

And, in the third and last place, it meant he was missing a lot of sure stuff. You go after a virgin, she's liable to still be a virgin after you leave her. You go after one that's been made before, you've got a better chance to make her again.

Three reasons, and all of them good ones. Vince spent a couple of days going over them, trying to talk himself out of this quest of the holy quail, then he strolled over to his father's car, slid behind the wheel, and drove off to see if this lousy lake could boast of even one single guaranteed virgin.

It could. Adele Christopher. And this time, he was absolutely sure. Never mind about appearances' being deceiving, they couldn't be all that deceiving. Adele Christopher was a virgin, no question about it.

Actually, she wasn't much Vince's type. She was a short, slender, mousy girl, with a boyish figure. She had breasts, but they were about the size of a bee-bite. And she had hips, but just barely. She did have good legs, at least, and a pleasant, oval face beneath short-cropped mouse-blonde hair, and she was definitely a virgin.

Adele was sixteen, but she looked more like twelve. She usually wandered around wearing scuffed loafers and frayed faded blue jeans and a white man's shirt with the tails tied in a knot beneath her bee-bites. But her little butt wiggled nicely inside the tight blue jeans, and her waist looked small enough to put his arm completely around it, and she had a nice friendly smile and clear blue eyes.

She wasn't precisely his type, but the more he looked at her, the more he had a feeling she could become his type without too much trouble at all. There was an old saying he'd heard once: The closer to the bone, the sweeter the meat. And you couldn't get much closer to the bone than skinny Adele.

He'd also heard it said that a thin woman is built for speed and a fat woman is built for comfort. A girl like Adele, being as thin as that—and it would be her first time, too, of that he was sure—she might just go wild. It didn't take much thinking-it-over before he really began to look forward to the experience.

The first thing, of course, was to get to know the girl better. He'd met her at the grocery store-post office around on the north shore of the lake, talked with her a bit, seen her a few times when he'd swum from his own cabin to the public beach near the store, but it had never been any more than talk about the weather and sunburn and how cold the lake water was. So the first thing to do was get to know her better.

That part was easy enough. He drove around the lake to the store, parked in the gravel parking lot beside the store, and there she was, at the public beach, sitting with a bunch of girls. She was dressed, as usual, in blue jeans, white shirt and scuffed loafers, and she looked, as usual, not a day over twelve.

He went over and talked for a while, talking with the whole group of girls. The usual vacation-at-the-lake crap, about the weather and the temperature of the water and all that; and when the right moment came, he asked her if she wanted to join him for a coke over at the store. Adele wouldn't be a wine girl like Rhonda. She'd be a coke and hot dogs girl.

And, of course, her Dream Man would be a coke and hot dogs boy. An outdoorsy type, young and kind of gawky, the kind of clown who'd wander around with Lassie at his heels. So that was the way Vince played it, young and gawky and full of coke. He fooled around with the notion of borrowing a dog from somebody, but decided it was too much trouble, and he could be gawky enough all by himself.

She went with him for the coke, but so did two of the other girls. That was the thing with girls, particularly short fat ugly girls like the two who came along to share the coke. They always ran in packs. You get a bunch of good-looking girls together, it's no trouble at all to cull one out of the herd. You get a bunch of beasts together, with one good-looking girl in their midst, and they'll cling to the looker as though she were a life-preserver. Vince thought that was probably because they knew the looker would attract males, and they didn't want to miss out if there were any extras. Or maybe they were just hoping some of the looks would rub off on them if they hung around long enough.

He knew better than to let the girls know he was less than overjoyed to have them along. He knew he had to make believe he liked Adele's bug-eyed monster friends if he wanted to get anywhere with her. So he grinned at them and talked with them, and waited half an hour before asking Adele if she wanted to go for a ride around the lake. She said yes, and he pulled her away before the beasts knew what was going on.

That first day, all they did was drive around the lake, looking at the cabins and the swimmers and the motorboats, while Vince did some strong groundwork on the Dream Man. By the time he brought her back to the store, where she wanted to be let off, he knew he had her hooked. She thought he was just the greatest thing since Claude Jarman, Jr. "I'll see you tomorrow," he said as she got out of the car, and she smiled and nodded, looking very pleased.

He spent four days that way, just driving her around the lake, going swimming with her either at the public beach or the little beach behind his parents' cabin, and all the time building up the young and gawky impression for her.

After the first day, he didn't have too much trouble with the beasts any more. It was obvious that Adele preferred to go off with him, rather than hang around with the tons of fun, and that was an excellent sign. There was only one of the beasts who caused any trouble at all; a short, heavy, stringy-haired mound named Bobbi. She even managed, on the second day, to come along for the ride around the lake—which pleased Vince no end. After that, he worked extra hard to keep himself and Adele away from lovable old Bobbi.

The fourth day was a Friday, and there was to be a dance that night in Cornwallville, a town about eight miles from the lake. In a Grange Hall, no less. While they were driving around that afternoon, Vince asked her if she wanted to go to the dance with him, and she said she'd be glad to. By that time, they were old hound-dog buddies.

So that Friday night was the first real date. He knew he was dealing with a genuine virgin this time—there wasn't the slightest doubt of that at all, he kept telling himself—so he played it very cautious on their first date. At the dance, which was lousy, consisting of a hillbilly jukebox alternating with some local hillbilly non-talent, he danced with her as though they were brother and sister. Afterward, he drove her right back to her cabin, and kissed her only once before saying good-night. She was surprised that he hadn't tried to kiss her again, he could tell that, and he knew she wanted him to kiss her again. She could keep wanting for a little while, he told himself. Work the anticipation bit.

At first, he'd been planning the defloration for the backseat of his father's car, but as the time grew nearer, he began to think about the mechanics of the thing again; that business of switching from front seat to back, of squirming around trying to get your clothes off in a cramped backseat, and he decided a grassy slope somewhere under a tree would be a hell of a lot better all the way around.

But not out at the island. Not after the fiasco with Rhonda. He didn't want to have anything to do with that lousy island ever again. Somewhere else.

He took some time out to look for a new spot, a place as secluded and handy as the island. He went looking on Monday afternoon, three days after the dance.

The thing was, this was a vacation-type lake. Every inch of shore was used by somebody or other, with cabins and docks and boathouses and beaches. A two-lane blacktop road circled the lake, and even the side of the road away from the lake was solidly lined with cabins.

Yet he couldn't roam too far away from the lake. He had to find a spot close enough so it would seem natural to go there. It would be in the afternoon, of course. An outdoorsy girl like Adele, you could only de-virginize her in the daytime, with the sun shining like mad.

He drove around Monday afternoon, looking for a secluded spot and not finding one. Then he noticed the little stream that fed into the lake from the east, tumbling down from the wooded hills back of the lake. There was a small bridge at the point where the road crossed the stream, and he noticed what looked like a narrow path leading off from the road along the streamside.

He stopped the car just beyond the bridge and walked back to look at the stream and the path. There was nothing up that way but woods. No roads and no cabins and no people. The path was overgrown, barely visible more than a few feet from the road.

This looked like the place. It would be the most natural thing in the world for a nature boy like Vince to suggest a little walk up that path. And it would be the most natural thing in the world for a nature girl like Adele to think it a great idea.

But it might also be a great idea to check first, to make sure there was some sort of clearing up that way, someplace where a couple of nature-lovers could lie down and have some room, if they happened to feel like it.

Vince didn't like to walk, not even on sidewalks. And he especially didn't like to walk along overgrown and weed-choked paths in the God-forsaken great outdoors. But a man with a goal will suffer a lot of inconvenience to reach that goal. And Vince was definitely a man with a goal. He started walking.

The stream meandered around like an idiot, curving back and forth and climbing erratically over hills, and the path followed right next to it, occasionally angling away from the stream for a few yards to cut through some particularly heavy underbrush. Vince fought his way along, and the farther he got the more overgrown the woods became, with trees crammed closer and closer together and all kinds of bushes and weeds stuffed in among the trunks. It looked as though there was no such thing as a clearing in these lousy woods.

But there was. And it was inhabited.

He heard the voices first, ahead of him. They sounded familiar, but they were still some distance ahead, and he couldn't figure out who it was. He had a sudden fear that it might be Rhonda, and he almost turned around right then and ran back to the car.

But he didn't. The voices might mean there was an open space ahead. Vince left the path, climbing up a steep slope away from the stream, planning to circle around and see who these people were before showing himself to them.

He was halfway up the slope when he suddenly realized that one of the voices was Adele's. He hesitated, wondering what the hell Adele was doing there, and all at once he had the horrible fear that he'd goofed again; that not even Adele was a virgin, that she was up here with some guy.

Maybe there just wasn't any such thing as a virgin, after all. Maybe virgins were myths, like unicorns. He suddenly remembered the legend that only a virgin could capture a unicorn, and now he understood that legend. It took a myth to catch a myth.

But as he stood there thinking about it, getting more disgusted every second, the other voice started talking again and, with a sigh of relief, he realized the other voice also belonged to a girl. So Adele wasn't up here with a guy, after all. It was just one of her little Brownie friends.

He thought he heard Adele mention his name. Sure, she was talking about him, she was telling the Brownie about him. Good old Adele.

He wondered what she was saying about him. He moved forward even more slowly and cautiously now, wanting to get close enough to hear what Adele had to say.

From the top of the slope, he could see them. It was Adele and the tons of fun, Bobbi, the menace who'd been hanging around so much all last week.

And there was a clearing. A great clearing, right out of a storybook. It was oval in shape, with the stream gurgling through the middle of the oval the long way. There were level grassy banks right down to the edge of the stream, and the whole place was ringed with slender-trunked young trees and dark green shrubbery.

Adele and Bobbi were sitting on the grass next to the stream, on the same side as Vince. They were both dressed in the uniform of the area, blue jeans and white men's shirts, and they were sitting chatting together about one thing and another. And mainly about Vince.

He lay prone on his stomach on the top of the slope, peering through the high grass, and watched and listened.

Bobbi was saying, "Vince wants to make love to you, you know."

"Oh, don't be silly," said Adele. "All boys think about it, but it doesn't mean anything. I mean, he isn't going to try anything."

Vince grinned down the slope at Adele. That's what you think, little baby, he thought. And what a great big surprise you've got coming. A great big surprise.

"I know why you're going around with him so much," Bobbi was saying. "It's to make me mad."

"I haven't been going around with him so much," objected Adele, but she smiled at the other girl, and she didn't deny the charge. "We've just gone riding in his car, that's all, just riding around the lake."

"You went to the dance with him Friday night," Bobbi said. Vince could see now that Bobbi was pouting. There was accusation in her voice.

Adele shrugged. "I wanted to go to the dance," she said. "What's wrong with that? And I couldn't very well have gone with you."

"Why not?" Bobbi demanded. "Girls go to dances together all the time. They even dance together. Who'd think anything?"

"I don't know about your parents," Adele told her, "but my mother and father are beginning to suspect."

Vince frowned, not following the conversation at all. Suspect? Suspect what?

Oh for God's sake, he thought suddenly, they're members of a non-virgin club. He knew it, he knew it, he'd known it all along, there just wasn't any such thing as a virgin. Virgins and unicorns, mythical beasties.

The conversation was still going on down there, and through his depression Vince continued to listen, and what they were saying down there just kept getting more mystifying all the time.

"They do not," Bobbi was saying. "Parents never suspect a thing like that. We could do it right in front of them, for Pete's sake, and they'd think we were just playing games."

"All I know," Adele said, "is that Mom's been hinting that I ought to stay away from you. And every time she gets on the subject, she gets too embarrassed for words."

"Then don't worry about it," Bobbi advised her. "Even if they think they know something, what difference does it make if they're afraid to call you on it?"

"I don't think I'd want them to know," Adele said soberly.

"Are you ashamed? I told you, Adele, there's nothing in the world to be ashamed of. There've been lots and lots of women—"

"I know all that. I just don't want my parents to know about it, that's all."

"You changed the subject," said Bobbi suddenly. "You didn't want to talk about that Vince any more."

Adele smiled, and lay back on the grass, staring up at the sky. "I think I like him," she said thoughtfully.

"Adele, don't be mean."

"I think maybe I'll let him make love to me," she said, still smiling at the sky.

Vince sat up and took notice. Now, *that* was the kind of thing he liked to hear!

"Adele, you're just teasing me," Bobbi said reproachfully. "Don't tease me like that."

"I wonder how it would be," mused Adele, ignoring the other girl. "I wonder how it would be to have a man make love to me." She turned and looked at Bobbi, grinning wickedly at her. "Don't you wonder sometimes how it would feel?"

Bobbi made a face and said, "Ugh!"

"I do," said Adele. She lay back on the grass again. "And I think I really will do it. I'll bring Vince up here and—"

"Adele, stop it!"

"After all," Adele went on, "I really ought to try it."

She was a virgin, Vince was thinking gleefully. This time, for sure, she was a virgin.

She went on, saying, "Just once, of course. But I ought to try it once, see what it's like. Maybe I'd enjoy it."

Oh, you would, little baby, thought Vince. You sure as hell would. And you sure as hell *will*.

"I think I'd like him to—"

"*Stop*!" Bobbi, her face contorted with rage, suddenly lunged forward and cracked Adele ringingly across the face, open-handed. "Stop that!" she screamed. "Stop tormenting me like that!"

"Don't you slap *me*!" Adele was suddenly enraged, too, and came up from the grass swinging.

Vince stared at them in blank-faced astonishment. Their conversation, their actions—none of it made any sense. And now they were rolling around on the ground down there, punching and scratching and biting each other, and he couldn't figure out for the life of him just what the hell they were fighting about

The two of them, fighting grimly and silently now, kept rolling around on the grass, slugging and clawing one another, until finally the inevitable happened, and they both tumbled off the bank and into the shallow stream.

They came up gurgling and thrashing, and all at once they weren't fighting any more. They looked at one another, solemnly, and both climbed back out of the stream; and sat down on the bank once more.

They sat in silence for a while, Vince watching and scratching his head, until at last Adele said, softly, "I'm sorry I teased you, Bobbi. I shouldn't be mean like that."

"And I'm sorry I slapped you," Bobbi said. "But when you talk that way, I just get so jealous I can't stand it. And when you keep going off with that Vince all the time—"

"I won't do that anymore," said Adele. "I'm really and truly sorry, Bobbi."

Vince blinked. What was this? A minute ago, she'd been talking about making it with him. Now she was saying she wasn't even going to go for rides with him anymore. He wondered what the hell was going on down there, and he also wondered just who in hell Bobbi thought she was, and where she came off, queering his deal that way.

Bobbi got to her feet, a round blob in the middle of the clearing. "My clothes are soaked," she said.

"Mine, too." Adele stood up beside her, and started undoing her shirt. "We better take them off and spread them out on the grass, so they'll dry."

"What if somebody sees us?" And Bobbi looked up the slope, straight at where Vince was hiding. Even though he knew it was impossible for her to see him, he winced and ducked lower into the grass.

"Nobody ever comes up here," Adele said offhandedly, and she stripped off her shirt. She was wearing a bra beneath it, which was a waste of good money. Those bee-bites of hers didn't need any support at all. She spread the shirt on the grass, then removed the bra, and her breasts barely cast a shadow.

Bobbi, still a little hesitant, also stripped off her wet clothes. Vince looked at them both, and he thought they really should have been cut closer to the middle of the deck. Where Adele was thin as a rail, with breasts smaller than the White Rock girl, and hips skinnier than a basketball player's; Bobbi was busting out all over. She had breasts that could have been used for sandbags, and a butt that was a sandbag. Nothing else in the world could be that wide and round and saggy.

They were both nude before it occurred to him that his status had just changed from eavesdropper, which wasn't really very bad, to peeping torn, which was very bad. He ought to get away from there before they found him and got the wrong idea.

But he was afraid to move, afraid he might make some small sound that they would hear. And now, with their clothes off, they'd be more alert for the sounds of other people. So he stayed where he was, and waited for a chance to slip away.

Besides, it was pleasant to have a preview of Adele's body. The legs, as he'd already known, were very good, with strong and supple thighs and good calves. And her stomach was flat, her waist delicate and tiny. The bee-bite breasts weren't much, but it might be fun to play with them a bit. Play delicately, of course, in relation to their size. Just with fingers, not with the whole hand.

Now stripped, Adele lay on her back, one arm across her eyes to keep out the sun, one knee raised. Vince nodded approvingly. That's the position, little baby, he thought. You just keep practicing that.

And then Bobbi's hand reached out and squeezed Adele's breast.

Vince blinked. What the hell was that all about?

He'd expected Adele to sit up like a shot, hollering, but she didn't do anything of the kind. Instead, she smiled and murmured, and reached up to press Bobbi's hand tighter against her breast.

"I do love you so," Bobbi said, and her voice was so soft that Vince could barely make out the words. "You know how much I love you. You shouldn't tease me the way you do."

"I know, honey," Adele said soothingly. She smiled up at Bobbi contritely and said, "I won't do that any more."

Bobbi leaned down and kissed Adele on the lips, and Adele's arms twined around the other girl, and soon they were lying side by side on the grass, stroking each other's body and murmuring.

After the first movement by Bobbi, Adele became the aggressor of the two. Bobbi lay flat on her back, and Adele leaned over her, stroking her breasts and stomach and thighs, kissing her, leaning down to nip at her breasts, kissing all over Bobbi's body.

When they really got into it, and Vince knew they wouldn't be paying any attention to outside sounds for a while, he crept slowly back down the slope, and headed down the path for the road and his car. He kept shaking his head in disgusted amazement, and trying to figure out what the hell kind of world it was he was living in anyway.

Well, he'd found his virgin. There was no getting around that, he'd found a guaranteed virgin. Guaranteed for life.

And that, he told himself, was definitely that. First two phonies, and now a dyke. Talk about queering the deal! Okay, the virgin-hunt was off. He was cured.

Back at the road, he got into the car and drove toward home. The virgin-hunt was off, and he was soured on the lake. He didn't want to be at any lake with Rhonda and Adele—the relationship kid and the dyke. He didn't know for sure where he did want to be, but he did know for sure he didn't want to be at the lake.

His father was reading the paper, inevitably, on the screened-in porch of the cabin. Vince went into his bedroom, which had a window looking out onto the porch, and grabbed his suitcase. As he stuffed clothes into it, he said through the window to his father, "You aren't going to be needing the car for about a week, are you?"

His father looked up from the paper, startled. "What?" His suitcase packed, Vince said,

"I'd like to take off in the car for about a week. You don't need it, do you?"

"Well—well, no. But—"

"Okay if I take it for a week? Don't worry, I won't crack it up or anything."

"I know that," his father said. "You're a good driver, Vince. But—"

"Then it's okay, huh?"

"Well, I suppose so, but—"

"Fine." He grabbed the suitcase and left the bedroom.

His father followed, the paper trailing from his hand. "Where are you going?"

Vince dumped the suitcase into the backseat of the car, slid behind the wheel, said, "See you in a week," and took off.

FOUR

THE TROUBLE WITH just pointing the car and heading down the road was that you might just happen to wind up in Brighton. And it wasn't easy to imagine a worse place than Brighton. Even the cruddy cabin by the cruddy lake, rustically rotten as it was, would have been better. Except, of course, for charmers like Rhonda and Adele.

The combination of Relationship Rhonda and Dykey Adele made it necessary to head for greener pastures. But Brighton wasn't exactly greener pastures. It was more on the order of a desert.

It was so simple at first, Vince thought. You got in the car, stepped on the gas, and drove. When you found a quarry worth pursuing, then you stopped.

Sure you did.

The problems occurred after you were heading down the old road. There were plenty of problems. For one thing, you didn't know where the hell you were going. For another thing, you had to get the damned car back to the damned cabin in a week, maybe ten days at the outside. That sort of ruled out a trip to any town that might be worth going to.

This limited things. He couldn't go to Florida, which might have been nice, and he couldn't go to California, which also might have been nice, and he couldn't go to Alaska, which might have been even nicer. But he still could have gone to New York, or Philadelphia, or Boston. New York, in some small way, meant Rhonda, which was disturbing, but Boston or Philadelphia would have been one hell of a lot better than Brighton.

Brighton.

But there was one more problem, one overwhelming problem, and the problem was money. More precisely, the lack of money. He had fifty dollars and change with him when he took off, and while fifty dollars was a small fortune when you lived with your folks, fifty dollars was very little when it was the sole support of both yourself and a car.

A hungry car. A car that, with a good tailwind, managed ten miles to the gallon. A car that drank oil like a Bowery bum with a thing for petroleum. A car that could easily burn up fifty dollars getting to Boston or Philadelphia or New York.

The smart thing to do was to turn back and give it up as a bad job. But that meant Rhonda, and Adele, and more than anything else it meant admitting defeat.

So he did the dumb thing—which meant Brighton.

He pushed the car seventy miles down the road, passing two towns even worse than Brighton, towns consisting of a gas pump and a general store and three empty houses. And then he reached Brighton, which had more empty houses and two general stores and an occasional hitching post. It was about time either to fill the gas tank or park the car. So he parked the car. It was cheaper.

He had a plan. The plan was the essence of simplicity. He would get the cheapest room he could find, eat the cheapest meals he could stomach, and lay the prettiest girl in the town. Not a virgin, and not a dyke, and not an Uninhibited Relationship. A girl, an ordinary girl. There had to be at least one pretty girl in Brighton, for God's sake.

So he got a room, a cubbyhole in a white frame Rooms-For-Rent run by a gray-headed keep-smiling tub of lard named Mrs. Rebecca Sharp. The room was fifteen dollars a week with meals, and by the looks of Mrs. Sharp, she could cook well. The room was clean, the meals turned out fine, and money was a little less of a problem.

And then, all settled, he went on the hunt for the prettiest girl in Brighton. And found her.

So Willing

HER name was Saralee Jenkins and she was beautiful. Her face was the best part, sort of along the lines of a small-town Grace Kelly, with long blonde hair and blue eyes and an occasional freckle on her nose. The body was good, too. Not quite as good as Rhonda, maybe, but a hell of a lot better than Adele the Dyke. She was kind of short, with well-established breasts and a very slim waist, with legs that were damned fine up to the knee and probably better and better as they went along.

And she was not a virgin. If anybody was not a virgin, she was not a virgin. No virgin looked at you in quite that way. No virgin moved her tail in quite that manner when she walked down the street. There might be a virgin somewhere in the civilized world, but this was definitely not the one.

She worked behind the counter at the drugstore, making sodas and sundaes for the local yokels and frying an occasional greasy hamburger for an occasional greasy kid. Vince saw her for the first time when he stopped in for a coke, and he knew right away that this was the girl; that she was the only one in Brighton worth bothering with, that she was fair game, and that she was not a virgin. This last point he knew instinctively, and later he found it out for certain.

And this was part of the problem. In fact, it was the problem, plain and simple.

She was married.

There were a few rules in the quail-hunting game, and one of them was that you did not fool around with a married woman. You just didn't. All you got out of it was trouble, and occasionally you got killed, and it just wasn't worth it. Vince had had enough opportunities in the past, and once or twice he had been genuinely tempted, but each time his guns had remained in his holster and the prize had not been shot down. There were women in Modnoc, available women, and they had made their availability obvious. But he had pictured himself in the saddle when the horse's owner walked into the room, and he had quietly forgotten the women involved.

But this was different.

For one thing, Saralee was too damned willing to play. That message hit him the minute he saw her, even before he saw the gold band on her finger. The way she looked at him, and the way she talked to him, and everything else about her—she was just there to be had.

Which was bad.

What was worse was that he wanted her, wanted her badly. The Adele episode had left him badly shaken. He needed a girl now, and without one he might go quietly mad. And the rest of the available talent in Brighton was either ugly or virginal. Saralee was neither.

He wanted her and she wanted him. And meanwhile her jerk of a husband, old Bradley Jenkins, stood in the back of the store filling prescriptions. That was all the dumb son-of-a-bitch seemed to know how to do. There was Saralee, itching for love, and the moron was filling prescriptions. It was ridiculous.

He talked with her for about half an hour the first day. She kept dropping hints and he pretended to be too dumb to see what she was getting at, which would have been very dumb indeed. Then, miraculously, the coke was gone, and he had a chance to leave.

So he did.

He spent the rest of the day trying to find someone else to spend the week with, but there wasn't anyone. The girls who had looked merely beastly at first, now looked downright nauseating. He walked all over town, which took all of fifteen minutes, and the more he walked and the more girls he looked at, the worse they looked and the better Saralee looked.

He got back to Mrs. Sharp's just in time for supper, which didn't taste as good this day as it had the day before. He didn't feel much like eating. He felt being alone, and after dinner he went to his room and stretched out on the bed.

There were so many reasons to stay away from Saralee Jenkins. Fine reasons. But the more he thought about them, the less important they became. There were other reasons, reasons why he should crawl between Saralee's anxious arms as soon as possible; and these reasons grew bigger and loomed larger and more significant the more he pondered them.

She was hungry for it, that was for sure. Her broken-down excuse for a husband wasn't doing his job. She needed a young man, and he needed her, and that was that.

She would be good. She would be damned good and hungry the way she was, hungry for him. It was good to have principles, and staying away from married women was a good principle to have, but there was a limit. She was worth stepping out of line for.

More important, it wasn't as if he was crapping in his own backyard. Nobody knew him in Brighton. He could creep up on her like a thief in the night, get what he'd come for, and then head back to the little cabin on the lake. That would be the end of her and the end of Brighton, and to hell with both of them.

He still didn't like it. Either way he didn't like it. Staying in Brighton without sleeping with her would be impossible, and creeping back to the lake with his tail between his legs would be unbearable, and heading onward and downward to still another hick town in the middle of nowhere would be even worse.

And, in the meantime, the second day was drawing to an uneventful close. There were just five more days, and then it was back to the lake, which meant he didn't have a hell of a lot of time to play games. Five days to get in and get out and go home.

The first thing to do, he told himself, was to relax. He counted his money, decided he couldn't really afford to see a movie but that he was going to do so anyway.

The price was a pleasant half a buck, which was a break, but the movie was a western, which wasn't. He sat through it, sighed with relief when it was over, and headed back to the room to sack out.

Before he went to sleep, his mind was made up. He was going to drop over to the drugstore the next afternoon. If anything happened, it happened. If nothing happened, nothing happened.

He drifted off to sleep hoping desperately that something would happen.

SOMETHING happened. It was a few minutes after two when he strolled into the drugstore, took a stool at the counter and ordered a coke. She gave him, in addition to the coke, a huge grin and a quick wink that was about as subtle as a blasting cap. When she shoved the coke at him she managed to lean so far over the counter that her uniform dropped about five inches away from her breasts. The breasts had looked damned good with the uniform around them and looked even better all by themselves. He tried to look away, but it wasn't easy.

"Like what you see?"

He stared at her.

"Because if you do—"

A customer came in and mercifully cut the discussion short before it really got going. The customer was a middle-aged woman with a pot belly who had the gall to order a double banana split with extra whipped cream. It took Saralee awhile to slap the garbage together, and while she was splitting bananas and scooping ice cream he tried to pull himself together.

She wasn't just forward. She was brazen, and eager, and ready. It wasn't a quail hunt, not this time. It was a rooster hunt. She was the one who was doing the hunting, and he was the one who was being hunted, and somehow this took the joy of the chase out of it.

But, at the same time....

It took the woman a lot less time to devour the double banana split than it had taken Saralee to prepare it. The sloppy old broad waddled out of the drugstore and off into the wilds of Brighton, and there they were again.

He felt trapped.

"He's old and he's ugly and he's no good," she was telling him. "And you're young and fresh and I want you. How old are you, Vince?"

"Seventeen."

"Is that all?"

"That's all."

"Most boys your age would have said they were older than that."

He shrugged. If she thought he was going to lie about his age just for a chance at her fair young body, she had another think coming.

"I never lie," he lied.

"I'm only nineteen," she said. "I guess it's all right. I mean, I'm two years older than you, but it doesn't make much difference. You're probably pretty mature for your age, anyway."

Sure, he thought. But only below the neck.

"And he's forty-three," she said, nodding in the direction of the prescription department. "Forty-three years old and no damn good at all. You know what it's like for a girl with a man like that?"

"Must be rough."

She nodded. "It's horrible."

He took a breath. "Look," he said. "I mean, there must be guys in town. You shouldn't have any trouble."

"That's just it, Vince. I'm not a tramp. If I did it with anybody from Brighton it would be all over town. Don't you see? But you're from out of town and nobody would have to know. We would just do it and it would be great and then it would be over."

"I guess I'm the answer to a maiden's prayers."

She leaned close, giving him another look at her navel. "I'm no maiden," she said. "But you're the answer. You got a car?"

"Sort of."

"Listen to me. You pick me up on the corner of Fourth and Schwerner at seven-thirty. We'll be done with dinner by then and I'll tell him I'm going out for a walk. But I won't be going for a walk. I'll be going for a ride, and then we'll stop the car, and then well both be going for a ride again. You understand?"

"Seven-thirty," he said stupidly.

"That's right. You'll be there, won't you? Because I'll be waiting."

"I guess so."

"You sound afraid. You're not afraid of me, are you? I don't think you're afraid. I'll bet you've had lots of girls. I'll bet you're real good at it."

"Don't worry," he advised her. "I'm not a virgin. There aren't any."

For a minute she looked bewildered, which was understandable. Then she did another deep knee bend and showed him her chest again.

"Look what I've got," she said. "All for you. And more, all for you. Anything you want, and it's all for you, Vince. Don't keep me waiting."

YOU'RE not afraid of me, are you?

Hell, no. Not him. He wasn't afraid. He was going to pick her up, and take her for a drive, and give her a workout that would keep her happy for the next hundred years. And then he would get back in the car and point the car away from Brighton and that would be that. Afraid? What in hell was there to be afraid of?

He was scared stiff.

He didn't taste dinner. But he finished it, somehow, and by seven-fifteen he was in the car. He drove to the gas station, put a couple bucks worth in the tank, and headed toward Schwerner Street. He drove along Schwerner to Second, and then to Third, and all the way he kept half-hoping that he would get to Fourth and she wouldn't be there.

She was, of course. He stopped the car and she was sitting next to him at once, her lips already parted for a kiss. His tongue darted between the lips and her arms wound around him and that chest of hers pressed tight against him. And then he wasn't scared any more.

"I couldn't wait," she said. "I thought you wouldn't come and I thought somebody might see us and I thought I would go out of my mind. But you came and nobody saw us and it's all right now. Take a right turn, there's an old road a few miles up. Nobody ever goes there. Well be all right."

He couldn't talk. He just drove, finding the old road, wondering absently how many other guys had taken her there, then stopping the car and not wondering or caring about anything but Saralee.

The chase was gone, but there was something far more exciting in its own way than the chase. There was a woman, a woman born for love, and there was Vince, and the two of them were getting along fine.

The old awkwardness of seduction in an automobile didn't come into the picture, not when the girl involved was so eager to be seduced. He was happily surprised when Saralee scampered over the seat and into the back the minute the brakes were on.

From there on it was ideal. He didn't have to undress her because she began tearing her own clothes off instantly. He had all he could do to get his own clothes off fast enough. Then she was in his arms, and she was kissing him again, and all of her was next to all of him.

"Sooooooo good, Vince. Touch me here and here and here. Touch me all over, touch me, kiss me, bite me, do everything to me. Don't ever stop, Vince. Please don't stop. I don't want it to stop. I want it to go on forever. Please, Vince. Oh, it's so good. So good, Vince, and I need it so much, and yes I need it, Vince, yes it's so good don't yes don't stop keep going yes I love it yes I love it yes I love it I need it I want it oh yes yes yes yes YES!"

It was over, suddenly, and the uncomfortable feeling of having been seduced was overridden by the joy of having been seduced so expertly. There was no getting around it—some girls were a lot better at it than other girls. And when a girl was good at it, and wanted it, it made a difference. One hell of a difference.

Of course, the car wasn't the best place in the world. It was cramped, even an old boat of a car like his father's. And it must have inhibited her performance, as good old Rhonda would have put it. Not that Saralee seemed at all inhibited, not in the least. But the poor girl didn't have enough room to move around in.

And she loved to move. Oh, how she loved to move. And she moved so nicely.

"Vince—"

He cupped one of her breasts and gave it a friendly squeeze.

"Vince, I needed that. You have no idea how much I needed that. It's been so long."

"Look," he said, "I don't want to get personal, but what the hell's wrong with your husband? Is he dead or something?"

"He's no good."

"Well...doesn't he even try?"

She giggled. "Once a night," she said. "Once a night, every goddamned night of the year."

He gaped. "Isn't once a night enough for you?"

"Well," she said, giggling, "to begin with, it isn't. Not tonight, anyway, because we're going to do it again as soon as I get my wind back."

"But—"

"Ordinarily, once a night would be enough. Once with you, for example, would be plenty. But Brad gets through before I even get started. All he does is get me the least bit hot and it's over and I have to crawl up the walls."

"Oh," he said.

"And I can't stand it, because I need it, and you came along and I knew you'd be good. And you are good, Vince. You're wonderful. You're the best ever."

"Well," he said. "Thanks."

"And we're going to do it again," she said. "Right here and right now, but we'll have to hurry a little so he doesn't get suspicious. We'll have to start right now, so get set, honey. Because we're going to do it and it's going to be great.

"Now," she said. "Now, yes, now, Vince, now!"

It was too soon, and he was tired, but she was persuasive.

Very persuasive.

And very skillful.

So skillful, in fact, that when in the course of things he pulled a small muscle in his back he didn't even notice it until later.

And it was worth it, anyway.

THERE was always the smart thing and the dumb thing, and it was beginning to seem as though the dumb thing was whatever he did. Or, rather, whatever the dumb thing was, he picked it.

Maybe he was just dumb.

Because, if he was smart, he would have gotten the hell out of Brighton the minute he dropped Saralee on the corner of Schwerner and Fourth. The game was won, the trophy would look good on the wall, and that was that.

But he wasn't smart.

He stayed the night at Mrs. Sharp's. That was dumb, of course, but it was also natural. He was just too damned tired to drive all the way back to the lake without a good night's sleep first. Besides, he'd paid up for a whole week. He might as well collect a night's sleep there and breakfast in the morning before he left.

Sure.

That, he told himself in the morning, was not exactly the truth. Vince, boy, you're not being honest with yourself. You don't give a lily-white damn about breakfast in the morning. You're wondering what Sexy Saralee would be like in a real bed.

Which was something he didn't have any right to think about.

For one thing, once with Saralee was enough. Twice with Saralee had almost been fatal, albeit wonderful, and a third time would be dangerous.

On the way to the drugstore, he told himself it was just to see her, to say good-bye. No sense running out without even telling her so long.

Uh-huh.

"Tonight," she said. "Tonight, Vince. Again tonight, and not in the car because it's better in a bed. Tonight we'll do it in a bed, Vince.

"Brad works late tonight," she went on. "You come over to my house and we'll do it and it'll be perfect, just perfect. In my bed. It's a big double bed and we'll have loads of room. You'll like it, Vince."

That sounded entirely possible.

"169 Hayes Street," she said. "Right on the corner of Fifth. Come up at eight o'clock and it'll give us two hours before he gets home. You come right up, Vince. You understand?"

He understood. Boy, did he understand. He understood so well he wanted to crawl in a hole.

"Look," he said, "Saralee, I mean, I have to get back home and—"

"Hush up," she said. "You better go now. I'll see you tonight."

So Willing

SO I'm stupid, he thought. So I'm a damned fool who ought to know better. So I'm a low-grade moron with a rock for a head. So what?

He parked the car around the corner from her house, then listened to his knees banging together on the way to her door. He rang the bell once, wondering what in God's name he would do if her husband answered the door, and then listened to his teeth chattering until she came to the door and opened it. She was stark naked.

He stood there, just staring, and then he managed to step inside and get the door shut.

"Jesus Christ," he said. "I mean, that's pretty stupid, Saralee. Suppose it wasn't me at the door, for God's sake. Suppose—"

"I saw you," she said. "From the window."

"But—"

"So I knew it was you and not somebody else. I didn't want to waste any time. I still don't want to waste any time. I want to get started, because we only have two hours, and I want to make the most of both of them. What's the matter? Don't you like the way I look?"

He couldn't answer. All he could do was look at her. Most girls, he had learned long ago, look a lot better with some clothes on. And a naked girl who was just sort of lying down looked a lot better than one walking around. But Saralee was an exception. She was perfect naked, perfect the way she wandered around without seeming conscious of the fact that she was nude.

She was lovely.

"Hurry," she was saying. "The bedroom is upstairs, and we want to go there right away, and you'd better hurry."

They hurried.

In the bedroom, with the door shut, she helped him get his clothes off. She really wasn't much help. Every time she touched him he got confused and fumbled with his clothing, but finally he managed it and they were both naked.

And both on the bed.

She was telling him to hurry up, that she couldn't wait, that she'd been going out of her mind all day waiting for him.

But this time he was going to play it the way he wanted to.

"You're going to wait," he told her. "I'm going to drive you out of your mind."

And he spent a lot of time kissing and touching her, and pretty soon she was squirming and moaning for him, making strange sounds from somewhere in the depths of her throat and begging him to hurry, for God's sake, to get the main event started and stop wasting time on the preliminaries, to hurry up because she was going mad.

It was time. His point was proved, and she had learned her lesson, and now he did not feel that he was the one being seduced. This time it would be good, and when he finally did get the hell out of Brighton this would be something to remember.

"Come on," she said. "Vince, please. I'll kill you, Vince. I'll kill myself. I'll go mad. I can't take it, you better start doing it and stop fooling around. I want it, Vince, I need it. Vince, please—"

He got ready, and was about to begin, and then he noticed that she wasn't talking any more, that she wasn't saying a word, that she was looking past him with something horrible in her eyes.

So he looked around.

And there, big as life, was Bradley Jenkins.

FIVE

IT WAS QUITE a tableau. There was Saralee Jenkins, flat upon her lovely back and reaching up with curving fingers for Vince. And there was Vince, naked as a jaybird, lowering himself to those waiting arms.

And there was Bradley Jenkins, standing in the doorway and staring at them both.

The next second just went on and on, while everybody stared at everybody else. And then that second was over, the next second had started, and everybody was in motion. Saralee gave a shriek and squirmed into a little ball, in a silly attempt to cover herself. Vince dove for his pants, on the chair beside the bed.

And Bradley Jenkins fell over in a faint.

That surprised Vince so much he missed the chair and went sailing into the wall. He clambered around, knocking things over, and when he got his balance and his footing back, he looked over at the door to be sure he'd seen right. Because he couldn't possibly have seen right. The husband who catches his wife in bed with another guy can do any number of things, from gunning the two of them down on the spot, through beating the guy up, to racing for his lawyer. But the one thing he doesn't do is faint.

But there was Bradley Jenkins on his face, passed out cold.

Vince thought fast. That was one thing he could do at least, he could think fast. And it was a good thing, because one thing he couldn't do was stay out of trouble.

The thoughts went flashing through his mind as he pulled his pants on. Number one, the husband was unconscious. Number two, he'd seen Vince for only a second, while in a state of shock, and while looking primarily at his wife, so he probably wouldn't even remember very clearly what Vince looked like. Not his face, anyway. Number three, if he moved fast enough he could get the hell out of here before the husband woke up again, and be out of town before Bradley Jenkins could figure out just what the hell was going on. Number four, Saralee knew his name, but she didn't know where he was from. Nobody in town did, not even Mrs. Sharp.

Which meant, number five, that with a little bit of luck and a lot of speed, he could get away with nothing worse than a bad scare.

Pants, shirt and shoes went on, and the rest of his clothes got stuffed into pockets. Then he jumped over the unconscious hubby and headed for the door.

Saralee grabbed him by the elbow as he was going through the doorway, swinging him around and practically slamming his nose into the jamb. She'd been busy, too, and was wearing blouse and skirt and loafers. "Take me with you!" she cried, and her eyes were wide with desperation.

"But—but—" He tried to slow down long enough to figure out the question, and the answer to it. "Your husband," he said.

"I'm through with him," she said. "I've been wanting to get out of this town for years. Take me with you."

"But—I'm only going home." The thought of going back to the lake, walking in to his mother and father, pointing to Saralee and saying, "She followed me home, can I keep her?" was a very strange one indeed.

She came up against him like a vibrating pad, jabbing him with the controls. "You don't have to go home," she said, seductively. "You can go anywhere you want, with that car of yours. And you could take me with you. We could go to New York." She vibrated some more. "We'd have a great time, Vince."

"But—I don't have any money. I don't have enough money to go to New York."

"Don't you worry about money, Vince," she said. She smiled and kissed him, and the vibrations got stronger and stronger. "Don't you worry about a thing, baby."

So Willing

SO there they were in Vince's car, driving hell for leather out of town. Saralee Jenkins, shed of her husband, sat very close beside him on the front seat. Vince's suitcase was in back, and so was Saralee's hastily packed overnight bag, and so was Saralee's bulging purse. The purse was stuffed with bills, ones and fives and tens and an occasional twenty, taken from hiding places all over the Jenkins house. "He didn't think I knew where he hid all this stuff," she'd said, grinning wickedly. "Brad underestimated me in every way, he did."

And now they were heading southeast in Vince's car, and Vince was having some second thoughts. Some very gloomy second thoughts.

What the hell is the use, he wondered, of being able to think fast in an emergency, if all of your thinking simply throws you pell-mell swell-hell into another emergency? No use, that's what use.

Question: Is it better to be caught by a husband with that husband's wife, or is it better to be caught by the police with the husband's wife and the husband's money? Don't answer.

It had all seemed so easy at the time, so simple and clear. Vince wasn't in any hurry to go back to Lake Lousy, and here was a chance for a trip to New York, all expenses paid, with a hot and willing female tossed in as an extra premium. Not an offer to pass up. That's the way it had seemed at the time.

So now Vince drove southeast through the night, and every pair of headlights reflected in the rear-view mirror shouted COP and every pair of headlights that shone through the windshield shouted TROOPER and Vince was beginning to get very very nervous.

Not Saralee, though. She wasn't worried at all. In fact, she was snuggling beside him and telling him all about her life in Brighton, and how she had happened to get tied up with a clunk like Bradley Jenkins.

"It seemed like such a good idea at the time," she was saying. "Mom was always after me about security, about how I shouldn't marry some randy bum who wouldn't support me. I should find some nice steady guy. And Brad had had the hots for me from the time I was fourteen and just beginning to push out my sweaters. So when I found out I was pregnant, two summers ago, and I wasn't sure who'd done it—and none of the possibilities would have made very good husbands—it seemed like a hell of a good idea to marry Brad. Security, you know, and a steady income, and a name for the kid."

"I didn't know you had a kid," Vince said. More complications, he thought. I'm not only stealing a wife from her husband, I'm stealing a mother from her child.

But Saralee said, "I don't." She curled her lip. "That's what made me so goddam mad," she said. "I had a miscarriage two months after I got married. So I didn't even have to marry the old jerk after all."

"Oh," Vince said. Well, that was a relief. Vince felt he was due for some relief.

Apparently, so did Saralee, for she suddenly said, "You know, we never did finish what we set out to do."

"I know," said Vince. At the moment, he wasn't thinking about things like that. He was thinking that the more distance he put between himself and Brighton, the better off he was going to be.

"Boy, you know how to get a girl ready." She rubbed herself against him, and nibbled on his earlobe a little.

"Hey," he said. "I'm driving."

"Well, stop driving," she said, reasonably.

"I don't know if we ought to take the chance."

"Don't be silly. Brad doesn't know who you are, or what kind of car you've got, or where we're going or anything."

"Yeah, well—"

"You know," she said, "I got dressed so fast back there I didn't even have time to put on a bra or panties or anything. See?" She pulled her skirt up.

He saw. And he saw the light gleaming in her eyes, and he saw her hand reaching out for him, and he knew if he didn't stop the car pretty soon he'd run it off the road and into a tree. "Hold on," he said desperately. "Wait'll I find a side road or something."

"Hurry," she whispered, and her hands were not a devil's workshop.

Driving all over the road, Vince managed to turn left onto a side road, jounce off among the trees, stop the car and turn the engine off.

"I did so want to do it in a bed," she sighed. "But it's all right this way. It's all right anyway, just so we do it."

"I think I've got a blanket in the trunk," he said, surprised to find himself out of breath, as though he'd been running. "That'll be better than the backseat, anyway."

"Hurry," she whispered again.

He hurried. He clambered out of the car, opened the trunk and found the blanket. It was pretty dirty, but one side of it was clean. He spread it out on the ground beside the car, turned around, and she was naked again.

"Slowpoke," she said, grinning, and wriggled.

"You spend half your life without any clothes on," he said.

Vince, too, had dressed in too much of a hurry to be wearing much. So there wasn't much to take off. And then he was lying on the blanket beside her, and all at once he wasn't worried about anything any more. He was enjoying the sight of this woman, enjoying in advance what they were going to be doing together. "Now, let's see," he said, grinning at her. "Where were we?"

"You know damn well where we were," she said. "Come on."

"That's right," he said. "I was warming you up."

"I was all warmed," she said quickly. "I'm all warm now. Come on!"

"No, no," he said, and his hand stroked her breasts. "Gotta be warmer."

"Oh, don't go through all that again, Vince. Come on!"

"In a minute."

He forced himself to wait. While he stroked her and kissed her and squeezed her and fondled her, while she clawed at him and shrieked at him and pulsated for him, he forced himself to wait just as long as he could. He wanted her, he wanted her so bad that if Bradley Jenkins had shown up again, this time he would have kept right on going.

He stopped waiting. Vince thought this was surely it, they were going to kill themselves this way, the human body wasn't meant for this sort of punishment.

And then they were punching each other, screaming and snarling, kicking and biting, hurting one another and loving to hurt, loving to be hurt, and there they were, doing it again.

When it was over for the second time, Vince was exhausted. He just lay pillowed on her flat stomach and her lush breasts, with her warm breath in his ear and her hands, gentle now, caressing his back.

He dozed for a while, and woke up to hear her whispering, "You're getting heavy, Vince." Then he rolled off her, and they lay quietly side by side for a while. He fumbled for his clothes, found his cigarettes, lit one for her and one for himself, and they smoked quietly, resting, nude on the blanket among the trees.

"I'm glad you came along, Vince," she said finally. "I've wanted to get away from that stupid town for I don't know how long. But I never had the guts to do it before."

Vince didn't answer her. He was thinking about the fact that he had to bring the car back to the lake in only four more days. He wondered if he should tell Saralee about that, or if he should just go along with the gag, and quietly disappear four days from now.

It wasn't that he was worried about how she'd make out in New York after he left. A girl like Saralee, he knew there wasn't a thing to worry about. She'd make out fine in New York.

So, there really wasn't any need to tell her about anything. If he told her he was going to be leaving in four days, she would either try to talk him into staying, or she'd start looking early for somebody else to pal around with. If she tried to talk him into staying, using that body of hers as the main argument, she just might succeed, and then Vince would be in dutch with his old man. And if she started looking for somebody else the minute she got to New York, she'd find somebody else right away, and Vince would be out in the cold.

So he didn't tell her anything. Instead, he sat up and said, "I suppose we ought to get going."

"I suppose so," she said. She sat up and looked at him. "I don't suppose you could do it again," she said.

"Not without eight hours sleep, three pounds of steak, five raw eggs and a quart of milk," he told her. "And even then, I might not be in top form. You're an awful lot of woman, Saralee."

She smiled, murmuring, "Aren't I, though?" She threw her arms around him and kissed him. "There," she said. "To remember me by until you've got that sleep and steak and everything."

"Yeah," he said. He had the feeling it was going to be a hectic four days in New York.

This time they put on all their clothes. Then they climbed into the car, Vince backed it to the highway, and they set off again for New York.

She slept most of the trip, and Vince was just as pleased. He'd heard before of people with one-track minds, but this girl had a one-track body as well. When she was awake, there was only one thing she seemed to think of. She didn't need a man, she needed a platoon. She'd do fine in New York, Saralee would. She'd do great.

So Willing

NEW York City at six in the morning of an already hot summer day doesn't look very much like Paradise. It looks and feels more like the other place. The streets are cluttered with papers and taxicabs and sweating human beings. The buildings are soot-darkened, the sky is a glaring white, the air is heavy with fumes and soot and humidity and the smell of eight million people.

Nevertheless, Vince was glad to see the George Washington bridge recede behind him. He'd been driving all night, after some pretty exhausting calisthenics, and he was ready for those eight hours sleep he'd been talking about. He prodded Saralee awake and said, "We're here. Now what?"

"Now," she said, "you park the car somewhere and we go find a hotel room."

Easier said than done, Vince thought. There was no place in New York to park a car, except the parking garages, where you had to pay. He told her so, and she said, "That's okay. I've got the money, remember?"

So they parked the car. Saralee did all the talking to the attendant at the garage, paying for a week's parking. "We won't need a car in New York," she explained to Vince, and he nodded, beginning to feel a little dirty for keeping silent about having to leave in four days.

Then they went to find a hotel. There was a convention in town, Vince learned at the first place they went to, and all the midtown hotels were full. The desk clerk suggested he try some of the hotels up around Broadway in the West Seventies. Vince thanked him, and they grabbed a cab, which Saralee paid for.

They found a hotel, finally, at Broadway and 72nd. Saralee had her wedding ring on, and they both had suitcases, and they were signing in for a week, so there was no trouble. Vince hesitated over the register, not knowing what name to put down, and then remembered a cat his Aunt Edith had once owned. So he put the cat's name down. "Mr. and Mrs. James Blue." James Blue was a pretty phony-sounding name, but the hell with it. The desk clerk didn't say anything, and the bellhop took their bags just as though they really were Mister and Mrs. James Blue from Philadelphia.

Up in the room, Vince dragged out a quarter for the bellhop. As soon as the door closed behind the bellhop, Saralee cried, "A bed!"

Eight hours sleep," Vince reminded her. "I've been driving all night."

"Oh, don't say things like that," she squealed. "It gives me goose flesh."

Vince blinked. "Say things like what?"

"That you've been driving all night. Wouldn't that be great?"

"Great," said Vince. He was beginning to suspect that Saralee Jenkins was nuts.

He managed to get undressed and crawl into the clean-sheeted double bed without anything worse from Saralee than dangerous looks. Then he said, "Wake me when I wake up," and closed his eyes.

"I'm all rested," she said. "I slept in the car. So I guess I'll go shopping."

"You do that," he said, and fell asleep at once. He didn't even hear her leave the room.

WHEN he woke up it was twilight, and the clock on the table beside the bed said seven-thirty. He'd been racked out for more than twelve hours.

Saralee wasn't there. For an awful second, Vince was afraid she'd found somebody else already, somebody who could supply his own money and who maybe didn't need as much sleep as Vince did. Maybe she'd found that platoon.

Then he saw the note beside the clock. He picked it up and read it. It was from Saralee, and it said she was starved. He was surprised to find she hungered for other things beside sex. Anyway, it went on to say that she had gone out for something to eat, and would be back around eight o'clock.

The mention of food reminded him that he, too, was starved. It was time for that steak.

He got up, dressed, and left a note for Saralee on the back of her note. "Can't wait," the note read. "I'm hungry enough to eat the furniture. I'll be back in about an hour." He propped the note up against the clock, and turned to leave.

Then he noticed all the packages on the chairs. Saralee had said she was going shopping, and it looked as though she'd been good to her word. Vince took a second to look in the packages, saw skirts and blouses and stockings and underwear and shoes. The kid had really gone wild with her stolen loot.

Stolen loot. Better not think about that. Better to think about food.

Vince took the elevator down, then wandered around Broadway for a while, finally stopping in at a luncheonette and having a too-dry hamburger and a too-bitter cup of coffee. Then it was time to go back to the hotel room.

But he didn't feel like it, not just yet. He knew Saralee would be there now, and he knew she would be hungry again, and this time not for food. And he didn't feel quite ready for another fast round with Saralee. He wasn't up to it yet, that's all there was to it.

So he wandered around some more. He strolled down West 69th Street to Columbus Avenue, headed up Columbus, and stopped in at the first bar he saw. He ordered a beer, and the bartender didn't give him any trouble about his age, which was a relief. He sat and sipped at his beer and tried not to think things over. That wasn't too difficult, since his stomach was acting up a bit. As soon as he put some beer down, the stomach let him know there hadn't been enough food put in yet. The old hunger pains were coming back. So he'd just finish this one beer, find someplace better than the greasy spoon where he'd had the hamburger and coffee, and this time really have a meal.

It was a goofy introduction to New York. A lousy hamburger, and living on Saralee Jenkins' money. No, not Saralee Jenkins' money. Saralee Jenkins' husband's money.

That thought was enough to drive Vince from the bar.

Vince went back to Broadway, and this time found a halfway decent restaurant, where he had his steak, blood rare, and a side order of poached eggs, and a couple glasses of milk. He finished it all off with two beers. He'd had some idea of filling himself with protein, so he could go back and at least have an even chance in the coming battle with Saralee, but instead he ate too much and wound up logey and stuffed and half-asleep. So he had to go out and walk around some more, and smoke lots of cigarettes until he felt like braving the hotel.

Saralee was coming out the door of the hotel just as he was going in. They both stopped on the sidewalk, and she said, "Where've you been? I've been going frantic. I was just going looking for you."

"I was pretty hungry," he said. "I've spent all this time eating."

"It's nine o'clock, Vince," she said.

"I was pretty hungry," he repeated.

"Well," she said, twining her arm with his and leading him back inside the hotel, "you're here now, at any rate." She pressed her hip against him as they walked. "And you know what we've got upstairs, don't you?"

"No," he said. "What?"

"A real bed," she whispered.

He took a deep breath. Saralee had told him, that first time they'd been together, that once a night with a normal guy was enough for her. But apparently she'd been wrong. No wonder Bradley Jenkins hadn't been able to keep her at home. Vince was beginning to doubt that anybody could keep Saralee Jenkins at home.

A stray ironic thought hit him. He'd started all this looking for a virgin. Instead, he'd found a nymphomaniac. How far a miss could you make?

Saralee wasn't a miss, but he could make her. He winced at that pun, and allowed Saralee to lead him into the self-service elevator.

She was a busy little girl in the elevator, all over him like a heavy fog, and when the elevator stopped at their floor, he had to readjust himself before he could step out to the hall.

The interlude in the elevator washed away all his apprehensions. As they headed down the hall for their own room, he was almost as eager as she was. It was impossible to be as eager as she.

They got into the room, and she pirouetted in delight. "A bed!" she cried, and started pulling off clothes.

Vince joined her in the disrobing act, and then he joined her in bed. "This time," she told him fiercely, "no warm-up. I'm ready to go right now. So you just come here."

"Right you are," he said.

Once was never enough for Saralee, that's all there was to it. It had to be twice.

It was eleven o'clock before she fell asleep. Vince lay there awake a little while longer, thinking about things. He had a feeling he was going to enjoy the hell out of these four days.

But he also had the feeling that he'd be ready for a vacation by the time they were through.

SIX

IT WAS A very strange vacation.

There was only one place in New York where they spent any time, and that was the hotel. And there was only one place in the hotel where they seemed to spend any time, and that was the bed. There were the mornings, and there were the afternoons, and there were the evenings. Some girls, Vince knew, had a time clock built into a very important part of their anatomy. Some could only do it properly in the morning, and others in the afternoon, and most of them at night.

Saralee wasn't the time clock type. She wasn't even the time bomb type. She was built more along the lines of a hundred-gallon drum of nitroglycerine, always ready to go off.

In the past, when Vince had gotten started in the role of a dungaree Don Juan, he had learned that you could get pretty sick of the same woman. That had happened with Rhonda. It was great, even if it did leave him feeling thoroughly conned by her mock virginity. It was great, but after a while it was the same damned thing over and over, and then all of a sudden it wasn't so great anymore.

Saralee was different. With Saralee it wasn't the same damned thing over and over. Far from it. Saralee was imaginative, and inventive, and insatiable. They had started off in the good old way, and after a while Vince had taught her a few things that he had always considered very advanced, and then she had taught him a few things that were absolutely unbelievable. If he had heard them described he would have sworn they were biologically impossible, but they weren't. Not with the two of them carrying through so successfully.

So he wasn't bored with Saralee. You couldn't be bored with Saralee, any more than you could be bored with sex in general. She just wasn't the boring sort.

Exhausting.... That was more the word for it.

Vince was exhausted. He ate eggs all the time, and plenty of nearly raw meat, and drank buckets of milk, and even bolted down a dozen raw oysters once in desperation. But it didn't work. In fact, the more fit he was for horizontal games (or vertical games, depending upon Saralee's particular state of mind at the moment) the more games they played.

In fact, if he had been out of condition it would have worked out a lot better. Then he could have said that he was too tired, which he did from time to time. It didn't seem to make much difference, though. She would find something to do that would make him untired again. She found a lot of things.

And they always worked.

Some of them were things that nice girls didn't do, and some of them were things that nice girls didn't think about, and some of them were things that nice girls didn't know about. Some of them, for that matter, were things that nice whores didn't think about.

But they always worked.

By the evening of the third day Vince realized that his time limit wasn't limited enough. He'd thought that four days with Saralee wouldn't be enough. He was wrong. Four days with Saralee would be enough. Enough to kill him.

It was eight o'clock now and he was mercifully alone, eating a plateful of fried potatoes and washing them down with black coffee. Fried potatoes and black coffee did nothing at all for your virility, and this was the main reason he was eating them. What he really wanted was a blood-rare steak, but he was afraid that if he had a blood-rare steak he would find it a good deal more difficult to run out on Saralee.

Which was precisely what he was planning to do.

He stirred the coffee and took a sip of it. It was simple—Saralee was out shopping, the only other activity she found enjoyable. The stores were open until nine and she was getting in her licks. She wouldn't be back until nine-thirty at the earliest, which gave him an hour and a half at the very least.

He was in a restaurant just a block from the hotel. He would go back, get the car which Saralee had moved to the hotel's parking lot, and get the merry hell out of New York. It would be too bad about Saralee, of course, but if it was too bad about Saralee that was just too bad. He couldn't feel particularly sympathetic toward her at the moment. She was a nice kid, and she meant well, and she was sweet and good and kind, but if he didn't get away from her soon he would be dead.

Besides, Saralee would make out okay. If worse came to worse, she could always get a job. He'd heard how rough it was for an inexperienced girl to get a job in New York, but fortunately Saralee had plenty of experience in two areas. She could get a job in a drugstore behind the counter, because of all her experience in Brighton. Or she could get a job in a cathouse because of all her experience, period.

He laughed an evil laugh. It was going to be easy now. Back to the hotel. Pack the suitcase. Get the car. Drive off into the night. Stay the hell away from New York because a man could get killed if he stayed in New York long enough.

The check came to a dollar and ten cents, which was too much, but he paid it and left the waiter a forty cent tip, which was ridiculous. What the hell. It was her money, not his. He couldn't take it along, because that would be stealing. But he could tip his head off, and that would be all right.

He no longer believed old Bradley Jenkins was over forty, the way Saralee said he was, and the way he looked. It seemed that way on the surface, but after you knew Saralee the way he knew Saralee, you got a different picture.

The way he figured it, Brad Jenkins was around twenty-three. When he married Saralee, Brad was big and broad-shouldered and hungry for sex. Being married to Saralee, Vince knew, would be a pretty debilitating experience. If three days with her could demolish a guy, a year could turn him into an old man before his time. More than a year was impossible to imagine.

Poor Brad Jenkins, fainting all over the place like that. The way Vince looked at it, Brad was fainting from sheer unadulterated joy. He was fainting because he couldn't believe he'd actually managed to unload Saralee on some poor goof.

Named Vince.

The elevator deposited him on his floor and Vince walked to the room. It was simple now, very simple. He opened the door with his key, closed it behind him, and started throwing things into his suitcase. There was very little to pack and it didn't take him long.

With the suitcase closed, he went to the door again, ready to ride back down to the main floor and get his car from the garage. And just about then something profound occurred to him. It was going to be difficult, very difficult indeed, to drive that car without the key. And he didn't have the goddamned key.

Saralee had it. Saralee moved the car from the original lot to the hotel garage, and somehow in the bed-to-bed-to-bed confusion of it all, he hadn't managed to get key away from her. At the time it hadn't mattered. What the hell, he wasn't going anywhere. He didn't need car, not then. So she kept the key. It was in her purse and her purse was with her, and she was not around.

Of all the brilliant, masterful, superb displays of creative stupidity, this won the Oscar. Of all the—

He didn't unpack the suitcase. It might have been the best thing to do, so she wouldn't suspect anything, but he was willing to bet she wouldn't look in his suitcase. Not her. She would look at him, and then she would take off her clothes, and off they would go again on the old merry-go-round.

He sat down on the edge of the bed and waited. While he waited, he found a few more things to call himself and a few more things to call her. At a quarter to ten the door finally opened.

"Hi!" she called gaily. "I'm home!"

"I'm glad to see you," he said honestly.

"Miss me?"

"Uh-huh."

"Wait'll you see what I bought." She wrestled with a package, a massive white box all messed up with red ribbon. She uncovered the box triumphantly, hauling out a garment.

I mean, Vince thought, you just had to call it a garment. Because there wasn't much else you could call it. Because there wasn't much there, when you came right down to it.

It was black, and it was flimsy, and it was sheer, and it was about as concealing as a pane of glass. "What the hell is it?" he asked.

"Can't you tell?"

"Frankly, no."

"Well, what does it look like?"

"Looks like a hairnet."

She laughed. "Here," she said. "I'll model it for you. I mean, I bought it for you."

"You bought it for me?"

She nodded.

"I'd look awfully silly—"

That got another laugh. "I bought it so I could look good to you," she said. "So you can look at me while I'm wearing it and get all excited."

Here we go, he thought. Here we go, off on the goddamned merry-go-round again. She began undressing, clothes soaring all over the room, until in a short time she wasn't wearing a damned thing. Then she was wearing something, but it was the hairnet, so the effect remained about the same. The hairnet, amazingly, covered all of her from shoulders to knees. It covered all of her and concealed none of her, all at once, which was fantastic.

"Vince," she cooed, homing in on him. "Good sweet Vince. My little Vince. My baby's going to be good to me, isn't he? My baby's going to make me feel good again."

Your baby, he thought, is going to crap out completely. Your baby is going to fold up like a murphy bed. And the word bed made him wince a little. He wondered whether he'd ever be able to see a bed again without thinking of Saralee.

Or a floor, for that matter. Or a bathroom rug. Or a bathtub. Or a coat closet, or an elevator, or—

"Take off your clothes, Vince. There, Vince. Now you're as naked as I am. Nakeder, because of this thing I'm wearing. It cost thirty-five dollars, can you imagine?"

At that price it cost about three times as much, ounce for ounce, as platinum. He looked at her, and he decided that maybe the thirty-five bucks had been well spent.

"Look at me, Vince. Don't I look good? Look at my breasts. They're nice, aren't they? You know, I think they've grown since I met you. I mean, they're getting all this exercise and everything. It's stimulating them, sort of, and they're getting bigger."

If they got much bigger she'd need a suitcase to carry them in. He looked at her. She was having that old effect on him again, the effect she invariably had. He didn't want to go another round, not mentally. But his body somehow wasn't listening to his mind. His body was acting as though it had a mind of its own, which was sort of disconcerting.

He grabbed her and heaved her down on the bed. The hairnet thing fell away and he threw himself down on her, hungry for her, but now it was her turn to play. She was being coquettish. It was sort of funny, but he didn't feel like laughing.

"Not so fast," she was saying. "Let's go nice and slow now, Vince. Remember the way you teased me that day I was on fire? Remember the way you made me wait and wait and wait and I almost went out of my mind waiting so long? Now you can wait, Vince. Now you can wait until I'm good and ready."

He was being placed in the difficult position of raping a girl he didn't want in the first place. Raping a nymphomaniac, which was even worse. How in the name of the Lord did you go about raping a nymphomaniac?

And she wouldn't stop squirming around. Every time he thought he had her, she would give a little twist and laugh a mean laugh and suddenly she wasn't where she had been a second ago. It was like banging your head against a brick wall. He got hold of a breast, and held it, and felt all that creamy flesh. And then he would reach for more of her, and, suddenly, the grand prize wasn't there any more.

Saralee, he thought, you are now about to be raped. Lie back and enjoy it.

The thirty-five dollar hairnet disappeared. It was an exhilarating feeling, ripping a thirty-five dollar hairnet into gossamer wisps. It was even more exhilarating when he hauled off and belted her in the belly with his closed fist.

She let out a roar.

So he belted her again.

Then the prize was his, and it began, and suddenly he heard her bellowing like a wounded steer. Except that she didn't sound wounded at all, or, for that matter, bovine.

When it was over and he was lying on his back staring vacantly at the ceiling, he knew just what he had to do. It was the only way out, and although it might well kill him, it was the best way to get out of the hotel without her. It would not be easy, not at all, but it was the only way. He had to tell himself over and over again that it was the only way or he could never possibly go through with it. And he had to go through with it, of course, because, after all, it was the only way.

It was a simple way. Very simple.

He simply had to keep doing it to her until she passed out. Over and over again, until she couldn't take it anymore and passed out. Then he would get up and get dressed and take the car key from her purse and off he would go and the hell with her.

The second time was tough, but he did it, and when he was through he looked hopefully for signs of weariness. But she didn't look very weary. She looked ready for more.

"That was good," she told him, her eyes shining. "You know, you seem to improve with practice. You just keep getting better."

More, he thought. Got to do it again. Then she'll be so tired she'll pass out, and that will be just ginger peachy. Then I'll spring out of bed and off I'll go, back to the pea-green waters of Lake Lugubrious.

"Come on, Vince," she said. "Let's do it again. Gee I haven't had this much fun in years. For a while there, I thought you were slowing down, but I must have been wrong. Three times in a row! Gee."

Gee, he thought savagely. Gee, oh, dee, dee, ay, em, en. Gee.

The third time was sort of like trying to climb a mountain with your hands and feet tied together. The third time was sort of like swimming through sand. The third time was torture.

But the third time did the trick. He rolled away from her when it was finally over and looked down into her eyes. They had a dreamy look to them and he knew it was only a matter of seconds before she would fall asleep. Then he would bound out of bed and get that cruddy key and off he would go.

He looked at her, waiting for her to fall asleep, hoping that she would have the decency to conk out before too long. He looked at her, and he felt envious of Bradley Jenkins. Jenkins might have lost a lot of money, but now he had the chance to get his health back. Lucky Jenkins.

Her eyes closed, and her breathing leveled off, and he was ready to get up and go. He was ready, but his body wasn't ready, and he waited for a minute or two to get his strength up.

And then, abruptly, Vince passed out.

He woke up. He sat up in bed and opened his eyes. He looked over at Saralee but she wasn't there. She had managed it, had gotten up before him and vanished into New York, leaving him there.

Her purse had gone with her, which meant that his key had gone with her, which in turn meant that he was right back where he started from.

Which was nowhere. Which was up the creek in a lead canoe.

Which was unpleasant.

And it had been such a perfect plan. He'd worked like a Turk, managed three masterful assaults on the castle, and then, with the prize within his grasp, he'd pulled a Bradley Jenkins. Not a faint, perhaps, but a crap-out, and it amounted to about the same thing.

His mind groped around and presented him with a marvelous mental picture. He would wait for her to return, and then they would do it again, and again, and again, and he would keep falling asleep, and he wouldn't get back to the cabin ever again. And, damn it, today was the last day he had. He couldn't afford to wait any longer.

Well, the hell with the key. He could always run a jumper wire and get the car started without it. He'd done that once before. It might look strange, might baffle the lot attendant a little, but what the hell, it was his car, and he could play games with it if he wanted to. The lot attendant's private opinion of him didn't count now. All that counted was getting back to the lake.

He pulled himself out of bed and jumped into his clothes. He picked up his suitcase, left the room and rang for the elevator. He wasn't even going to wait for breakfast, not now. He could grab a bite to eat on the road. For the time being, all he wanted was to put as much distance as possible between himself and New York.

He left the elevator, walked around to the garage and found the attendant. "I'm James Blue," he lied. "I'd like my car, please."

"Sure," the guy said. "Hang on a minute and I'll run her out for you."

The attendant disappeared and Vince steadied himself. It was suspicious, him leaving with a suitcase. Almost as though he was trying to skip out on his bill. Which, come to think of it, he was.

Well, if the attendant made any trouble, he could always leave the suitcase behind. The suitcase didn't matter. He mattered, though, and the car mattered. To hell with the suitcase.

The attendant came back smiling. "Sorry," he said. "Guess you and the missus got your signals crossed."

Vince looked blank.

"It's in the book," the attendant explained. "I wasn't on then so I didn't know, but your wife picked up the car a few minutes before eight."

Vince *felt* blank.

"If you don't have too far to go," the attendant said, "you can always go out front and grab a hack. Easier than driving, especially if you don't know the city. Doorman'll flag down a hack for you if you ask him."

He headed back to the room. All of a sudden he didn't feel too good.

HE felt worse when he got back to the room. Much worse, because he gave the room a quick going-over and saw something, something he hadn't noticed when he jumped out of bed and headed for freedom.

The room looked the same as ever, with boxes piled all over it. But this time he looked in the boxes and made a rather startling discovery.

They were empty. Every last one of them was completely empty. So was the closet.

Which meant, pure and simple, that Saralee had decided to clear out. It wasn't enough that she had left him, but she had also made off with his car. And, undoubtedly, had also left him with the hotel bill unpaid. And no money except for the ten bucks and change he had in his wallet.

Or did he? He looked in the wallet and shuddered. The little bitch had gone through it and it was empty. Quite empty.

He was broke, and his car was gone, and the bill wasn't paid, and he had to bring the car back to his father by nightfall, and he didn't have a car to bring back, and he was broke, and he owed the damned hotel a fortune, and he had to get back to Lake Ludicrous, and....

First things first. First he had to get out of the hotel, and this time, of course, he couldn't take his suitcase with him. If he did, they might stop him. And if they stopped him there were several things they would find out. They would learn that Saralee was gone, and that all Saralee's luggage had somehow managed to accompany Saralee, and that the car was gone, and that he had been trying to get lost himself. They would also discover that he was neither James Blue nor a resident of Philadelphia, and at that point they would solve all his problems for him. They would chuck him in the tank, and they would lose the key, and that would be the end.

He left the suitcase, took the elevator to the main floor and headed for the door. He felt his hands trembling a little and hid them in his pockets.

Then he heard the voice, just behind him, saying: "Mister Blue? Could I talk to you for a minute?"

SEVEN

VINCE WAS NEVER quite sure how he did it. When he turned, slowly, in answer to that ominous question, and saw facing him a bald man wearing a pinstriped suit who could have been nothing in this world but a hotel manager, his blood sank to his shoes, his heart jumped up into his throat, and he went blank. And someone else, some total stranger, using his body and his voice, snapped with obvious irritation, "What is it?"

"About this bill, Mister Blue," said the manager, holding up a squarish sheet of thin paper. "I hate to—"

"Bill?" snapped the person using Vince's body and voice. "*Bill*? When my wife walks out on me, takes my car and goes God knows where, *you* come jabbering at me about a bill?"

The manager managed to back speedily away without moving a step. "Well," he said, his face a symphony of sympathetic smiling, "well, I didn't realize—of course, I had no intention—"

"You'll get your money," the genius in Vince's body said contemptuously. "Let me worry about one thing at a time, will you?"

"Yes, of course," said the manager. He was bowing from the waist now. "Of course."

"I'll straighten things out with you," the genius in Vince said, "once I've found my goddam wife."

"Certainly, sir," said the manager. "Of course, sir."

The genius who had control of Vince's body glared with Vince's eyes at the manager for a second longer, then spun Vince's body on Vince's heel and marched Vince the hell out of the lobby and out to the sidewalk. Then the genius went away to wherever he'd popped up from, and left Vince standing there, shaking like a leaf.

He'd gotten away with it. He'd gotten away with it! *He'd gotten away with it!*

Now, all he needed was a place to sit down for a while, until his knees could carry his weight again. Now, all he needed was a place to sit down and a strong black cup of coffee and a dime to pay for the coffee. And his father's car back, so he could go home again. And Saralee standing in front of him, so he could beat her lovely face in.

It was so clear now, so goddam clear. She'd gotten up—it must have been seven o'clock or earlier, since the garage attendant said she took off with the car at eight—she'd gotten up, and she'd noticed Vince's suitcase all packed and ready to go. And she had realized that Vince was on the verge of taking a fast powder. So she had decided that she would take that fast powder herself, before little Vince had the chance.

It was now just about noon. She had a four-hour start on him. She also had money, and he didn't, not a dime. She also had a means of transportation, and he didn't, not a pogo stick.

What Vince had been doing to her physically all week, she had just done to him figuratively. And she'd been a lot better at it than him. When *she* did it, she was thorough. There wasn't any need for seconds.

Coffee. He needed coffee, and a place to sit down and try to think. That was the first thing. He couldn't just stand here, on the sidewalk in front of the hotel, until that manager in there had a chance to think things over and decide maybe Mister James Blue ought to hang around the hotel awhile and wait for his erring wife where the manager could keep an eye on him.

As if in answer to his thoughts about coffee, a bum picked that minute to panhandle him. He was a short, scrawny, scrubby little bum, with a short, scrawny, scrubby little beard. He came staggering up, dressed like a picture on a CARE poster, with a pathetic expression on his rummy face and his filthy hand held out, palm up, and he whined, "You got a dime for a cup of coffee, Mister?"

Vince just looked at him. He opened his mouth, and closed it, and opened it again, and closed it again, and finally said, in a calm and reasonable voice, "If I had a dime for a cup of coffee, you stupid son-of-a-bitch, I would *drink* a cup of coffee."

The bum blinked, and looked aggrieved. "Jeez," he whined. "You don't have to get that way about it." And he went staggering off to panhandle somebody else.

Vince took off in the opposite direction. It was too dangerous to hang around in front of the hotel any longer.

He'd walked two blocks, trying to think about what to do about Saralee and the car but managing only to think about the fact that what he needed now was a cup of coffee and a place to sit down and think things out, when he suddenly had a brilliant idea.

He stepped into the next doorway he saw. He took off his tie and slipped it into his coat pocket. Then he turned his coat collar up, unbuttoned his white shirt halfway down and pulled one shirt tail out so it dangled down below the bottom of the suit coat. He rubbed his hands on the sidewalk until they were good and sooty, then rubbed them on his face until *it* was good and sooty. Then he stepped back out among the pedestrians and looked for a likely prospect.

One came along almost immediately. A youngish guy in his mid-twenties, walking arm in arm with his girl. Vince figured a guy with a girl would be afraid to look cheap in her eyes, and so would be an easy touch. He stepped in front of the couple, a pathetic expression on his face and his now-filthy hand extended palm upward, and whined, "You got a dime for a cup of coffee, Mister?"

The victim looked embarrassed. He stopped and fidgeted for a second, and mumbled something, while the girl with him looked curiously at Vince, and then he stuck his hand into his pocket and came out with a handful of change. "Here," he mumbled, and dropped half a buck into Vince's waiting palm. Then he hurried on by.

Not only a cup of coffee. A cup of coffee and a hamburger. With onions.

Sitting in the luncheonette, dawdling over his coffee and hamburger, Vince thought it out.

Saralee was gone. So was the car. They were together, Saralee and the car.

Vince needed the car. He was supposed to go back to the lake today, so his father could drive the car home and get back to work when his vacation ended.

Vince wanted to kick the crap out of Saralee while wearing hobnail boots and brass knuckles.

Vince had to have the car, and he wanted to get his hands on Saralee. And since the car and Saralee were together, once he had found one of them, he would have both of them.

That brought up the first question. Where would Saralee have gone? Where would an ambitious, unscrupulous, good-looking nymphomaniac with a stolen car and about three hundred stolen dollars go?

She wouldn't go east because there was nothing east of New York but New England, and New England was kind of famous for prudery, and a girl like Saralee wouldn't even think of going to an area that was famous, rightly or wrongly, for prudery. And she wouldn't go north, because there was nothing to the north but lots of New York State, and then the Canadian border, and she'd never get over the Canadian border in a stolen car for which she didn't have any registration.

Come to think of it, Saralee didn't even have a license. He remembered her telling him that, after she had driven the car from the parking lot to the hotel, and how relieved he'd been that she hadn't been involved in any of the thousand minor accidents that happened every day in midtown Manhattan.

Getting back to the geography, she wouldn't head west because that way lay Brighton. The only direction left was south. Okay, she would go south. Now what?

He turned it around and looked at it from another point of view. Where would a girl like Saralee fit in? Where would a girl like Saralee naturally gravitate for?

Only two places: California and Miami.

There were lots of things against California. In the first place, it was three thousand miles away. And Saralee only had about three hundred bucks left out of the five hundred she'd lifted from Bradley Jenkins. You don't take a car three thousand miles on three hundred bucks. Not if you plan to do any eating yourself.

In the second place, in order to get to California she would first have to drive toward Brighton.

In the third place, Miami was to the south, which is the direction she would naturally take anyway.

In the fourth place, Miami was only one thousand miles away, which a girl could do on three hundred dollars.

Okay, that answered question number one. Saralee, without a shred of doubt, was headed for Miami. Now for question number two.

Question two: How the hell was Vince going to get to Miami? Once he was there, how the hell was he going to find one sharp broad in a town full of sharp broads?

He sat there for a long while, and he just didn't get any answers to question number two. The coffee got cold, and the hamburger got colder, and the hamburger bun got hard, and he still didn't have any answers to question number two. The waitress began to glare at him and he still didn't have any answers to question number two.

He finally left the place, noticing that it was now one o'clock, and Saralee now had a five-hour start on him.

Saralee didn't have a driver's license and she was driving a stolen car. Therefore, Saralee was going to be obeying every speed law she came across. Which meant it would take her two days at the very least to get to Miami, and probably three. The first day, she would maybe be able to drive four or five hundred miles. Then she'd clock out at a motel somewhere, and start off bright and early tomorrow morning.

If Vince had a car, he'd be able to at least catch up with her. He could drive all night, if need be, and finally he'd catch up with her, because she'd be obeying the speed limits, and she'd be stopping for sleep.

But Vince didn't have a car.

And he didn't have lots of time either. He was supposed to be back at the lake today. He might be able to get away with overshooting for a day, coming back tomorrow, but it just wasn't possible to never go back there, or to go back without his father's car.

He wandered around and occasionally, when he saw a likely customer, he panhandled a bit, because he at least needed eating money, and within half an hour he had three bucks. Which was a pretty good wage, averaging out to six dollars an hour.

He could always stay in New York, of course. Stay here forever, panhandling at six bucks an hour. Because he definitely could not go back to the lake without his father's car. He definitely could not, and that was all there was to it.

He saw a gas station, one of the cramped little hole-in-the-wall gas stations common to Manhattan, and stopped in, on impulse, to get some road maps. There wasn't any one road map for all of the Eastern Seaboard, but he got a bunch of state maps, and could go from one to the next, and follow Saralee's route from New York to Miami. Then he went down to 72nd Street and Broadway, where they had benches on the mall, and sat down to look at the maps.

The thing was, there were so many roads. You had your choice of half a dozen roads going out of New York, and about half a dozen roads the rest of the way.

But Saralee would be in a hurry. She would take the shortest, straightest route. Vince searched his pockets for a pencil, found one, and marked out on the maps what he thought would probably be her route. He worked at it slowly and carefully, and by the time was finished, he was ninety-nine percent sure he knew every inch of road Saralee would be traveling.

It was two o'clock. Saralee was six hours ahead of him.

He looked at his maps, and he swore under his breath, and he felt horribly frustrated. And all at once, he got his idea.

It wasn't a very good idea, but that didn't matter. That didn't matter, because it was the only idea. It was his only chance. He was sure of his reasoning all the way, sure that Saralee would be heading for Miami, almost dead sure he had figured out her complete route. If his reasoning was correct, his idea just might work. If his reasoning wasn't correct, his idea didn't matter and it didn't matter what he did, because Saralee and the car and everything else were gone forever anyway.

So the idea was worth trying, even though it wasn't very good.

He got to his feet and crossed the street to the subway station. He paid fifteen cents of his panhandled money and took the subway downtown. He made a couple of transfers, paid another quarter, and wound up on the H&M tubes, headed for Jersey. While in that last train, he put his tie back on, buttoned his shirt, turned his coat collar back down, and tucked his shirt-tail in. When the train reached the last stop in Jersey, everybody got off, and Vince was alone in the car for a minute. He pulled one of the advertising posters down from the row above the windows, hid it under his coat, and left the station.

The Delaware, Lackawanna and Western railroad station was right next to the last H&M tube stop. Vince went over there and stopped off in the men's room. There he washed the panhandling dirt from his face and hands, and carefully wrote "UNIVERSITY OF MIAMI" on the back of the poster, in large, thick, letters. Then he went out to the waiting room, found a likely-looking untended suitcase, picked it up, and left the depot. He spent a dollar and a quarter on a cab to take him to the highway, and then he stood beside the road, the stolen suitcase next to his feet, the sign in his left hand, and his right hand out, thumb extended.

He waited five minutes before a new DeSoto screeched to a halt. He picked up the suitcase, ran to the car, and the driver, a thirtyish salesman type with horn-rimmed glasses, said, "I'm only going as far as Baltimore."

"That's fine," Vince told him. "Every little bit counts."

He tossed his suitcase into the backseat, slid into the front seat beside the driver, and said it again, his eyes staring down the road, southward. "Every little bit counts."

A truck took him from Baltimore to Washington. He didn't get to see much of the country, because he slept most of the way. He knew he was going to have to be wide-awake later on, so he forced himself to relax and sleep while he could.

Actually, it wasn't that tough to get to sleep. He'd had a very active four days, coupled with some nervous running around today, and whizzing along a superhighway on a sunny summer afternoon was pretty relaxing anyway. He conked out within ten minutes in the salesman's car, and didn't wake up till they reached Baltimore. Then the salesman wished him luck, Vince thanked the guy for the ride, closed the door, stuck out his thumb, and a truck stopped. Just like that. He was running in luck, and he hoped it kept up that way.

By the time he got to Washington, he was pretty hopeful. The salesman had driven like a madman, and the truck driver hadn't been any slouch either. Both of them had gone a hell of a lot faster than Saralee would dare to, and Vince figured by now he couldn't be more than four hours behind her.

Then came Washington, and things slowed down to a crawl. For one thing, the truck driver let him off at the northern edge of the city, which meant he was going to have to work his way all the way through Washington, and he knew from experience that hitchhiking within a city is hell. For another thing, he was beginning to feel starved, and the money he could have spent on a fast cab-ride through town had to go for food. And the eating of the food took time, too, no matter how fast he tried to chew.

Then he was back on the street again, thumbing once more. And, as he'd expected, hitchhiking through the city was hell. He did it in four short rides, with long waits in between. And the fourth ride didn't turn out to be so short after all.

It was a woman, driving a new Pontiac convertible, the incredibly expensive car for people with enough money to buy a Cadillac convertible and not enough sense to come in out of the rain.

This woman was about forty. He didn't know whether she had any sense or not, but she very obviously had money. She was dressed in an obviously expensive blue suit and, even though it was warm as hell in Washington, a waist-length fur jacket over it. On her head was one of those goofy hats that was one-tenth hat and nine-tenths veil. She was a good-looking woman for forty, as far as the face was concerned. The fur made it impossible to tell much about the body, though her nylon-sheathed legs looked pretty good from the knee down.

She stopped the car next to him, smiled, and said, "Hop in."

"Thank you, ma'am," he said, and hopped in. He'd barely had his thumb out, not expecting a woman to stop for a hitchhiker, and the fact that she had stopped surprised him so much it took him a second or two to react.

Once his suitcase and University of Miami sign were stowed in back, and he was seated in front beside the woman, the Pontiac slid away from the curb and purred southward through the evening traffic.

After a minute, the woman said, "I went to Miami, too. Quite a number of years ago."

Vince tensed. He knew what was coming next, a lot of talk about the new buildings and the old professors and how the old town is getting on and all that garbage, none of which Vince would be able to handle, since he'd never been near either Miami or its university in his life. "Well, uh," he said. "Uh, as a matter of fact I don't go there myself. My brother does. I'm going down to visit him. This'll be my first trip down there." There, he thought, that ought to do it.

The woman turned to look at him for a second, smiled and said, "Crap." Then she looked back at the street.

Vince blinked. He gaped at the woman, and waited for her to explain what that had been all about, but apparently she had no intention of doing so. She just kept driving along, a half-smile on her lips. He noticed that they were good lips, just slightly touched with lipstick, and that her hair was in a tight permanent that wasn't blowing around even though the convertible's top was down. Black hair it was, with just a touch of gray in some of the hairs at the side. It looked good on her, very sophisticated. She looked like a real heller who had grown older gracefully.

They drove two blocks in silence, and then the woman said, "Well? Aren't you going to defend yourself?"

Vince decided the only thing to do was let this graying chick have the lead, until he could figure out where she thought she was going. "Defend myself?" he asked. "From what?"

"You don't have any brother in the University of Miami," she said. She glanced over at him, smiled again, and looked back at the traffic. "That sign of yours is just something to make it easier for you to get a ride."

Vince shrugged. This time, he thought, the best thing to do was admit everything and say nothing. "It's pretty tough to get a ride," he said, "unless you do something like that."

The woman nodded. "I know it is," she said. "You're absolutely right." She glanced at him again, looked back at the road, and said, "What's that bulge inside your coat? Is that a gun?"

"Gun?" Vince hadn't even known he had a bulge inside his coat. He looked down, and realized all the road maps tuck into his inside coat pocket did make a healthy bulge. Now that he thought about it, with a bulge like that in his coat, it was a miracle he'd gotten any rides at all. And here this was the sixth person to pick him up. And this one was even a woman.

"Well?" she asked him. "Is it a gun?"

"No," he said. He grinned uneasily, not sure what this crazy woman was leading up to. "Heck, no," he said, playing it boyish. "Nothing like that. It's just road maps. See?" He dragged them out of his pocket and showed them to her. "I really am going to Miami," he said. "And I've got these road maps so I won't get lost."

The woman looked at the road maps, looked at him, stopped smiling, looked out at the street again, and said, "How disappointing."

A nut, decided Vince. That's what she was, a grade A, first-prize, number one nut.

He didn't know just how nutty she was. They were in the southern part of the city now, near the Potomac, and Vince was surprised to see that they were coming to wooded sections among the built-up areas. And he had the crazy feeling they were going the wrong way.

The feeling got stronger, a lot stronger, when the woman suddenly made a turn onto an unpaved street and drove down past two rows of unfinished ranch-style houses to the end, and stopped.

Vince looked around, half-expecting a couple of guys to come running out of one of the half-built houses and grab him. "What's going on?" he demanded. "What is this?"

"You're an awful disappointment," the woman said. She was sitting half-turned in the seat, facing him, and she was half-smiling again, her eyes shining at him in the moonlit darkness. "I certainly didn't expect anything like this when I picked you up," she said. "You turned out to be a complete flop, do you know that?"

"Well, for God's sake," Vince cried, "what the hell do you want from me?"

"Isn't that obvious?" she asked him. "I want you to rape me."

He could only stare at her. He couldn't say a word or do a thing or move a muscle, all he could do was just sit there in the car in the moonlight and stare at her.

"If you look over that way," she said, pointing beyond him, "you'll see lights. There are lots of houses all around here full of people. If you don't rape me, I'll throw you out of the car, and then I'll tear my clothes and go to one of those houses and say you *did* rape me. And I don't suppose it would take the police very long to find you. You'd be on foot, and you don't know Washington at all."

A nut, thought Vince for the thousandth time. A complete and utter nut.

The woman watched him, growing impatient. "Well?" she demanded.

"Well—" said Vince. He was trying to think. This nut wanted to be raped, that's all. That's why she'd picked him up, because she heard women who picked up hitchhikers got raped, and she got it into her head she'd liked to get raped herself.

So, what the hell, how long could it take? And it might even be fun.

But then a sudden thought struck him. "How do I know," he asked her, "that you won't call the cops afterward, anyway?"

"I won't," she said. "I promise you I won't."

"Yeah, sure, but how do I know?"

"You *know*," she reminded him, "that I *will* call the police if you *don't* rape me."

He thought that one over for a minute. It looked as though he didn't have much choice. "Okay," he said, and reached for her.

She slapped his hand away. "I didn't say make me," she said. "I said rape me. You're going to have to work for it." And she pushed the door open on her side and scampered out of the car.

She didn't run very fast. In the first place, she was wearing one of those tight hobble skirts it was impossible to walk in, much less run. And in the second place, she wasn't trying very hard.

Vince caught her after six steps. They were on ground that was going to be somebody's front lawn some day, but was now just churned-up dry earth. Vince caught the woman by one shoulder, twisted her around, and she lost her balance and fell heavily onto the ground. He dropped to his knees beside her and grabbed.

"Don't rip my clothes!" she cried, in a shrill half-whisper. "Don't rip them!"

Vince looked at her, her straining face staring up at him, and he knew this woman wanted to be roughed up. And he was willing to go along with that. All he had to do was think about the fact that she was delaying him, and that she had threatened him with the law. And all he had to do was make believe she was Saralee Jenkins. That's all he had to do, and then he could rough her up to her heart's content. And then some.

So he belted her open-handed across the face, and snapped, "If you don't want them ripped, pull them off. And do it fast."

"Yes. Yes." She struggled, lying on the ground next to him, pulling her skirt up and her panties off, and he saw that she had surprisingly good legs, that she was a woman who had cared for her body all of her life, and it had responded by staying firm and shapely long after most women were well into the sag-stage.

He slapped her again and said, "Get that fur thing off too."

She did. She was panting and moaning and half-crying, staring up at him with a crazy combination of terror and desire on her face, and she struggled around until she got the fur piece and the jacket and blouse off, and then he reached down, inserted his fingers under her bra between the breasts, and yanked upward, ripping the bra in two. The bra fell away on both sides, and he slapped her hard, forehand and backhand.

She moaned and rolled over, trying to crawl away. He smacked her naked buttocks, grabbed her hip with pinching fingers and digging nails, and pulled her back around and down again. He had his own clothes open, and he was ready, and he fell on her.

She lashed at him, screaming through clenched teeth, trying to buck him off her, but he held on grimly. All the workouts he'd had with Saralee had made it possible for him to last a long time, and he was glad of it. He wanted the time, he wanted to give this woman all she wanted and then some, he wanted to make her sorry she'd ever threatened him, sorry she'd ever come out looking for this tonight. His hands slapped and pinched and pummeled her body, until finally she opened her mouth in a full-throated scream, and her fighting changed, became more real, and she shrieked, "Stop! Stop! Stop!"

But he couldn't stop, and he wouldn't stop. And now she wasn't fighting him, either make-believe or real, now she was blending with him.

Slowly, his breath came back, slowly his awareness, of the place and the circumstances came back, and slowly he crawled off her and got shakily to his feet, readjusting his clothes. And the woman lay on her back, her skirt a wrinkled mess around her waist, her jacket and blouse and panties lying dirt-stained around her, and she smiled up at him, sighing, and whispered, "You weren't such a disappointment, after all. Once you got started, you weren't a disappointment at all."

Now, he was sick of her. He felt used, cheapened, as he had never felt with a girl before. This woman had dragged him down into her own sickness and made him a part of it. He remembered how he had slapped her and clawed her, and how he had enjoyed doing it, and he felt sick and ashamed, and wanted nothing but to get away from here.

She got slowly to her feet, straightening her skirt as best she could, donning again her blouse and jacket and fur. Balling up her panties and ripped bra, she said, "Come on. I'll drive you across the Potomac."

He thought of saying no, but then he remembered how important time was, that he had to make up for a lot of lost time, and so he nodded and walked back to the car with her. There, she put the panties and bra on the floor in back and slid in behind the wheel, as Vince got in on the other side. All at once, he noticed that she was still wearing that nine-tenths veil hat, that she'd worn it all the way through the fake rape-scene. And for some reason, that struck him as the sickest part of it all, that she'd worn that stupid little Sunday-tea hat all during the phony rape scene.

She drove him out of Washington, then across the Potomac and through Alexandria to a good spot for him to hitchhike from. As he was getting out of the car, she leaned toward him, her hand held out, and said, "Thanks. You did a good job."

He had the suitcase and sign in his left hand. He reached out the right hand, she dropped something into it, and her car spun around and headed back for Washington. Puzzled, Vince looked at what she had given him. A roll of bills. Ten tens. One hundred dollars.

HE got another truck ride out of Alexandria, and this time he was really in luck. The guy was going all the way to Miami. Vince was about six hours behind by now and he was glad he wasn't going to be losing any more time between rides.

This guy was driving an overload of tile pipe, so he didn't exceed any speed limits. Vince was just as well pleased. He was coming into the territory where he was going to be very interested in the roadside scenery, particularly around the motels, so he was glad the truck wasn't going to be whipping by too fast to see anything.

What he was looking for was his father's Packard. He was glad, for one of the few times in his life, that it was a Packard. There were damn few of them on the road anymore, particularly dull gray ones. He wouldn't be likely to miss it.

They headed on down across Virginia and into North, Carolina, following the route Vince had marked out on the roadmaps back in New York, and every time they passed a motel, Vince took careful inventory of the cars parked in front.

He struck paydirt just south of Charlotte, almost into South Carolina. A dull-gray Packard, right year, what looked like the right license plates in the dim motel light. She'd gotten pretty far in one day.

"Stop here," Vince told the driver. "I get out here."

"I thought you were going to Miami."

"I just saw my roommate's car back at that motel. He can take me the rest of the way."

The truck driver was plainly puzzled, but he stopped the car. "Anything you say, buddy," he said.

"Thanks a lot for the lift," Vince told him. "I really appreciate it."

Then the truck was gone, and Vince was walking back toward the motel. He threw the sign and suitcase away. He wouldn't be needing those anymore.

He went up to the motel, noticing that the office was dark, which wasn't surprising. It was almost four in the morning. He walked on down the row of motel units to the one with the Packard in front, and tried the door. It was locked, which didn't faze him. He took one step back, took careful aim, raised one foot, and kicked the doorknob a good one.

As he'd supposed, the lock was pretty flimsy. The door flew open, and he walked on in. The light switch was beside the door. He flicked it on, closed the door behind him, and grinned at the wide-eyed girl sitting up in the bed.

"Hello, Saralee," he said. "Surprised to see me?"

EIGHT

THE KID WAS awfully nervous. He was about Vince's age but looked a lot younger. His face was round and rosy like a highly polished apple. His eyes were the kind that were scared to look back when you looked at them. It was a shame, Vince thought, that you had to deal with people like this. But money was money. You couldn't be too choosy, not when money was money and you needed it in a hurry.

"Hot as a pistol," Vince went on, coaxing the boy, leading him gently by the nose. "Built like a bomb shelter. Young, too. Good stuff. You won't regret it, believe me. Money well spent and all that. You know."

"Gee," the kid said. "I mean…gee."

"And she'll do anything," said Vince, giving the kid a sly man-of-the-world grin. "Anything you want. Anything at all."

"Anything?"

"Anything," Vince emphasized. He would have sworn the stupid bastard's mouth was beginning to water.

"Well," said the kid. "I mean, twenty bucks is a lot of money. You can't just reach out your hand and there's twenty bucks."

Vince reminded him that the motel where the kid staying with his folks cost more than that for a day. Then he went into another profound description of Saralee's assets. That did it.

"I'll get the money," the kid said. "Hang on."

Vince stood there with his face hanging out while the kid went to get the money. *Maybe he'll steal it from his old man,* he thought. *Or maybe he'll just tell the old man Hey, gimme twenty bucks so I can get laid, and the old man'll come across with the twenty.*

It was a pretty horrible thought.

"I got it," the kid said, returning. "Let's get going. I mean, we might as well get it over with, don't you think? I mean, there's no point in wasting any time."

Vince didn't feel like talking anymore. He pointed at the Packard and the kid got in. Vince slipped behind the wheel, played games with the ignition, leaned on the accelerator and aimed the car at Saralee's motel. The kid would be tossing another twenty bucks in the sack, and Saralee would be tossing another kid in the sack, and this should be cause for rejoicing. Somehow it wasn't. Somehow he felt pretty cruddy.

It was, he reflected, damned hard work being a pimp.

Vince was standing outside the door, smoking a cigarette and listening to Saralee showing the kid what it was all about. If anybody had told him he'd be pimping in North Carolina, he would have laughed. But here he was, pimping in North Carolina. And what the hell was so funny?

When he broke in on Saralee, first she tried to explain, and then she tried to apologize, and finally she tried to seduce him. But this time her attempts at seduction were as ineffectual as her apologies and her explanations. Maybe he was growing immune to Saralee or something. Whatever it was, her body did nothing to change his mind.

At first he had wanted to beat the living crap out of her, but the phony rape bit with the tired old broad in Washington had taken it out of his system. He just didn't feel up to slapping another woman. Some guys got their kicks that way, but he didn't seem to be one of them. Besides, he'd come a long way. You don't hitchhike all the way from New York to North Carolina just to knock some girl's head in.

And there were more important considerations. The most important consideration was getting the car back to his old man, and this turned out to be impossible. Saralee wasn't much of a driver. The Packard was a wreck to begin with, but she hadn't bothered to put any oil into it. The poor heap knocked and rattled and huffed and puffed. It wouldn't make Baltimore, much less New York. And if he gave the car back to his old man in that shape, he might as well hang himself.

That's where the money came in. With enough money, he could fly back to New York and take a bus to the lake. His father would be annoyed, but he'd get back soon enough so that the old man wouldn't exactly hit the roof. Then, with enough money, he could pay his father for the car. Make up some story about how it got wrecked, and hand his father a mittful of money. That might do the trick.

The problem, then, was money. He had the hundred bills from the Rape-Me Relic, and Saralee, he found out quickly, had almost three hundred of her own.

Which wasn't enough.

It would cost him, say, a hundred dollars to get back to the lake. The car might bring a hot fifty bucks on the open market now, but his father would expect at least five hundred for it. And he didn't dare sell the car.

THE thing was, he and Saralee had a little less than four hundred between them. And he needed a bare minimum of six hundred—one hundred to get back to the lake and five hundred to pay for the car. Seven hundred would be more like it, and eight hundred would be fine, but six hundred would do in a pinch.

And if this wasn't a pinch, nothing was.

The answer had been simple. Saralee would hustle for the money. She would stay in the room, and he would scout likely prospects and bring them to the room where she would accommodate them. He told Saralee about it, and she was against it, claiming that she would give it away to anybody but the idea of selling it repelled her.

"It's the same as giving it away," he told her. "Because I'll be taking all the money. You won't get a nickel of it."

This didn't placate her. But pretty soon she managed to see that she didn't have a hell of a lot of choice in the matter. First of all, he took all of her clothes and put them in the trunk of the car. That left her naked, and restricted her movements to the immediate vicinity of the room itself. Then he told her precisely what she would look like after he got through with her if she didn't do as expected. She shuddered a little.

Getting customers could have been easier, but it also could have been harder. Vince knew the type to work on. Kids his age, rich kids on vacation.

Nice virginal type kids who wouldn't make any trouble and who would pay plenty for a chance to be with Saralee. The South seemed to swarm with kids like that. They were all over the place.

The door opened and the kid walked out. He had a stupid grin all over his polished apple face. "Everything okay?" Vince asked him. "You get what you paid for?"

The kid nodded, still grinning, and headed off down the road. It was a good mile to the motel where he was staying and Vince started to offer him a ride. Then he decided the kid was so high on Saralee he could probably *fly* back.

Vince walked into the room, closing the door behind him. "That's six of them," he told her. "How's it going? How's the old machinery holding up?"

He expected her to be a little bitter, but she wasn't. She smiled dreamily, running her hot hands over her hot body and purring like a kitten.

"Wonderful," she said. "Just wonderful. I never had so many boys at once before. One after the other. It's wonderful."

"Well," Vince said. "Well, a few more and we can call it quits. We've got over five hundred now. As soon as we hit six, you can take it easy."

"I am taking it easy," she insisted. "This is fun. Hurry up and get some more, will you?"

"You're insatiable."

"What's that mean?"

"It means you never get enough."

She licked her lips. "You hurry up and get some more," she said, "or I'll rape you."

He shook his head, then walked out and got in the car. The next motel he came to was like striking gold. There were six of them there, six kids seventeen and eighteen years old, and all of them were about as interested in Saralee as it was possible for a person to be. They were ready to go, and they didn't haggle over the price, and that meant a very fast hundred and twenty dollars, which was enough to retire on. He loaded them into the Packard and stepped on the gas.

On the way the boys kept talking about what they were going to do. They had some fairly unusual ideas. They weren't going to stand around waiting in line, not them. They wanted sort of a party with all of them in there at once. Vince felt like telling them they were sick, but he had decided that pimping was one of those occupations where the customer was always right.

But he did have a good money idea.

"Look," he said, "something like you got in mind, you got to have what is known as a package deal. That's what we call it in the trade. A package deal."

He sounded so professional that he scared himself. But right away they asked him what he meant by a package deal.

"Well," he said, "the twenty dollar price, that's for one man. You understand? But if you want sort of a party, then the price arrangement is different. What it is, you pay a lump sum by the hour. Then you can do whatever you want, all of you, as much as you want. It's like you were renting the girl for the hour."

He left it dangling there, waiting for them to bite, and they bit. They asked how much it was by the hour, and he told them it was a hundred dollars an hour, with a two-hour minimum. That way they wouldn't have to worry about how many times, or what they were doing, or anything. They would pay him the two hundred dollars and do whatever they wanted.

They went for it. They got all excited, as a matter of fact, and before long he was standing in front of the door again, counting the money and waiting for the two hours to pass. He didn't want to wait for two hours, not really. He didn't want to stand outside the door while all that nonsense was going on inside the door, either, and it suddenly occurred to him that there was no reason in the world for him to stick around. He had the money, and he didn't give a hydroelectric dam what happened to Saralee.

So why stay around?

He hopped into the car again, and drove to the Charlotte Airport. There was a flight to Idlewild leaving in half an hour, and because of a last-minute cancellation there was a seat open, and he took it. He got on the plane and studied the pretty breasts of the stewardess, which made him think once more of Saralee.

Poor Saralee. He'd played a dirty trick on her, all things considered. A hell of a dirty trick. She didn't have a dime, and she didn't have a car—not with the Packard parked at the airport. And, he realized all at once, she didn't have a goddamned thing to wear. All her clothing was stashed in the trunk of the Packard. He'd put it there to keep her from running out, and now it looked as though she was going to do very little running out indeed. He tried to feel sorry for her, but it seemed as though every time he tried to feel really sympathetic towards her, he burst into uncontrollable laughter.

Poor Saralee, he would think. Then Ha-ha-ha-ha-ha. And so on, with all the other passengers staring at this idiot who kept breaking up and laughing all over the place. Let 'em stare, he thought. Hell with them.

He settled back finally, and relaxed in his chair, and, because he was very tired, fell asleep. He woke up as the plane was bouncing through some air pockets. His ears were popping and his head ached dully. Then the pilot set the plane on the ground and everything was all right again.

He took a bus to the East Side Terminal, and a cab to the Port Authority bus terminal, and another bus that made fifteen stops, the last of which was Lake Ludicrous. And then, finally, he was at the lake, and then at the cabin, and there was his father.

"You're late," his father said, "and the car's gone, and what the hell happened to you?"

Vince took a deep breath. "The car," he began. "Some idiot came down the wrong way on a one-way street and hit the car. Knocked it for a loop."

His father stared.

"I was lucky I wasn't killed," Vince added, which was true in a way. "But don't worry about the car. The guy paid for it."

"Paid for it?"

"He wasn't insured," Vince said. "I could have sued him down the river, and he was all shook up, so he offered to pay for it. I've got the money. I figured suing him would just take a lot of time and get him into all kinds of trouble. He was a pretty nice guy, too. Stupid, and a hell of a driver, but a nice guy."

"How much?"

"Huh?"

"For the car," his father said. "How much did you get for it?"

"Oh," Vince said. "Well, six hundred dollars."

His father stared. "You're kidding," he said. "You have to be kidding. You can't mean it."

"It wasn't enough?"

Softly, his father said: "Perhaps, on a good day, I could have sold the car for a hundred and fifty dollars. On a bad day, maybe half of that. And you—" he said reverently, "—got six hundred beautiful round dollars for it."

Vince took the money from his pocket. "The guy was scared," he elaborated, "and he just wanted to get rid of me, I guess. Here's the money."

His father counted the money, his eyes shining happily. "Vince," he said. "Good old Vince. My son. Chip off the old block. Only kid in creation who could make a pile of dough by cracking up a car. You're a good boy, Vince. Any car I ever have, you be sure and borrow it. Borrow all of 'em. Great boy, Vince."

"Gee," Vince said. This was going much better than he had expected.

"Vince, I can't keep all of this. You were the one who swung the deal. You ought to get sort of a commission. You know—a piece of the profit."

His father was pushing money at him, telling him go out and have himself a big time. Vince walked away shaken, and looked at the money in his hand. He counted it, after awhile, and discovered that there was a hundred and fifty bucks there. Which was quite a bit of money. Even with inflation, and all that, and the shrinking dollar, and the high cost of living, even with all those things to take into consideration, one hundred and fifty bucks was a lot of money.

So here we are, he thought. Back at old Lake Lollapalooza, with a fistful of dough and no place to go. Now just where in hell do we go from here?

THE first place he went was to take a shower, because he stank a little, and to change his clothes, because they stank a lot. Then he went down to the lake and slept in the sunshine, which was fun, sort of. Then, because he was hungry, he went and had something to eat. After lunch he went back to the lake, on the prowl again for female flesh. There were plenty of likely-looking prospects, but somehow he couldn't get interested. He would look at the girls and imagine what they would look like without any clothes on. Then he would imagine how they would be in the hay, and he would decide that it probably wouldn't be much fun at all.

He was frightened. Maybe he was losing his interest in sex. Maybe he had burned himself out, or something, and he couldn't get excited by a woman again.

That didn't seem too likely. But there was something he found out that day, and it became more apparent during the next week. They spent part of the next week there at the lake, and then his father picked up a second-hand car at a good price and they drove back to Modnoc. At Modnoc it became obvious. The domestic life just wasn't exciting enough. Modnoc and the lake, both at once, were totally lacking in points of interest. He was bored stiff.

Well, he told himself, it was no wonder. In the past month or so he'd done one hell of a boatload of fascinating things. He had had two virgins who weren't virgins, and then he had put the blocks to a married woman, and then the married woman turned out to be a nymphomaniac. Then he and the married woman ran off to New York, with the married woman's husband's hard-earned cash, and registered in a hotel and played sex marathon.

Then the gal left him, and he begged on street corners, and skipped a hotel bill, and hitchhiked to Carolina, and raped a girl on command, and found the married woman, and made her whore for him, and left her naked and penniless, and flew back to New York, and here he was.

Which was a lot of activity. And which made Modnoc seem more than ever a tasteless, lifeless, useless place to spend his life.

He thought what it would be like to spend his life in Modnoc. He would go back to school in the fall, graduate the following June, and then go to college. Four dull years at a dull college and he would be back, taking a "good job" with the Modnoc Plastics company, marrying some stupid virgin or near-virgin, raising a batch of grubby kids and playing the good old American game.

For three days in Modnoc he lay around the house waiting for time to pass. He thought about how nice it would be to leave Modnoc, to go somewhere else on his own. Hell, it wasn't hard to be on your own. He'd managed well enough there with Saralee. She had conned him, of course, but then he turned around and conned her right back and came out of it smelling like a rose. If he left Modnoc now he would not have a car to worry about, and he would not have to come back at any set time. He could work things whatever way he wanted to work things. He would have all the room he needed to move around in. It would be a pleasure. He would go wherever he wanted, and he would do whatever he wanted, and if anybody didn't like it, to hell with them.

It sounded good. But he spent his time thinking about it rather than doing anything about it. The days dragged by until he couldn't stand it any longer. So Friday night he finally went out of the house, anxious to find something to do.

He found Sheila Kirk, who was slightly better than nothing.

So Willing

SHEILA Kirk had always been around, and Vince had been convinced that she had always been available. There were no stories about her one way or the other, but she had that "Available" look in her eyes. For some reason, he had never taken her up on it. It didn't make any sense, really, because she was one hell of a good-looking girl.

One *hell* of a good-looking girl. Soft brown hair and very pale skin and a pretty face and good legs and an almost unbelievable pair of mammaries. She was good-looking, and she was available, and somehow he had never answered the door when this particular opportunity had come knocking.

Well, that would have to change.

He spotted her on the street, and he walked over to her, and he said hello, and she said hello, and from there it went according to formula. She told him how lucky he was to get to the lake because Modnoc was dead as a doornail in the summer, and he told her it couldn't be that dead if she was around, and they went for a coke, and from there on it was pattern, pure pattern. It was as easy as rolling off a girl.

He had it all figured out in a few minutes. Two dates, and a long ride in the country, and a blanket on the grass, and Sheila Kirk would be his. He was going along with the pattern, riding it out, when something snapped. He just couldn't stand it another minute. It was part of the Modnoc routine, the dulldom capital of the western world, and he wasn't going to play it that way.

He broke off in the middle of a sentence, turned to her, caught her pointed chin in one hand and looked hard into her eyes. "Look," he said to her, "how about walking over to the park and having a go at it?"

She stared. Her mouth opened, then closed again, and she went on staring some more. He felt like laughing at her.

"C'mon," he said. "We'll take a nice walk in the park and then I'll take your cruddy clothes off and it'll be good. I'm pretty great at it by now. I've been making a study of all the finer points and I'm an old pro already. What do you say to that, Sheila, old kid?"

She didn't say anything. Not a thing. She just stared.

"Come on, old girl." He took her arm and started off toward the park. She didn't seem too enthusiastic, but at the same time she walked along with him, not pulling away, not fighting a bit. It was going to be easy.

"The direct approach," he announced. "Nothing like the direct approach. You and me, Sheila, we don't have to pretend for each other. We can be honest. We can both stand a little action. We don't have to play games. We just go to the park, and lie down in the sweet-smelling grass, and we have ourselves a ball."

Which, when you come right down to it, is what they did.

He led her to a nice private place in the park, one he had used before, and there he undressed her. He didn't kiss her, mainly because he had no desire to kiss her. He took off her blouse, and he took off her bra, and he played around with two things that were closer to mountains than mole-hills. Then he took off the rest of her clothing, and played some more little games, and took off his own clothes, and got going.

She had been had before, and she had been had properly, and she was good at it. The shock of his approach seemed to have worn off because whatever state she was in now, it was not shock. She was squirming all over the place, and her nails were raking his back, and it was, by all rules, great.

Then they got dressed, and walked back to town, and he told her goodnight and left her to find her own way back to her house.

It was, by all rules, great. But somehow it wasn't so great at all. Somehow it was lousy, and it shouldn't have been lousy, but it was and this annoyed him. She had done a good job, and he had done a good job, and the sum total of their efforts had been highly charged monotony.

Which was a shame.

He was tired, so he went to sleep. But it took him awhile to drop off into blissful unconsciousness. He tossed around for awhile, thinking that he had to get out of Modnoc before he went out of his skull. It just wasn't fun anymore. All Modnoc ever had to offer was female flesh, and now even that was beginning to pale. It was time to go.

"I don't understand," his father said. "Don't you like it here? Don't you like living with us?"

"Frankly," Vince said, "no."

"We try to make a good home for you. We try to give you everything you want. And you just want to up and leave us. Where are you going? What are you going to do?"

Vince shrugged. "Who knows?"

"Crazy," his father said. "That's what it is, crazy. You won't finish high school and you won't go to college and you won't get a good job and—"

"Dad."

"And you'll be a bum. That's a hell of a note. I don't want a bum for a son. A thief, yes. A con man, maybe. But a bum?"

"Dad," he said. "Dad, I'm not going to be a bum."

"You're not?"

He shook his head. "I'm going to be a great success," he said. "Horatio Alger style. Spirit that made this nation the great and powerful country it is today. Young man out for success. Flash Gordon conquers the Universe. You know."

"Really?"

"Sure," Vince said, getting slightly carried away with himself. "No opportunities in a town like this. A young guy like me has a great chance in the world. Opportunities galore. Money, fame, power. All these things are waiting for a man with courage and initiative and imagination."

"You sound like an ad for door-to-door shoe salesmen."

"I'm not kidding, I'm serious, I mean it," Vince said, meaning it.

"Really?"

"Sure," Vince said. "The world is waiting for me. Maybe I'll do some traveling. Paris, Rome, Berlin. The Mysterious Orient. The South Seas. Latin America. All over the globe, challenging chances await earnest young men."

"You're not kidding," his father said, glowing.

"Nope."

"You're serious," his father said, beaming.

"Right you are."

"You mean it," his father said, bursting with pride. "My boy. My son, out for glory. A chip off the old block, that's what you are. I should have known it the minute you sold the car for six hundred dollars. You've got a head on your shoulders, Vince. A real head."

"Thanks, Dad."

"I'm proud of you, Vince. Really proud. Where are you going? Any ideas?"

"I'm not sure, Dad."

"Of course," his father said. "Of course. Got to feel your way around. Got to see which way the wind is blowing. Got to keep both feet on the ground, your nose to the grindstone, your shoulder to the wheel, all that. Hell of a position to get any work done in, but you'll manage."

"Right."

"When do you figure on leaving?"

"Well," Vince said, "I was thinking of getting started tomorrow morning."

"That's pretty soon, Vince."

"I know, but—"

"But you're one hundred percent right, boy. No time like the present. Can't let the grass grow under your feet. You know what they say about rolling stones. Don't gather any moss. But who wants moss? Right?"

"Right."

"Better let me tell your mother," Vince's father said. "You know how mothers are. Probably be all upset that her boy is leaving her. That's the way mothers are. They sort of carry on about things like that. A tendency they have."

"Okay, Dad."

"She'll probably cry," his father said.

She did.

VINCE'S father didn't get enthusiastic too often, but when he did, his enthusiasm was contagious. Before she quite knew what was happening, Vince's mother agreed that Vince should go out into the cruel world. She wasn't quite sure why she thought so, but she was the type of woman who had most of her decisions made for her. She was a fine woman, a good mother and all that, but Vince's father was the real brains of the family.

Which didn't say too much for the family.

It worked out, though. Before too long, Vince had a suitcase packed and a wallet full of money. He still had most of the hundred and a half from the car, plus a little extra left over from the Saralee episode, plus the extra hundred his father pressed on him as a going-away present. When morning came, he was on his way to the bus depot. And when the bus left, he was on it.

The bus was bound for New York. That seemed like a good place to start. He had to avoid the hotel where he was known as James Blue, but in a city the size of New York that shouldn't be too hard to do. He also had to avoid Rhonda, who lived in New York, but the chances of running into her seemed pretty small. And if he did see her, he could always cross the street. It wouldn't be much trouble.

The bus moved along, the wheels churning, and Vince hummed softly to himself. The crap he had fed his father had been, strangely enough, partly true. He felt like a pioneer, a Forty-Niner heading for gold in California. Not many pioneers rode the bus, he knew, but times were changing. It was a brand-new world, a brave new world. His world.

The sun was up and the roads were clear. The bus went along at a good clip and Vince could hear the wheels singing a little song to him. He couldn't make out the words, but it was a cheerful, optimistic little song and he was happy.

Modnoc faded off into the distance. New York was ahead of him.

NINE

WELL, NOW, THE best laid plans of mice and men, of mouse and man, of moose and Mau Mau, mink and marigold, as the trite and true old phrase doth say, often go astray.

Well, there was New York, and here came Vince, roaring down from the upstate foothills like a one-man tidal wave, like a timebomb ready to go off in any girl who got in his way. Well, and then here was New York and here was Vince, in the middle of Manhattan with a suitcase in his hand and a gleam in his eye. Well, and then there was New York, and where was Vince?

Vince was in Boston.

The tale of how Vince ricocheted and rebounded, how he was bank-shotted off the biggest city in the world and basketed in Boston, is one of those long sad stories without even a happy ending to make it all worthwhile. Or much of any ending at all, except that he went to Boston.

It started with the Port Authority Terminal where the bus emptied, Vince with it. He went out to the street, which was Eighth Avenue, with 41st Street to his left and 40th Street to his right. So he turned left, having had seventeen years of not going right and not wanting to change things at this late date, and a block and a half with the suitcase brought him to 42nd Street, which is the hub of half-a-dozen very strange worlds, most which Vince had no interest in.

But he had to turn right now, because the bright lights were off to the right, and there was nothing off to the left but some more street and the river, and he was too young for the river. So he turned right, in spite of himself, and lugged the suitcase toward the milling people and the flashing lights.

And a girl walked by him, crying her pretty blue eyes out.

"Hey!" That was Vince, and he said it again: "Hey!"And dropped the suitcase and started back and touched her on the arm and said it again. "Hey. What's the matter?"

"He's a bastard," the girl said, and went right on weeping. A good-looking girl she was, what the pulp-writers call class, and she was wearing a short-sleeved, full-skirted, pale blue dress of the kind that's too expensive for Saks to carry, and she had a nice young body like Spring and soft blonde hair that had been molded by the loving touch of a professional hairdresser, and even though she was weeping and strolling down 42nd Street past midnight, she had the look of lots of money, of Newport money and Palm Beach money, of private estate money and private girl's college money.

Vince took all this in while he was saying, "Who's a bastard?"

She stopped walking then, but she didn't stop weeping, and when she turned to face Vince, he saw that all that loveliness had been callously flawed by a swift right to the eye. And not too long ago either, because the swelling hadn't yet finished and the skin around the eye was only just beginning to darken. But she was going to wake up in the morning with the kind of shiner that looks cute on boys of ten but distinctly out of place on girls of twenty, particularly rich young girls who look like Spring.

"Archer is," she told him, which was the answer to his question, but he'd already forgotten all about that question and instead said, "Hey! Who hit you?"

"Archer," she said again, still crying. And started walking again.

"Hey, listen!" Vince cried. He had done a number of things in his young life, but the attempted destruction of beauty hadn't been among them, and the stirrings of a brand-new indignation was causing a flurry in his chest. "Hey, listen!" he cried. "Where is this guy? He can't do a thing like that to you!" He was trotting along after her, and glanced back once at his suitcase, sitting in the middle of the empty sidewalk, then trotted on because suitcases always come second after beauty.

"He's a bastard," she said again, and the word seemed as out-of-place on her lips as the shiner did on her eye.

"Listen!" Vince cried, caught up in the romance of the thing. "Tell me where he is! Tell me where he is, and I'll take care of him for you!"

She stopped and turned to him with a glad cry. "Would you?"

Vince had never before felt like a knight-errant, but there's a first time for everything. "Damn right I will!" he cried, and shook his fist.

The girl had stopped weeping to beam at him, and now she stopped beaming to frown and look doubtful. "But why would you?" she wanted to know. "You don't even know me."

Vince tried to put it into words, and it wasn't all that easy. "A girl like you," he started. "A girl as good-looking as you—to punch a girl in the eye—" He stopped, took a deep breath, and shouted, "He can't do a thing like that, that's all!"

"Do you really mean it?" she demanded.

"Of course I mean it!"

"He's gone home," she said. She reached out and touched his arm and she must have been carrying a load of static electricity because the touch of her fingers on his arm jolted him to his soul. "He's gone back to his apartment," she went on. "I'll take you there."

"I'll show him!" cried Vince.

"My car is down here," said the girl. "In the parking lot."

He went with her three steps, then stopped. "My suitcase," he said. "Wait, I'll only be a minute." She waited, and he ran back, to discover that an agitator with a Bible had taken up a stance on the sidewalk next to his bag, and a crowd had gathered around to punctuate his appeal with good-natured obscenities, and it took Vince a couple minutes to worm his way through the Philistines to the suitcase and back. "Are you saved?" cried the agitator, and Vince shouted, "I'm going to be!" and ran back to the girl who looked like Spring.

She led him to the parking lot and to her car, which not surprisingly turned out to be a Mercedes-Benz 190 SL which, while not the hottest car on the road today, is the hottest one that isn't actually on fire.

They got in the car and she drove. She wasn't crying anymore, but looking furious and determined, and as they snaked through the cabs she told him one or two things. "His name is Archer Danile," she said. And a minute later: "I'm Anita Merriweather."

"Vince," he told her.

She nodded and was silent and sneaked between a cab and a truck and shot through a red light and made a right turn without taking her foot off the accelerator. “We were out tonight,” she said all at once. “And we got into an argument. He was drunk, and he hit me.”

“The bastard!” Vince cried. The girl’s wild driving didn’t scare him, it exhilarated him. This was all he’d been missing in Modnoc. Action and adventure and romance, and the feeling of adrenalin coursing through him and his pulse pounding and he was, by God, a bloody knight errant.

She drove and drove and then stopped, and they were on East 63rd Street between Madison and Park Avenue, which is what you call a ritzy address. They got out of the car and went into a building, and they were in a square little place that was mainly marble. The street doors were behind them, another set of doors was ahead of them, and the square metal bank of mailboxes and doorbells was to their right.

“When he asks who it is,” she said, “I’ll answer. He’ll let me in. Then we can go up and you can take care of him.”

“Right,” Vince said. He clenched his fists and hunched his shoulders and knew he could lick the world.

The girl—Anita—pressed a button and a minute later a blurry voice said, “Who’s there?” and she leaned close to the mouthpiece to answer, “Anita.” And a buzzing sound came immediately from the door.

They went in and there was a wide long room like a hall, with a mirror and a table and a vase full of flowers and a self-service elevator. They zoomed up to the eleventh floor and down the hall, and Vince waited beside the door, out of sight of the peephole, while Anita rang the bell.

Click went the peephole, and click again, and then the door opened, and Anita walked in. Vince followed.

The door led to a hall, which went away to the left, to the living room. Anita walked down the hall and Vince followed, and there didn’t seem to be anyone else in the apartment at all, which was ridiculous.

Anita turned around to frown in puzzlement at Vince, and her eyes widened and she cried, “Behind you!”

Vince turned. This Archer Danile had been behind the door, which was now closed, and he was coming grinning down the hall toward Vince. He was tall and blond and Greek-goddish, which is to say somewhere between Apollo and Bacchus. And Vince looked at him and knew he had better smite the first blow, because there might not be a second.

So he stepped forward to the grinning Greek god and punched him square in the nose. And Archer Danile went, “Uck!” and half-turned, and leaned against the wall. His profile was plain before Vince's eyes, all manly nose and manly jaw, and Vince snapped another fist out, lacing across the manly jaw, and Danile went "Urk!" again, and fell down.

"Hit him!" cried Anita. "Hit him!" More strange words to come from the mouth of a girl who looked like Spring.

"Quite enough," Danile said clumsily. He was sitting on the floor, looking at the opposite wall, and trying quite unsuccessfully to smile. "Quite enough," he repeated, just as clumsily. "You've already broken my jaw."

"Your jaw?" Vince had been standing there, fists clenched, waiting for Danile to get up and rejoin the fray. Now he eased the taut fingers and leaned forward to look at Danile's face. It did seem different now, he noticed, a trifle unbalanced. The jaw seemed to be a bit too far to the left.

"You've done it this time, Anita," said Danile, still trying to smile and still looking across at the opposite wall. "You've really done it this time."

"Well, look what you did to me!" The girl pushed past Vince and leaned forward, pointing at her eye.

Vince all at once felt left out. The two were comparing wounds, and Vince didn't have any interesting malfunctions worth mentioning. Not only that, but the romance and high adventure were quite rapidly leaving this whole episode. The whole thing was suddenly a disappointment. For one thing, it hadn't actually been a fight he'd had with Archer Danile. He'd punched the man twice, knocked him down, and broken his jaw. And he didn't even *know* him!

For another thing, he didn't even know Anita Merriweather. He'd been walking along, minding his own business—

She was tugging him by the elbow. "Come on," she was saying. "We've got to get out of here."

"You've done it this time, Anita," said Archer Danile mildly.

Vince allowed her to lead him from the apartment and down the hall to the elevator and down the elevator to the first floor and out the door and into the Mercedes-Benz 190 SL.

"You'll have to come home with me," said Anita.

"Okay," said Vince. He had given up thought for the duration and was simply letting things happen.

Anita jumped on the accelerator as though it were Archer Danile's head, and they shot away from the curb and down the street.

After one or two blocks, Vince's mind began once more to work. And, Vince's mind being what it was, the first thing he thought of was sex.

Sex with Anita Merriweather, that was. If anything was obvious in this green world, it was that Anita Merriweather wasn't part of the greenery. That is, she wasn't green. To put it simply, she was unvirginal. It was plain, that is, that she was not a virgin.

Because, of course, she'd been living with that guy. Right? Of course. There wasn't any question. And besides, she was rich, and everyone knew what the rich did. Even more often than the poor. And with more people. And started younger.

And besides that, she had invited him to her place. Which meant only one thing. He had beaten up her old boyfriend for her, and he was on his way to get his reward. And his reward would be—Anita.

There had been a time when such a reward would have filled Vince with mouth-watering anticipation. But that time had ended somewhere in the last month, and now, instead, he wondered where the romance and adventure had gone, and he wondered further if it wouldn't be a good idea to just step out of this hot little car the next time Anita decided to obey a traffic light, and wander off into the city again.

But it was nearly one o'clock in the morning, and Anita was offering, besides her body, a place to sleep. That would be nice. And in the morning he could begin again and afresh, and henceforward he would ignore all weeping girls, even weeping girls who look like Spring and dress like money.

Anita was silent now, and so was Vince, and they drove and they drove. They crossed a bridge, and that startled him at first, until he realized that a girl like this, wealthy and all, undoubtedly would live on Long Island. So he relaxed and lit a cigarette, and they drove and drove.

And they kept on driving, they just kept on diving, and Vince noticed that they were on a major highway.

"Hey! Where do you live, anyway?" he asked.

"Boston," she said, and kept on driving.

SO that was how Vince happened to go to Boston. He hadn't planned on going to Boston, he hadn't even ever thought much about Boston, one way or the other. But there he was, at six o'clock in the morning, in Boston. They drove around the Common, and up Beacon Hill, and then they stopped, and they were parked in a driveway beside a mansion.

"Come in," said Anita, and she got out of the car and walked away, toward the back of the mansion.

Vince scrabbled for his suitcase, and once more he trotted after the girl, and they went in a back door and down three steps and they were in a kitchen. A huge kitchen, with three white walls and the fourth wall of unpainted brick. There was a big wooden table and wooden chairs and a strange combination of the most modern (refrigerator and freezer and dishwasher) with the most antique (a wood-burning stove and shelves lined with intricately designed china).

"Sit down," Anita said, and Vince sat down.

"I bet you could use some coffee," Anita said, and Vince nodded.

He was stunned and he was exhausted. It had been quite a while since he'd slept, and so everything that happened in the world outside his eyes happened in a strange slow-motion sort of way, and he had plenty of leisure to be stunned about things that were surprising.

And Anita was surprising. And Boston was surprising. And his presence in this kitchen was surprising. So he just sat there and waited for whatever was going to happen next.

And he knew something was going to happen next. He'd been feeling strange ever since he'd first noticed Anita, weeping and black-eyed, go walking by him, back on 42nd Street in New York. And now, like Anita's shiner, that strange feeling within him had grown and grown, and he knew that something fantastic was going to happen, and he didn't know what it was, and he didn't even know if it were going to be good or bad.

She had a hell of a shiner by now, a swollen black discoloration around the left eye, but instead of marring her, it merely emphasized the beauty of the rest of her. A beautiful girl, who moved like a racehorse and looked like a debutante's self-delusion, and who was going to be a prime mover in the strange happenstance that Vince could feel coming upon him.

She sat down with him at the table, bringing with her two steaming mugs of black coffee, and she said, "Tell me about yourself."

"You first," he countered, not knowing why, but only knowing that that was the thing to say.

"All right," she said. She smiled and shrugged, and said, "I'm Anita Merriweather. My parents have lots of money. I'm twenty years old and I don't know what I want, but it isn't anything I have. I hate Archer Danile and everybody like him, parasites, drifters. That's what the argument was about. I went to college two years and then I stopped, because there wasn't anything there I wanted. I've been to Europe and I've been to Japan, and I don't feel as though I've been anywhere. I'm young and I *feel* young, and I want to grow up. And now it's your turn."

"I'm Vince," he said. And then he told her about himself, and he told her the truth. He told her about his summer, about his virgin hunt and about Saralee and about pimping and leaving the car and telling his father he was going out into the big wide world to seek his fortune. She laughed at the right places, and she looked serious at the right places, and when he was finished she said, "I wish I'd been with you. I wish I'd been along for every minute of that. I don't know anything. I've never had anything except money, and that isn't enough."

He looked at her, and he felt the happening coming on, getting ready to burst, and he opened his mouth to give it a chance to happen, and when his mouth was open he said, "Will you marry me?" And he hadn't known that was what was going to happen.

And she smiled at him. And she said, "Yes."

"Anita," he said. It was all he could say. He didn't even know her, and a million pieces of common sense were clamoring for his attention, were hollering at him that he couldn't propose marriage to a girl he'd met six hours ago, and he ignored them all.

"Vince," she said, and looked at him, and her one good eye was as deep as a bottomless abyss, and he knew he was teetering on the edge of that bottomless abyss, and he knew he was going to topple in.

He got to his feet. "Come on," he said.

"Yes," she said.

She had to lead the way, because it was her house and not his and he didn't know where her room was. They left the kitchen and they walked through one room after another, and through halls and corridors, and up a flight of stairs, and around them all the way was the kind of richness Vince had only seen in old movies on television.

And finally they came to a closed door and Anita opened it and they went in and she closed the door behind them. It was a big room, as big as the whole cottage had been back at the miserable lake, and across on the other side of the room were three windows, with the early morning sunshine pouring in. And midway between the door and the windows, its headboard against the right-hand wall, was a bed, Anita's bed.

She turned to him to say, "You haven't even kissed me yet." And her voice broke when she said it, and he knew that she was as terrified as he.

He reached for her, and she came slim-waisted and eager into his arms, and he kissed her. And her lips were soft and cool-warm, and her tongue was a slender reed playing with his thick bear of a tongue, and her body was slender and like Spring against him.

He kissed her, and then she moved away, crossing the room, making a wide berth around the bed, going to the window, looking out and down, her face and hair highlighted by the sun, and she was the slimmest, youngest, most beautiful, most heart-wrenchingly perfect thing he had ever seen in all his life. Betty and Rhonda and Del and Saralee and all the others ceased to exist. He could feel them receding away from him, like smoke, evaporating, and he felt a momentary sadness at their departure, and then he didn't care anymore, because the blonde-haired girl dressed in blue, made up for all of them, and was all he would ever need.

He came across the room to her, feeling himself lumbering and clumsy, wishing he were lighter, more graceful, more accomplished, more an ideal, to match the ideal that she was. He came across the room, and he touched her arm, as he had done years ago in New York on 42nd Street near Eighth Avenue, and he said, "I love you, Anita."

"I love you, Vince," she said.

It was a ritual, like the marriage ceremony, except that it was much more solemn and much more binding. And he held her arm and turned her around and kissed her again. And their clothes seemed to float away, like gossamer and lace in the barest of breezes. They were naked, and hand in hand they walked to the wide sunlit bed.

Her body was Spring, was young and Spring.

She was closed to him at first, and her clear brow ruffled in a frown as her lips whispered, "Vince." And then she sighed, and her good eye closed, and his lips were by her cheek, and he murmured her name, "Anita. Anita. Anita."

And they flowed together, blended together, and the sweatiness of the past disappeared, and he understood now why he had lost interest in all those others. It was because he had needed this completion, this unhurried blending, this oneness.

"YOU were a virgin!"

"Yes," she said.

The sound of the door opening spun him around on the bed.

A woman, fiftyish, tall and prim, obviously Anita's mother, stood wide-eyed on the threshold. Her eyebrows lifted and she looked at Vince. "I don't believe I know you," she said.

TEN

"ALL I HAVE to say," Anita was saying, "is that Baltimore is an unusual place for a honeymoon."

"What's wrong with Baltimore?"

"Nothing," Anita said, "is wrong with Baltimore. Nothing could possibly be wrong with Baltimore. Don't misunderstand me. I like Baltimore. I love Baltimore. I—"

"How about the Lord Baltimore Hotel?"

"A wonderful hotel," Anita said. "A magnificent hotel. The food in the Oak Room is delicious. The decor in the lobby is exquisite. The service is impeccable. The furniture is posh and the rugs are thick. The view breathtaking. The—"

"How about the room?'

"The room," said Anita, "is sumptuous. It has a television set with a thirty-inch screen. You don't even have to drop in a quarter to make it operate. And—"

"How about the bed?"

"Mmmmmmmmm," said Anita.

"You like the bed?"

"I love the bed."

"Well," said Vince, "we're on it."

"True."

"And, after all, it's our honeymoon."

"True."

"Sooooo—"

"A good idea," said Anita. "An excellent idea. A commendable idea. But do you think we ought to again?"

"It's our wedding night," Vince reminded her. "Wedding nights only come once a marriage."

"Well," said Anita, running her hands over him, "I wouldn't want to put up a fight. But you have to be gentle. After all, I used to be a virgin. You have to bear that in mind."

"Yes, Santa Claus," Vince murmured. "There was a virgin."

THE chain of circumstances that got Vince and Anita from a bed in Boston to a bed in Baltimore is a curious chain of circumstances indeed. When we last saw Vince, as you may recall, he was under the watchful eyes of Mrs. Merriweather, who happened to be Anita's mother. Anita's mother, strange to say, was not too pleased with the spectacle of Vince and her daughter lying belly-to-belly. She was, as a matter of fact, somewhat livid with rage.

"I'll have you thrown in jail," she ranted. "I carry a lot of weight in this country, young man. I'll have your father thrown off the stock exchange. I'll ruin your entire family. I'll—"

"Mother," said Anita gently, "shut up."

Mrs. Merriweather shut up.

"In the first place," Anita said, "we haven't all been properly introduced. Vince, this is Helen Merriweather, my mother. Mother, this is Vince. Uh...I don't know your last name—"

Vince supplied his last name.

"That," said Anita, "is the first place. In the second place, you are not going to have anybody thrown into jail. Vince has done nothing wrong. If anybody is going to land in jail, it will be me."

"You?" said Vince and Mrs. Merriweather in one voice.

"Me. I am twenty years old and Vince is only seventeen. This makes me guilty of statutory rape, mother. You wouldn't want to see your daughter in jail, would you?"

Mrs. Merriweather shuddered.

"That," said Anita, "takes care of two places. In the third and final place, Vince and I are going to be married.

"Married?" said Mrs. Merriweather.

"Married," said Vince and Anita in one voice.

"What you just had the unmitigated gall to intrude upon the aftermath of," said Anita, "is what is technically referred to as premarital intercourse. While you and Beacon Hill may feel that it is not proper form, it has happened. Once. Tonight. Tomorrow we will be married, and tonight's escapade will be justified ex post facto. I feel certain you can see the value of that."

"Anita," Mrs. Merriweather said, "you must remember that you are not old enough to marry without my consent. I have some voice in this matter."

"True," said Anita. "But you will give your consent."

"I will?"

"Of course," said Anita. "Otherwise Vince and I will live in sin on the front lawn. Just think how the neighbors would react to *that*."

Mrs. Merriweather thought how the neighbors would react to *that*. "You wouldn't do it," she said levelly. "You wouldn't."

Anita said nothing.

"You wouldn't," Mrs. Merriweather repeated weakly. "Would you?"

"Yes," said Anita. "I would."

"You probably would," Mrs. Merriweather agreed. "Knowing you, you probably would. I wouldn't put it past you."

Mrs. Merriweather smiled. It was, Vince thought, a strange smile. Any smile under such circumstances had to be a strange smile. Perhaps, Vince guessed, the hallmark of the wealthy was their ability to smile when there was nothing to smile about. At any rate, Mrs. Merriweather seemed determined to make the best of a bad thing. Vince was the bad thing.

"Well," said Mrs. Merriweather, "I shall give my consent. Not gleefully, I admit. But stoically. However, I don't see how you can arrange to be married tomorrow. There's a waiting period, you know. Two or three days."

"We can't wait that long," Anita said.

And Vince, who had felt for a few minutes as though they were going to have the wedding without him because he was so thoroughly excluded from the conversation, chimed in with a valuable thought. "There's no waiting period in Maryland," he said. "We can fly down to Baltimore and be married immediately."

"Baltimore," said Anita thoughtfully.

"Baltimore," said Mrs. Merriweather, heavily.

"Baltimore," said Vince, happily.

"Baltimore," said Anita, decisively. "Now, mother, if you'll leave us alone, Vince and I would like to get some sleep."

"Together?"

"Together," Vince and Anita said, together.

"But—"

"Of course," said Anita, "there's always the front lawn—"

Mrs. Merriweather sighed. Then, with the air of someone making the best of a bad thing, she suggested: "Vince, Anita, before you go to sleep again, there's one thing I'd like to do for you."

"What is it?"

"You may object," Mrs. Merriweather said. "Old practical people sometimes have old practical ideas which conflict with the notions of romantic youth. But still—"

"Get to the point, Mother."

"If you don't mind," Mrs. Merriweather said timorously, "I'd rather like to change that sheet."

THERE was, inevitably, a two-day waiting period in Baltimore. There had to be a two-day waiting period in Baltimore, of course. The wedding would not have been complete without it. The two of them, Anita and Vince, taxied at breathtaking speed from the Baltimore airport to City Hall, raced hysterically down the corridor to the License Bureau, and were informed that there was a two-day waiting period in the state of Maryland. Anita threw a fit, and then they laughed, and then they prepared to spend two days in Baltimore waiting for it to be time to get married.

Which is to say that they had their honeymoon before the wedding.

"It's not really that bad," Vince explained. "After all, we don't really know each other. This way we have a chance to know each other. By the time the two days are up, we will be prepared for marriage. It's a lucky break, this waiting period."

"Sure," Anita said. "Except I'm in a rush to be married. I hate this waiting."

"You hate *this*?"

"Not that."

"And *this*?"

"Well, not that."

"How about…*this*?"

"Vince—"

"Well, do you?"

"Vince," she whispered throatily. "Vince, you shouldn't do that. It gets me all excited. It gets me so excited I can't stand it. It makes me want you to make love to me."

"Good," Vince said. "I was beginning to think along those lines myself."

They were married, finally, after two heavenly but interminable days had come and gone. They were married in a minister's study, with Vince wearing a once-pressed suit and with Anita wearing a black dress. It was, all things considered, a somewhat bizarre ceremony. Vince was shaking throughout it, wondering what, in addition to Anita, he was getting into. But it went more or less according to plan, and then they were married, and away they went, back to the hotel and to bed.

And to bed. And to bed. And to bed. And to bed.

The night lasted a long time. So, for that matter, did the morning. Then, suddenly, it was noon, and time to leave the hotel, and face the world. They showered, dressed, packed, and left.

"We have to see my parents," Vince said, remembering that he had some and that they had something of a right to know of his new station in life. "They live in Modnoc. I think I told you about them."

"You did."

"We have to see them," Vince repeated. "Tell them we're married. Get their blessing. That sort of thing."

"They won't like me," Anita said.

"Of course they will. They'll love you. You're young and sweet and beautiful."

"I'm older than you."

"So what?"

"They'll think I'm an old lady corrupting an innocent youth. Actually, of course, it's the other way around. You corrupted me. Nobody on earth could corrupt you. You're as corrupt as can be."

"And," Vince reminded her, "you like it that way."

"Love it," said Anita. "But your parents will hate me."

They didn't. Vince cleverly managed to see his father first. He and Anita walked into the office while his father was working. And his father was his usual self.

"Vince," he said. "Vince. My boy. You're back already. Good to see you, Vince. Did you take the world by storm? Carve your name on the face of the nation? Eh, boy? What stories of success have you brought back to your old Dad?"

"Dad," Vince said, "this is Anita."

Eyes glanced briefly at Anita, took her in. Teeth flashed briefly in a smile. Then the eyes flashed back to Vince. "That's nice," he said. "Nice girl. Always glad to meet one of your girlfriends, Vince. But let's get back to you. How have you been doing, my boy? Making your way in the world? Getting ahead by bounds and leaps? Setting the world on fire?"

"Well," said Vince.

"If it's money," Vince's father said, "I understand. I'll be glad to help out. World's a tough place. How much do you need?"

"Dad," Vince said, "Anita isn't a girlfriend."

Vince's father looked a little stunned. He had more or less forgotten Anita, and now the conversation was back to her for some incomprehensible reason, and his son was telling him that she wasn't a girlfriend. "Then what is she?"

"My wife," Vince said.

"Your *what*?"

"My wife," Vince said firmly.

"Your WHAT?"

Anita put a small tentative hand on the shaking shoulder of Vince's father. "Steady," she said. "You mustn't let yourself get upset. Bad for the heart."

Vince's father relaxed. Somewhat.

"Vince and I were married," Anita was saying now. "Two days ago in Baltimore. We fell in love and decided to get married. Now we are man and wife. For better or for worse. That sort of thing."

"For worse," Vince's father said. "Obviously, for worse. Vince is only seventeen. You can't get married at seventeen. It doesn't make any sense."

"We're in love," Vince said.

"Then sleep together," his father suggested, taking a totally opposite stand from that of Anita's mother. "Sleep together. On the front lawn, if you want. But don't get married. For God's sake, don't get married."

"We already did," Anita said.

"In Baltimore," Vince added.

"WHY?"

"Because we're in love," Anita said.

"Deeply in love," Vince added.

"Oh," said Vince's father. Then: "But how in the name of heaven do you expect to keep body and soul together? You don't know what it costs to support a wife, Vince. Takes a lot of money. And you were going to be a success, remember? Horatio Alger? That sort of thing? There's an old saying, my boy. He who takes on wife and children gives hostages to fame and fortune."

"Children?" Anita said. "Not for a while, I hope."

"You never know," Vince's father said darkly. "They have a way of coming up when you least expect them." And he looked at Vince with a reminiscent gleam in his eye.

"But," he said suddenly, "let's get back to money. Maybe it'll work if you're planning on having Anita get a job. Maybe the two of you can get to work together. Can you type, Anita? Take shorthand? Keep books?"

"I can't do anything," Anita said.

"Oh," Vince's father said. "Well, where there's a will, there's a way. Old saying. You can learn. You're young. You—"

Vince felt called upon to explain. His father didn't understand the basic nature of the situation. He had to fill his old man in. He meant well, his father did, but he was missing a few salient points.

"Dad," he said slowly, "money is no problem."

"Ah," his father said, "it never is when you're seventeen. But it becomes more of a problem as you grow older. You probably think you can live on love. All the old myths. Two can live as cheaply as one. Not true, young lovers. Two can live as cheaply as one if only one eats. Otherwise it doesn't work out that way. Has a way of surprising you. Oh, I know I sound like a materialistic old fool. But money matters, Vince. Money makes a big difference. Why, I remember when your mother and I got married. Didn't have a pot to cook in, as the old expression goes. We thought it would be easy. But—"

"Dad," Vince broke in desperately, "Anita's father has better than five million dollars."

For perhaps the first time in his life, Vince's father was at a loss for words. He stood there with his mouth hanging open. He looked as though someone had hit him over the head with a bankbook.

"Five million dollars," Vince repeated reverently. "So money is no problem. Not for us. I mean—"

"Excuse me," Vince's father said, recovering slightly. He looked at Anita. "What did you say your name was?"

"It was Anita Merriweather. Now it's—"

"I know what it is now," Vince's father said. "Merriweather. Not the iron-and-steel Merriweathers?"

"That's my uncle," Anita said. "Dad is the brokerage Merriweathers."

Vince's father sat down. Heavily. "Five million dollars," he said softly. "Five million dollars. Vince, my boy, I don't know how you do it. You know, I had my doubts when you set out to conquer the world. Didn't want to voice them, but I'll admit now that I had my doubts. Couldn't figure out how you'd make a lot of money. Oh, I know you've got the brains for it. No question about that. But the way the tax set-up goes these days, I didn't think you could come out ahead of the game. Hell, a man can't get rich by earning money these days. But you found the answer, you genius. You did it, you hero. There's only one way to get money, and that's to marry it, and that's just what you did."

"Not for money," Vince said.

"For love," Anita explained.

"We're in love," Vince said.

"Deeply in love," Anita said.

"Forever and ever," Vince said.

"Amen," Vince's father said. "Amen and amen. Well, I guess money's no problem, after all. How about that?" Vince and Anita smiled.

"Vince," his father said, "you're mother doesn't know yet, does she? I mean, you haven't told her about the wedding, have you?"

"Not yet. We wanted to tell you first."

"Good idea. Fine idea. Well, I think you ought to let me break it to her. Sort of let her in on it a little at a time. You know how mothers are. But I'm sure she'll like Anita. Of course she will. Wonderful girl, Anita."

Vince and Anita beamed.

"She'll probably cry," Vince's father said thoughtfully.

She did.

But tears have a way of stopping. Vince's mother, being a woman all the way, was considerably less impressed by five million dollars than was Vince's father. She thought the money was nice, of course, and of course she wasn't going to hold it against Anita, but that wasn't the turning point. Neither, as it happened, was Vince's father's firm assurance that they had not lost a son but had gained a daughter. This turned out to be about as reassuring as it was original. The big thing was not what was said but Anita herself.

Vince's mother talked to Anita, and Vince's mother looked at Anita, and before long Vince's mother decided that Anita happened to be just what Vince needed. Since Vince and Anita had already agreed on this point, there was no conflict there. Before long Vince's mother was writing out little file cards with Vince's favorite recipes on them, and otherwise preparing Anita for what was obviously the most important role in life, that of Vince's wife. Anita cared about as much for cooking as she cared for crocheting lace doilies, but she wisely kept quiet. Everybody approved of everybody. The parents thought Anita was a darling girl, and Anita thought the parents were darling parents, and life was suddenly very much worth living.

They stayed in Modnoc for two weeks. They stayed in Vince's room, and that made Vince understand that they were very definitely married and that it was very definitely right for them to be married. He had slept with many women in his young life, but this was the first time he had ever slept with a woman in his own room in his own house. He thought it would feel wrong, but it didn't, and when things really got going he barely knew where he was, so everything was all right.

And then, at last, it was time to leave Modnoc. It was time to go back to Boston, to meet Anita's father, who somehow had been left out of the picture. Vince wasn't especially looking forward to the meeting. From one standpoint, Mr. Merriweather was the great benefactor, the man with the five million dollars, the great white father who would see to it that Vince never had to work for the rest of his life. That was one way of looking at it, but it was not necessarily the right way.

The other side of the coin had Mr. Merriweather playing the role of indignant papa, prepared to disown his willful daughter and to cast his new son-in-law out into the street, penniless. This was a far less attractive picture. From what Anita had said of her father, old man Merriweather was a twentieth-century improvement on the concept of the self-made man. He hadn't exactly dragged himself up out of the gutter. But he had taken the three hundred thousand dollars his father had left him and turned it into five million. Which, all things considered, was no mean accomplishment. Even if you're born with a silver spoon in your mouth, it's a neat trick turning it into a platinum one.

And what self-made man was going to look with favor upon a penniless son-in-law with the hand out? Not Mr. Merriweather. Not in a million years.

Actually, Vince didn't find either prospect particularly attractive. He wasn't too keen on being disinherited, for obvious reasons. But at the same time he wasn't too hot on the notion of living off Papa for the rest of his life. Somehow that took the kicks out of the game. It was sort of like settling down in Modnoc, except without a job. The same monotony, on a solid gold Cadillac level. The same lack of incentive and stimulation. It would be easier to bear, due to the presence of the most wonderful girl in the world, but he couldn't help wondering how long it would take for even that to wear thin. If he didn't work, and if everything got handed to him on a platinum platter, then he and Anita were going to have a rough time of it.

"Don't you worry about a thing," Anita would say. "Papa will be perfectly wonderful about the whole thing. There's an answer, somewhere in the middle, maybe. We'll find it."

Vince pretended to be very optimistic about the whole thing, but he remained scared. And the scared feeling did not vanish when he met Mr. Merriweather. It grew.

Mr. Merriweather wasn't the type of man with whom you felt instantly relaxed. He was the type of man who made you feel as though your tie was crooked. Even if you didn't happen to be wearing a tie. He was big, and he was white-haired, and he stood at attention even when he was sitting down. He smelled of money and hard work simultaneously and Vince felt intimidated.

"Always figured Anita would do something like this," he said. "Type of girl she is. High-spirited. Red-blooded. Sets her head and heart on something and doesn't let go. Can't fight her, whether I approve or not. Don't know whether I approve or not. You good for anything, Vince? You got any ambitions? Any ideas? Or are you going to sponge off the old man and wait for him to die?"

Vince was struck dumb. He hoped he didn't look stupid but was sure that he did. He felt stupid. That much was certain.

"Maybe you don't want to be a playboy," Mr. Merriweather said. "Maybe you want me to get you started in my business. Slip you into a junior executive slot at, say, twenty thousand a year. Move you up quickly, make a branch manager out of you or something. Wouldn't have to do much of anything. Take a vacation whenever you felt like it, put in a couple hours a day at a desk the rest of the time. Give you a good position with enough money and enough respectability. That what you're angling for?"

"No," said a voice. Vince looked around. Then he realized that it was his voice.

"No?"

"No," Vince said, more positively this time. "I don't want any favors. Whatever I get I'm going to work for. It's not my fault if your daughter happened to be blessed with a rich father. I didn't have anything to do with that. Neither did she. Whatever Anita and I have, we're going to have for ourselves. And we're going to get it by ourselves. Without any handouts."

Mr. Merriweather's eyebrows went up. "You're a good actor," he said. "You almost make me believe that you're sincere."

"Almost?"

"Almost," Anita's father said. "But not entirely. Nobody throws money away. Self-respect is all well and good, but nobody turns down the sort of opportunity I just offered you. I'm afraid I don't believe you, son."

Vince bristled. "That's just too goddamned bad," he said. "Because I don't happen to give a damn whether you believe me or not. You can take your job and stick it up your—"

"Vince!" Merriweather's eyes blazed. "No one talks to me like that."

"I do," Vince said.

"Maybe more people should," Merriweather said. "You know, I do believe you now. It's ridiculous, of course, but I believe you. You're a fool, of course, but maybe the world needs more fools."

Vince, naturally, kept his fat mouth shut. He was wondering why he hadn't kept his fat mouth shut before, when he had an offer of twenty thousand dollars a year for doing nothing. Now he had no offer at all, which was substantially less.

"Vince," Mr. Merriweather was saying, "perhaps I have something else you might be interested in. Not as attractive, but something."

"I don't want a handout, Mr. Merriweather.

"This isn't a handout. Are you interested?"

"Maybe."

Merriweather laughed. It was quite a laugh. He threw back his head and broke the room in half with his laughter. "You little wise guy," he said. "You sharpie. How old are you, Vince?"

"Seventeen."

"Just seventeen? You certainly aren't the normal seventeen-year-old. What made you grow up so fast? Good Lord, the average youngster these days is a perfect example of stunted development. Four years of high school, four years of college, four years of graduate study—and the result is less mature than you are. Can you explain that? Was there any particular factor that made you grow up?"

Someone—it couldn't possibly have been Vince—said: "Women."

Merriweather's laugh made the other laugh sound like a chuckle. "That's it!" he said. "That's the trouble with modern man. No rakes left in the world. A batch of sincere idiots. You must have been a real lady killer, Vince."

Vince lowered his head modestly.

"That's the secret," Merriweather said. "Love 'em and leave 'em before you marry. Then stick to one woman. That's the way I did it. I must have had...oh, I don't know, but there were a hell of a lot of them. Then I met Helen and that was it for me. Strict fidelity. Uh...you will be faithful to Anita, won't you?"

"Of course," Vince said. "When you've had the best—"

"Precisely," Mr. Merriweather said. "Vince, if someone had said you would turn out to be a boy after my own heart, I would have laughed in his face. But you're all right, Vince. You're too young for the offer I have in mind, but I think you might be able to handle it. Know what I'm getting at?"

"No."

"Simple," Merriweather said. "Our house is thinking of opening a Brazilian branch; dealing primarily in Brazilian securities. There's a fortune to be made down there. They're short of capital. The right investments will move at triple the speed of comparable investments Stateside. A Brazilian realty syndicate will pay thirty percent compared to an American ten percent. Brazilian stocks either fall flat or double every two months. It's the perfect spot for a brokerage office. A smart man down there can get rich overnight. Or go completely broke. It's up to the man involved."

Vince wisely didn't say anything.

"Interested?"

"In what?"

Merriweather smiled. "You'll spend three months in the New York office," he said. "You'll make fifty dollars a week and you'll hustle your behind off for it. Then you go down to Brazil—if you can stand the gaff. You'll be second-in-command of the Sao Paolo office. You'll put in twenty hours a day for a relatively small salary. But if you play your cards right, you'll come out of there with a fortune in your pocket. It's all up to you, Vince. If you make money, it's your own money. If you lose, I won't be around to bail you out. It's all up to you."

"I'll take it," Vince said.

"It's not soft," Merriweather said. "It's hard. I don't know if I would take it myself, come to think of it. I don't know if I'd have the guts."

"I think you would," Vince said.

Merriweather studied him. "I think you'll wind up broke," he said. "I think you'll come out of Brazil with your hat in your hand, begging me for a soft touch."

"Don't bet on it," Vince said.

IT was the middle of January and the sun was hotter than hell. The summer in Brazil came in the middle of winter. And when it was hot, hell was no hotter.

"I picked a winner," Anita said. "I picked a real winner. You keep surprising me, Vince. And you keep winning."

"Write your father," Vince said. "Let him know about it."

"He knows."

"It looks as though the Moreno Dam is going through," Vince said. "We've got a piece of it."

"Good," Anita said.

"We're doing all right," Vince said. "We're doing fine. By the way, I love you."

"You do?"

"Uh-huh. Quit hogging the pillow."

"Sorry."

"Comfortable bed," Vince said. "Comfortable girl. You busy, little girl?"

"It's awfully hot."

"It can get hotter."

"In this heat?"

"I'm strong," Vince said. "And young. Come here, little one."

The bed creaked and the world sang.

Sin
Hellcat

ONE

I SAW JODI again the other day. She's a whore now making twelve thou a year, doing quite well at it. I remember, way back in college days, thinking to myself, now, Jodi's not the marrying type. There stands (or sits or lies prone) a career woman if there ever lived one. It was nice to know I'd been right, and that she was doing so well.

She offered me some, no charge of course, for old time's sake, but I just couldn't get into the mood. I mean, it would be like taking free legal advice. I mean, it's the girl's *profession*.

So we sat around at her place—lovely little apartment in a hotel on Lexington Avenue—and talked over old times together, college days and what happened to so-and-so, and what we've both been doing since, and we both got a little smashed on Scotch—a bottle of Vat 69 given her by one of her admirers for some symbolic reason or other.

It had been ten years since I'd seen Jodi, and Lord how she'd changed! Those huge soulful dark eyes were even deeper and more level and piercing than they'd been when she was twenty-one and could still remember back to the loss of her virginity. And her body had filled out very nicely—lovely surging breasts and firm hips and the kind of solid thighs that can constrict a man if he doesn't watch himself—the inevitable result, I suppose, all that filling out, of her constant activity. She'd had two more abortions since last we'd met, she told me, making a grand total of three, and the unlicensed fraud who committed (I can't say performed) the third one slipped a bit, and now dear Jodi can rest assured that there will never be opportunity or necessity for a fourth.

It was mid-afternoon, a Tuesday in fact, and so both early in the day and early in the week for Jodi to be down and about, making a living. She was wearing a green knit sheath dress—it went well with her naturally-tanned complexion and honey-blonde hair—and she persisted in crossing her legs, revealing the long tanned underslope of one rounded thigh. That was distracting as hell, but I averted my eyes, and compromised by looking intently at her breasts instead, outlined individually by the tight green knit, proclaiming twice that she wore no bra beneath.

I knew I'd get a grumbly sort of hell from Marty for not coming back to the office after lunch, but this old school reunion was just too good to miss. Besides, I had all my copy in on the Dexter Frozen Dinners—"A Square Deal On A Square Meal"—and didn't really have anything to do until I got the go-ahead from the Dexter people. So old time-clock Marty could go to hell with himself. I would spend a quiet afternoon here with dear old Jodi, and take my normal train back to Helen.

I thought of Helen, my wifey-wife, the frigid witch of the Ramopos, icily waiting off in our Rockland County suburban hideawee, and I glanced again up under Jodi's green skirt, and I shuddered at the contrast.

We sat and chatted and got quietly snockered, and I contemplated sliding the palm of my hand up along that thigh, fingers extended, and in a happy glow composed of one part Vat 69 to one part reminiscence, I remembered the first time I had ever taken dear old Jodi to bed....

SPRING of my sophomore year, it was, twelve years ago. I was nineteen, only recently devirginized myself, and suddenly discovering in me some of the common aspects of the bull, with the exception that I seemed to be eager all the time.

It was Friday afternoon, I remember, in late May, and a bunch of us had cut classes to go down to the lake and swim. There were about twelve of us, evenly divided into boys and girls—which is always the best way, I think, after all—and we'd begun as simply an amorphous pack, only gradually pairing off. I'd taken Jodi to a movie once upon a time, but aside from some sporadic breast-clutching in the darkened balcony of the theater, nothing much had happened. I looked at her that afternoon, and I knew at once that that was a mistake that had to be rectified, and the sooner the better.

God, she was lovely! Picture this, if you'll be so kind: A girl of eighteen, just tall enough so that the top of her head was even with my shoulder. Long slender legs, tanned an amber gold. Smooth tanned arms, cameo shoulders and neck, the softest downiest throat in all creation. A longish pixyish face shaped somewhat like an inverted triangle. No! What a ghastly picture, that isn't what I mean at all! Picture an elf, with the straight slanting jawline, the high cheekbones, and somehow *hungry* look. Add to this picture a flawless tanned complexion, two huge round dark eyes as deep as night, a straight not-too-narrow nose, and cupid-bow lips of a red that would put Titian to shame. That was her face, framed by honey-blonde hair cut rather short and brushed very straight, curling around the shells of the ears.

I purposely left the portion encased in the bathing suit till last. The bathing suit itself, of course, was black. Two straps curved over those lovely shoulders and shot down toward the breasts. Firm breasts, not yet very large, but exciting to touch for all that. And, below, the bathing suit hugged down across a perfectly flat belly. And now we turn her around, as though she were a work of art upon a pedestal, and we stare for a while at the back view.

The lovely breasts around front distracted us so that we didn't really notice her waist. Now, with the aft portion facing us, we can see that she has a hell of a good waist indeed, the sides sloping in from beneath the arms—that's just a hint of breast-curve we can see there, when she raises her arm that way, and isn't that the most beautiful sight in all the world?—and the sloping-in ends at a waist that is just the perfect degree of slenderness, without the malnutrition look that goes over so big in the clothing ads. And below the waist, the whole business starts to slope out again, curving this way and that, in the cutest rear you've ever seen. You just want to walk up behind her and pinch, and lean your chin on that soft shoulder and whisper into that soft ear, "Hiya, Jodi."

That was Jodi.

At any rate, we all cut classes and went off to the lake for an afternoon of swimming and fooling around. It was, as I said, late May, and too early for the lake to be filled with tourists and vacationers and cabin-owners, so we had the place pretty much to ourselves. We ran shouting into the chilly water at the public beach and immediately swam around to one of the better private beaches, where we knew the owners hadn't yet put in their annual arrival. One poor fool—old Jack Fleming, I think it was—tried to swim the whole way one-handed, holding a portable radio up in the air with the other arm, and of course the result was that he practically drowned himself and gave that radio a hell of a good soaking.

But they really made radios in those days. We opened the silly thing up and let it dry in the sun for two or three minutes, and then we slapped it back together and turned it on, and by God it played! It played mainly static, of course, but here and there you could detect a note of music in the garble, so we turned it up to top volume and then spent the afternoon screaming over it.

I went after Jodi right away. She'd spent a short while going steady with a guy named Andy Clark, but he wasn't there that afternoon, and the whole thing between them was finished with anyway, so she was unattached, and I made damn sure I was the first one to attach myself to her.

It was the usual routine that afternoon. We swam around a while, and then we splashed each other, and chased each other around in the shoulder-deep water, and I dunked her a couple of times, and then I kissed her. Her lips were cool from the water, the rounded double-front of her bathing-suit-covered breasts was rough and exciting against my chest, and her waist, way down beneath the water's surface, was cool, the perfect size for my arm.

And she responded beautifully. She clung to me, her arms around my back, returning the kiss—eyes closed, in the manner of young girls everywhere—and when I parted my lips and probed hesitantly with a quivering tongue, she opened her mouth at once to accept it.

That was all, for a while. We splashed and chased and occasionally kissed, and finally I got my courage up—I was only nineteen, after all—and hidden beneath the water I slid my arm around her side, beneath her arm, and clutched her tender breast.

There was a difference. Why was there a difference? Even now, I don't know. All I know is that there was that difference, and that the difference always holds true. In the balcony of the movie theater Jodi's breasts had been soft and pliant, in feeling they were whipped cream mountains topped by wrinkled cherries. To touch those cherries was to make dear Jodi moan and writhe in delight. Underwater, encased in a bathing suit rather than blouse and bra, the breasts were firm and strong, the cherries as hard as anything one would want, and the whole thing, if possible, even more exciting than before.

The second time my hand fondled those wonderful breasts as we kissed, my other hand encircled her and cupped a rounded buttock, and she closed her eyes and moved against me, the water cool and invigorating, the vibrant girl in my arms too exciting to be stood, and I confess a wild oat was lost in the depths of the sea.

It was a long and—now I look back on it—horribly frustrating afternoon. We stayed in the water awhile, and then we stretched out on a blanket onshore, a bit away from the others, ostensibly to get some sun, but actually to get some fondling done. I caressed that precious body, leaned down to kiss the breasts with lips that grew stronger and harsher until at last her moans of pleasure were muffled by a stifled scream of pain, and my hand roamed the front of her body, building courage, stroking the coarse front of that bathing suit, moving ever closer, until finally she sighed and gripped me tighter and kissed me so furiously I thought she would break my neck.

But farther than that we could not go. Her bathing suit, top and bottom, was too snug-fitting. And there were, after all, ten other youngsters right nearby.

And so the afternoon was played away, with mutual frustration. Around seven, one of the more organizational-minded males of our group took up a collection for food and drink—I donated two dollars, I remember—and went away, to shortly return with pizza and beer, the pizzas cold and the beer warm. But we were all young, and hardships didn't bother us, so we ate the cold pizza and drank the warm beer, and at every opportunity I caressed Jodi's fantastic body.

It must have been around eight o'clock when one of our group mentioned the baseball game. Now, here's the situation: Every college worthy of the name has the three intercollegiate sports, football and basketball and baseball. And our college was, in that respect, worthy of the name. Now, everyone attends the football games, of course, particularly when one's own team is an odds-on favorite to win, which ours inevitably was, and about half the normal student body jumps at the chance to watch a basketball game. But no one in college goes to look at a collegiate baseball game, absolutely no one. Why this is I don't know, but it is. We twelve had, therefore, neither the knowledge that a baseball game was to be played by our jolly team tonight, nor much interest in what the hell our baseball team was doing *any* night.

And so it was that the announcement that our baseball team was playing an away game that very night was met, at first, with an overwhelming display of public apathy. At first. But then someone else—or it might have been the same person, I no longer remember—suggested that it might be a great oddball idea to go watch this here baseball game, cheer our team extravagantly, and get happily mashed.

The concept of going to a college baseball game was so radical, so unexpected, so completely absurd, that we all, naturally, agreed at once, and immediately began to pack the remaining beer into auto backseats, while two of the drivers huddled together over a roadmap, trying to find out (1) where the hell Ylicaw, where the game was to take place, might be, and (2) how the hell to get there.

Then someone came up with a disgusting thought. "Hey!" cried this someone. "What kind of baseball team do we have, anyway? Are they good or are they lousy?"

A quick headcount demonstrated that no one present knew what kind of baseball team we had.

"I don't want," said this someone, "to watch our lousy baseball team get beat."

True enough. But the problem was solved by someone else, who said, "Hell, we won't know which team is ours, anyway. What difference does it make?"

None at all, obviously. We piled into cars—Jodi curled beautifully upon my lap—and tore away in the general direction of Ylicaw.

We got lost, of course—several times—which didn't bother me in the least. I was scrunched into a corner of the back seat, Jodi on my lap, and my hands and lips were kept very busy indeed. By the time we finally did straggle into Ylicaw, I was as eager as a Cape Canaveral launching pad and as frustrated as a soap opera heroine. You could have fried an egg on me.

Ylicaw, by the by, was the other side of a state line or two, so I suppose I should have spent the next twenty years in jail. My purposes, concerning Jodi, were about as basic as it is possible to get.

At any rate, what with leaving the lake so late and getting lost now and again, we arrived at the green-wood stadium in Ylicaw just in time to watch our school bus pull away, toting the ball team back home again. We had managed to miss the game.

So there we were in the thriving metropolis of Ylicaw at ten-thirty of a weekday evening. None of us had ever been in that town before—what possible reason would anyone have for going to Ylicaw?—and from the look of the place we had arrived too late to watch them roll up the sidewalks.

We clambered out of our two-car caravan and conferenced around a lonely streetlight. There were no other pedestrians in sight. The stadium—barely large enough to deserve the name—lay shrouded in darkness, a condition shared by all the buildings we could see up and down the street. The only bit of neon in sight belonged, believe it or not, to a feed store.

And so we talked it over. We had come all this way, with great difficulty, and none of us wanted to simply turn around again and drive all the way back. We had to *do* something first, doggone it!

Unfortunately, Ylicaw was about the most unlikely spot for *doing* something that any of us had ever seen. At least that portion of it in view was pretty unlikely.

We finally decided to split into scouting groups, each heading off in a different direction, and we would all reassemble here at the cars in half an hour. If there was any life to be found anywhere in Ylicaw, one of our scouting parties would find it.

Jodi and I were a complete scouting party. We started walking, turned two corners, walked and additional block, and discovered a park. It was a small and dark and empty little park, about the size of a desktop, sporting grass and trees and assorted shrubbery and a couple of footpaths.

We looked at one another, and we looked at the park, and we looked at one another again. Jodi squeezed my hand, and her eyes were brighter than the streetlight across the way.

Without a word being spoken between us, we both turned as one and strolled into the park. We had half an hour before we were to return to the others. Half an hour would surely be sufficient. In fact, the condition I was in, an hour would be *more* than sufficient.

We strolled along the footpath, passing a bench to our right, two trees to our left, shrubbery to our right—

We turned right.

It was pitch black in there. Twigs crackled underfoot, bushes tugged at our knees and entrapped our ankles, a low-hanging tree branch brushed my face with coarse leaves. Jodi held my hand clenched tight in hers, and in all that blackness the only thing I could see was the bright gleam of her eyes, and above the thunder of our passage I could hear her breathing, as loud and irregular as my own.

We blundered and crashed our way into the shrubbery and came, all at once, to a cleared spot, completely encircled. Jodi whispered "Whew!" and immediately sat down. I flopped down beside her, reached for her, kissed her, and we toppled backward, lying prone on the barren ground.

Active hands, active hands. We were still in our bathing suits, and I had the straps of her suit unhooked and the top half folded down, and I was doing all sorts of interesting things to her bare and beautiful breasts, when the cop suddenly put in his appearance.

He shone a flashlight on us, the blasted Peeping Tom, the beam centered on Jodi's tanned and pink-tipped breasts and she screamed. I didn't blame her, I felt like screaming myself.

I was blinded by the light at first, but then I could make out the shadowy form leaning over the bushes on the side opposite the direction of our entry. As I peered trying to make out who or what this was, a voice said, rather gruffly and much too loudly, "What's going on here?" So I knew that it had to be an officer of the law. Anyone else would have *known* what was going on there. And had the decency not to interrupt.

The long and the short of it is that Jodi and I—her top half once again barely covered by the bathing suit—were bundled into what Ylicaw apparently considered a prowl car (a dilapidated Chevy, three or four years old) and driven away to what Ylicaw apparently considered a police headquarters (a dilapidated brick structure, perhaps a hundred years old), where a short fat bald man with a red face and a red head threatened us with all sorts of unlikely punishments, grumbled at us, and wrote endlessly on sheet after sheet of paper.

Jodi, wearing only her bathing suit, carried, of course, neither money nor identification. I, however, as supply sergeant of our scouting party, had tucked my wallet into the waist of my bathing suit, and so I had identification and eight dollars. The bald man—a desk sergeant or some such thing, I suppose—took my wallet with claws that snatched, and wrote my name and home address down at least half a dozen times. I gave him a phony name for Jodi—what the name was I have no idea, at this late date—and he lectured and threatened and grumbled at us for a while again, finally releasing us with a warning to leave town at once.

By then, it was midnight. We walked, we hoped, toward the Ylicaw stadium, found it at last and, to our dismay, discovered that the cars were gone. We learned the next day that the others hadn't even noticed our non-appearance. There were ten of them, all somewhat high, and with that number in that condition it was easy to lose track of two people.

For a few minutes, we didn't know what to do. My eight dollars wasn't enough to get us back to campus, not even by bus, assuming we could find a route—changing buses, changing buses, changing buses—that would take us from the nondescript out-of-the-way dinky little hick town of Ylicaw to the equally non-descript out-of-the-way dinky little hick town where the campus was situated. At any rate, we couldn't afford a bus anyway. And it was too far to walk, of course. And far too late at night to hitchhike, on the secondary and tertiary roads that would be our inevitable route.

Jodi suggested calling someone on campus, preferably one of those who had so unceremoniously just dumped us here, at the edge of beyond. But of course we couldn't expect them to get back to the dorms before three at the earliest. In the morning, I could call someone to come and get us, but for the moment we were stuck.

The long and short of it was that we were going to have to spend the night in Ylicaw.

We talked around the subject for a few minutes and finally brought it out into the open. We were going to have to spend the night in Ylicaw.

Now, what with piercing flashlights and threatening fat men and being abandoned by our friends and whatnot, we had pretty well lost the fervor that had driven us all day long. We were neither passionate anymore, nor were we coy. And so when we spoke of staying the night here, we discussed the subject with clinical coldness.

We couldn't very well sleep in the park; neither of us was in a particular hurry to meet the flashlight-bearing patrolman or his red-faced superior again. And, dressed only in bathing suits, carrying no luggage, and with no ring on Jodi's third-finger-left-hand, staying at a hotel seemed a remote possibility. Nor were we particularly happy about the idea of spending the next nine or ten hours wandering around the streets. We were somewhat tired, from our day's exertions.

We strolled, talking it over, irritated and worried. We strolled for perhaps fifteen minutes and then we saw the hotel.

It was the western edge of town. Every town in the country has a section like this, on one edge which is neither fringe nor outskirt but seems to be a small hunk of downtown broken off and rolled into a corner. A few seedy-looking stores, some equally seedy offices, and, down at the corner there, a rambling structure two stories high, fronted by a neon sign reading "BAR-HOTEL."

"I'm going to take a chance," I said, the minute I saw that sign. "Places like that usually aren't too particular."

"I'll wait here," she said, tiredly.

And so she waited there. I continued down to the corner and stepped into the bar. A hotel like this, of course, had no lobby.

I made quite a stir in the bar. There were six or seven locals, hulks in hunting jackets, draped over beers at the bar, while another hulk, this one in a filthy white shirt and apron, played bartender in front of them. And here I walked in, a nineteen-year-old kid in a bathing suit.

They watched me, with stoic interest, and I got a bad case of stage fright. I sidled to the bar, the bartender ambled over, and I said—whispered, rather, for I was completely intimidated by the surroundings—"Have you a room?"

"Sure I got rooms," he said. He looked me up and down, slowly, looked beyond me through the fly-specked window at the empty street, and said, "Single or double?"

My hesitation should have been a dead giveaway. Finally, I said, "Single."

He didn't seem to notice the hesitation at all. He simply nodded and told me the charge was three dollars, and that he wanted it in advance, since I had no luggage. I paid him, gratefully, and he came out from behind the bar and led the way to my room.

We went through a door in the side wall, coming into a long narrow hall, with a street door at one end and a flight of stairs at the other. The bartender pointed at the stairs. "Up there," he said. "First door on your right." He handed me the key.

I thanked him, in a frightened whisper, and he nodded and started back to his bartending duties, pausing to look at me and point at the street door. "Bring her through there," he said. "And try to keep it quiet." Then he went back into the bar, closing the door after him.

After only a few seconds of paralysis, I raced to the street door, opened it, and waved frantically at Jodi. She came down the street at a half-trot, and when she reached me I whispered, "We've got a room. It's okay, the bartender's on our side."

"I've got to get off my feet," was all she said.

We hurried upstairs and into our room.

This time, there was no caressing, there was no physical play. We entered the room—a small barren linoleum-floored monstrosity with bed and dresser and chair—and the both of us immediately stripped off our bathing suits and crawled into bed. I switched off the light, a glaring overhead affair, and Jodi and I lay together in the dark, almost touching, but a million miles apart.

We lay there, side by side, unmoving, for perhaps fifteen minutes, and then Jodi exhaled in a long sibilant sigh and whispered, "My God, it feels good to lie down."

"This sure turned into a mess," I answered. I was beginning to feel very sorry for myself.

"Poor Harvey," she murmured. She rolled over her side—demonstrating, in the process, that we were aboard a bed with a particularly virulent squeak—and patted my arm consolingly. "Fate was against us," she whispered.

"I'm sorry about that thing in the park," I said.

"Hush. It wasn't your fault."

"Damn it, Jodi."

"Poor Harvey," she whispered again, and leaned over to kiss me on the cheek. When she did so, her breast brushed my arm, hard and electric.

Passion, in a manner of speaking, came back in a rush.

Squeak! went the bed, as I flipped over onto my side and gathered Jodi into my arms. *Squeak!* it went again, as she pressed herself close against me, and then all was silence as we kissed, kissing with lips and tongues and hands and pushing bodies.

The feel of her beneath my hand, her breasts crushed against my chest, her hair around my face, drove me in seconds to the same fever pitch that had originally taken me all afternoon to work up. I kissed her, caressed her body, and she responded like the passionate nymph she was.

Squeak! went the bed as I pushed her over onto her back again, and *squeak!* it went once more, as I followed, moving at her and *squeak!* and *squeak!* and *squeak!* and *squeaksqueaksqueaksqueak*....

Long and painful as the frustration of the afternoon and evening and night had been, I was suddenly grateful for it. If I had been able to take Jodi at once, this afternoon, right off the bat, it would have been fast and furious and finished before barely begun. Even had our commingling in the park been consummated, it wouldn't have been the love that lasts. But the day's events had temporarily aged my body somewhat. No longer the randy rooster, picapicapica*puc,* I was now a mighty javelin in my very first marathon mating.

The sweat started from us, our bodies were slick and hot in the dark on the wrinkling sheets. Jodi, but eighteen then, was even less experienced than I, and at first she simply lay passive, receiving me, but the force of the rhythm awoke her body, and all at once she surged beneath me, and the bed screamed, and she moved as lustily as I. Her moaning gasping breath was hot in my ear, her arms clutched my back, her body drove and drove. Like a rolling liner on the rolling sea we rolled together.

I felt her passion climbing, up and up, and knew myself to still be strong, and knew I would last, and when she went rigid beneath me, nails sunk in the flesh of my back, legs straining upward, head arched back, I only drove harder and harder and harder still, and it wasn't till the second time for her that I finally surged to immobility, and held my breath, and squeezed my eyes shut, and bit the soft flesh of her shoulder.

We lingered together, calming slowly, our breathing gradually becoming more normal, and at last I moved over to my own side of the bed again, and Jodi kissed me, and we fell asleep in one another's arms.

We awoke late the next morning, both ravenous. We left the bar-hotel, had breakfast together at a diner, and I called one of our compatriots from last night, who promised to drive out for us at once. While waiting, Jodi and I, incredibly conspicuous on the quiet streets of Ylicaw in our bathing suits, strolled and window-shopped and held hands and, whenever no one could see us, touched one another in fond reminiscence.

Our driver, apologizing profusely for last night's oversight—for which we were, of course, no longer *angry*—arrived at about two in the afternoon, and drove us back. We had already worked out our story, and told everyone that we had been picked up by the police for wandering around in bathing suits in the park at midnight, and had spent the night in separate cells in the local hoosegow. Jodi told all her girlfriends that, and I told the same story to all the guys in the dormitory. But I, in my telling, made damn sure no one was going to believe me. Jodi was too lovely a conquest, too desirable a bedmate, for me, at callow and loud-mouthed nineteen, to be able to keep it all a secret....

TALKING together now, Jodi more desirable and more exciting than ever in that green knit dress with the revealed expanse of thigh, we laughed over that first time, and Jodi said, "In a way, I'm glad the cop caught us. That bed was a lot softer than the ground in the park." She gave me a melting smile. "And you were a lot firmer."

TWO

IF HELEN HAD been waiting for me, preferably nervous and dynamically concerned, I could at least have permitted myself the luxury of delicious guilt feelings. But such luck was not to be mine. The train let me off and the chrome-plated ranch wagon was waiting for me, emptily metallic. I turned a key in it and drove along tree-lined streets to our little hate-nest among the crab grass. I buried the car in the carport—garages are sadly out of style; all that space to waste on cars that don't fit in them anyway—and I walked around to look at the outside of our deluxe split-level colonial.

There is something reassuringly schizoid about a split-level to begin with. Ours looks as though it couldn't possibly continue to exist if the various floors were level all across the board. The imbalance of its design is essential if it's going to survive all the concentrated imbalance of the people who live in it. But when you take this split-level and make it colonial as well—colonial, for the love of the lord—well, the result is nice to visit, but wouldn't you just *hate* to live there?

The other car, Detroit's most recent attempt to barrelhouse into the compact field, was missing. It stood to reason that Helen was missing as well. She never goes anywhere without the car—in fact I was once thinking of buying her a bicycle to get into the house from the carport—and by extension the car never goes anywhere without her. I rang the bell anyway, sort of for the hell of it. If a doorbell rings and there's nobody in the house, did it really ring? It really rang. I heard it. Then I opened the door with my key and went inside.

Experience told me to go first to the kitchen. It's an electric kitchen, of course. Electric range, electric icebox, electric garbage disposal, electric washing machine, electric dishwasher, electric frying pan, electric sink, electric pop-up toaster. The sad thing is that if you put your head in the oven you can't turn on the gas. You can only turn on the electricity. Shocking, but harmless.

The kitchen had a pegboard. It came with the kitchen, of course, and it is a huge flattened-out cork shaped like a kidney where husbands and wives leave notes for each other. A last-ditch attempt at eliminating conversation forever from the domestic scene. I looked at the pegboard and there, of course, was a note from Helen.

Harv—it began, quaintly enough. *Couldn't wait dinner for you. The girls are playing at Betty's tonight. You know the number if something comes up.* Now what in the world could come up? I pushed onward. *There's a teevee dinner in the fridge. Just pop it on the stove and eat hearty.* The note was unsigned but I had a fairly sound idea who had written it.

I opened the fridge and stared thoughtfully at the teevee dinner. It was a Dexter Frozen Dinner. A Square Deal on a Square Meal, I thought. And just how square could you get? It was unsettling. I was selling my own wife.

I took out the teevee dinner, the Dexter Frozen Dinner thoughtfully provided by Harvey Christopher's Frozen Wife. I put it on the electric range and turned the dial. The burner unit glowed like neon. I looked at Dexter's creation—pieces of unhappy chicken swimming with leaden wings through a sea of à la king. I watched the green peas in one section of the aluminum foil container grow slowly warm. The frozen French fries thawed and heated.

When the chicken bubbled the dish was prepared. Scientific eating. Scientific cooking. I took the container—dishes are a waste of time, of course, even with an electric dishwasher to care for them, and besides you can only get them in boxes of soap, and soap makes too many suds and is harmful to your new automatic, and—I took the container into the family-style living room carpeted protectively from wall to wall to hide the bad job they'd done on the floor, and I sat down in a chair no more comfortable than it looked. I placed the container on the arm of the chair, then flicked the remote switch that clued in the television set to the fact that someone, by God, was eating a teevee dinner, and while the set woke up and came to life I plunged a fork into the chicken mess and brought it to my mouth. I chewed it—it wasn't really necessary, because the Dexterino people sort of chew the food *for* you, scientifically, of course, as an unbeatable aid to digestion. A western was happening on the screen. I studied it for a moment, pausing before attempting another forkful of Dexter's Death Warmed Over.

And I thought about Jodi, and bed with Jodi, and Jodi's happy apartment on Lexington in the very heart of Madcap Manhattan. Jodi's apartment was not schizoid. It didn't even have a sunken living room. It was all on one level, as, for that matter, was Jodi.

And something happened. I reached for the remote switch and killed the television set in the middle of a howdy. I stood up, slowly but quite firmly, and I carried the Dexter's Frozen Tundra to the bathroom.

The toilet wasn't electric but it tried. I poured the teevee dinner into it. There was no chain to pull, no handle to yank. There was instead a pedal on the floor. I trod lightly upon the pedal and the toilet gurgled pleasantly at me while Dexter's Frozen Folderol disappeared to wherever bad food goes when it dies.

I had a shaker of martinis mixed before I remembered that I didn't really like martinis. I poured them down the toilet and pedaled the pedal. It was damned enjoyable. Then I looked for the Scotch, and we were out of it. I started for the carport, stopped suddenly, and returned to the kitchen. I scrawled a note for Helen *Hel*—it began. *Went out for Scotch. Couldn't wait until you got home.* I didn't sign it, because I figured she would know who it was from.

Then I got into the ranch wagon and pointed it at Manhattan. I didn't really have to do much more than that. The car knew the way. I pointed it, and I let it drive, which it did very well with its automatic transmission and its power steering and its power brakes and its power windows and power doors. And while we rode along, the car and I, I thought about Jodi some more, and about me. My mind must have been as properly primed as the car. The memories flowed easily....

IT was a strange affair, if you could call it an affair. I don't think you could. *Affair* means several things, and none of the things is what we had. *Affair*

means contemporary adultery, or it means modern people having a go at it, or it means a Radcliffe girl having a mad fling before she marries a stock-broker's son. And Jodi and I were none of these things, so what we had wasn't really an affair, evidently.

But whatever it was, it was fine with me. We were at college, and we were young, and there is no better time nor place for falling happily and heedlessly into the hay. We were at college, and we were young, and we were not in love, and we realized this.

After the wonderful night in the wonderful hotel, after the wonderful leading up to it and the wonderful doing it and the wonderful lying there and thinking about it, there was a period of about a week during which I avoided Jodi. No, that's not it, not quite. I didn't avoid her like the plague, or walk away when I saw her coming, or steer clear of her favorite haunts. I simply made no attempt to seek her out. Our paths did not cross by accident and I did not cause them to cross by design.

I suppose I was shy, or embarrassed, or merely young. It was the way my mind worked at that period of my life. I had made love to Jodi, and it had been more fun than a beer-drinking contest, but it was over. Make love to her again? Hell, man, I already *did!* Why do it again, for God's sake?

Fear of foreign alliances, perhaps, or fear of rejection, or just stupidity. But I went on with classes and beer and rides and assorted nonsense, and I dated a few girls and caressed their breasts. Their breasts were nice, if not quite so nice as Jodi's. And at that stage of my life, the skirt of one girl was much the same as the skirt of another. If something was missing with those other girls I was barely conscious of it. Something *was* missing, of course. I didn't get to sleep with them. But I would, in due time, and I was busy making plans.

Then I ran into Jodi. Quite literally, as a matter of fact. I was strolling down the campus oblivious to mostly everything, and so was she. I didn't see her coming and I don't know whether she saw me or not, but we bumped chests, always a nice way to say hello. She started to topple over and I grabbed her and hoisted her upright again and we looked deeply into one another's eyes. I remember feeling very ashamed of myself and not knowing why.

"Harvey," she said. "I've missed you."

There was not much to say, so I mulled bashfully and took her arm. "Buy you a beer," I suggested.

"Wine," she said.

The liquor store in the silly little town closed at dusk. "I don't have any wine," I said. "And it's too late to buy any. Unless you want to go to the bar." I left the rest unsaid. You didn't go to the bar for anything but beer. If you had hard liquor you were a lush. If you had wine you were obviously trying too hard. So the hell with it.

"I have wine," she said, "In my room."

"Fine. Where will we drink it?"

"In my room."

I thought that one over. It was against the rules, a boy and a girl in a dormitory room, but so, for that matter, was a love bout in a faraway hotel. As seems to be usual, the rules of the college had little connection with reality. But, since the fundamental rule was *Don't get caught,* this being a Spartan sort of a college, and since we stood a great chance of getting caught in her room, I was a little bit worried.

"We'll get caught," I said.

She tossed her head, sort of, and looked every inch a queen. I mean it. There was something regal about her, something I should have been able to notice long ago. It was an air that said that she not only didn't give a warmed-over damn for the rules but that the punishment was equally unimportant to her. A sound attitude. One that I, unfortunately, was unable to carry off.

"If they catch us," I said, "they'll give us the old heave-ho. We won't graduate."

"So what?"

"You need a diploma," quoth I, "to be a success."

"At what?"

I wondered at what, since I had not made up my mind just what I was going to be a success at. There was a cartoon once which summed things up—a guidance counselor studying a small boy, both counselor and boy wearing thick glasses. *But Arnold,* said the caption, plaintively, *it's not enough to be a genius. You have to be a genius AT something.* That was I, with *success* instead of *genius.* I was majoring, theoretically, in English, which meant that I read books instead of tables. But I didn't want to be a writer or a reader or, God save us, a professor.

"At something," I said to Jodi.

"If you come up to my room," she said, "and if we drink the wine there, you are going to be a success. At something. At something that's fun." And she stepped so close to me that I could feel her. We were smack dab in the middle of the campus, and there were probably people around, and I did not care. Her breasts bumped into me and I remembered them—in the water, in the bed, firm and lovely in my hands. She did something with her hips, sort of throwing them at me. and I remembered things that were very nice to remember.

I looked at her. She was in uniform—sweater and skirt, saddle shoes. I looked at her and sweater and skirt melted away in a dissolve no Hollywood studio could attempt to duplicate. I saw a naked Jodi in Technicolor and cinemascope. She bounced at me again and naked breasts banged into me, naked hips offered themselves.

I had nothing to say. But I had things to do. I took her arm in my arm, possessive as a papa bear, and off we went to the little dormitory room that she called home.

"The best way," she said, "is nonchalance. We'd better not try to sneak in. If we do, somebody will see us, and we'll look sneaky. That's no good."

That sounded reasonable enough.

"But if we walk in as though we have every reason in the world to be there," she went on, "we'll look natural enough. They'll think we're studying together or something."

"We will be."

She giggled a charming giggle. "Studying," she mused. "It's a shame. I mean, you ought to get a diploma for it. If you're good enough."

"So you think you'd be good enough?" Remember, she was less experienced than I was. Not many people could have made that statement. So here, for a change, I was the Voice of Authority, the old man on the mountain, the accomplished lecher teaching the young prodigy how to get ahead on a horizontal basis.

"Practice," she said, "makes perfect."

"So let's practice."

Her room was on the third floor of the sterile brick dormitory. She led the way and up the stairs we went. A girl met us, stopped to chat. We chatted amiably about something or other. And, incredibly, it was working. The girl noticed me, all right. And there I was, leading the lovely Jodi up the primrose stairway, and there was this girl, noticing the fact and thinking nothing of it. Nonchalance, then, was the ticket.

Then we were in the room. Jodi, happily, did not have a roommate. She barely had a room. It was the single, the room the architects had made a mistake about, the little cubicle crouched precariously across the narrow hall from the community bathroom. The room had a bed, sort of, and a dresser, and an excuse for a closet. The dresser and the closet were unnecessary for the time being. The bed was there—inviting, beckoning—and we were there—hungry, eager—and the wine was there, red and sour.

"I really would like some wine," she said. "Unless you're in a hurry."

There was something strange about that line. We were there to make love, you see, and her attitude was that, while she'd like to sip Chianti and talk for a moment or two, she'd be perfectly willing to stretch out on the rack if I was in a rush. Generosity? No, more than that. Here was a girl who understood the place of woman in the total scheme of things. Here was a girl who knew the proper position of woman in the social order.

"Let's have some wine, then."

"We'll have to drink it out of the bottle."

I said that was fine, and she yanked out the cork, and she took a drink. She could drink magnificently. I watched with mute admiration while the level of wine in the bottle went steadily down. Then she passed the bottle to me. I almost wiped off the neck instinctively, the way you always do when someone hands you a bottle, but I remembered that I was going to make love to this girl in a minute or two and there didn't seem to be much point in such health precautions. I drank, taking as much as she had taken, and passed the bottle back to her.

She finished it and heaved it at the wastebasket. It missed and struck first the wall and then the floor. It bounced twice on the floor before it cracked, and when it cracked it did not fool around. It shattered into splintered glass.

"Damn," she said thoughtfully. "We'd better not go barefoot. Not over there, anyhow."

She turned to me. We were sitting on the edge of that very narrow bed, and when she turned to me I took her in my arms and I kissed her. It was not one of those kisses that sent a striking bolt of passion shooting through the last atom of one's being. It was a much more contemplative sort of kiss. She was there, and I was there too, and our mouths were together and it was nice.

Her lips parted and my tongue stole past them like a thief in the night.

The kiss was long. It was one of those slow kisses that let us think over and decide that everything was going very well indeed. The kiss ended and she stood up. She peeled the sweater over her head. She was not wearing a bra, and it was just as well, because if she had been I would have torn the damned thing off of her. She did not need a bra—it would have been like harnessing a whirlwind. The whirlwind was unharnessed and my hands reached for cool soft flesh. Her nipples were buds a-blooming.

"That's nice," she said. "Very nice. When you stroke them and like that. It feels good." There was something detached about her words and about the way she said them, as if she were carefully taking stock of just what I was doing and just how good it felt. I bent down and put one of those nipples to lips and she very suddenly stopped talking. Her muscles went tense and then her body began to move with something that had to be passion.

"Let me take everything off," she said. "All my clothes. Then we can fool around for a while and then we can do it. But I don't want to mess my skirt."

"Fine," I said. It may well go down in history as the understatement of the century.

She got undressed. Rather, the skirt flowed off of her, and the panties flowed off of her, and the silly saddle shoes fell from her feet, and the socks followed them, and everything that I was looking at belonged to Jodi, and consequently to me as well.

"You like?"

A silly question.

"Now you get undressed, Harvey. I want to watch. Unless you're bashful."

If I was, I decided, I could get over it. I felt a wee bit self-conscious stripping my clothes off, especially the way she stared at me with a cross between curiosity and desire, but I managed.

"You like?" I asked. I had to say *something.*

"Mmmmmm."

And then toppled we to the bed, as Time might put it. And then kissed we, as backward rolled sentences while whirled the mind. And then fondled we, and stroked me, and touched we, and then, whee!

"Harvey—"

I wondered what she wanted.

"Harvey, do you have a thing?"

I was lost.

"So I won't get a baby," she said.

"Oh."

"Because that wouldn't be any good. Getting a baby, I mean. Inconvenient."

I did not have a thing. For weeks I had carried one around in my wallet, just as most college students do. But, sad to say, I had used it. Before I met Jodi. Before I got next to Jodi, anyway. And, thinking about it, I had an unhappy thought.

"Last time—"

She was right there with me. "Last time," she said, "there was nothing to worry about. But—"

"I don't have one."

"Then we can't do it."

That was something to ponder. "We can start to," I said thoughtfully. "And before anything happens, we can stop, and then—"

"A friend of mine did that."

"Yeah? What happened?"

"She had a baby."

"Oh," I said hollowly. "Then...do you want to wait while I...uh...find a drugstore?"

Alarm was an ugly black shadow across her pretty face. "That will take too long," she said. "I couldn't possibly wait. It would tear me apart."

I had to admit that I couldn't wait either. The dilemma grew. And grew. And grew.

"Harvey," she said plaintively. "Harvey, there is a way. I...you might not like it. I mean, it's not...some people would say it isn't normal. If that makes a difference. But I wouldn't get a baby that way."

I asked her what way she meant and she told me.

Is there anyone in the world so prudish as a college boy? The young lotharic type, out to conquer the female half of the universe, is in his own weak way as puritanical as any spinster from here to Bessarabia. If they have spinsters in Bessarabia. And I was quite roundly shocked.

But I was also quite roundly ready, and it was easier to conceal the shock than the evidence of my interest in Jodi. So I reached for her, playing the scene by ear as it were, and it began.

It was her first time at that particular fun-and-games method, but she took to it like a mallard to hydrous oxide, and away we went, off into outer space. It was good, and it was fun, and Jodi's particular brand of Scotch was chosen forever.

I spent the night with her. Ill-advised, in a way—any damned fool could have wandered into her little room and loused things up for both of us as far as the college was concerned. But I was unable to see myself tiptoeing out of the girl's dorm at three in the morning. Nonchalance is only good for so long. Then the roof falls in on you.

So we topped the world by being a bit much in the line of nonchalance. We slept, body to body, and when we woke up the idea of her getting pregnant seemed far less important, and we risked it. Then she went off to breakfast, bringing me a very modest repast in a paper bag, and we crawled back in the sack for another go at it.

I left that dorm at high noon and no one looked at me twice.

Youth. She didn't get pregnant from that delightful evening. And after that I was careful, very careful. And, for some reason which eluded me then but which was very important nevertheless, my conquest became a secret one. I suppose it was Jodi's change in status from conquest to partner. We were having an affair, not playing a seduction scene. There was no need to ply her with liquor, to woo her with words of love, to con her in one perverse way or another. There was no need to do anything but ask her, and that was enough.

I was clever and conscientious. I kept up-to-date in my scholastic endeavors, such as they were. I slept alone, confining our amours to an hour here and an hour there. I worked at my books and I gave her the hours that were left, because school was important and the future, the glowing shiny chrome-plated future, it was more important. And Jodi—well, Jodi was important, too, because Jodi was a valuable outlet and a pleasant way to spend an hour here and an hour there. But Jodi was not important enough.

"It's a shame," she said, one afternoon on a blanket on the golf course—a common abode of lovers; no one in the history of the college ever committed the cardinal sin of playing *golf* there, for the love of God—"that you don't love me. And that I don't love you."

"Why?"

"I don't know," she said, dreamily, her hand doing magical things. "I don't know, exactly. Except that I think it would be nice."

"Love," I said. "Nice."

"Kind of."

I put my hand inside her blouse and felt a nipple stiffen. I caressed and she purred. I put another hand up her skirt and she gasped. Not a gasp of surprise and not a gasp of passion but something harder to define. As if she was thrilled by the fact that I was touching her and that she was responding, and wasn't it nice?

It was that. And the afternoon was a trip to the moon on the gossamer-est of wings, and, in the words of the bard, the world moved. No sleeping bag, but you can't have everything.

She remembered the next day. "Love," she said.

"Love," I said. "Moon and June. Do you know that there are only four words in the English language that rhyme with love?" I told her erroneously.

She hadn't known that.

"Glove, dove, shove and above," I said. "Want to write a poem? Sing a song?"

She didn't. She wanted to be somber. "I don't think I'll ever fall in love," she said. "I'd like to, kind of. But I don't think it will ever happen to me."

It was the regal Jodi speaking, the far-off look in the lovely eye. One did not speak when the queen spoke. One listened thoughtfully and hung on every word.

"Some women are made for love," she said, "and some are not. I'm made for sex, I guess. Or something like that. But not for love."

"How can you tell?"

The spell was broken the mood shattered. Wherever she had been, she was there no longer. "Let's make love," she said happily. "Or let's make sex. Let's make something, for goodness sake, and let's do it as well as we possibly can." Which was very well indeed....

I garaged the car, not wanting to carry the memory any further. It had carried me as far as Manhattan and that was quite far enough. Any more would be bad, because the only course for memory to follow was the course of an affair that went downhill from there in a way I did not enjoy reminiscing about. And after that there were ten more years of my life to consider, and the less I considered them, the better.

So I garaged the car and paid the man and walked into Manhattan. I don't know what I was looking for, exactly, except that I was thirsty. The bar I found was on 47th Street between Fifth and Madison. It was late, businesswise, but the boys were still there.

I heard phrases that I didn't want to listen to. I heard the fey patter and the unhip hipness, and I drank Vat 69 and did not talk to anybody. I was roundly bored, and the only thing that could have been more boring was the little split-personality home in Rockland County, with or without my barren witch aboard to louse things up.

The liquor was good and I drank quite a bit of it. I'd had no dinner, of course—just a mouthful of Dexter's Deflavored Dishwater—and I still had a little of the edge from the Scotch I'd shared with Jodi. And the more I drank the more sploshed I got, and the more sploshed I got the less I wanted to spend the evening sitting in an ad man's bar.

I left the place, left the unasked-for twist of lemon curling around the rim of my glass, and I walked. I did not know where I was going.

I was actually surprised when I found out that I was on Lexington Avenue. Surprised, but not confused. Lexington rang its bell at once and I knew where I was and why, and I only hoped she wasn't busy with a customer.

I stopped for a drink on the way. Then I stopped again, this time in a liquor store, and I asked the clerk for a bottle of Vat 69. He gave it to me and took my money and I waltzed out into the street again.

The desk clerk at her hotel called her on the phone. "Let me talk to him," she must have said, because he presented me with the receiver and I held it to my ear.

"Harvey," she said, sounding pleased. Her voice was a throaty whisper. "Honey, can you come back in half an hour? Or forty-five minutes, that would be better. I'm busy right now, honey, but forty-five minutes—"

I found a bar for the forty-five minutes. I felt silly, paying bar prices for liquor with a paper bag full of better liquor at my foot. I felt even sillier, waiting for three quarters of an hour to see a girl I'd seen that afternoon, waiting until my friend, who happened to be a whore, got rid of her guest, who could only be a customer. I drank a little more than I'd planned on drinking and when I left the bar and returned to the hotel, exactly forty-five minutes after I had talked to her, I was pretty well stoned.

The desk clerk recognized me, called up, spoke softly for a moment or three, and gave me the nod. The elevator took me to her floor and her door was open, her face smiling at me.

"Harvey," she said, looking at me oddly. "Is something wrong, baby?"

"Long time no see," I muttered vacantly. I poured myself into her room and her arms swallowed me.

THREE

I WAS TWENTY-TWO. A lovely age to be; I hadn't been twenty-two for years. *How many years? No, no, that required counting, and counting hurt the head, and there was the dim possibility I would wake up. Voices murmured.*

Back, back, back down into unconsciousness. Where was I? I was twenty-two.

Yes, that's it. I was twenty-two, and it was summer. Oh, my *God,* was it summer! It was summer like the inside of an oven, which one shared with the biggest klieg light of them all. Too hot and too bright, and the humidity was fantastic. The air was about eighty per cent water; one didn't walk down the street, one did the breaststroke. And that's the only kind of breaststroke one did; it was much too hot for any other kind, and besides that I was living at the Y.

That's it! I was twenty-two, and it was summer, and it was New York, and I was living at the Y. "I'm going to New York after graduation," I said to everybody. "But I hear it's awful expensive to live in New York. I don't know what to do about an apartment." And everybody said. "Live at the Y. It's cheap, and it's clean." So I lived at the Y.

And nobody told me I was going to be pawed surreptitiously all the time. And in that heat, too. All these heavy-breathing dark-eyed boys prowling the clean cheap halls at the Y, panting. They were the only things around hotter than the sidewalks.

And the sidewalks were hot. I walked on them, and the bottoms of my shoes got hot. And then I walked some more, and the bottoms of my feet got hot. And then my feet, which were encased by shoes, got hot. And then my ankles got hot. And then I walked into a bar and sat down at a table, because I couldn't take my shoes off if I sat on a stool at the bar, and I spent a dime of what was left of my savings on a glass of draft, and I sat holding the cold glass in both hands and wiggling my toes. I was twenty-two, and despite it all it was delicious to be alive.

A man came over to my table. It was three-thirty in the afternoon, there were only about eight or nine people in the entire bar, and this man came over to my table. He wasn't one of the ones like at the Y, he was one of the ones like at the bar, gray-suited and somber-faced, with twenty-year-old bodies and thirty-year-old faces and forty-year-old jowls and fifty-year-old appetites for booze.

This man came over to my table. "You've got your shoes off," he said.

I was twenty-two and my shoes were off and it was delicious to be alive. "By God, sir," I said, "you are absolutely right."

"I think that's great," he said. He wasn't drunk, but then he wasn't sober either. He waved a hand that more or less held a glass containing an amber fluid and two clear unfogged ice cubes with holes in their tummies. "I think that's absolutely great," he said, expanding on his last remark, and added, "Mind if I sit down?"

"By all means, sir," I said. I was twenty-two, and I called everyone over twenty-five 'sir,' because that's the way I was brought up, buddy.

He sat down, lowered the glass to the black Formica table top, and leaned forward to study me, one might say, piercingly. After too long a time of this activity, he straightened up, leaned forward again, and said, "You married?"

"Not as yet," I said, so there would be no misunderstanding.

"Hah!" he cried, and sloshed drink on the Formica "I knew it," he announced. "The minute I looked at you, and I saw your shoes was off—were off—I said to myself, 'There is a free man. That man over there with his shoes off is not married to anybody at all, not even once.' That's what I said to myself."

"You converse rather well," I complimented him. God, it was *delicious* to be alive!

"Do you want to know something?" he asked me. Accepting my millisecond of silence for consent, he hastened on. "I have been coming into this bar every afternoon," he announced, adding parenthetically and inaccurately, "at the coffee break, for the last eight years. Summer, winter, hot weather, rainy weather, *all* of that stuff. And do you want to know something?"

"Something else?" I asked him.

"I have never," he said emphasizing his words by rhythmically sloshing drink in the general neighborhood, "never in all that time seen anyone in here take off his shoes. What do you think of that?"

"Not much," I said.

"Exactly!" he cried.

At that moment, a waiter came by. I could tell he was a waiter by the filthy apron wrapped round his middle. Everything else in the bar, including the bartender, the customers, the glasses, the tables and the floor, all were clean, except this dour-faced man in his rape-of-Troy apron. "You can't have your shoes off in here," is what he said to me.

I had just about decided that my shoes were getting a lot more attention than they deserved. They were just a cheap pair of old black shoes. I'd worn them for three years now, practically all the way through college. Not to bed, of course, but almost always else.

The man opposite me said, "Never mind," to the waiter.

The waiter looked at him, and then looked questioningly at the bartender over there, and the bartender shook his head in a leave-them-alone gesture, and I knew at once that I was talking to an Important Man, and I thought of all the success stories I knew which opened in bars, but practically all of them were sexual, so I dropped that line of thought. I was living in the Y, and it had been five weeks since I had last seen Jodi, and there was little likelihood I would ever see her again, and I hadn't yet found a job so that I could have an apartment and meet girls and start all over again with someone else, so I did my level best not to even think about sex. The heat helped, that way.

The Important Man then said, "What's your line, my friend? "

"I don't have one yet," I admitted. "I came to New York three weeks ago," I explained, "armed with my brand-new sheepskin, and I've been prowling the streets, turning down management-trainee jobs, ever since."

"Good," he said. "What kind of college? You an engineer or something? Or what?"

Did I look like an engineer? "It was a Liberal Arts College," I said, rather stiffly, "and quite a good one at that, where I obtained a Bachelor of Arts, with a major in English, primarily American and British Literature."

"Now, what the hell," he said. He looked at me, frowning, puzzled, obviously ready and willing to learn something. "Now what the hell did you do that for?" he asked me.

I blinked. I'm sure I did. "What the hell did I do what for?" I parried.

"Get your degree," he explained patiently, "in English. Now, you could of got your degree in anything you wanted, history or science or even philosophy, and you could of been adapted into American industry, some way or another. But English? Let me tell you something, my friend. By the way, the name's Tom Stanton."

"Harvey Christopher," I told him, and we solemnly shook hands. His hand was wet. From the drink. I surreptitiously dried my hand on my trousers.

"Let me tell you something, Harv," he said, for which I never forgave him. After all, I had been calling *him* 'sir.' "It's this way," he went on, ignoring my reaction. "American industry, now, distrusts the English major. And for very good reasons, too. The English major is very liable to be a guy who thinks like mad, all the time, but what he's thinking about is very rarely much use to American industry. You see what I mean? What, do you figure to be—a writer?"

"No," I said. "Nothing like that. I would simply like to get a job in American industry. But not, frankly, any of the management trainee positions I've been offered in the last few weeks. They look very much like dead-end streets to me."

"You're right there," he said at once. "There, you are one hundred per cent right. Tell me something, Harv? What do you think about advertising?"

"Advertising? I don't suppose I've ever thought much about it at all," I admitted, "except when a particularly horrendous singing commercial comes on the radio."

"Sure," he said. "But what about advertising men? You know, the scapegoats, the ones the people all the time make the funny remarks about. What about them?"

"What *about* them?" I asked him right back.

"Have you ever thought of being one?"

I hadn't. I said so, adding, "Though now that you mention it, it sounds like a good idea. After all, an English major—"

He shook his head. "English majors," he said somberly, "come to advertising agencies only long enough to soak up the atmosphere. Then they go write a nasty book. Either that, or they stay around forever and have guilt feelings, and they keep missing work and coming in the next day with a note from their psychiatrist. That's the way it is with English majors in advertising."

I considered the problem, wriggling my toes beneath the table, After due consideration, I said, "I don't think I'd be that way."

"Neither do I," he said at once. "I think you're the exception to the rule. There's an exception to every rule, you know."

"I'd heard rumors," I admitted.

"The minute I looked at you," he said, starting off on that again, "and saw you sitting there with your shoes off, I said to myself, 'There's an exception to the rule.' And I think I was right. You want a job?"

There were a million possible things to say. I said, "What?"

There were a million possible things *he* could have said, too. He said, "A job."

My keen analytical mind flashed hither and yon over our preceding conversation, correlating, comparing, combining implications, grouping subject matters, following the thin threads of cortical reasoning, and in less than a second I had the whole knotty problem doped out. "You mean," I said, "a job in advertising."

"You have," he said indistinctly, "a keen analytical mind. A job in advertising is *exactly* what I mean."

"Well," I said. "Gosh. I hadn't exactly thought much about it."

"Harv," he said with the disgusting familiarity that is so prevalent in certain otherwise-genteel sections of this city, "I'll tell you who I am. Ever heard of MGSR&S?"

I allowed as how I hadn't.

"Well," he said, "I'm S sub-two."

My keen analytical mind couldn't quite analytic that one. Apparently my mental floundering showed on my face, because he returned to English. "MGSR&S," he told me, "is Manning, Greenville, Silverstein, Rorschach and Stanton. Stanton is me."

"Ah," I said. "I see."

He looked at his watch. "Coffee break's over," he said, and engulfed the liquid in the glass. He spared the ice cubes. "Come on over to the office," he suggested, rising with surprising steadiness to his feet, "and well talk it over "

"Why, thank you," I said. I stood, and we started toward the door. We'd gone no more than five paces when he looked at me oddly, and said, "Don't you want your shoes?"

"Oh, yes!" I exclaimed. "My shoes!"

I went back to the table, feeling like a fool, and fished around among the crumpled cigarette packages until I found my shoes. Shod, I returned to Stanton, S sub-two. He was surveying me somewhat oddly.

I felt called upon to defend myself, albeit timidly. "It's the first time I ever forgot them," I said. It was a weak defense.

"That's all right," he said. "Come along." A bit of doubt had come into his voice. Perhaps he was growing more sober, and the prospect of hiring a man solely on the basis of him having his shoes off no longer seemed so enjoyable to him.

But I was twenty-two, and it was summer, and I was newly in New York, and the unreality of this man's conversation and job offer was of such a high level that I wasn't a bit confused or worried or nervous during the following employment interview, and I got the job.

And so I learned about advertising.

Do you know about advertising? When an otherwise-desirable young lady appears on your television screen and, to a Neanderthalic melody, sings, "Winky dinky hinky rink, Goolash beer is the beer to drink," do you have the idea that it all came out of her own little head in just a second or two? Well, you're wrong. Shakespeare wrote *Macbeth* in less time than it took a whole staff of people at MGSR&S to write those eleven words. Of course, Shakespeare had the edge. He just used English; he didn't have to *make up* exciting new words, like 'winky.'

I won't go into the entire hierarchy and nomenclature of an advertising agency, of the little bitsy contribution of every member of that crowd to the epic quoted above. I am not avoiding this naming of parts out of a fear of boring the reader, I am doing so out of a fear of boring *me*. Twelve years, let me tell you, can be a long long time.

I *will* tell you however, out of an obvious bid for sympathy, what *my* contribution to that Cro-Magnon couplet was. I made it rhyme. When it came to me, the meter had already been established—though the melody hadn't yet surged out of our symphonic department—and the first line read (do you mind?), "Goulash beer is hotsy tots." I changed 'hotsy tots' to 'hinky dink.' Someone else changed the first half of the line, and altered my contribution to hinky *rink*. Whether one man added winky and one man added dinky or one man doubted up and added both words I don't know. Having contributed of my talents already, I slept through the rest of the conferences. And, at those rare conferential moments when I was awake, I wiled the time away drawing nonsensical pictures on my notepad.

Such was my job, but I didn't begin at that exalted level. Oh, no, one doesn't simply step into an important job like that. I began in the mailroom.

(I seem to be waking up. I'd much rather not wake up; if I do my head will explode. People are talking, I can hear the murmur of their conversation distantly, and I don't imagine I want them to start talking to me. I must go back to sleep. Be twenty-two again, remember back, float back and down, back and down, find something on which to pin my floating psyche and avoid consciousness.)

Laura Gray.

Ah, yes, Laura Gray. Her first name wasn't Laura, it was Natalie. And her last name wasn't Gray, it was Gregenbaum. Why is it that depressed minorities invariably express agreement with the unflattering opinions of their depressors?

At any rate I know these horrible secrets about Laura Gray because I snuck into the Personnel offices and looked at her records. I'm not sure why I did that except that I was twenty-two. And I would dearly have loved to have Laura Gray as the replacement for Jodi, and because Laura invariably cut me dead every time she saw me.

She was a secretary, Laura was. She was from the secretarial pool (I always get a picture of a bunch of laughing nude girls at a round shallow swimming pool with a statue of Cupid in the middle when I hear that phrase, don't you?) and she sat all day typing revelations granted her by a Dictaphone machine. My mailroom job consisted of distributing incoming mail all morning and picking up outgoing mail all afternoon, so I saw Laura Gray rather often, and she always cut me dead. After all, I was just a nobody from the mailroom.

Then I snuck into the Personnel office and found out her name and age and home address and other fascinating information and I went around smirking at her for a few days, and she went on cutting me just as dead as if I didn't know that she'd changed her name

Invariably, she irked me. There finally came the day when she had irked me just a little too much, and I no longer even *wanted* her to replace

Jodi. On that fateful day, out of a meanness of spirit that until then I hadn't known I possessed, I became snide with dear Laura Gray.

It was a Wednesday afternoon, and I was gathering correspondence from outbaskets all over the place. I paused beside Laura's desk, looking at her as she typed glaze-eyed the orders being whispered to her by the ubiquitous Dictaphone machine, and waited for her to notice me.

She did, at last, and raised her foot from the machine pedal, cutting off its dictation. "What do *you* want?" she demanded, and there was a whole world of scorn in those four syllables.

"I was just wondering," I said, my voice as sweet as blueberry pie.

"Wondering *what?"* she snapped, with Olympian impatience.

"If it's true what they say about Jewish girls," I said.

She blinked. *"What?"*

"You know. About it being sideways."

Now, of course there were about ten thousand possible answers to that remark, any one of which would have been enough to get me fired, but I just didn't care. I was irked. So I stood blandly and waited for her answer.

Lo and behold! The color fled her face at first, but then rushed right back again, all in the space of a second. And then she *smiled!* Laura *smiled!*

And said, all trace of hostility gone from her voice, "No, silly. That's *Chinese* girls."

"Oh, go on," I said. That's all I could manage, under the circumstances.

Laura was being very arch all of a sudden, smiling coyly and generally being flirtatious as all get-out. It just goes to show you, you never know the right approach.

At any rate, we discussed anatomy a little while longer, and before I returned to the mailroom we had made a date for that very night.

There are many similarities between the young man on Madison Avenue who works in the mailroom and a young man on Madison Avenue who works as, say, an account executive. They dress in precisely the same uniform, they wear precisely the same horn-rimmed glasses, they eat precisely the same lunch in precisely the same luncheonettes, they read precisely the same magazines, and they work precisely the same hours. There is only one difference between them. The account executive earns about five times as much as the mailroom boy.

Which is simply to say that I did not take Laura Gray to the Ruban Bleu. Nor did I take her to see a Broadway show. I took her to a cheap movie theater in the Village and we saw two depressing flicks from Italy. Then I took her to a cheap coffee house, and I swear the customers were the same people we'd just seen in the movies. And then I took her home. To *her* home, I mean. I was still living at the Y. Mailroom salaries and all that.

She lived up on West 69th Street, in one of those buildings that looks as though it must have grown like a tree because nobody in the world would be idiotic enough to *build* a building that way, and I accompanied her all the way up in the elevator and to her apartment door.

Where she said, "Thank you for a lovely evening." Scarcely original.

"The evening," I said, also with scant originality, "is a pup."

"I don't hear it barking," she said.

Now, there's no possible answer to a nonsense line like that. So I didn't try to answer it. Instead, I wrapped my manly arms around her womanly body, and I kissed her.

She kissed very well. She curved against me as though she wanted to be glued in place, and her fingers played at the back of my neck, and her waist was just the perfect size for my arm.

We broke at last, and she smiled. "Thank you again," she said, her voice huskier than normal.

"Thank *you,*" I said gallantly, and reached for her again.

She backed away, bumping into her apartment door. "I have to go to bed now," she said.

"Of course," I said.

"Now, Harvey," she said. "You've been a perfect gentleman all evening."

"Ridiculous," I exclaimed, stung to the quick. "Who did you think that was in the movie, the little old lady on the other side of you?"

"You know what I mean," she said, smiling again.

I coughed, not too convincingly. "I'm dying," I told her, "for a cup of coffee."

"That isn't what you're really after," she said. She was being coy again.

"Let's talk about it," I said, "while I drink the coffee."

"Well, all right."

She unlocked her door, and we went in. I drank the coffee—it was instant, and terrible—and then she started talking about me going home again. We were in the kitchen, so I merely backed her up against the refrigerator and kissed her again. She responded just as nicely as she had the last time. I was emboldened, certain that she was simply putting up token resistance, and so I started to waltz. Still kissing her, I waltzed her out of the kitchen and across the living room, headed for the bedroom beyond. But midway across the room she took the lead away from me and veered us away from the bedroom door and toward the sofa. I went along with the gag, figuring that if she wanted to make an intermediate stop it was okay with me, and we tumbled onto the sofa together, our arms still around one another and our lips still pressed firmly one to one.

When we came up for air at last, she murmured, "We shouldn't, Harv," and sort of wriggled against me.

"You're absolutely right," I told her, and unbuttoned her blouse.

We discussed the situation, amid kisses and caresses and other amusements, for about half an hour, which is to say until we were both nude. And then I suggested that it was time we went on into the bedroom.

"Harv, we shouldn't," she said, a line that was getting progressively sillier as we went along.

"At this point," I told her, "I think we absolutely should. Not only that, I think we must, if you see what I mean."

She giggled, seeing what I meant.

But she wouldn't get up from the sofa. And so, at last, I simply got to my feet, gathered her into my arms, and carried her into the bedroom, where I plopped her down on the bed during another, "Harv, we shouldn't."

Perhaps we shouldn't, but we did.

Did you ever see a fan with ribbons tied on the front grill? When the fan is turned on, the ribbons fly straight out, fluttering and jumping around like mad. Change this picture from the horizontal to the vertical, change the ribbons to arms and legs, and you have some idea what I had to contend with, once we decided to do that which we shouldn't.

Talk about explosions! Another thing those ribbons lack are claws. I was certain that by the time it was all over I was going to be black and blue everywhere except where I was clawed bright red. Very colorful, no doubt, but not too comfortable.

But such mundane thoughts cannot hold one's attention long under circumstances of that type, nor did they hold me for very long. I simply gave as good as I got, discovered that both of us enjoyed the mutual pummeling no end, and so we hurtled on across the bed to ecstasy.

When it was all over but the heavy breathing, Laura smiled at me and stroked my cheek with soft hands, and lit me a cigarette. I smoked it, contented, and Laura said, "You see? Not true at all."

"Must be the Chinese," I said.

After a while, we put our cigarettes out, turned out the light, and prepared ourselves for sleep. Shortly before sleep came, I whispered, "I'll get my things from the Y tomorrow."

She murmured, "Mmmmm." And we went to sleep...

...*Only to be awakened by somebody shaking my shoulder,* and a gruff male voice said, "Okay, buddy, you've slept it off long enough."

I tried to say, "Go away," but I think what actually came out was, "Gremmmfff."

"It's time to join the conversation, little man," said the gruff male voice.

I opened my eyes.

That was a mistake. In the first place, I wasn't twenty-two any more. In the second place, I wasn't in Laura Gray's bed any more, I was in Jodi's bed. In the *third place, I had* the kind of hangover that made Grant such a surly general. And in the fourth place, there was a man I'd never seen before leaning over me, waking me up.

I'd never seen him before. Up till that moment, I hadn't known how lucky I was. Now my luck had changed.

This guy would scare little children. This guy would also scare mothers and Marines and Mau Maus. He looked like a boxer who'd lost a close decision to a meat-grinder.

"Time to join the party, little man," this apparition told me. A meaty hand descended from on high and love-tapped me on the cheek. I think it loosened teeth.

"I'm awake," I said.

"Good boy," said the monster. He backed away, saying, "Now, sit up like a good little man."

I sat up, like a good little man, to discover that I wasn't in Jodi's bed after all, I was on Jodi's sofa in Jodi's living room. And I was fully dressed, including my shoes. I had slept with my shoes on and now my feet felt like boiled turnips. All puffy and yellow.

I sat there, blinking miserably, and slowly it came home to me that I was in a *woman's* apartment, but I had been awakened by a *man*.

A husband! No, that was ridiculous, Jodi was a whore. That didn't mean she couldn't have a husband, though I didn't think she did have one, but it did mean that her husband—real or hypothetical—would stay away from her place of work.

A policeman?

Maybe I was being arrested. Maybe it was a vice raid. That was a charming thought.

I peered blearily at the monster again. He might have been a policeman—there are policemen who have that orangutan quality—but he didn't seem particularly anxious to arrest me.

Then I noticed Jodi, sitting in the armchair across the room. She was still wearing the knit green dress, and still had one leg crossed over the other to reveal all that gleaming thigh, but now she was simply sitting there, her face a careful blank as she smoked a cigarette.

"Jodi," I said. "What's going on?"

"I'm about to tell you, little man," said the monster.

Jodi didn't look at me, she looked at the monster. "Al," she said, her voice tired, as though she didn't expect any answer at all, "why don't we just leave him alone? Harvey's a nice guy."

"Am I going to hurt him?" demanded Al. I would have liked to have known the answer to that one myself.

I said, "I have to go home."

"Not just yet," said Al. He pulled over a chair and sat down in front of me. He offered me a cigarette, and when we had both lighted up he said, "Now you're a married man, am I right?"

"Yes," I said.

"And Jodi here's a whore, right?"

"Yes," I said.

He pointed the cigarette to the right. "And that thing over on the table there is a camera, right?"

I just stared at it. It had one eye, and that eye was baleful.

"Now, little man," said Al cheerfully, "I got a proposition for you."

FOUR

NOW I HAVE gone through something very much like thirty-four years of reacting incorrectly. Whenever confronted by the sort of situation in which my response ought to be thoroughly predictable, I cross up the experts and do something wrong. When I was twelve, and cooped up in a coatroom with an apprentice Lolita, a warm-blooded moppet with auburn tresses who kissed me with lips and tongue, with arms tight around me and budding breasts rampant, I was not excited, not shocked, not even taken back. I stepped away from her and asked her, solicitous as a student nurse, what brand of toothpaste she used.

I could cite other examples, but this should suffice. Take heed—I am not boasting. Perhaps there is something wrong with me, perhaps certain cerebral connections have been disconnected within my cranial cavity. I do not know, nor do I particularly care. What I *do* know, as sure as Luther Burbank made little blue apples, is that I am a perennial source of disappointment to persons who bounce supposed-to-be-shocking bits of news off me.

I disappointed Al.

There I was, disturbingly respectable, thoroughly married and gainfully employed. And there was Jodi, recently ravished. And there was this camera which had purportedly caught us *in flagrante delectable*. According to all the established rules, I was supposed to fall on my knees and beg, or race to heave the camera through the nearest open or shut window, or simply do a lap-dissolve into saline tears.

Perhaps it was the afterglow of a tumble with Jodi—which had obviously taken place, and which had undoubtedly been enjoyable, and which, damn it to hell and back, I could not recall. Perhaps it was the Vat 69, which left me with no hangover but with a delicious sense of well-being and security. Perhaps it was the elementary fact that the possible loss of my Spiritless Spouse did not terrify me. If a slew of pictures would send Helen flying to Reno, I would shed no tears. I would even supply transportation, in the form of a new broom.

So I did not fall to my knees in the manner of a sorrowful supplicant. Nor did I make a grab for the camera. Nor did I abandon my masculinity and weep.

What I said was: "Has anybody got a cigarette?"

Al didn't, or didn't care. Jodi passed me a flip-top box which I glumly recognized as an account of MGSR&S. I took one and set it aflame, sucking in smoke and expelling perfect smoke rings, wispy symbols of what Jodi meant to me. Al waited patiently, the perfect anthropoid. Jodi looked sorrowful.

Then I said: "When you print the roll, send me three copies of each shot."

I looked at Al while Jodi laughed happily somewhere in the background. I watched animal expressions play across Al's face. Any moment, I thought, he was going to hit me.

He didn't. "Look," he said. "Don't be a stupid, huh? You know what I can do with those pictures?"

"You can't sell them to the *Daily News,*" I said. "They draw the line at cheesecake. You can peddle them to school kids, I suppose, but I hear the competition is keen. When you come right down to it, what in hell *can* you do with them?"

"Jesus," he said. "I can show 'em to your wife."

"She'd blush."

"Look—"

"She might even cry," I went on thoughtfully. "Helen cries easily. When she needs a new dress, for example. But she wouldn't get physically aroused, if that's what's on your mind. Nothing gets Helen physically aroused."

He was nonplussed, or un-plussed. Or plussed. "Listen," he said. "You got a job, huh?"

"Huh," I said.

"You know what happens when your boss sees these shots?"

"Now that's a different story," I said. "Not at all similar to Helen's case. *He* wouldn't blush."

"Look—"

Look, listen, huh. A spectacular vocabulary. "He wouldn't cry either. He's not exactly the tearful type."

"Listen—"

"Huh," I concluded. "On the other hand, he would get physically aroused. In marked contrast to Helen, he would get very much aroused. He'd probably spend his lunch hour with Jodi, or someone comparable. Or locked in his private bathroom with the pictures."

Al looked uncomfortable. Jodi was still laughing, louder and more happily than ever. I seemed to have fallen upon an advantage, though I wasn't too sure how or why. I stood up, dropped my cigarette onto the rug and squashed it. When you had an advantage, you were supposed to press it. They teach you that on Madison Avenue.

"You said something about a proposition," I said forcefully. "Let's hear it." I almost added *My time is valuable,* but that phrase just then would have been uncomfortably ludicrous.

"Yeah," Al said, slowly. "Yeah, a proposition. I don't know, little man. I think you're all bluff, you know that?"

I didn't answer.

"Then again," he went on, "I don't know if maybe I don't have enough chips to call."

He turned from me to Jodi. "I think this one is a waste of film," he told her. "He don't seem to scare. I could shove him around but that won't do any good. I think we should find somebody else."

"I told you," she cooed. "Harvey's a nice guy."

"That's a matter of opinion," Al said. "I think he just might be a louse. But unless he runs one hell of a bluff, he honestly don't give a damn." He raised both arms to heaven. "Now how in hell," he wanted to know, "can you pressure someone who doesn't give a damn?"

There was a moment of silence. I looked at Jodi, at green knit dress, at crossed legs, at expanse of thigh. I wished Al would go away.

"The proposition," I said.

"Forget it, little man. We'll get somebody else. Go home to your wife."

I shuddered at the very thought. "Let's hear the proposition."

"I told you—"

"Oh, tell him, Al." Jodi smiled. "Harvey's a nice guy."

"Why tell him? What the hell good—"

"I just might go along with it," I said. "Without the pressure. I'm a real oddball."

Looking back on this conversation, the inference is inescapable that I could have sounded like the damnedest dolt on earth. The whole episode, complete with whore and photographs, resembled nothing so much as blackmail pitch. The "proposition" could only be a demand for money. And here was I, successfully excavated from the pressure, suggesting that I might go along with the proposition for the hell of it. *Just tell me about it,* I was saying in effect, *I'll pay through the nose just to be a good sport.*

But at the time blackmail did not even enter my mind. Perhaps I had watched too many television crime shows—they filled the time between various commercials that I had to catch. Blackmail was too simple. I expected more complicated plotting. At a grand for a half-hour script, one has a right to expect complicated plotting.

Besides, if Jodi was whoring herself into twelve thou a year, money could hardly be their problem. And Jodi was not the blackmailing type. There was something far too honest in her emotional makeup. She wasn't that sneaky.

So I took it for granted that they wanted a patsy, not to pay them, but to perform some task for them. I had no idea what such a task might be. And I was tremendously curious. Chalk it up to the monotony of the day-to-day existence. Chalk it up, if you will, to Hellish Helen who was waiting for me, and who would be so not nice to come home to. Chalk it up to the Vat 69, or to Jodi's creamy thigh. Or to profit and loss.

Al said: "Jodi, I think he's nuts."

"He always was," she said. "A little. But he's a nice guy."

"They finish last."

She looked thoughtful now. I studied her face and her expression was disturbingly familiar. Then it came back to me. She had had just such a look in her pretty eyes when, in bed, she was engaged in figuring out a new way to do it.

"Al," she said, "maybe we ought to tell him."

"Don't be a stupid."

"We should," she said, positive now. "I'm sure of it."

"And if he blabs?"

"He won't, Al. Harvey's a—"

"—nice guy," I put in.

"A nice guy," Jodi said. "Besides, I think he really might go along with it. And he'd be perfect, Al. You know damned well he would be perfect."

The *damned* took me aback. Jodi was not the swearing type.

"I *know* he's perfect," Al was saying now. "That's what I was telling you, and you tried to tell me to leave him out of it. Now I want to leave him out, and *he* wants in, and *you* say he's perfect." He paused a moment to let that sink in. "I think," he wound up, "that *I'm* maybe going nuts."

"Maybe," Jodi said. "But just think about it, Al. He's perfect, just as you said. And if he goes along with it, because he *wants* to, he'll be a lot better than if he's forced into it. When you rape a girl, she doesn't put her heart into it the way she does when she's interested in the game. Right?"

He nodded. The image must have been right up his sewer. I wondered how many girls he had raped, and whether they had put their hearts into it. They evidently had not, because this was the argument which convinced him. He resumed nodding his head, so forcefully that I thought for a moment it might part company with his body, which would have been no major loss. Then he stepped over to me (I was still standing, and smoking a second of Jodi's cigarettes by this time) and jabbed a forceful finger into my chest, as if pushing a doorbell.

"Little man," he said, "I think maybe you've got rocks in your head. But if you want in, you have in. If you don't want it, you will have to for everything which Jodi tells you, because otherwise you could have a bad accident."

"Huh." I said.

"Listen," he said, to both of us. "Look. I am getting out of here, Jodi. This has been a very bad night for me, Jodi. First I take a roll of pictures, which as it turns out we can use for wall paper, or maybe to start a fire in the furnace. Then you and this bird play some kind of Ring Around The Rosie and I don't quite get what is coming off. I am going home, Jodi, and I am going to bed."

"You aren't telling Harvey?"

"You tell him," Al said. "You tell him whatever you want to tell him. and tomorrow you can tell me what the hell is coming off. Okay?"

"Okay," Jodi said.

"Huh," I chimed in.

If you can picture an orangutan stalking off in a huff, you can picture the exit of the Abominable Cameraman. He picked up his sneaky little camera, a pudgy finger smearing the baleful lens, and he hulked haughtily to the door. He opened it, and stepped outside, and the door slammed shut.

That left me alone with Jodi, which was a marked improvement. Jodi paced the floor for a moment or two, and I sat down once again on the couch and time passed on little cat feet. Now and then Jodi turned to me, and cleared her throat, and opened her mouth as if to speak, and closed her mouth, and looked away, and resumed pacing.

"Harvey," she said finally, tired of parading like a caged lion, "I am very sorry."

"Why?"

"That I let Al...take pictures. And try to put you on the spot."

"Forget it."

"I'm horribly sorry, Harvey."

"Don't be." I extended a hand plaintively and she put a fresh cigarette between two of my fingers. I let her light it for me. She sank down onto the couch, her rear nestled neatly on top of the long legs that she folded under herself. This pretty process made her dress ride a little higher, so that it was roughly halfway up her thighs and all bunched from hem to waist. She leaned forward, her eyes soulful, and her breasts leaped at me.

"About the proposition—"

"Forget the proposition," I said.

"You mean you're not really interested?"

"I'm interested, Jodi. But let's get to it chronologically. Not too long ago I came floating through your door. You let me in, and I said something inane like *Long time no see*, and then Al slapped me back to the land of the living. Now, something happened in the middle."

She waited for me to say something more. This was awkward, because I was waiting for *her* to say something. Rather lamely I said: "In the middle. What happened?"

"You don't remember?"

"Not a bit of it. woman. Fill me in."

"Why, you silly! We made love, Harvey What did you think we did, you silly?"

"That's what I thought. It seemed painfully logical. But I don't remember it."

"Well, I do. It was kind of fun."

"Oh," I said.

"It's a shame you don't remember."

"More than a shame," I said, hanging my head. "The memory is half of it. Now it's as if we never did it at all. Of course there are pictures to prove it, but no memories to warm my later years."

"Poor Harvey."

"Did we do anything unusual?"

She wrinkled up her forehead, thinking back. She threw her shoulders back, and this only pushed her breasts out at me a little more dramatically. I let my eyes take a guided tour of her, let myself get mesmerized by the way her perfect body was shaped and molded by the loving hand of a benevolent God. The body was magnificent.

And yet magnificence of form was less than half the story. The sensual appeal of feminine curves cannot be measured in inches or feet, in pounds, shillings or ounces. In her own unpleasant way, my good wife Helen had a body not overwhelmingly dissimilar to Jodi's. The breasts were smaller, but hardly miniscule. The thighs were not so plump, not so well-muscled, but they were by no means bad. There was something else—an aura of excitement, an artistic quality to the twists and turns, the curves and planes. Something that told you at a glance (provided you knew what to look for) that Jodi was a potential source of delight, while Helen could set ice floating in the Caribbean.

"Nothing too unusual," she said, dragging me back to our conversation. "Nothing we hadn't done years ago. In college."

"That doesn't rule much out."

"I know."

"And it was good?"

"Kind of, Harvey. Except you were pretty stoned, weren't you? You didn't exactly know what you were doing. And then I knew Al was there, snapping his silly camera. That took some of the fun out of it. Poor Harvey."

"Poor Jodi," I said.

She uncoiled like a striking serpent, came to her feet and stretched her arms to the skies, or at least to the ceiling. She stood high on the tips of her toes and my eyes were with her every glorious inch of the way. This had been mine once, I remembered. This had brightened college days, this had taught me what my manhood was. And now, because in those long-lost days I had confused success with happiness, Jodi was a whore who loved her work and I was an ad man who hated mine. Now, when I did make love to her, I could not even remember it.

"The proposition," I reminded her.

Slowly she pirouetted, turning her back to me. Slowly her arms descended from the ceiling and she leaned three miles over and touched her toes. I let my eyes focus on her rear. This they did of their own accord.

"The proposition," I managed to say. "With Al."

She straightened up again, slowly, and she turned around, slowly, and her cheeks were roses in bloom, her eyes huge and shining, her lips parted and moist.

"I've got another proposition in mind," she said. "And we can leave Al out of this one."

Her green knit second-skin buttoned down the back. I would have gladly unbuttoned it for her but she did not require my help. Her hands stole behind her back and toyed expertly with buttons. This did more things with her breasts. They leaped across the room at me.

"One button at a time," she said. "There are a lot of buttons. You'll have to be patient, Harvey. You don't look patient at all."

The room was a steambath. After four years she finished with the buttons. She stepped back, suddenly, and the dress fell off. That's precisely what happened—the dress *fell off*. One moment she was clothed, and the next moment the dress was a green pile upon the carpet, and all that had been under it was my Jodi.

I've mentioned her body, haven't I? Her body of college days, and how perfect that body was, and how the breasts jutted and the waist tucked itself in and the hips flared and the buttocks quivered? How the thighs reached up to the universal V, V for vigor, for vitality, for vim, for voom? I've mentioned all this, haven't I?

I have; I'm sure I have. And I've mentioned, too, how that body had filled out with time, how time did not wither nor custom stale her infinite variety I had seen the old Jodi nude, and I had seen the new Jodi with clothes on, and now I was seeing the new Jodi nude, a flawless combination of old and new retaining the finest features of each.

She did not walk to me. She flowed to me, her body a symphony of fleshy poetry in motion. She came in like the tide, and her voice was a panther's purr.

"Harvey," she said. "You don't remember the last time, do you?"

"Don't you even move," she said now. "I undressed *you* before. Did *you* know that? And then dressed you again when we were done. Now you just sit there without moving and I'll undress you again, honey."

I sat there, as motionless as possible, and she did just that. Her hands were cold as Dexter's Frozen Dinners. I was not. She took off my shoes and my socks and my slacks and my shirt and my underwear. She ran those soft hands over my body and I reached for her.

"Not here," she breathed. "Not on the couch. The bedroom is right this way. A bed is more comfortable than a couch, don't you think?"

"Sure," I gulped. My mouth was dry. Now why on earth should my mouth be dry?

"This way, Harvey."

Then we were in her bedroom. I could describe her bedroom—the kind of furniture, the type of carpet, the prints on the wall. But why describe her bedroom? It had a bed in it. Enough? More than enough.

"This is my office," she said. And she giggled then, and we were both naked, and I needed her now far more than I needed her years ago. Our arms went around each other, and her big breasts bundled themselves up against my chest.

"Harvey—"

"Jodi—"

Uninspired dialogue at that. My mouth was dry again, and then my mouth was no longer dry because we were kissing and her wet tongue was a long drink. Breasts and belly and thighs, and all there, and all close, and all warm.

As Dempsey hit Firpo, so did we hit the bed. As Cortez explored Mexico, so did we explore each other. I filled my hands with her breasts. I kissed those breasts, and I touched those buttocks, and my hands shouted Open Sesame, and the command was heeded.

Well, it had been a long time. A good many years (or a bad many years) since college and Jodi. A bad many years of Helen, whose hips had sunk a thousand ships. In that length of time a man can forget excellence and accept mediocrity as the normal course of events. Then, if you are very, very fortunate, the spectacular happens upon you.

The spectacular happened upon me—or beneath me, to be more nearly precise. And bombs went off, and choirs sang, and whistles tooted, and Grant took Richmond, and Socrates took poison. I had Jodi's breast for a cushion and Jodi's hips for a safety belt and Jodi's body for a fine and private place. She squirmed and tossed, the ultimate synthesis of genuine passion and the technical virtuosity only a professional can display. She moved and I moved, and she moved and I moved, and she moved, and I moved, and she moved and everything moved—

Slowly the world came back into its own. Slowly the clouds drifted away, the fog lifted, and reality returned. I was lying on my back and Jodi's face hovered above, inches from my own. Her mouth opened.

"There," she whispered. "You won't forget this time, will you?"

I did not have to answer. She turned away from me, her face nestled against her pillow. She fell asleep at once, the healthy sleep of the healthy animal. I lay on my back, my eyes tightly shut, but I did not sleep. I thought instead of Jodi, and I thought of just how far I had come, how I lived now with a streamlined iceberg and peddled monotonous meals and stale cigarettes to Mr. & Mrs. Middle Majority.

It seemed to be my day for reminiscence. There had been Jodi, in the beginning, shortly after God created the heavens and the earth. Then there had been the shoeless time in the bar, and the *Harv, we shouldn't* interlude with Laura Gray. Even then I had been a human being, living a human life. But somewhere, in the course of it all, things changed....

AS it turned out, it took even longer to get out of the mailroom than it had taken to get into Laura Gray. One year longer, more or less. For the first two months of that year I lived at Laura's humble flat. I dragged my suitcase from the Y and moved in with little ceremony, and Laura and I set sail upon the placid sea of domesticity.

Every morning we awoke together to the farm news, furnished by a nasal-voiced announcer who held sway on her clock-radio. Every morning we turned off the farm news and played hayloft for a spell, after which we showered and brushed out teeth. Then I would shave while she applied make-up, and then she cooked either bacon and eggs or ham and eggs, each an equally valid rebellion against her ancestry. And then off to work went we, she to the secretarial pool and I to the mailroom. Then home came we, sweat-stained and weary, grabbing dinner at a luncheonette around the corner from our 69th Street home, and killing time one way or another until it was a respectable hour for mattress machinations.

A scant two months, and then our mad and passionate affair withered and turned to dust. There were a great many reasons. On the purely physical side, I think another month of Laura would have killed me. She liked to bite, and to scratch, and to dig with her claws and to hit—in fact, I finally took to calling her *Justine*. This was before Lawrence Durrell, I was thinking of De Sade. The scratches and bites didn't embarrass me too much—I probably wore them with an air of callow triumph—but the pain, in time, grew unbearable.

Then there was our different position in the lists of commerce. She was a secretary while I was a mail clerk, and this fact remained no matter who was on top during the night. Account executives made passes at her, and copywriters made passes at her, and once in a while a partner of the firm cast a sidelong look at her. And here she was, shacking up with a clod from the mailroom, for the love of God.

Besides, domesticity paled. I was too young for it. The delight of having a sure conquest at home failed eventually to compensate for the moral obligation to refrain from making a fresh conquest. Our affair ran its course and died and despite mutual tears at parting, I am sure we were both equally delighted to be on the loose again.

This time the Y didn't snare me. It was autumn. I went downtown and shared a one-room apartment with four hundred and thirty-seven cockroaches, a fourth-floor walk up on Barrow Street in the heart of Greenwich Village. It should have been romantic—I was young enough to appreciate that sort of thing. Somehow, it was only verminous.

And so I toiled, and toiled. The months went by and the seasons changed, and I remained in the mailroom, carting correspondence from desk to free-form desk and waiting patiently for a promotion. There were five of us in the mailroom, all hungry to break into the ad game, and all of us united by one other common bond.

We were never promoted.

No one, it seemed, was promoted. Periodically one of us was fired, and periodically one of us quit, and the agency quickly replaced the departed one with still another young hopeful. I decided that Tom Stanton, S-sub-two, was the most hilarious practical joker since Guy Fawkes. I was doomed to a lifetime in the mailroom, a lifetime of $40-a-week minus deductions.

Then came August. And somewhere, I suppose, someone died, because a man named John Fehringer came up to me, tapped me on the shoulder, and said *See you a min, keed.*

I translated this mentally—I had learned, in my year with MGSR&S branch of the post office, how to translate Newspeak into English automatically. I went off with Fehringer, and he gave me a filtered cigarette and a filtered smile, in that order. I accepted both.

"I hear good things about you," he said. "The word from up high has it that you should be given room to grow. Like to try a stint of copywriting, Harv Boy?"

"Well," I said, "sure."

He took me to another huge room, into which I had occasionally delivered pieces of copy and mysterious manila envelopes. He showed me a desk and told me that it was going to be my desk. It was old and wobbly, the kind they sell for ten dollars, but, by God, it was all mine. There were drawers in it, and I could fill those drawers with my things. There was a top on that desk, and when no one was looking I could put my feet on it. It was my desk, my first desk, and I shelved it in my mind next to my first love affair.

Fehringer brought me some artwork for a magazine ad, with the key copy penciled in and with catchwords scrawled on a batch of file cards. "This is the ad," he said. "Like?"

The artwork showed a half-naked girl drawing the string on a sixty-pound bow. It was an advertisement for Bull's-Eye Spaghetti.

"Like," I said.

"In here," he said, pointing at the white space at the bottom of the layout, "is where we tell them that if they buy this cruddy spaghetti they can grow boobs like the broad in the picture. Or whatever we're telling 'em this week. It's all on the file cards. You turn it into English and put it in there."

"I see," I said.

"It's a pipe," he told me. "Easy-do does it, Harv Boy. If it sails smoothly you can keep this desk."

"And if it doesn't?"

"Then you're fired," he said sweetly. "Have fun, keed. Just take your time and hurry. Run it up the flagpole and see who salutes."

He left. I sat in my desk for a minute, getting the feel of it, and then I started to turn Bull's-Eye Spaghetti into English. It was a pipe, and easy-do did it. I got a head-swelling collection of compliments from the goof I turned the gunk over to, and I celebrated that night by picking up a Bohemian girl in Greenwich Village.

Her name was Saundra. She had long black hair and purple eye shadow, and she was not quite as bad as she sounds. Or maybe she was. She seemed all right at the time. I found her over a cup of cappuccino in something called *Le Cul de Sac,* where she was telling a group of bearded young men just how horrible Madison Avenue was. It was amusing, because I was certain she got nosebleeds every time she went north of Fourteenth Street. But I kept a straight face.

"You have some interesting ideas," I butted in, "but I don't think you have a straight line on the ad game. It's a little more complex than all that."

"Oh?" She favored me with a look. "Are you in advertising?"

"I handle the Bull's-Eye Spaghetti account over at MGSR&S." It was a more-than-slight exaggeration, but I could have told her I was a Third Assistant Skyhook at TWA&T. She was duly impressed.

"I've had too much coffee," I said. "Let's get a drink."

We got a drink. She was terribly young, and terribly naive, and, when you came right down to it, stupid as the whole Jukes family, I cried on her shoulder about the Ulcer Gulch rat race, told her how I ached to get away from it and write the Great American Novel in a humble garret. Midway through the fourth drink she was deciding to be my constant inspiration in the wars against crass commercialism. Midway through the fifth drink I had my hand in her leotards. We had the sixth drink in my Barrow Street roach farm, where she took off all her clothes so that she wouldn't feel inhibited.

As it turned out, she did not feel inhibited, not in the least. She was thin, with cute if bite-sized breasts. I could have counted her ribs, if I had been so inclined. A lean horse for a long ride, say the Arabs knowingly, and Saundra proved them right.

I snacked on her little bite-sized breasts while she warbled about the meeting of true minds. I dined on her body with hungry hands while she told me how I was selling my soul to the devil of commerce.

Then I ran her up the flagpole, and everybody saluted....

THERE my reverie gave way to sleep. I'd sort of planned on thinking back to the beginning with Helen, but sleep saved me from such heartache, and I forgot all about Helen and dreamed pleasant dreams of Jodi. The night passed slowly in slumber, and then dawn winked too bright an eye at me, and Jodi was beaming at me.

A wonderful girl, Jodi. She cooked breakfast and fed it to me without saying a word, and I for my part said nothing at all. I finished my third cup of coffee, thinking all the while of a suitable explanation to heave at Helen, and then, finally, I said: "Good morning, Jodi."

"Good morning," she said. "Did you forget?"

"Forget what?"

"Last night."

"Jodi," I said, "I shall sooner forget my name."

"You're nice, Harvey."

I lit the ends of a pair of cigarettes and passed one to her. Then I remembered in part why I was still at Jodi's, instead of being on the 8:12 out of Rockland County.

"Jodi," I said, "the proposition."

She nodded sagely. "Listen to this, Harvey," she said. "You may like it."

FIVE

THERE WAS TIME, in my not particularly innocent youth, when I considered myself an essentially moral type, a young man who was a bit shrewd perhaps, something of a corner-cutter and a doubt-benefiter, but nevertheless containing a solidly moral and ethical core.

We all believe that when young, I suppose. Some men—I imagine they should be considered the lucky ones—never do find out the truth. Alas, those self-ignorant ones are not to be found in the advertising profession, not outside the mailroom at any rate. It was relatively early in the game that I discovered what was really at the core of me—a black, sinful, unashamed and overwhelming concern, interest and fascination for number one. Or, I should say, Number One. Me. I quite frankly don't know what I'd do without me.

"You may like it," said Jodi, and I'd never realized till then just how well she really knew me. Her proposition, if it included someone like Al the Neanderthalus Chicagus, would inevitably be something highly illegal. Only a man who has learned to live with his nasty true self can be expected to sit still when someone begins a criminal or sinful proposition with the words, "You may like it."

She expected me to sit still. Ergo, and all that.

I gained my precious self-understanding, by the by, at just around the same time as I was promoted from the ten-dollar desk and the Bull's-Eye Spaghetti account, as so often happens in real life or whatever it is I've been doing for the past thirty-one years. The promotion and the self-understanding both were the end result of a little conversation I had with Fehringer one day after I'd been hitting the bull's eye for about seven months.

I looked up from my pencil that day, and saw Furry Fehringer approaching my desk. He wore one of those smiles that makes you instinctively look to see if there's a knife in his hand.

As a matter of fact, there was. But not for me.

"Min, keed," he said. I think his years in the racket had made him learn to hate the English language, and he was gradually trying to divorce himself from it completely. He was doing a pretty good job.

"Sure thing," I said. Both sensible English words, pronounced the way schoolteachers do it in Iowa, which just goes to show how new I was.

"Around the quad," he said. "Kay?"

"Kay." I was learning.

I got to my feet, and we roamed together around the quad. That is, we traversed the corridors of MGRS&S, up one pastel alleyway and down another, every once in a while passing that section of translucent glass-brick wall with the eight-foot free-form pink beer bottle in it celebrating a five-year-old MGRS&S coup, and Fehringer newspoke about this and that, mostly conversational chaff, from which I herewith extract the wheat, with my responses:

"You know Tom Stanton, eh, keed?"

"Uh huh."

"Brought you into the corps, didn't he?"

"Uh huh." (My responses gained in directness what they may have lacked in vivacity.)

"Feeling of loyalty, eh?"

(Dangerous ground, that. I wasn't *that* new. Was Fehringer a loyal Stanton man, or was his suzerain in our hierarchy? The best answer, I decided, was no answer at all.) "Well," I said, "you know how it is."

"Mmm. Just traded the flivver in, did I tell you?"

"Oh?"

"Mmm. Trade in every two years. Like to keep the old boat, sentimental attachment and all, but got to be practical. New one cuts the mustard. Sense?"

I nodded. "Sense," I said.

"Pity about Tom," he said.

I endeavored to look as blank as I felt. "Pity?"

"Booze. Fifteen to one in the club car lab now, you know. Poured into Westport every night."

"I didn't know that."

"Been covering for him, holding the flanks. Loyalty myself, you know. Sentimental attachment. Grand guy."

"Sure."

"Pity," he said again, and gloomed at the pink beer bottle on the way by. "Used to cut the mustard."

"Uh huh."

"Got to look out for myself," he said. "Wife and kiddies, that bit. Name and game, you know. Expect a hassle on the Wilmot Toothpaste. Sales on the downydoo."

"Oh?"

"Like to have you in my corner, Harv. Step up, eh? Think it over."

And we went back to our respective desks.

I thought it over. Fehringer claimed he'd been doing Tom Stanton's work for a while now. He had the game, and he wanted the name. All I had to do was manufacture a little damaging evidence concerning Bull's-Eye Spaghetti—which was also, ultimately, in Tom Stanton's bailiwick—and I could have a piece of the game for myself. When Fehringer moved up, so would I.

I thought it over. All afternoon at the desk I thought it over, and homeward bound on the IRT I thought it over some more.

Come to think of it, I wonder just how many decisions to foreswear goodness and virtue in favor of evil and degradation were made homeward bound on the rush-hour trains of the IRT, between Lexington-51st and the depths of the Village. (For the benefit of foreign citizens the IRT is the Metro. Geh?) This daily voyage involves three trams and a lot of subterranean walking, all in the close company of a surly mob which, for pure meanness of spirit and nastiness of behavior, holds no equal in all history with the possible exception of Robespierre's crowd in the French Revolution. (Could it be that old Tom Jefferson's—what a copywriter!—second revolution never came about simply because, for the urban masses, all revolutionary humors are dissipated in the mere process of getting to and from work? A thought I toss out for political scientists in the arena.)

At any rate, I thought Friend Fehringer's proposition over all afternoon at my desk, and couldn't see myself being such a dastard as he proposed, not for anything in the world. How could I possibly look myself in the eye ever again, having betrayed a kindness in such a manner? For it was, truly, Tom Stanton S-sub two who had given me my start in this rewarding (sic) profession.

On the Lex local, straphanging, between 51st Street and Grand Central, I thought it over some more. And subtly, without my really noticing it at all, my thinking began its insidious change. My thoughts were still in opposition to Fehringer the Ferret, but my reasoning had metamorphosed. Now, I was thinking: What if Fehringer doesn't get away with it? After all, Tom Stanton is S-sub two, no easy man to diddle. Wouldn't my smart move be to avoid the issue entirely? Thus remaining both morally pure and occupationally safe.

Walking underground from the Lex local to the 42nd Street shuttle, my busy brain turned to contemplation of the Bull's-Eye Spaghetti account. Was that an occupation, after all, worthy of safeguarding?

Wedged amid the snarling weasels on the cross-town shuttle from Grand Central to Times Square, I thought about Fehringer's job. I might, could possibly have that job myself, if Fehringer bootstrapped (or bootlicked, or booted) himself upward. With its increments, ah, yes. One could taxi homeward, lollygagging in blissful solitude in acres of back seat, whilst the taxi driver did all the sweating and snarling in one's stead.

Traversing the tile-walled corridors from shuttle to 7th Avenue Express, and riding that Profane Comedy southward, I began to see the justice of Fehringer's proposal. He was absolutely right actually. Tom Stanton *was* a rather heavy boozer. He'd been glowing rather brightly, in fact, when he'd met and hired me. Feral Fehringer was undoubtedly accurate in his claim that he had been carrying the ball for Tom Stanton lo these many moons. Name and game, indeed and exactly. A ball carrier in need is a ball carrier indeed. And I was surely worthy of promotion myself. Hadn't my earnest efforts on behalf of Italian clotheslines been met with universal and unequivocal approval among the higher-ups?

By the time I made the change at 14th Street from the express to the local, I had made another change as well, and somewhat more significant. What, I was currently asking myself, had Tom Stanton really done for me after all? Hired me to the mailroom, that was what, something any personnel manager or employment agency in the business could have done just as well. And what had Furtive Fehringer done for me? He'd rescued me from the mailroom and started my upward climb via Bull's-Eye Spaghetti, for number one. And he'd offered me a helping hand to climb yet another rung of the ladder of excess. Fehringer the bellringer. Put your money on Fraternal Fehringer, the pupil's choice.

But still, you know, some tattered remnant of my earlier self-respect still clung to my hunched shoulders. Rationalizations were all well and good, but something more was needed.

I was still living with Saundra at that time, and so I broached the subject to her that evening. I felt the need for a confidante, for someone to assure me that my choice was right and proper and good and beneficial, and that I could get away with it.

Saundra seemed, at the time, like the logical choice. She hated Madison Avenue so. Our nocturnal exertions were punctuated by manifestoes, our foreplay was fortified by foreign-born philosophies, our sex was ever seasoned with sociology.

According to Saundra, the capitalist society was a jungle, of the most primitive kind. For the individual in such a jungle, there were three choices open, three avenues of life: First, one could choose to be a timid tiny creature, with a burrow in which one hid from the ferociousness outside. Wage slaves and other roamers of the rutted routine were such stuff as timid tiny creatures were made on. Second, one could choose to be a lion or a panther, stalking the jungle, tearing from its richness whatever one could get. Financiers and Wall Street and Madison Avenue were panthers. Third, one could choose to be an eagle, and get the hell out of the jungle completely, by soaring above it all, swooping down into it only rarely for sustenance and otherwise wafting among the clods, thinking higher thoughts. Saundra and her unwashed friends were, if you could believe it, eagles.

According to Saundra, timid tiny creatures deserved everything they got, and in all justice were fit prey for panther and eagle alike. Panthers, on the other hand, were contemptible for their lack of intellectualism or morality, but were worthy of respect for their graceful ferocity. Eagles, of course, were the chosen few.

Saundra, I think, was never quite sure exactly what yours truly was. I lived more or less like a timid creature, but I had moments of aspiration toward pantherdom, and I seemed somehow able to converse with eagles on their own air.

In essence, therefore, I believed it reasonably safe to inform Saundra of my decision to join the ranks of panthers with one mighty bound upon the back of Tom Stanton. Her contempt for Stanton—for all advertising men who compounded their original sin by living in a commuter suburb—seemed to be sufficient to keep her away from any pity for the man. And her grudging respect for panthers should keep her at my side after the announcement was made.

I arrived at our den of iniquity—the term 'pad' was not at that time as yet hip, nor was the term 'hip'—exhausted not from my labors but from my homewending, and over platters of Dinty Moore beef stew I told her of Philistine Fehringer's proposition, and of my own decisions thereunto.

Alas, it only goes to show that one never knows women! At least not emancipated Bohemian women who have left the middle class behind but haven't yet decided whether that makes them upper class or lower class. Saundra's reaction to my disclosure was as violent as it was unexpected.

"Harvey, you don't mean it? You'd—you'd stick a knife in the back of the man who befriended you? Who got you your *job?*"

"Well," I said, "he *is* a lush."

"That only proves," she snapped back, "that he has a conscience. I wouldn't be surprised if he had a very delicate soul. Look at the way you two met. He came to you instantly because you didn't have any shoes on."

"So did the waiter," I said.

"Don't try to be funny, Harvey," she said commandingly. "I think that's a terrible thing. If I thought for one minute that the man to whose bosom I had—"

"And a lovely bosom it is," I said.

"Don't try to change the subject. Mr. Stanton was very good to you. How you could even think of—"

She went on and on that way. I had forgotten one important truth: Early upbringing remains behind, no matter how many logical or emotional overlays are laminated on it. And had I ever mentioned that Saundra hailed originally from Doughboy, Nebraska? (If you don't believe that such a place exists, friend, you just look it up in that miserable encyclopedia that smooth-talking door-to-door son-of-a-bitch sold you last year.) Way down beneath all the eagles and panthers and timid tiny creatures, Doughboy, Nebraska still burned in the heart of my raven-stressed Saundra. It was Doughboy that was talking now, not pinko sociology professors from

Czechoslovakia. And Doughboy, it seemed, was just as long-winded as that other Saundra I had come to know and love so well.

And all at once I realized she was right, though for the wrong reason. Of *course* I should remain loyal to Tom Stanton! My evil little brain went clickety-click, and the whole frabjous plot lay nekkid before me. Alors!

I leaped up from the table. I never did care much for beef stew anyway. Rushing around to Saundra's side, I embraced her, crying, "You're right! You've made me see the light, Saundra, and tomorrow morning I will go straight to Tom Stanton and warn him of Fehringer's evil scheme."

She studied me suspiciously. "Do you mean that?"

"Cross my heart," I said, crossing my heart.

"Because if you don't," she said, "I certainly wouldn't want to have anything to do with—"

She was far from finished, of course. She intended to talk all night, no matter how often I agreed with her. So I pinched her left nipple and said, "Darling, speak to me only with thine eyes." That was a little euphemistic cue-phrase we'd developed for a certain amorous variant of which I had become quite a devotee of late, since it prohibited speech on Saundra's part.

"You haven't finished supper," she said.

"It isn't beef stew I want to eat," I said gallantly. My future had suddenly opened before me, rosy and soft, elating me in all sorts of ways. As the caveman returned from a successful hunt or joust, full of his triumph, and could find no better capper for the whole thing than to throw his mate onto the floor of the cave and prod her with his maledom a while, so I.

I grabbed my Saundra's little breasts—as hard as young rocks, but much more delicious—and led her by them to the bedroom. By the time we passed the threshold, she was giggling and her little tail was wagging just fine. Bohemian ranter or Doughboy doughgirl, both of those were finally incidental. Saundra was, elementally, a sex machine. She had two buttons in front, and both were marked ON.

I'm a lazy man, all in all, and Saundra loved to pander to my laziness. Our conjunction now took its usual—but far from routine—course. Fully clothed, I reclined upon our wrinkled bed, still musky from this morning's pre-breakfast calisthenics. Saundra, narrow body and all awiggle, pink tongue-tip trembling between her lips, proceeded to undress me while thus I lay in regal lassitude. My shoes and socks she removed, then nibbled my toes a while and tickled my soles. Pulling off her sweater and bra, she next knelt at the foot of the bed and carefully placed my feet. Right foot to left breast, the hard dark burning nipple between first and second toes, likewise left foot to right breast, and then I wiggled my toes for her benefit, while she giggled and wiggled and squealed. A silly thing, but we both enjoyed it.

Then, her eyes now gleaming bright, she would push my feet away and come climbing up over me, to sit astride my waist and unbutton my shirt while I unzipped her dungarees. Man's dungarees, thank God. The female variety has the fly on the side, designed no doubt by some anti-social type or a believer in the theories of Malthus.

In order to remove my shirt, she would have to lean close over me, while I propped up a bit on my elbows. This position was perfect for windshield wiper: Left breast, kiss, right breast, kiss, left breast, kiss, and so on. The T-shirt involved a bit more work, but was worth it.

At this juncture, Saundra liked to lie prone upon me a moment or two, and nibble on my chest. I always took this opportunity to push her dungarees and panties down over her hips and halfway down her thighs, which was as far as I could reach in that position. I then liked to treat her buttocks like a drum, slapping little stinging syncopated rhythms on them, while she squirmed in delight beneath my hands.

When we'd worked this routine as far as we could stand, Saundra would next writhe off me and, standing beside the bed, finish removing her dungarees and panties. Then she would stand close enough for me to do some in-fighting while she wrestled with my belt, and stripped away the last two pieces of my clothing.

Then she spoke to me, for a while, only with her eyes. For very good and obvious reasons.

There were times when I preferred to simply lie in state during this interlude, passively appreciating her attentions upon me. But there were other times, and this was one of them, when I was in high spirits and wanted to reciprocate in kind, a treat that Saundra found absolutely delightful. She was, as I have said, a lean and bony thing, all flesh and bone, but with wiry muscles and unquenchable energies. She found it impossible to remain still whenever I so much as touched her. Her shoulders twitched, waggling her bite-size breasts, her hips gyrated, her legs trembled, her arms waved around, and she was generally and delightfully in motion. This motion increased tenfold when I chose to perform upon her the equivalent of her service for me. The dear hard nipples of her lovely breasts would scrape upon my belly, her head would nod in staccato agreement, her hips would pulse madly upon me as I once more slapped the small globes of her buttocks, her knees would beat upon the bed beyond my ears, and her hands would caress in fine imitation of my own handiwork upon her.

Yet she was always the one who first ended this preliminary bout, coming up gasping for air, her face bright with sweat, her mouth lax and passion-drugged. "Now," she would whisper, unable to talk aloud. "Oh, now, Harvey, do it to me now, take me, do it!"

And I would slap her ringingly, here and there, which only made her desire more intense, and she would squirm around, sitting now in position similar to the one she'd taken when unbuttoning my shirt, though now with a significant difference, and thus she would sit, writhing and pulsing, the muscles working beneath the skin of her flat stomach, her breasts bouncing with her exertions, her head flung back, eyes squeezed shut and mouth hanging open, her hands prodding me like a lifeguard performing artificial respiration. And I, lazy and comfortable and effete male, would lie in pleasant bliss upon my back, a silly smile upon my face, a passive but interested observer as Saundra agitated over me, working herself to a climax.

What a wonder that girl was! Undoubtedly stupid, as I have earlier said, and full of all sorts of philosophical eyewash, Bohemianism interwoven with Doughboyism, but Lord love a duck was she good in bed! And making love was such a natural and basic thing to her that she crested more readily and more often than any other girl I have ever known, before or since.

So we would continue, until she would suddenly go rigid, arms twisted upward and fingers curled, mouth wide-stretched in a silent scream, and my hands would rub her, finding every muscle taut and tense, her nipples fairly tingling beneath my touch, her abdomen as hard as a wall.

Thus she would climb to the peak before I, but she was good about it. She always rushed back down the mountain to join me again, so that now we could climb together.

And for our second stage, our positions would be more or less reversed. She would be tired now, worn from her labors, and I chivalrously would allow her to take my place. In legend, men have owed their strength to the length of their hair or the whim of some deity or some other such unlikely source. My own strength would arise much more directly. Saundra's first exertions never failed to inspire me, and I believe that I have never risen to the occasion with any other woman as strongly or as well as with Saundra.

Ah, if only she hadn't been such an utter bean-brain! I might have never become involved with Helen. And who knows, then, what my future might have been. Surely not Jodi and her illegal proposition.

At any rate, the day that I decided to remain true to Tom Stanton turned out to be one of the best encounters that Saundra and I ever had together. And the next day, refreshed in body and mind, I waited till I saw an important client enter Fetid Fehringer's office—so I was certain he would be in there for a while, and wouldn't see me leave my desk nor know my destination—and then I went up to talk to Tom Stanton.

It was one of the very few times I'd seen the man since he'd hired me. Looking at him now, I saw the increased puffiness of face, laxity of expression, since that day so many months before when I sat unshod in the bar. Fehringer undoubtedly was right; Tom Stanton was drinking himself out of efficiency.

But this was no time for soulless calculation. This was a time for loyalty. And I was full of loyalty, stoked to the gunwales with loyalty, fairly reeking with loyalty.

Once I got past Tom's receptionist—a nice bit that, and available from what I'd heard around the water cooler—and saw Tom himself, I got directly to the meat of the problem.

"Tom," I said, using his first name for the first time, "you're the man who brought me into MGSR&S in the first place and I want you to know that I'm grateful."

"That's good," he said. A faint aroma of bourbon was in the air.

"And so," I continued, "when I heard of something in the wind that could be dangerous to you, I knew at once what my duty was."

He became a bit more alert. "Dangerous? To me?"

"Your boy Fehringer came to see me yesterday," I said, and went on from there, outlining everything that Fehringer had said and everything that Fehringer had implied.

When I was finished my tale of deception and intrigue, a dejected and beaten man slumped in his easy-foam chair before me. "He's right, Harv," said Tom Stanton. "I've been slipping lately. I've left myself wide open for a back-stabbing like this. Old Fehringer! I might have known."

"I thought I'd let you know at once," I said, "so you'd have time to plan your counterattack."

"Counterattack," he echoed hopelessly. "What can I do? The man's an intriguer, he's been planning this for months. Old Fehringer! Got the knife out for me, and nothing I can do."

"Ah, but there is," I said. "Tom, I'm loyal to you, you know that. I want to help."

He looked up at me, hope springing into his eyes. "Is there something cooking in your double-boiler, Harv, boy?" he asked me.

"There sure is, Tom. Fehringer's going to play the eager-beaver a while now, till he's ready to spring the double whammo. All you have to do is let him swipe a project, and let the big men see him at it."

"Bad tactics, Harv," he said, shaking his head. "Right away, they'll know old Tom is slipping."

"For the nonce, Tom, for the nonce. But catch this: You work up a presentation anyway, you see? Meanwhile. I'm in Fehringer's bailiwick, and I sabotagerooney *his* little effort, and at the next conference *splat!*"

He sat up, the light of battle dawning in his eyes. "You'll do that for me, Harv, boy?"

"I'm loyal, Tom," I said simply.

...Now there was a thing that year called the sailor hat, only for girls not for boys. At a conference, Tom allowed Fehringer to grab the project away from him, and said only one sentence to Fehringer, which would ring in the big boy's minds a few weeks later: "I'll be glad to have you take a stab at this, boy; I want to know if you're ready for the big time."

And Fehringer, poor Fehringer, smiled his little smile and said, "I think I'm ready, Tom."

Six weeks later, I had Fehringer's job, and the sailor hat account was using Tom Stanton's presentation. *Don't say no till you've seen the proposition from every side.* No one told me that, I thought of it all by myself. If you're going to be immoral, you really ought to be smart about it.

Which was why I replied to Jodi, "Yes, I may like it. Let's hear it."

"It's a one-shot proposition, Harv," she said. "There may be repeat jobs, but I'm not sure of that. Here's the story: There's a man in Brazil right now, and he wants something that happens to be in New York right now. This thing can't just be sent to him, because the federal government would grab it, and there'd be a lot of trouble all around. So it has to be smuggled out of the United States and smuggled into Brazil."

"But surely," I said, "there are regular smuggling routes already. For dope, say, or gold."

"There's very little smuggling going *out* of the country," she said. "Besides, this is too dangerous to be trusted to the regular systems. What the boys have been looking for is an honest Joe, a guy with no record and no file, and a guy rich enough to take a trip to Brazil anyway. He can carry the stuff, and nobody the wiser."

"And?"

She smiled. "You want to know what's in it for you. Five thousand dollars, and a two-week all-expense-paid trip to Brazil. With me."

"With you?"

"A man traveling with his wife," she said sweetly, "is less suspect than any other kind of man."

"And what is this cargo I'm supposed to deliver?"

She shook her head. "I don't know. Except it's valuable." She lit a new cigarette. "Well, Harv? Are you interested?"

I suddenly remembered the slogan in Fehringer's sailor hat presentation and I burst into laughter. "Spend your summer under a great big sailor," I said. "That means yes."

SIX

HASTE MAKES WASTE. Look before you leap. Rome was not built in a day. The mills of the Gods grind slow but they grind exceeding small.

I quote the above, not to demonstrate my familiarity with banality down through the ages, but to point out just how thoroughly our platitudes have lost touch with the era in which we live. Tell the twentieth century male that haste makes waste and he'll reply—quickly—that ours is an economy of waste and he's merely being economical. Look before you leap, friend, and the door will be shut before you're through it. And, while Rome may not have been *built* in a day, it was certainly *sacked* in a day. As for the mills of the Gods...well, forget about them.

Which is all just a lap-dissolve into the message of the moment. Jodi and I leaped quickly, without wasting time looking around. We leaped furiously. There was no time to play games.

In the first place, the cargo, whatever it might be, had to be in Brazil in a hurry. This man in Brazil (and here I pictured a fat Sidney Greenstreet type with a tropical suit and overactive perspiration glands) was impatient. He needed this cargo. And, while I had a mental image of this Man In Brazil, I had no image whatsoever of the cargo. But he needed it, by Allah's beard, and he needed it with bells on.

In the second place, this was smuggling, and smuggling was illegal. Now neither Jodi nor I were traditional law-abiders, but smuggling in the eyes of the federal government is somewhat more serious an offense than either prostitution (Jodi's crime) or false advertising (mine, repeatedly). Both Jodi and I, though more than willing to do the deed, echoed Macbeth in hoping that if it were done, would it were done quickly. The sooner we were in Brazil, and the sooner the cargo was delivered, and the sooner we were *back* from Brazil, the sooner we would be safe, again.

"Passports," Jodi said. "I think you have to have a passport to go to Brazil, Harvey. Or to get back from Brazil. I forget which."

"Either way," I said, "we need them."

"How long does it take to get a passport?"

"Months," I said hollowly. "Many months. Red tape, and all."

For five or ten minutes we sat in Jodi's apartment and thought about the many months we would have to wait before we could get our passports. For five or ten minutes we sat, chewing our tongues, and preparing to cry. And then, casually, I said: "Of course, I already have a passport."

"You do?"

"Mmmmm," I said. "I took Helen to Europe a year ago. We went and looked at all the things you're supposed to look at, and I met a Pigalle whore while she went shopping for shoes."

"Is yours still good, Harvey?"

"Sure," I said.

"Why, you silly! Then we don't have anything to worry about."

"We don't?"

"I have a passport," she said. "I have a perfectly fine passport, because six months ago there was this gentleman who was going to Europe, and he wanted me to—"

She broke off, snapping the poor sentence right in the middle. Jodi, alas, was somewhat embarrassed to talk about her professional career in front of me. This embarrassment was something relatively new, since she'd been delighted to discuss the theory and practice of whoring the day we renewed our happy acquaintance. And, strangely, the same reserve was developing within me; I was unwilling to discuss my profession, a subtler sort of whoring, now that Jodi and I were fleshmates once more.

"Wait," I said. "We're supposed to be husband and wife."

"That's right."

"But we aren't," I said. "Your passport is in your name, and mine is in my name, and we're not married. So how on earth can we travel as husband and wife?"

She poured me a fresh cup of coffee, passed the Vat 69 bottle to me, and pointed from the Scotch to the coffee. I took the hint and sweetened my Brazilian brew.

"Harvey," she said, sounding a little like a melodious version of Al, "don't be a stupid."

I looked at my watch. It was getting to be eleven o'clock, and around that time even a casual sort of person is expected to report to MGSR&S and get to work running somebody up some flagpole or other. I took a sip of the alcoholic coffee and squinted at her over the brim of the cup.

"A stupid?"

"A very stupid," she said. "You have a passport and I have a passport. And all we need to travel as man and wife is a marriage license."

"A marriage license?"

"Of course. Then everyone will realize we got married *after* we got the passports. Which is perfectly valid, and which leaves the passports every bit as valid."

Now she was beginning to make sense. I may or may not have been a stupid, but I could see the merit in what she was saying. Still, I had to get to the office. So all I had to do was hurry on to MGSR&S, while she went out and picked us up a marriage license—Wait.

"Jodi," I said. "Really, girl, that's all well and good, but you don't understand. I mean, girl, bow can we come by a little thing like a marriage license?"

"Easy."

"Have it forged?" I asked brightly. "I suppose Anthropoid Al knows someone who's handy with a pen but—"

"Not a forged one, Harvey. A real one."

"So much the better," quoth I. "Very much the better. But how and where does one acquire a real marriage license?"

"I'm not sure where," she said. "Anyplace, I guess. But the how part is easy, Harvey "

I watched while she carefully broke a seeded roll in two, spread butter upon each half in turn, and stuffed bites down her throat. When the roll was gone I was still patiently waiting.

She said: "It's simple, Harvey. We get married."

SO I never did get to the office that day. Instead, I got married.

First, of course, I explained to Jodi that I already *was* married, for better or for worse, as they say in ceremonies. And while divorcing Helen may have been an admirable notion, it was an unwieldy solution. It would take even longer than arranging for fresh passports.

"You really ought to divorce Helen," Jodi told me. her eyes calm and serious. "I mean afterward, when we get back from Brazil. Not now, but later on."

"Jodi—"

"I know what you're going to tell me," she said. "You are already married. I know that, Harvey. And you know it, and maybe even your wife knows it, though from what you said about her it's hard to tell. But somewhere in Maryland there's a little guy behind a marriage license counter, and *he* doesn't know you're married."

"That," I said, "is bigamy."

"So," she said, "what?"

So what indeed. I went, not to my office, but to the garage wherein I had deposited my ranch wagon the night before. Just a night ago, a night that seemed like ages. I took the car back, power-steered to Jodi's hotel, power-braked at the curb, and went in for her. She came out with two suitcases. We were taking virtually nothing, but one suitcase, she insisted, would make a bad impression upon the Justice of the Peace. So we took two empty ones instead of a single full one, and we loaded them into the rear end of the wagon, and we loaded ourselves into the front end of the wagon, and I pointed the wagon at Maryland's marriage mill, and we set out.

The town for which we were bound was providentially named Cherry Park, for obvious reasons. It was on Maryland's northern border, and it was the marriage capital of the area, since neither a blood test nor a waiting period was required there. This made it a paradise for impulsive souls and syphilitics, and Jodi and I qualified on the first count if not the second. Huzzah for Cherry Park, where all roads lead to City Hall, and where an astounding number of young things park their cherries every day!

Huzzah, indeed.

We went to City Hall, found the marriage license bureau (which was not hard, since it dominated two rooms of three-room city hall), and filled out brief forms. We walked next door, where there was a line at the Justice of the Peace's little shantie. Finally it was our turn. She said she did, and I said I did, and he said we could. I gave the license, signed and duly noted in Maryland's ledgers, to Jodi, who folded it neatly and placed it in her purse. And back we climbed into the ranch wagon.

"Now what?" I wondered aloud. "Back to New York?"

"No," she said.

"No?"

"No." She let out a long breath. "I've never been married before," she said. "And I have never before had a wedding night, and I would feel rotten spending my wedding night in my own apartment. Find a good motel, Harvey. And then we'll have a good wedding night."

It was not hard locating a motel. The motel industry is a natural in a marriage mill, and the enterprising fellows of Cherry Park were missing no bets. We found a place called Honeymooner Lodge, and I parked the wagon and carried our two suitcases out of it. They were part of a set of matched luggage, which should have shattered the we-never-did-this-before illusion, but this hardly mattered. I walked to the desk and signed the book Mr. and Mrs. Harvey Christopher and only felt like half a liar. The son behind the desk didn't even ask to see our license, and I could have killed him. I mean, we had a license, and I wished he would ask for it.

Our room was clean and spacious. It had a huge double bed, and almost before I had closed the door Jodi was leaping happily upon the bed, bouncing hither and yon to test the springs.

"I'll bet you're starved," I said. "I mean, nothing to eat since breakfast, and that was long ago. We ought to be able to find a decent restaurant down the road, and—"

"We will," she said. "After."

"After?"

"After," she said positively. She was wearing a black dress (inappropriate as hell; whoever heard of getting married in a black dress?) and she proceeded to correct the inappropriateness of the garment by the simple expedient of removing it. The girl had not only gotten married without an unblack dress, but beneath it she wore a black bra. Lacy, and peekaboo in style, and provocative. Then she took it off, and her big boobs beamed at me, and I stopped thinking about bras and dresses and began thinking very seriously about Jodi.

"We have to consummate our marriage," she said, her eyes a-twinkle. "If we don't, you could get an annulment. I don't want you to get an annulment, Harvey."

"But our marriage is bigamous to begin with."

"Still," she said, "I don't want us to get an annulment. So let's make sure we can't."

We made doubly sure.

We made very doubly sure. We knocked ourselves out, and we had a wonderful time.

And afterward she said: "That was wonderful, Harvey."

"Which?"

"Both. This what every woman should have. This is just what a wedding night ought to be."

WHICH put me in mind of my own wedding night, which in turn was *not* all that a wedding night should be. Not by a long shot, and not by a damn sight, and not by any stretch of the imagination. I didn't *feel* like being put in mind of my wedding night with Helen, but Jodi was sleeping the sleep of the just, or the just-laid, and I was somehow not sleepy. I closed my eyes, and that didn't work either.

Now if you've been following this little narrative closely, and if you've also duly taken note of my reference to Helen Christopher, the frigid witch of the Ramapos, you may have come up with a jim-dandy question. You just may be wondering, as you sit or stand or lie there, just what in the world made me to do a stupid thing like getting married.

A good question.

It started, I suppose, after Saundra and I came to a parting of ways. Saundra, tasteful though she was in bed (and tasty though she was, and willing though she was to do tasting of her own) was too much a product of Doughboy, Nebraska and too much a case-study in belligerent bohemianism to be a lasting thing in my life.

She ran out on me, she did, ran off to Province-town with a lunatic bearded painter who drew watercolors of ax handles and similarly startling items. They didn't even look like ax handles, either. And, while I was a bit pained at being jilted, I was also a bit thrilled at being Saundraless. Harv Boy was free again, footloose and fancy-free.

And, although I didn't know it, I was on the road to Helen.

There were other girls between Saundra and Helen. Their names and faces have faded from memory, but I know one thing about them all. Each was not so delightful as Saundra, and each was better than Helen. I can be very sure of the final part of that sentence. If *any* woman were ever *worse* than Helen, I am sure I would not forget her so easily.

I was living the fine life of a bachelor, and I was secure at MGSR&S, having proved my dedication to the advertising profession by planting a stiletto in Faggy Fehringer's gray flannel back. I was living Riley's proverbial life, and do you know what I did?

I decided I was making a mistake.

It was the old Mad-Ave hard sell, I suppose. All my colleagues were married men, most of them with children. Most of my colleagues lived in Fairfield County or Westchester county or Rockland County, and all of that group chatted amiably about crabgrass and commuting and the club car of the old 8:02.

And I was left out.

The others were also married, only they lived in cooperative apartments in Manhattan, and they chatted amiably about bomb shelters and maintenance fees and such.

So again I was left out. I was there, snug in my Barrow Street bunghole, sleeping with every passable woman who crossed my path, and envying the married ones their security and stability and stodginess. I looked out at Barrow Street and wished I had crabgrass to mow. I looked at my current paramour and wished she would have children so that we could go to PTA meetings.

The beginning of the end—

When a man shops for a car, he determines just how much money he is going to spend, and he determines where he can get the best car for his money, and then he goes out and test-drives that car. If he likes what he's driving, he buys. If not, he keeps looking.

You would think that a man would be just as careful when choosing a wife. If nothing else, there's the fact that you can't trade in your wife every two years. If you do, the expense is overpowering. Your wife is most usually a lifetime acquisition, for either your lifetime or hers, and such an acquisition should be acquired intelligently. A man should be careful, finding out first just what he wants, and then finding the girl to fill those requirements to the nth degree.

I was a poor shopper. In the first place, I selected a girl whom, I thought, I had much in common with. I based this guess on the fact that she, too, was in advertising. I ignored her personality, and I ignored her background, and in short I ignored everything other than the fact that she was a minor copywriter at Stafford & Bean, a competing firm a few doors down the Avenue. She was a copywriter, a rising star with a college diploma and a pretty face. Obviously, I would always love to look at that face across the crabgrass.

Ah, indeed.

Her name, as you may well have guessed by now, was Helen. Helen Wall, to be exact, and there was never a harder wall to climb, including Hadrian's and the Great one of China. I courted her like a goofy gallant. I took her to dinners and shows and hip cocktail lounges. I even, God save me, sent her flowers. She was asthmatic, as it turned out, and the roses I plied her with made her break out with a horrid rash. There's something symbolic there, I'd say.

Helen Wall, an insurmountable wall, and a wall I simply could not mount. I committed a cardinal error here. I bought a car without test-driving it, and few men are so foolish. But at the time it was easy to delude myself. Every thin-blooded American male has been told from the cradle that he wants a virginal bride, and in weak moments some of us believe this pap. I managed to con myself into thinking thusly. Helen was virginal as the driven snow, I would say in odd moments to myself. She shall be a perfect helpmate, a wife I can truly respect. Why a square inch of tradition-ness tissue should make her worthy of respect is now outside my ken, but at the time it seemed flawlessly logical.

I proposed, on bended knee.

She accepted, with tears in her eyes. We were married, she in a white gown and I in a rented tuxedo, and we cruised Bermudaward on our honeymoon. We spent our wedding night on the ship, and quite a night it was....

Sin Hellcat

BUT I digress. To Hell, for the moment, with Helen. Let us get back to Jodi, my newer bride.

We awoke the next morning, arm in arm, and we greeted the day as days should be greeted. Then, an hour or so later, we got out of our big double bed, took a big double shower together, dressed, and drove to New York. I dropped her at the hotel and told her to call Al for the cargo and the airlines office for reservations to Rio de Janeiro. Meanwhile, I hurried for my passport. It was in a safe deposit box at a Fifth Avenue bank along with such invaluable documents as my life insurance policies and a few old savings bonds. I took it back to the hotel and rushed upward in the elevator to Jodi.

She had a strange light in her eyes.

"Al was already here," she said. "He came and went, sort of."

"Great! He leave the cargo?"

"He left the cargo," Jodi said. "Harvey, I didn't know about this. I honestly didn't. If I had, maybe this wouldn't have happened."

"What are you talking about?"

She opened the door wider and stepped inside. I walked inside. "Our cargo," she said, pointing.

On the bed, smiling, was a five-year old boy.

"I didn't know about this," Jodi was saying. "We have to take him, and I think it's too late to back out, and I'm sorry I got you into this, Harvey. I'm awfully sorry."

I looked at Jodi, and at the moppet. He was a cute kid, tow-headed and blue-eyed. The eyes were wide now.

He said: "Hello, mister."

SEVEN

I'VE NEVER BEEN to Brazil before," said the moppet.

"Golly," I said.

"Harvey, I'm sorry," said Jodi, of the furrowed brow.

"My name's Everett," said the urchin.

"Who asked you?" I asked him.

"Now, Harv," said Jodi. "It isn't *his* fault."

"Everett Whittington," said the talking albatross.

"Hail and farewell, Everett Whittington." I told him and, to Jodi: "Remember me to the gang."

"Harvey, please!"

My hand on the doorknob, I made the biggest mistake of my entire life. I turned about, and I looked at them. I looked into the trusting innocent saucer eyes of the five-year-old kiddie kargo, and I looked into the pleading promising deep-well eyes of Jodi, and I was lost. Lost lost losterooneyed.

I undid my fingers from around the doorknob, and I sighed an all-is-lost-anyway sigh, and I went over to the nearest chair and I sat down. "All right," I said. "All right."

"You aren't going to run out on me, Harvey, are you?"

"No, Jodi, I suppose I'm not."

"You're a funny man, mister."

"Contraband," I told him, "should be seen and not heard."

That broke him up. He thought that was the funniest thing since the Three Stooges. He slapped his little knee and whooped in his little falsetto and generally overacted all over the room.

"You know," I said into the racket, "if I'd had a child five years ago, he'd be just about your age now. And that's the strongest argument for celibacy I've ever heard of."

But I was lying. There was an even stronger argument, had he but known it. And the argument's name was Helen.

Helen. I married her, if you recall. I recall, worse luck.

Bermuda bound we were, on one of those Technicolor cruise ships, with a crew entirely composed of gigolos, and passengers from Central Casting. The Captain was a humdrum middle-aged fag, than which there is nothing sadder, and the third night out I saw Charon pass us, smirking up his sleeve.

But I wanted to tell you about the first night out, though I hardly know why. Some masochistic desire within me for public humiliation, I suppose. Herewith, therefore, the tale of my virgin bride and I upon our wedding night, heading southward through the glistening seas o'er the turning orb toward the beauteous pearl of the Atlantic, Bermuda, tourist trap of the British Commonwealth, where wealth is common and so are the British. Very common. In more ways than one.

But I digress. Perhaps I don't really *want* to tell you about my wedding night. Nevertheless, I've promised, and so I'll do it. I really will.

That day, our wedding day, had been hectic from dawn to dusk, with split-second timing being the rule throughout. The wedding had started at precisely such-and-such—attended primarily by office friends from her office and my office—and had finished at exactly thus-and-so, in order for the reception to commence *here* and end *there,* so that the two of us could whisk away to the pier and board our vessel of delight specifically at *then,* milliseconds before the gangplank was taken away and the vessel of delight drifted away from Manhattan Island, southbound for a warmer but not really much different island, seven hundred miles away.

Honeymooners, of course, made up a large part of the passenger complement aboard the ship, intermixed with intermixers of various kinds and sexes, divorcees anxious for another try, kept boys and kept girls and kept tweeners looking for somebody to keep them, single girls and boys looking for romance (which is the ladies' word for sex), and even a couple of fussy

British retirees who'd apparently been playing tourist in New York and were now homeward bound to Bermuda. Greener pastures and all that, and their presence did make everybody else look a little silly. At least, I thought so. No one else seemed to notice the irony at all. But, after the first night, I must admit that I had an eye for irony.

After all the timetable rushing around of the wedding day, it was good at first to simply sit and relax awhile aboard the ship. Manhattan Island, that crowded three-dimensional Monopoly board fell away to the stern, and the rolling ocean rose up before us to the horizon. We wandered around on deck, hand in hand, watching the sun go down, looking at our fellow passengers, and generally breathing deeply and getting ourselves unjangled.

You could pick out the newlyweds with absolutely no trouble at all. The grooms all looked gently lustful, as though mentally practicing the line, "I won't hurt you, I won't hurt you, I won't hurt you." And the brides all looked apprehensively lustful, as though they didn't believe it.

I don't know for sure whether Helen and I could have been spotted as newlyweds or not. It depends, I suppose, on how much showed on my face. Nothing at all showed on hers, that much I'm sure of. At the time, I thought it was simply unusual control. I didn't realize that it was a perfectly accurate portrayal of what was on the inside. Nothing, in other words.

As to me, my feelings weren't precisely those reflected on the faces around me. I was lustful, certainly, but there was nothing gentle about my feelings at all. I didn't much care at that point whether I hurt her or not. I had been biding my time for far too long, had been respecting her maidenhood and maidenhead till a few mumbled and overpriced words had been said over us, and now I was anxious to get to it, get at it, and get with it. I wouldn't say that I was lustful; I would say I was rapacious.

At the same time, a kind of contented lethargy—you've seen that on the faces of the cows on the Carnation milk cans—had come over her. After all this waiting and all this preparation and all this buildup, at last it was mine, it was legitimately and completely and exclusively mine, and there wasn't any particular hurry in demonstrating my proprietary control. We could relax a while from the exertions of the day, we could stroll the deck, we could take our time and take it slow, knowing that soon or late what I had come here for would be mine, all mine, mine, mine, mine.

I have the feeling, then, that the expression on my face was that of a sex maniac with a low metabolic rate. I looked, I imagine, insatiable but calm.

And since Helen had no expression at all on *her* lovely physiogoomy. Gods knows what our combination looked like. Trilby and Svengali, maybe.

Yeah, well let me tell you something. *I* was Trilby.

At any rate, we roamed the deck anon and anon, and around us the ranks of newly weds diminished. A gently lustful groom would all at once grab the hand of his apprehensively lustful bride, and the two would scuttle away toward their cabin, hips already awag. This couple so departed, and that couple, and that couple over there, and gradually the decks emptied of their panting cargo, leaving only the singletons—none of whom would be making out that well this first night out—and the returning Britishers, who wanted nothing more than to sit morosely on deck chairs and think about how they'd been taken in New York.

Until finally there wasn't a newlywed to be seen. Except for Svengali and me, I mean. And I at last suggested that we make the retreat complete. "What do you say?" I murmured in my true love's ear. "Shall we, ah, go below?"

"Oh, but look at the ocean," she said, turning away from me and pointing out away from the ship. "Look at it in the moonlight."

"Let's look at it through our cabin porthole," I suggested.

"I think I'm hungry," she said.

"I *know* I'm hungry," I told her. "Let's go to our cabin."

"I wonder if the dining room is open," she said. "Or do they have a snack bar or something like that?"

Maidenly modesty, I thought. Virginal apprehension. I thought it was cute, this big and lovely girl, so well-endowed for calisthenics of the kind I was envisioning, as delicate and innocent as *Her Wedding Night*. I really thought it was cute.

At the same time. I had to admit to myself that it was somewhat irritating. I had been patient. I had been patient through courtship and engagement, and I had been patient through an overlong ceremony, and I had been patient through the reception. I had been patient during the waning of the afternoon and evening aboard this ship, allowing us both plenty of time to be rested up for the labors ahead, and it seemed to me that the time had come when patience ought to step aside for action to take over.

These two attitudes, indulgence and impatience, combined within me to cancel one another out and leave only compromise. "All right," I said. I even smiled, making the best of it. "As a matter of fact, I'm kind of hungry myself. Let's see what we can get to eat, before we go down to the cabin."

"Fine, Harvey." She gave me that beautiful smile of hers, and linked her arm in mine, and off we went in search of edibles.

As it turned out, there was something like a snack bar, adjunct to the cocktail lounge. We had sandwiches, and I plied my darling with daiquiris, on the theory that alcohol makes the heart grow fonder, and warms the virgin blood. I wolfed my sandwich, and she hesitated over hers, and at last our dining and drinking were done, and back on deck we were, for more staring at the sea.

Another hour of this, promenading on the nearly deserted deck, and I was beginning to get just a wee impatient. Every blasted time I importuned my darling about coming down to our cabin for some fun and games, she played sightseeing guide some more, pointing at this and that, exclaiming over one sight or another, and generally changing the subject by the simple method of beating it over the head. This got to be a little strained after a while—face it, there's a paucity of varied sights in mid-ocean—and at last I took the bull by the horns—that isn't quite right, is it?—and said, "Listen, Helen, it's time for us to go down to the cabin. Now, I understand, you're nervous and all that, but the time has come. Believe me, I'll be understanding and I'll be gentle and I'll be sympathetic, but we just can't stall around any longer."

She raised a hand, as though to point out a particularly charming whitecap to the westward, but then she seemed to think better of it. Her hand drooped, and she turned reluctantly to gaze at me, and she nodded her lovely head "You're right, Harvey," she said. "It's got to happen sometime. We might as well get it over with."

"Of course," I said, too delighted by her acquiescence to see the snapper in that sentence. Any of the snappers.

Snapper number one: When you say you might as well get something over with, you're talking about something distasteful, that you aren't looking forward to at all, in any way shape or form.

Snapper number two: When you say you might as well get something over with, you're talking about something you have to do *once*. After that, it's over with, it's done, you don't have to do it anymore.

Snapper number three: When you say you might as well get something over with, you're talking about something *you* aren't going to enjoy and something nobody *around* you is going to enjoy.

There are more snappers in there, but those three will do for a starter. The point being that I didn't notice any of them. I just lit up like a pinball machine, and escorted my baby away from the deck and down the long narrow hall to our wee cabin.

Where Helen all of a sudden found a whole new vista of things to point at. We hadn't been to our cabin before—a steward or somebody had delivered our luggage, and we'd stayed up on deck ever since boarding the ship—and Helen just couldn't get over the place. She kept saying, "Oh, look at—" and pointing at things. She pointed at the portholes, and the Mae Wests, and the leaping-fish paintings on the walls. She pointed at the chairs, and the bureau, and the writing desk. She pointed at the carpet, and the lamps, and the doorknobs, and the light switch, and everything else she could think of.

She did not point at the bed.

I kissed her. I had to grab her and turn her around in order to do so, but I managed it, and I kissed her, and for the duration of the kiss she was still. She didn't respond at all, she was merely subservient and passive. For the duration of the kiss. And then she was off again.

I finally allowed my irritation to take command. "Now, hold it a goddamn minute, Helen," I said. "Maidenly hesitation is all very well, but let's quit fooling around. At this rate, our grandchildren will be grown up before we start their parents. Now, come on."

"We have to unpack," she said hurriedly. Our luggage was on the bed, and that was the only reason she went anywhere near that particular piece of furniture. She hurried over to the bed, and bent over, and proceeded to open a suitcase.

I goosed her. I goosed her a good one. After all that while, believe me, I had to do *something.*

She jumped a mile, and when she spun around to face me there was nothing on her face but outrage. "Harvey!" she cried. "How *dare* you! How *could* you?"

"It was easy," I said. "I extended my middle finger like this, see, and then I took aim like this, and then I—"

"Harvey, what has gotten into you?"

"Nothing compared to what's going to get into you if you'll only settle down for a goddamn minute."

"Harvey, I want our wedding night to be perfect."

"And I want it to be tonight.'

"It *will* be, Harvey, don't be so impatient for Heaven's sake."

"We've been married seven hours, Helen. Other people have consummated their marriages half a dozen times by now. We really ought to take care of it at least once, you know what I mean?"

"We will, Harvey, honestly. Don't you think I know how you feel?" (Another snapper I missed at the time: How I felt, not how *we* felt. The reason being that she didn't feel anything. Then or ever.)

"If you know how I feel," I said, missing the snapper, "then come over here and let's get going."

"Darling, all I want to do is get ready for you. Unpack our luggage, so we'll have a nice room, and put on that beautiful nightgown I picked out for just this occasion, and be really ready for you."

"I'm really ready for you," I told her.

"It won't be long, Harvey," she said. "Honestly."

"When won't it be? It is now."

She looked puzzled. "What?"

"Never mind. How much longer am I supposed to wait?"

"Oh, please don't be angry, Harvey dear. Don't spoil things."

"There isn't anything to spoil, yet," I said. I was growing surly, and I knew it, but I felt that I had some justification.

"Darling," she said, "I tell you what. You go back out on deck—"

"What?"

"Please, now, listen to me. You go back out on deck, for half an hour. I'll get the cabin ready, and myself ready, and when you come back everything will be perfect. All right?"

"All right," I said. Anything, to be assured of a time limit on the stalling. "Half an hour it is," I said. "Let's synchronize our watches."

"Oh, don't be silly."

So I wasn't silly. I left the cabin like a good boy, and went back up on deck, and wandered around, looking at my watch every thirty seconds or so, and waited for the half hour to go by.

As I walked, my thoughts quite naturally were sexual in nature. And, since I had not yet tasted the joys of union with Helen, I had no choice but to fall back on my memories of the other women in my life, those who had preceded Helen as my bedmates. They included the tall and the short, the lean and the not-so-lean, the good-looking and the better-looking. There were the slow and passive receivers of the male, the fast and furious engulfers, and a host of variations in between. There were all kinds of girls, and I thought about them all, and I thought about the act which had bound me to each of them and which had given them all something in common, and then I thought about Helen. And I looked at my watch again, and fourteen minutes had gone by.

I thought about Helen. My activities in the past with those other human females would be of the same approximate type as my activities in the to-be-hoped-for immediate future with Helen, so I combined memory with imagination with my knowledge of Helen's appearance, and long before I ever got into Helen's bed in actuality I had done so a gross of times in my mind. We would do *thus,* and then we would do *so,* and then we would do *suchandsuch.* It was fine in imagining, but it would be far far better in reality.

That's what I thought.

At any rate, thirty minutes oozed by at last, and I streaked back to the cabin, moving like one of those cartoon characters on television; nothing but a cloud of dust and a rifle-like *twang!* And there I was at the cabin door.

At the locked cabin door.

I knocked on the door. "Helen," I called. "It's me. It's Harvey. Unlock the door."

"Not yet!" she cried, and there was a touch of desperation in her voice. "I'm not ready yet! Come back in half an hour!"

"I already have," I announced. "Your half hour is up. It's time to drop the coin in the slot, baby."

"Not yet, not yet!"

"God damn it!" I pounded on the door with both fists, shouting, "Open up this door, Helen! Enough is enough!"

Then a muttonchops Britisher and his frau came down the hall, looking at me with ill-concealed astonishment, and I ceased and desisted from battering at the door. I offered our friends in NATO a weakish grin, and they went on by in seemly haste, not looking back.

Once they were gene, I took to kicking the door, shouting Helen's name amid imprecations. Then a few other doors up and down the hall opened, and some irate sleepers told me where to head in. I bitched back at them, being mad enough by then to want to hit anybody within range, and it looked for a while as though a dandy Donneybrook would get going in that hallway, without even John Wayne or Victor McLaglen to give the thing the proper feeling.

Until a ship's officer, called for by someone or other, put in an appearance and wanted to know, in clipped British monosyllables, just what the hell was going on around here. What the devil is what he actually said, if I remember it all right.

Well, of course, everybody answered him at once for a while, and it was impossible to get his attention, much less explain the situation to him. So I took the easy way out. I ignored them all, and went back to kicking the door again. That got me the officer's attention, and when he demanded of me specifically just what the devil was going on, I replied, "*You* I'll tell. These rubbernecks here can go to hell for themselves."

"He started it all," announced a snippy-type woman, pointing at me. I made a gesture at her involving a specific adjustment of the fingers of the right hand, and she looked shocked.

"All right," said the officer, "all right now. Let's just clear the hall here. I'll take care of things. If you good people will return to your cabins now, I assure you there will be no more noise. Just move along now, please, back to your cabins, that's it."

They finally *did* all go back where they belonged, leaving the officer and I alone in the hallway. "Now, then," he said, turning back to me. "Just what seems to be the ruckus here?"

"My wife and I," I told him, "just got married today, just before we boarded this ship. And now she's locked herself in our cabin, and she won't let me in. I mean, uh, she won't let me in the cabin. That, either. She won't let me, in other words. Anything."

"I see," he said. I suddenly had the impression that this sort of thing had happened on this particular ship more than once in the past. He covered his amusement well, considering, and acted promptly and properly, as though there were a tried and true Standard Operating Procedure for this sort of situation. I could see it; Manual on Procedure when Faced with a Groom whose Bride has just Locked him out of their Connubial Cabin.

The procedure was a simple one, all in all. He reached into his pocket, pulled out a ring of keys, selected the one he wanted, and unlocked the cabin door. "If you want," he said sotto voce, "I can have a bottle of something or other sent along to you."

"Thank you anyway," I said, rather grimly. "We won't be needing anything at all. Not for quite a *while*."

"Righto, sir," he said. "Oh, and by the by. This *does* happen, you know. Try not to be too angry with the lady. They get skittish."

"So do I," I said. "Thank you, and good night."

But it wasn't good night to the good officer just yet. A moment later I had to chase down the hall after him and bring him back to unlock the bathroom door. Helen just wouldn't give up.

When he left this time, I marched into the bathroom and confronted my reluctant bride. She stood cowering in a corner, fully dressed. I had already noted the fact that the luggage, still unpacked, had not been moved from the bed. Just what the hell had she been *doing* down here for the last half hour? Not that it mattered. She'd be doing something else for the next half hour.

My bride's first words to her returning husband were, "Don't you touch me! Don't you dare touch me!"

"I'm going to do a hell of a lot more than touch you, baby," I told her grimly. And then I told her some more. Graphically, in specific Anglo-Saxon detail, I told her exactly what I intended to do to her, what I expected her to do to me, and what we would be doing together.

She covered her ears. She squeezed her eyes shut. She cringed into the corner. She did her damnedest to squeeze through the wall and escape.

But there wasn't any escape. I ripped her clothing off, not because I wanted to rip her clothing off but because I didn't have any choice. She was doing her damnedest to keep her clothing on.

I've always wanted to punch Helen's mother in the nose. Unfortunately, the old witch is dead, and I don't have the energy to dig her up just to punch her posthumously. At any rate, she was one of those mothers who spends her entire life figuratively sewing her daughter up. *Sex*, in Helen's household, was the second syllable of a two-syllable English name. That's all it was. Things of the body were revolting, all and every. Family members had to apologize to one another whenever they sneezed, had to leave the room to blow their noses, had to be sure no one was looking before they scratched. Banishment was the only punishment possible for someone who broke wind. They all made believe that they didn't excrete, and Helen still had a sneaking suspicion that the stork bit was the actual truth about her birth after all.

This shapely sack of horrors was then presented to me as marriageable, and I fell for it. I married it. And all of a sudden Helen realized that she had gotten herself into the worst horror of all. I didn't merely intend to *sneeze* in front of her, oh, no. I had this plan to *violate* her. You've heard the word. Violate. Yecch.

Violate the witch I did, too. In the bathtub. She hopped into it, and wouldn't get out of it, so by God I hopped in after her.

Once in the tub, I grabbed her nearest knee and yanked. She flipped from a sitting position in the corner to a prone position on her back, her legs all balled up against me.

I readjusted them, and she tried to get them together again. So I reached over and smacked her open-handed across the face, and then she stopped kicking and just stared at me, unmoving.

I held her knees apart, and all at once she started fighting like a wildcat. She scratched and bit and punched and butted, she writhed around trying to keep me from finding my objective, and she generally gave me a bad time.

I gave her a worse one. Making a girl in a bathtub isn't all that easy anyway, even if she's willing. If she's opposed, it's next to impossible. And if she's a virgin and therefore more than normally difficult to get at, it becomes totally impossible.

So I did the impossible.

I kept my weight on her, hampering her defenses, and every time she punched me I punched her twice, every time she bit me I bit her harder, and all the while I slammed a battering ram at the closed and bolted gate of the city. I hit the city walls as often as I hit the gate, but I had determination, and when a man has enough determination there are times when he can do the impossible after all, like the poem says.

The city fell.

And it was a ghost town.

Once Helen realized the battle was all over, the city had fallen, she suddenly quit. Completely. She just up and stopped. She lay there like a board. That beautiful body, so cleverly muscled to afford the finest in nocturnal pleasure, just lay there beneath me like a corpse. She might just as well have been alone, for all the effect I had on her.

And when it was all over, she refused to talk to me. She wouldn't even acknowledge my existence for the next two days. And we were at Bermuda before we ever tried it again.

I've got to say this much for Helen, the second time she actually did try. The whole thing revolted her, but she put on the stiff upper lip and did her best not to show it.

And that selfsame night I became an adulterer for the first time, with a young lady named Linda Holmes, a bikini-clad beach girl with all the right equipment and all the right attitudes, whose mother had apparently minded her own business, which is as unusual as it is delightful.

So that, in essence, was my wedding night. My *first* wedding night. Is it any wonder I leaped at the opportunity to have another chance at a wedding night? No, it isn't any wonder at all.

Of course, you win a little and you lose a little. Helen had not culminated our wedding night with the presentation of a five-year-old boy. I mean, there's always that consolation.

On the other hand, Jodi did. Looking apologetic and worried, but nevertheless fatalistic, she presented me with a five-year-old boy, name of Everett Whittington, and she asked me quite seriously to smuggle him out of the country and down to South America and into Brazil.

Having traded banter with the moppet for a few minutes, I sat down in Jodi's living room for some heavy thinking and some heavy smoking. Jodi sat across from me, still looking worried, but also looking hopeful now, and the tad scampered around like an innocent five-year-old.

The wretch.

At last, I said, "Tell me straight, Jodi. Is this a kidnapping?"

She shook her head. "No, it isn't. Al promised me it wasn't. It isn't anything like that at all."

"I mean, kidnapping is bad enough if you just take the kid across a *state* line. If you take him across national boundaries, God knows what they're liable to do to you."

"It isn't anything like that," she said.

"Then what is it?"

She took a deep breath. "I'll tell you as much as Al told me," she said.

EIGHT

AFTER SHE TOLD me, we did the only thing possible under the circumstances. We put young Everett in the bathroom, ostensibly to splash splendidly in the tub, and we locked the door on him by wedging the top of a chair under the knob. An old college trick, that, and whoever maintained that a college education is less than essential in the modern world?

Then, as you might almost have guessed unaided, we played the games all newlyweds play. Not all newlyweds play such games with a brat locked in the bathroom, although said brat's imminent appearance on the scene within a matter of six or seven months is often enough the cause of their newlywed state. Be that as it may, there were we, a-tumbling and a-loving, and there in the powder room was Young Everett Whittington.

There was, of course, a bad moment. It came at a bad time, this bad moment did. At the moment of crisis, the delicious moment of crisis, came a shrill five-year-old cry from the bathroom.

"Hey," bubbled Everett, "let me out of here!"

Did we ignore him? One could sooner ignore a typhoon. But did we let him out? One would sooner liberate an evil imp from a bottle. So we pressed onward, with youthful wails in our ears, and I realized just how fortunate I was that Helen was barren. Life with Helen was all too unbearable without an offspring.

Helen, I thought, abstinence makes the heart grow fonder.

But it didn't. Not really.

And then we were up and dressed, Jodi and I, and Evil Everett was liberated from his prison of plumbing, and it was rushing time. So rush we did. We rushed to the West Side Terminal, and we missed the last bus to Newark that would get us to our plane on time, and we leaped into a cab and pressed an outrageous twenty dollars upon the sardonic little man behind the wheel, and we sped to Newark, checked our overweight luggage, boarded a gleaming jet, and spent at least ten minutes convincing our moppet that he ought to fasten his seat belt.

"Listen," I told him, "you don't fasten that belt and you'll bump your head on the seat in from of you."

This did not impress him.

"Listen," Jodi told him, after I had made other dire threats, all quite ineffectual, "you don't fasten that belt and I'll wrap it around your neck until your eyes pop out of your head."

This impressed him. I assured Jodi that she had a way with wee ones, and all at once there was a tear in her eye. A small tear, a tear that looked out of place, a tear that looked infinitely sad.

"I can never have children," Jodi said.

I remembered what she had told me on that first afternoon of our reunion—a batch of abortions, the last one a final one because more than a fetus had been removed. A whore shedding tears for her unborn children.

"I'm sorry, Jodi," I said. And she squeezed my hand.

The plane taxied down the runway (imagine a taxi planing down a runway, if you will) and suddenly we were in the air, going like a bat from hell. The FASTEN BELTS sign went out, and we loosened our own belts. Everett could not read. His belt remained fastened. Why mobilize an enemy? Why unchain the forces of destruction? The NO SMOKING sign went out, too, and I lit two cigarettes and put one between Jodi's red lips.

She took a long drag and filled the plane with smoke. "Sometimes," she said, "I wonder about them." I asked her about whom, and the tear appeared again. I leaned across to wipe it from her eye with a finger tip, but as soon as I did this another tear took its place.

"The dead ones," she said. "The ones they cut out of me. The poor little kids never had a chance, Harvey. I asked the doctor one time whether it was a boy or a girl. He said it was too early to tell, so I don't know. Those kids never had a chance to be born."

I suggested that they might have been better off that way—that, as far as it went, everyone might have been better off unborn. But Jodi shook her head sadly.

"You have to have a chance," she said. "You have to live. Then, when you make a mess out of it all, you know at least that you had that first chance somewhere along the way."

It was a fairly profound speech, and I for once had no answer to it. I started to say that we were getting into deep water for a honeymoon trip. I didn't say this, though.

"I shouldn't go on this way," she said, reading my mind. "It's just depressing, Harvey. And you can't be too interested."

I told her, not altogether untruthfully, that I was interested in anything she had to say.

"But you've never had an abortion," she said. "It's not exactly up your alley."

It wasn't? True, I had never had an abortion. But I had been involved in one, had even paid for one. All of which happened after I was married, but not long after. And the abortee—is that the word? It might as well be—was not my wife, but Linda Holmes.

REMEMBER the wedding, and the wedding night?

All on the good ship Lollypop bound Bermudaward? You must remember. I remember. As though it were yesterday, or perhaps the day before.

Every night has a morning after, and the manufacturers of Bromo-Seltzer remain ever grateful for this fact. Even wedding nights have mornings after, and mine was no exception. The exceptional element lay in the fact that upon that evil morning after I awoke in bed, not with my good wife Helen, but with another girl entirely.

Her name was Linda Holmes, of course. She had red hair and green eyes and breasts like someone in Swedish movies. Anita Ekberg, for example. Not Ingmar Bergman.

I rolled over that fine morning and almost called her *Helen*. But she had awakened before me, and when my eyes opened she came into my arms as soft and fresh and sweet and willing as—well, quite soft and fresh and sweet and willing, metaphor be damned. And I knew full well that this was not Helen. Not at all.

"Let's play a game," she whispered, her little pink tongue darting into my ear to blur the words—and to blur my vision, as well, and to make my knees knock together. "Mister Bridegroom, let's play a game."

We had played games a-plenty the night before. Did I tell you that Linda's mother had a laissez-faire attitude toward sex? I must have, and she did. Linda had somehow escaped the puritanical upbringing of my fair Helen. Salemites might have burned her as a witch, had she not charmed them first.

"What kind of a game?"

"An Oriental game," she said. "You'll be a Jaded sheik in an Oriental pleasure dome in Asia Minor, or something like that."

"In Xanadu," I suggested. "That's the best place to decree stately pleasure domes."

"In Xanadu," she echoed. "And do you know what I'll be?"

"A slave girl."

She shook her head.

"A harem favorite," I suggested.

"No. Remember, you're a jaded old sheik. The harem favorites don't jolt you any more."

"A tender virgin," I said, wincing slightly because after Helen the whole idea of virginity was somehow nauseating. "A tender virgin at the sheik's mercy."

"Too jaded," she insisted stubbornly. "You eat virgins for breakfast."

The idea was not entirely without appeal, I must admit. I put a hand on one of those fair Swedish peaks, and I felt a nipple go stiff, and I squeezed. A hand came for me—a soft little hand attached to a strong little arm attached to Linda Holmes—and the hand found the object of its search, and the hand held and stroked.

"Linda," I said.

"Not Linda," she said. "You're old and jaded, Pukka Sahib. Countless nights of dissipation have ruined your appetite for normal lust. And now, oh Great Leader, you are hard to arouse."

I put my hand on her hand, raising my eyebrows as I did so. "Linda," I said, "believe the evidence of your senses. Hard to arouse, no."

She giggled. Her hand did things, and my hand did things and for a moment passion caught hold of us. But suddenly she stiffened, pulled away playfully, and regarded my hungry eyes with mirthful ones.

"Women no longer excite you," she said. "Do you know what you need now?"

"Yes."

"What?"

I told her in four letters and she shook her head solemnly. "You need a young boy," she said. "Huh?"

"A young boy. You see—"

"You," I said, "have the wrong number."

She sighed. "It's a game, silly. Listen, you're the sheik, or the harem leader, or whatever the hell it is. Get it? I think we've got our geography all balled up, and so on, but you're the Lord High Everything Else of Xanadu, see, and I'm the young boy assigned to bring you pleasure. Now, you have to make love to me as though I were a boy."

I told her that if she were a boy I was the Lord High Whatzit of Xanadu.

"Exactly," she said.

But once we caught the spirit of the thing it was fine. I stroked her not-at-all boyish body, disobeying her injunctions to leave her breasts alone. "You're a boy," I insisted, pinching pink nipples and cupping globes of soft firmness. "I'm just rubbing your flat chest. Use your imagination, for God's sake."

Finally she was kneeling before me on the bed. I looked at the back of her head, her flaming red hair. I ran my hands over her back, feeling skin that was wondrously soft. I cupped her buttocks, and no buttocks in the world were as butty as they. Round and pink, firm and delicious—I have never felt particularly cannibalistic, but if I ever were to begin a diet of human flesh, I think I should like to start with buttocks like hers. Roasted Buttocks of Succulent Girl—one could do worse.

She writhed and moaned while I caressed her bouncy behind, wiggled and squirmed and told me what a great Lord High Whatever I was. And then I came between them like a family feud between Romeo and Juliet, and my hands went around her to grip her breasts while I surged again and again into her.

You may understand, I suspect, how surprised I was to discover, two months later, that she was pregnant.

She called me in New York. I was back at the agency, swinging away madly in a mad effort to keep my wife from driving me to suicide. The phone rang one fine day, it did, and there, by God, was Linda Holmes.

"Harvey," she said, clear as a bell, "this is Linda Holmes. Remember?"

I remembered—some things are not so easily forgotten, and Linda was one of the unforgettables. I smiled at her memory, and thought to myself that it would be very fine indeed to see her again, and wondered what sort of games we would play this time. I decided to leave the choice up to her.

"Harvey," she said, clear as an open window, "I am going to have a baby."

Now remember please what we had done, she and I. Remember that I had entered, as it were, by the back door, the servant's entrance. Remember this.

I said, "That's impossible."

"Harvey," she said, clear as a Windex commercial, "I am pregnant."

"Not pregnant. Constipated, maybe, but not pregnant. Listen, don't you remember—"

She remembered, of course. But she also remembered that the Jaded Sheik was not my only role, although it remained most memorable. Lovable Linda was pregnant. Layable Linda was going to have a baby. Lousy Linda was making a father out of me.

"I'd marry you," I said. "But I already did that."

"I don't want to get married, Harvey."

"What do you want?"

"First I want to go to bed with you," she said, clear as a bell, as clear no doubt to the switchboard girl as to me. "Because I miss you, I mean. But what I really want is to have an abortion."

I got her phone number and her address, and then I left the office early and found a run-down bar on Sixth Avenue. There are times when liquor is a tongue-loosener, and I could ill afford a loose tongue in the presence of mine enemies, and all the hucksters I might encounter in Ulcer Gulch drinkeries were to be counted amongst mine enemies. So I chose a bar where the draft beer was fifteen cents and the bar rye was varnish, and I drank boilermakers that could not have tasted worse without killing me.

There I thought about Linda.

And drank.

In the morning, I woke in an alleyway, cleaned up a bit in a convenient men's room, bought a new set of clothes with my Diners' Club card, rented a hotel room with my Diners' Club card, ate a meal with my Diners' Club card, and quite systematically made phone calls until I located an abortionist. I made another phone call to Linda, cabbed to her apartment, and spent two hours in bed with her to prime her for the ordeal ahead. On the way to the greedy little rabbit-snatcher I stopped at my bank and cashed a check for a thousand dollars. The abortionist, God love him, did not honor Diners' Club cards.

I had the unhappy thought, while I waited for Linda to come out of it all, that she might die under the knife. This would have been properly dramatic, but it did not happen that way. She recovered, and I kissed her, and never saw her again. Yet the experience, as I thought of it now, was jarring.

I had conceived a child, sure enough. Had gotten a woman to conceive one, at any rate. The entire arrangement was incomprehensible. The notion that a few idle moments—well, not so idle, but hardly serious ones—a few moments, call them what you will, of sack time with Linda Holmes had resulted in this entity, this child. And now this child like Macduff was untimely ripped from its mother's womb, and was gone, flushed down the toilet of a friendly abortionist who didn't honor my Diners' Club card.

So I think I knew how Jodi felt, God bless her.

IT was evening when the plane landed in Rio. It was winter, of course, but a winter in Brazil is not like a winter in New York. If we had been further south, there would have been snow around and all that. As it was, it was more like a New York spring. Cool, clear, a little muggy but not uncomfortable.

The combined officialdom of Rio de Janeiro passed us through Customs with no difficulty at all. Our passports, proclaiming us to be Mr. and Mrs. Harvey Christopher, were in good order. Our wee one, who behaved lamb-like by calling us Mom and Dad in front of the baleful eye of a Portuguese-speaking flunkey, was received with smiles from every corner. He belonged to us, obviously, and they gave him no more trouble than they gave the rest of our luggage. We found a taxi, loaded ourselves and our suitcases and our moppet into the back seat, and gave the driver our destination a hotel named El Punto Finale.

"I think he's cheating us," I whispered to Jodi. "We've passed this corner before." This after a long and round-about ride.

"But there's no meter in the cab," she said.

There wasn't. By the time I had an explanation figured out, we were somehow in front of the hotel, and the driver was asking in English only slightly better than my Portuguese (and I speak *no* Portuguese) for a dollar, sir. Obviously, he hadn't conned us. Obviously, everything was fine. I gave him two dollars because I had misjudged him and he grabbed up our suitcases, beaming crazily, and toted them into the lobby.

The clerk had our reservations, made for us via redoutable Al. We had a penthouse suite with a view of most of Rio—a room for us, a room for the kid, a room to sit around in, a room with a bar in it, and a pair of bathrooms. There was a thick carpet all over, and the bellhop told us in flawless English that he could get us anything we wanted.

I told him a bottle of Scotch would be nice. He asked us what brand, and I mentioned Vat 69.

He went away. He came back with ice, Vat 69, soda, and ginger ale. I made him take away the soda and the ginger ale—only in Brazil would anyone conceive of mixing Scotch with ginger ale. I poured drinks for Jodi and myself, glowered at Everett until he ran off to his own room, and drank.

"He could have gotten us anything," I told Jodi. "Maybe I should have asked for something tougher."

"Like what?"

"I should have told him to send up a girl," I said.

"But you've got a girl."

"Two would be twice as much fun."

Jodi licked her lower lip pensively. "I knew a man who thought that way." she said. "That two would be twice as much fun."

"Who?"

"I don't remember his name," she said. "I knew him professionally, Harvey."

"A client?"

"A client. It was a call job, Harvey. I was working through this agency, like any agent except their cut was more than ten percent. Closer to half, really. I got a call to go over to a coop apartment in the east sixties. Money—you know?"

"I know."

"So I went over there. There was this guy, maybe forty-five, and there was this girl, maybe thirty. I was maybe twenty-five myself at the time. A few years ago."

She smiled. I poured more Vat 69 in her and more Vat 69 in my glass, and we touched glasses together. It's an old custom you can get neatly fried. A colleague of mine once theorized that it was the clinking that stoned you.

that if you did the same thing with glasses of skim milk you would have the same hangover in the morning. A theory, for better or for worse

"She was a sort of sloe-eyed thing," Jodi was saying over the brim of her glass. "And I thought it was a mistake, that they had sent us both there or something because some bonehead got his wires crossed. Or his fingers, or his signals. I can never keep my clichés straight."

I told her to go on.

"But it wasn't a mistake," she said hazily. "It was for real. This forty-five type had a taste for orgies, I guess. He thought two would be twice as much fun you see."

I say "What did he want you to do? I mean, two could be trouble. Unless the guy had managed to grow a second—"

"No." she said firmly. "He only had one of those, and it was a pretty ordinary one anyway. You know what he wanted us to do, Harvey? Do you have any idea?"

"Well, don't keep me in suspense."

She waited while I refilled the glasses. Then she said, "He had us take off all our clothes. Both of us."

"That sounds like a pretty fair beginning."

"And then he had me lie down on a bed, Harvey. On my back naked."

"It figures."

"And what do you think happened next?"

I made a pretty decent guess. It was what I would have done under the circumstances, and I figured, well, what the hell.

"*He* didn't," she said. "*She* did."

"Huh?"

"She got on the bed with me," said dear Jodi, "And she started to do things. Like feel my breasts. Here, give me your hand, Harvey, and I'll show you—"

"And here, too. *You* know."

Damn right I knew.

"And so she made love to me," Jodi said. "This sloe-eyed thing made love to me, and the guy who was picking up the tab just stood there watching, and drooling a little. She did things for about half an hour and she damn well knew what she was doing."

"How was it?"

Jodi thought about it. "Not bad," she said. "Because I could close my eyes, Harvey, and pretend that it wasn't a girl but a man. And you know what she was doing to me, of course. With her hands and her mouth. I've had men do that to me—"

"Like me," I said, "for a starter."

"That's right. And I like it."

"Damn right you do."

"Don't growl," she said. "Anyway, it was just the same thing, and she was okay at it. And besides, I knew it was all an act, what she was doing. She was just a poor whore hired for the occasion, same as I was, and it wasn't as though she was a lesbian or anything. So I didn't mind it too much."

Somehow in the course of all this I had managed to get rid of two glasses and one blouse. I took off Jodi's bra. I have often been a vicarious sort, despite the rather active sex life of which I have boasted in foregoing chapters, and books and movies never fail to arouse me. A story, recounted to me by a beautiful woman, can have an even more erotic effect. Perhaps the profession is partially responsible—when you sell sex night and day, as you do on Mad Ave, you become every jot as suggestible as the rank fools who buy the products you sell.

Thus, as I stood there listening to Jodi's little narrative, my profile became somewhat annular in one particular area. And Jodi's bra went away, and her breasts were warm in my hands.

"There's more," she said.

"I know there is. It's under your skirt."

"More to the story," she said. "Don't you want to hear it, Harvey? It's kind of interesting."

"Well, make it fast."

Jodi giggled. I was still holding her breasts and they seemed to be growing in my hands. Maybe flesh expands as it grows warmer, like metal. Another story.

"So this sloe-eyed dame finished making love to me." Jodi said "And she got up, and hot-shot took her place. And he made love to me, and then he made love to her."

"That's sort of anticlimactic," I said, "And no puns intended."

"That's not all."

"I think you're stalling. Jodi."

She giggled again, lewdly again. "I'll make it short," she said.

"You already made it long." I squeezed her breasts. "Long and drawn-out."

"The story, I mean. I got dressed, finally, and he gave me a hundred dollars, and I started to leave. And I asked Miss Sloe Eyes if she was coming. I figured we could have a drink somewhere, or talk about this nutty trick, or something."

"So did you?"

"No," she said. "She stayed with him."

"Maybe he wanted her for the night."

"He wanted her all the time, Harvey," she said. "The sloe-eyed one was his wife. His wife, for God's sake!"

It might have been a nice story for us to talk about, and to cluck tongues over, or something of the sort. But if you have read this far, you have no doubt gathered there was a strong physical attraction betwixt and between dear Jodi and I, and that we were both rather physical types. And you may have established a pattern in our relationship. And, if this is so, you know very well that we did not sit around and talk about the Rich Bastard and his Dyke Wife.

You know very well what we did.

IN the morning, which was clear and dry, we had breakfast downstairs in the hotel's coffee shop. The food was good if not exotic, and the bill of fare seemed divided between American items and German food; Rio itself seemed divided between American tourists and escaped Nazis, and our waiter bore a striking resemblance to Martin Bormann. One never knows.

Jodi and I had schnitzel Holstein, veal with eggs on it, and I felt only mildly ridiculous ordering the dish in English in a Brazilian restaurant. The coffee was hot and thick and black. There's an awful lot of it in Brazil, as says the song. But very few Brazilians—just Americans and Germans.

Everett Whittington (or Everett Christopher, as his passport swore up and down) had flapjacks with maple syrup and a hearty glass of milk. He ate as though food was a new discovery and Jodi beamed at him.

"This is so nice," she said.

"The schnitzel?"

"No, silly. No, just all of us here. You and me and Ev."

"Ev?"

The moppet beamed at Jodi. And at me. He was sort of a cute little one.

"I can pretend," Jodi said. "Do you know what I'm pretending, Harvey?"

"What?"

"That we're married," she said simply. "We're a pair of married tourists, off to Brazil on a spree, and Ev is our little boy, and we are all very much in love. Isn't that a nice pretend?"

"Uh-huh."

"Isn't it, Harvey?"

"It really is," I said, meaning it. "But couldn't we call the little tyke something besides Ev? It gets to me."

"What's a tyke?" Everett asked.

We ignored the question. Jodi smiled at him and patted his hand, and I said, "Why not Rhett?"

"Rhett?"

"Sure," I said. "It's better than Ev, for God's good sake."

Jodi tested the name on her tongue, deciding that she liked it. "But it doesn't really matter," she said. "We have to turn him over to Whittington, damn it. That old bastard."

"What's a bastard?" Everett asked.

While Jodi tried to tell him what a bastard wasn't, I thought about Dixon Whittington, the old bastard. Whittington was an executive of some company or other, or had been, until he did the only truly sensible thing in his life and absconded to Brazil with seven hundred thousand dollars of company funds, partly in bearer bonds and the rest in cash. He stopped in Mexico to divorce his wife, then headed to Brazil and married a slut of some sort to make extradition impossible. His wife, scandalized, leaped out a window. Everett—Rhett, damn it—was now half an orphan, and the other half was in Brazil.

So Dixon Whittington wanted the kid—more because he was a possession than anything else. And, because people with seven hundred thousand dollars can get in contact with almost anyone, he had reached our animalistic friend Al, who swiped the kid and shipped him, via us, to his rightful owner.

The way Jodi had explained it, it wasn't kidnapping. A father couldn't kidnap his own son, not unless the courts had awarded custody to somebody else, and this they had not yet done. But because the U.S. government was rather anxious to bait Papa Whittington into returning to the States, Rhett was not allowed to make the trek to Brazil.

Thus the deception.

"It's a shame," Jodi said. "I know."

"But I guess we have to give him back, Harvey."

I looked at Rhett. Never again could I think of him as Everett, and hardly Ev.

"Son," I said in fatherly tones, "what does your old man call you?"

"The little bastard," he said. "That's a funny word, isn't it? Why won't you tell me what it means?"

"It's a term of endearment," I told him. And to Jodi I said, "You're right, of course. It's a damn shame."

"Couldn't we wait awhile?"

"Not according to instructions."

"Today," Jodi said sadly.

"Today. This morning, in fact. Pronto. We bundle Rhett into a cab, drop him in the old bastard's arms, and scram. I think we should start now."

"Now?" she said glumly.

"Now."

"Can't we even—even have another cup of coffee?"

"Honey, we can drink every cup of coffee in this whole country," I said. "We can ruin our kidneys stalling around. But sooner or later Mr. Whittington's seven hundred grand is going to be calling for its mate—or his kid, or whatever; let's quit trying to push fancy metaphor. We have to give up sometime." I felt pretty hopeless, all of a sudden.

We were sadder than hell. We got up from the table, signed a check, left a tip. We walked to the elevator to get Rhett's suitcase. The moppet walked between us, and each of us held one of his wee little hands.

"I like you," said Rhett.

I swallowed but there was still that lump in my gullet. Ad men are horribly emotional. It's the kind of work they do, naturally.

"I like you both," said Rhett. "And I'm going to live with you forever."

I looked at Jodi. She had that tear back, in her eye, and I didn't even try to wipe it away.

NINE

DON'T TALK TO me about fate. It's 1946 and you're offered some IBM stock at seventy percent of market price and you turn it down and today that block is worth about five million dollars more than what you would have had to pay for it, and you try to console yourself by saying it's fate, that's the way it goes with fate, you can't fight fate.

Phaugh. It ain't fate, comrade, it's *you*. You decide not to buy that stock, *you*. Nobody twisted your arm. It's just that you're an imbecile that's all.

But don't feel bad, brother of mine, don't feel badedoo, I'm an imbecile, too. We're all imbeciles, marching along arm in arm together, with Corrigan leading the way. It isn't the fluke of fate when we make a wrong decision, podnuh, it's the fickle finger when we make a *right* one.

When was the last time you made a right decision? Yeah, you, hiding over there behind that eight ball.

What gets me mad is that we didn't even talk about it. Jodi and I, I mean. We rode up in the elevator, and we were both thinking the same thought, and we both knew that the other was thinking the same thought, and we didn't even talk about it. Arm in arm, brother, imbeciles we.

You know what I'm talking about, don't act coy. Jodi and I and the little bastard, that's what I'm talking about. A series of really monumental wrong decisions had brought me thus far to Rio de Janeiro of all places, in company with a college-educated whore and a five year old basketball who wanted to live with us forever. Do you realize how long forever is? More than a *year.*

And we didn't even discuss it. Never mind right decision wrong decision, I'm not talking about that. It was far too late for a right decision by then. What we had to do was choose which wrong decision to plummet into. And the *best* wrong decision we didn't even talk about.

There are shades and shades of rightness and wrongness. Now the *blackest* wrong decision we could have made, the wrongest wrong decision, was to act sensibly, in line with our previous wrong decisions, and simply turn Everett Whittington over to his dear papa and take our next plane back to New York and never see one another again. And the *whitest* wrong decision we could have made, the rightest wrong decision, was to act with total incoherence, to run off somewhere with Rhett, and the three of us remain an unlikely trio forever. Of course, there were complications of legality and income and language and a few dozen other hurdles far too high to leap so we didn't even talk about it. *That's* what makes me so mad, brother, that we didn't even talk about it. I don't mind being an imbecile, it's part of my humanity, but I hate being a coward as well.

So I bit my tongue as a punishment, and we went up in the elevator again, and Rhett looked up at me and said, loud and clear. "Whatcha gonna do with my suitcase?" And the elevator operator glanced around, wondering too.

I said, "Hush, Rhett, we're skipping out on the bill." So then the operator figured we couldn't possibly be skipping out on the bill, so he ignored us again, and I bit my tongue harder for even more of a punishment because it wasn't a bill we were skipping out on; we were skipping out on Rhett.

Outside, a gaily colored taxi was a reminder of our gaily colored homeland far to the north. I looked at it, standing there in the Southern Hemisphere sunshine, and a strange thought went gliding unasked through my mind: *I never have liked New York.*

The lemmings rush to the sea. The bright young humans rush to New York. I think now that the lemmings have the smarter idea. Drowning is so much cleaner a death.

We boarded this northern chariot and I withdrew from my pocket the slip of paper and read from it the address, and on the second try the driver comprehended, and we jolted away into traffic.

"Where are we going?" That was Rhett.

"To see your father, dear." That was Jodi.

"Are we all going to live with my father?" That was Rhett again.

"Grrrrr." That was me.

"I don't remember what my father looks like." Rhett once more.

"Oh, Harvey." Jodi again. "Oh, *hell.*" Me.

The conversation continued in that vein, sporadically, until we turned through a blacktop turnoff between pale stone walls and along the curving drive to a low rambling white manor which lacked only the darkies' quarters out back. We emerged from the cab, and I'm certain that this time I was overcharged, and we rang the bell.

A haughty male servant allowed us ingress, and ordered us to wait upon the marble entrance hall. He went away toward the back of the house, and when he opened the distant massive door sounds of revelry poured forth, snipped off again when he closed the door once more behind him.

Guilt and indecision faded for a time from my mind, as I stood waiting for Dixon Whittington to put in his appearance. I was, like unto bird and snake, fascinated by the man. I wanted to know what he would look like. What would a corporate thief look like? What would be the physical appearance of a man who entrusted his son for a three thousand mile journey to the hirelings of mobsters? What possible face could front such a mind?

Renewed revelric reverberations signaled the reopening of the door. I looked up and saw the face I'd been wondering about.

One thing was certain. No Dorianesque painting was locked away above stairs in this villa. The face of Dixon Whittington reflected the man. The eyes, of course, were the features one noticed first. Small and nearly round, with a darkish gray-green tinge, they were set deep in the forepart of his skull, widely separated by pasty flesh. The nose was thick and veined, with flaring deep-lined wings and black gaping hair-filled nostrils. Lines of sour discontent fanned down across the flesh from his nose to the corners of his mouth. His cheeks were rounded and mottled, though meticulously shaved, and his small mouth was thick lipped, the lower lip protruding in a moneyed pout. His forehead was high and pale and gleaming, with thick black brows hung awninglike over those beetle eyes. In ridiculous contrast to the jungly underbrush of brows, his coal-black hair was plastered straight back on his bulky head in the style of Valentino.

The body on which this head sat solidly and truculently was, in a word, gross. Is that the right word? Does it get the idea across? What I'm trying to picture for you is, see, a businessman. You know what businessmen are built like, they're the ones for whom the double-breasted suit was invented. Kind of barrely. Chunky. Now, you take that businessman, and you give him a nasty mind and a life of ease and dissipation, and pretty soon that same double-breasted suit, when he puts it on, is single-breasted. And he isn't chunky any more, he's soft and flabby. Gross, in other words. But the original businessman body is still down inside there someplace. You have the feeling that if you prodded him with a finger, it would be like prodding a thick layer of dough over a honeydew melon. Soft and flabby, with the original chunkiness down underneath. Gross. See?

I looked at this thing, this seven hundred thousand dollar mistake, this Dixon Whittington, and then I looked at Rhett. The gross mistake before us had created this tiny child, and what that proves I don't really know. I'd have to see the mother first. But of course, the mother had flung herself from a window, and was unavailable for the viewing.

Come to think of it, that fact alone made the viewing unnecessary. It didn't matter what the mother looked like. Having been betrayed by this dank troll here in front of me, she had taken the easy way out, totally ignoring her own responsibility to the child she had brought into the world.

Isn't it amazing? The most utter wretches of creation, civilization's anal excretion, the vilest black souls of Newgate, still are capable with their scabrous swords and gaping maws, in an act of loveless conquest, of producing beauty and value. Rhett, now, was surely the only even remotely possible excuse for the existence of Dixon Whittington or his cowardly spouse. How had they done it? The rose on the dung pile, and it never fails.

The troll advanced. "You got him," he said. He might have said exactly the same thing, in precisely the same tone, to a servant who had finally bagged the rat in the basement.

"Yes," I said. I looked once again from father to son, and this time I looked at Jodi. She looked ill.

The troll had closed the door behind him when coming out to this hall, and now the door opened again, drenching us with another burst of alcoholic vivacity, and a slut emerged.

Here we go again. You never know, really, what words mean. Such as gross previously, which can also mean twenty of something. Or is that a score? Or a stone? Maybe a gross is twelve twelves. A hell of a point to make, at any rate.

But about words. Take slut, for instance. By dictionary definition, Jodi was a slut, and the woman who came toward us from the revels was not a slut. By dictionary definition. But dictionaries are usually wrong. I don't know whether you've ever noticed that before, but it's true. Being a Mad Ave word purveyor for so long, it was brought home to me fairly often.

A slut, for instance, is *not* a prostitute, though the dictionary might claim so. No, a slut by *usage* is a promiscuous slattern, a sloppy slobby easy make. Jodi, though she worked the midnight trampoline for pay, was not a slut. The woman who had just joined our little group *was* a slut. Not the dictionary definition. She looked like the kind of woman *you* would mean if you said the word slut. Okay?

So that's what she looked like in loose wrinkled clothing, barefoot. Black-haired, by the way. A good-looking woman about three or four years ago, before she decided to be a slut. Also, she was drunk.

She arrived and cast a jewel-fingered hand upon the troll's elbow. She smiled sickeningly at Rhett, her unfocused eyes damply gleaming. "And is this Everett?" she said, the way women like that say things like that to little children, trying to be cute and motherly simultaneously and missing both by a mile.

The troll—no, I'm not going to call him Dixon Whittington—pushed her hand away ungraciously. "Go on back to the party," he said.

She went down on one knee, but not too steadily, so she went down on both knees. Then she extended her arms—both draped with gold bracelets—toward Rhett and mulched, "I'm your new mama, honey. Come to mama."

Rhett, understandably, did his best to fade into the material of Jodi's skirt.

"Sober up first," said the troll to mamacita. He had the grace, surprisingly, to look embarrassed.

Me, too. Hadn't I brought Rhett here?

I suddenly remembered something that I had successfully managed to avoid conscious thought about for eight years. This was before Helen, when I was still a normally oversexed bachelor grinding away at the prevarication factory, finding my physical ease wherever I could, and a fellow pulser on advertising's bed of gold told me about Will Brockheimer's wife.

Will Brockheimer was then, and still is so far as I know, an accountant executive with a fantastic knack for liquor ad copy. Actually, it wasn't so fantastic as all that if you understood that by Will Brockheimer, liquor ad copy was a love letter. Will has lived on the product of the distiller's art for fifteen or twenty years by now, and I don't believe there's anything else in the world he loves half so much as booze, not even himself. And particularly not his wife.

You know how it is with booze. You drink a lot of it and then you think about sex, and you discover that the spirit is willing but the flesh is weak. There's nothing like good Scotch or rye or bourbon or blended whiskey or vodka to make you crave what you can't perform. After a while, as in Will's case, this results in even the craving fading away.

Will Brockheimer was married. Will Brockheimer was alcoholically undersexed. Will Brockheimer, so I was told, had a wife who welcomed all substitutes for her booze-limp husband. All you had to do was go along with Will one night after work. He would head immediately for the nearest bar, and drink steadily till around midnight or one in the morning. If you stayed with him, and made sure he swallowed enough to be really reeling, then of course you'd have to take him home. His wife would help you put him to bed, and then, so the scuttlebutt ran, she would help you put *her* to bed.

I heard about this interesting possibility during a particularly dry spell in my sexual life, all puns intended. And so, two days after first hearing of it, I took action. Seeing to it that I boarded the elevator with Will Brockheimer, whom I knew only casually, I started up a conversation with him on the way down to the ground, and the two of us wound up in a cozy dark joint off Madison Avenue, and Will proceeded to get smashed.

What a strange oblique seduction that was! Plying a girl with liquor in hopeful preparation of later plying her with me, that was something I understood and was familiar with. But plying a man with liquor, in hopeful preparation of later plying his wife, that was strangely twisted, and not entirely enjoyable by any stretch of the imagination.

And he wanted to talk. This man on whom I was even attaching the cuckold's horn wanted to talk to me, and I must, perforce, talk back. I must smile at him in all guile, and tell him stories, and listen to his stories, and be his pal. And all the time thrust down the quirks of conscience plucking at my mind. For isn't it drummed into us from earliest childhood that it is more important in life to get laid than anything else? Isn't copulation our chiefest goal, over mere honesty or truth or pity? Given all the choices of all the magic rings or Araby, comrade of mine, what would *your* first wish be?

And so, when at the witching hour out he passed, strode I unto the street and flagged a cab. It cost a dollar to get that worthy's worthless assistance in carting the carcass from bar to car, and then all at once I realized that I didn't know my drinking pal's address.

Are you paying attention? Not only did I cuckold this sweet and sodden creature, I even picked his pocket. Out came his wallet, and from the identification card therein I parroted the address to the surly hacky, then nicked back the dollar I'd so far paid the driver, plus another for the trip, before stuffing the wallet back into his pocket.

They lived uptown a ways on the West Side. Not too far uptown, not far enough for a police lock to be necessary or for housewives to feel frightened of tripping down to the corner grocery after dark. Just far enough uptown to be expensive without being too expensive. (I'm going around the bush this away, to be honest, because I don't properly remember exactly *what* the address was. Somewhere between Broadway and the park, between Columbus Circle and the Planetarium. Up in there.)

Will blessedly recovered somewhat by the time the cab reached his apartment building. It was at least possible, once the driver had helped me drag him out of the backseat and get him vertical on the sidewalk, for him to stand and even to walk, so long as one held onto his arm and guided him.

Entering the apartment building, the amount and intensity of qualms and queasiness I had to ignore suddenly increased, and it became effectively impossible for me to ransack Will's pockets once more, in search of keys. Instead, I found the button tagged Brockheimer and pressed it firmly.

In a moment, I heard the voice of the object of my desires, albeit electronically distorted to something similar to the croaking of a frog, and saying only: "Who is it?"

That stumped me. She didn't know my name, she didn't even know *me.* The whole project suddenly seemed absurd. I had been planning to go up to an apartment and have intercourse with a respectable married woman whom I'd never even met before. Ridiculous.

The object of my waning desires spake again, in precisely the same words: "Who is it?"

Since I couldn't answer that question, I answered another one instead: "I have your husband here, Mrs. Brockheimer."

There was a pause, and then Mrs. Brockheimer strained the building's electronics to the utmost, by forcing it to reproduce a sigh. Even through the distortion, it came through as a bitter and fatalistic sigh, a there's-no-way-out sigh. And she said, "All right. Come on up."

I wonder now what that sigh meant. Was she being fatalistic about Will, or about herself, or about me? Or all of us, equally though divergently doomed.

At any rate, she told me to come on up, and the door buzzed. I pushed, it opened, and Will plodded docilely if unsteadily to the elevator. Up seven flights we groaned, and down the hall to where she stood waiting for us.

I remember her clearly. Not because she was stunningly beautiful, for she wasn't. And not because she was startlingly ugly, for she wasn't that either. I remember her because she was so fantastically ordinary. She wore a housewife sort of dress, and old bedroom slippers, and no stockings. She had no makeup on, and her features were regular and plain to the point of invisibility. That slightly idealized housewife in the washing machine ads was this woman, without the idealization. Hair black and neither short nor long, done in a style of total anonymity. You have seen this woman a thousand times, usually in supermarkets, and you see that she was probably a striking teenager, but marriage and cookery had made her sexless. She still has the slender body and the good breasts and the clear unblemished features, but domesticity has leeched her blood, the fire is out. Or so you think. You look at her and feel none of the stirrings aroused by palpitating femininity in bikinis on the beaches. No spark shoots out from her, and so no answering spark is ignited in you, and you glance at her and that is all, you walk on.

Trepidation, I'm afraid, was the order of my day as I steered the lurching Will down the hall toward home and wife. Not only was she my drinking companion's wife, not only had she never even met me before, she was a *housewife!* Do you get it? A housewife! You don't lay housewives, for Pete's sake.

Will providentially afforded a diversion by passing out again, across his own threshold. Mrs. Brockheimer and I had to drag him into the living room. When she bent beside me to grab his arm, the loose neck of her dress fell open a bit, enough to show me the first swelling of a breast hung for the hand, strong yet yielding, full and desirable. And beneath that housewife disguise, she wore no bra!

Get thee behind me, trepidation! Housewives wear bras!

Mrs. Brockheimer, of course, had had plenty of experience of putting her husband to bed unconscious, and so she directed me in assisting her.

We half-carried and half-dragged his hulk down the hall into the bedroom, rolled it onto the bed, and stripped it. Iwas for leaving the poor man whatever dignity can be afforded by a pair of boxer shorts, but the woman stripped him naked, and thus bare and sodden he lay before us on the bed.

She tweaked a portion of his anatomy with a contemptuous linger. "Look at that thing!" she said, her voice low with controlled anger and disgust. "What good is it? I ought to cut it off him."

"The amount he drinks," I said, "he still does need it for something."

She looked at me unsmiling. "You want some coffee?"

"Yes, please."

I followed her back to the living room, where she unexpectedly turned around and said, "Do you really want coffee?"

Perhaps brutal honesty was what this woman wanted. "No," I said. "It isn't coffee I want."

"What's your name?"

"Harvey."

"Sit down here on the sofa with me, Harvey. Tell me about yourself."

We sat down, and neither of us said a word. She leaned forward, as though listening attentively, and once again the front of her dress hung away from her body. I reached out and slipped my hand inside and cupped her left breast, feeling the tip hard against my palm, the swelling slopes soft against my fingers. She smiled, then, a smile of cynicism and animal pleasure, and quickly opened my trousers. Then her face slipped down out of my vision, and her mouth was warm.

The dress was all she wore. My hand slid up her leg, beneath the dress, to equatorial climes, and busy fingers spoke in sign language. She lay half prone now on the sofa, her head in my lap, and down the slope of my side her hips twisted and writhed With my free hand I stroked the upper rise of hip, feeling the muscles moving beneath dress and flesh.

Then she sat up, all at once, and pushed my hands away, and harshly whispered, "Take your shoes off. Take them off." And leaped up to pull the dress over her head, wriggling her body energetically as she did *so*.

The housewife, with the dress, was gone. Beneath was a panther, a leopard, a cheetah. A female animal demanding the male. A musk rose from her, the scent of carnal battle. As I stood up to strip away my trousers and shorts, leaving shirt and T-shirt on—having removed my tie already and tucked it in my jacket pocket several bars ago—she dove back onto the sofa, twisting around onto her back, knees up-thrust at outward angles, belly hot and quivering, hips alive and vibrant, demanding their fulfillment. "Come on," she whispered, harshly, urgently, straining fingers reaching up for me. "Come on, *come on.*"

I came on.

It has always been my technique to tease with small nibbles, finding this works wonders in increasing the receptivity of the female, but this woman would have none of such dandification. I lowered slowly between her shaking impatient knees, pointing at my target, and she lunged upward to grab me in her hands and yank me down atop her. The legs shot out straight, then in-curved, met above my back, and locked, squeezing me down and in and under. Her arms embraced me, her mouth was hot on mine, and it seemed that she wanted to absorb me, to assimilate me entirely to pull all of me down inside her skin and make us one body.

A driving female like that destroys her own purpose, of course. Hardly had we begun when I for one was done. But that mattered not to her at all. She pulsated on, thrusting and squeezing and clamping me tight, and lo and behold I was begun again.

And a teeny tiny voice from far away across the room said, "Mommy."

I was off her like a shot, staring madly around in all directions, and seeing a teeny tiny girl-child, no more than three or four, garbed in cotton pajamas with feet rubbing her little eyes in the doorway to the bedroom.

The woman disentangled herself from me, and hurried across the room, her flanks gleaming in the dim light of the room, her half-crouch as she ran, breasts hanging, feral and magnificent. I heard the girl-child murmur sleepily, "What are you doing, Mommy?" and then the mother had removed her, and I was alone in the room.

When she came back, to tell me that the child had been put back to bed and was now definitely asleep for the night, I was smoking a cigarette and seriously studying my trousers. Though my second beginning had not yet had its finis, I too seemed to be definitely asleep for the night.

She would have none of it. She snatched the cigarette from my hand and stubbed it angrily in a tray, then knelt before me, cajoling, threatening, stroking, pleading, kissing, urging, mouthing her need, until I found myself—despite myself—coming awake again. And we finished what we had begun. I got no enjoyment from that, but we finished anyway. Because *she* wanted to, and what she wanted in that line of things she surely got.

Though she assured me I would always be welcome, I never returned to Mrs. Brockheimer. Nor did I ever manage to feel comfortable around Will Brockheimer after that. It was guilt, of course, at least partially. Guilt and embarrassment at what I had done to Will. But it was also embarrassed humiliation at what Will's wife—you know, I never learned her name?—had done to me, emasculating me, unmanning me in the very act of proving my manhood.

And the child. I hadn't known they had a child. And I had come in stealth by night to copulate upon the child's mother, and she the child had seen me and wondered what her Mommy was doing. There was a guilt and an embarrassment in that that transcended all else.

And now I felt much the same sort of feeling toward little Rhett. I looked upon the physical father to whom I was delivering this child, and the slut who would mother him, and I felt that guilt and shame and embarrassment again, and it was almost as though I could square things with both Rhett and the Brockheimer child at one.

There was only one course of action I could, in all dignity and self-respect, allow myself to take. And so I made my decision, and my course of action was chosen.

To begin with, just sort of as an opening gun, you might say, I stepped forward and punched the troll smack in the nose.

TEN

I AM NOT a violent man by nature. My earliest memories are memories of acute physical cowardice, and I have been known to go to great lengths to avoid a fight. And that is one of the tragedies of the modern world. All our brain-workers (for this is the term they persistently apply to us boys who make the yokels buy things they don't need) have gone physically soft. We are vicious enough, and we will twist a verbal knife as deftly as Cyrano ever wielded a blade, but the physical sends us scrambling for the exits. We have but one sword, and it is a poor thing used only upon women, and our hands are better at holding pencils than making fists.

A sad affair.

Which makes it all the more amazing. Because, while my fist was in the air and on the way to the nose of Dixon Whittington, a most unseemly thought raced through my feverish brain. *I won't hit him hard enough,* I thought sickly. *I haven't hit anyone in years, I don't know how anymore, and I was never much good at it to begin with. I watch Kirk Douglas movies and an occasional prize fight, but I haven't hit anybody and I am about to mess it up. I'll pull the punch or something. Or, oh, God, I'll miss him. I'll just flail at empty air and seem like a total fool.*

A lot of thinking while throwing a punch. But my thoughts stopped suddenly, you see, because my hand ached. And my hand ached because my fist had just collided quite magnificently with the nose of Dixon Whittington. The punch, by God, had landed. I hadn't, by George, pulled it.

Not a wee bit.

I stood there for a moment and merely watched things. I watched Dixon Whittington, the troll, with his thick veined nose more misshapen than ever. Blood streamed from those black hair-filled nostrils. The color combination at least was passable—like red leather seats in a black Jaguar. And I watched him reel backward, ever so slightly, until he was sitting on the floor and covering his revolting nose with a hairy paw.

I watched. And out of the corner of one eye I saw Jodi gaping and smiling at once, and reaching to take my arm. And out of the corner of my other eye I saw Rhett, laughing like an Indian and slapping his hands to his knees. And out of the corner of my third eye—

No, that's wrong.

"You socked him," Jodi was saying, hysterically.

"You socked him," Rhett was saying, jubilantly.

"Socked the old bastard," Jodi squealed.

"What's a bastard?" Rhett asked, undaunted.

The old bastard, speak of the devil, was getting to his feet. He pawed at the air with his hands, and that was a mistake because it let the blood come pouring through those black holes of Calcutta once again. There was blood on his fingers, too. I looked down at my hands, and there was blood on the knuckles of the hand I had hit him with.

"Now what the hell," the troll grunted. "Now what the hell."

"Old bastard," Rhett chirped. "Old bastard old bastard old bastard old bastard—"

Jodi covered his mouth with her hand, demonstrating again that she had a way with children. And the slut appeared in the doorway, looking thoroughly puzzled, and Dixon Whittington swung a heavy hand to the side of her face, demonstrating that he had a way with women. The slut went back, presumably, to her bottle. And the troll fixed two uncertain eyes upon me.

"I don't get it," he said.

I probably should have hit him again. But picture please the scene in its entirety. Picture driving a furious fist into the nose of a total stranger, and imagine him getting up bloody and bowed, and staring at you, and telling you he doesn't get it. Would you have hit him again? Would Kirk Douglas?

I didn't. I placed hands upon hips and played a waiting game, and he looked from me to Jodi to Rhett to Jodi to me. And then he looked at Jodi, and he seemed to be concentrating on her ample bust, and I'll be damned before I'll let a troll look at my unlawful wife that way. So I hit him.

I got that poor old nose again, and he sat down again, and there was more of that red stuff. He tried to hold it in with his hands and the damned blood leaked through his fingers. I thought of a few speeches from *Macbeth*. I tried to decide whether a person could have a fatal hemorrhage through his nostrils. And the troll stayed right where he was again, which was on the floor.

He looked up at me. Not at Jodi now. Not at Rhett.

At me.

"Listen," he said, "just tell me what it's all about. That's all."

I'D heard that question at least once before. I quite possibly had heard it on many an occasion, since a desire to know what it's all about is universal in human experience and particularly prevalent in my circle of friends, but there was one time that sprang at once to mind.

It happened at our house.

Remember the house? I've mentioned it, haven't I? The suburban hide-a-wee, the Rockland County Split-Level Colonial with wall-to-wall carpets and floor-to-ceiling walls? I'm sure I have. Our hate nest amongst the crab-grass, where Helen and I lived a life of mutual animosity in rustic splendor.

I've mentioned it, all right. But I haven't told you how we acquired it, or when. We acquired it shortly after the wedding, and we acquired it because Helen wanted it. I had wanted it myself, during those moments when visions of domestic bliss had not yet been washed away entirely by the realization that Helen was colder than a well-digger's ass in Little America. But after we left Bermuda I would have been as happy to remain in Manhattan forever.

Not so with Helen. She wanted charge accounts and heavy furniture, and she wanted a massive life insurance policy with herself as beneficiary, and above all she wanted a house.

Why, you ask, do women want houses? Why did this woman, who had no children and seemed totally uninterested in accumulating any, want a big house instead of a tidy little apartment? That house, my friend, was security. That house, holding a pair of the most secure souls who ever should have graced a psychiatrist's waiting room, was warmth and stability and everything nice, as far as my icebound bride was concerned.

You see, it's easy to run out on your wife when you live in an apartment. You pack a suitcase and you go. There's no car, because you don't own one, and there's no money tied up in the house, and you just get on a plane and don't come back. But once that breezy broad has conned you into buying a house, you're stuck with her for life. You can't put the house on your back and go away. You either leave her the house when you run or you get a divorce and divide the house down the middle. And either way she wins.

Anyway, we bought this house. We bought it during one of my relatively rare I-married-this-bitch-and-maybe-if-I-make-nice-she-won't-be-so-hard-to-live-with moods, and I would have done anything then to make her happy, so I bought a house. We went out looking for houses. We saw majestic old pre-revolutionary homes in upper Westchester with high ceilings and a view of the Hudson, and I liked them. We saw Frankllloydwrightish contemporaries with planes and angles and zip level colonial with an attached carport, and we bought it. I'll leave you to guess who liked it.

And there were we, anyway, Helen and I, in our house. Linda Holmes was a thing of the past, aborted and forgotten, and I was living the commuter's life. I put in my two hours daily on the 8:12 to New York and the 5:15 to Boondocks Station, and I mowed my crabgrass and wrote my ad copy and functioned, all things considered, as a model citizen of twentieth-century America. Suburban model, that is.

Until I discovered the next door neighbors.

Now *there's* something about Suburbia. In Manhattan I had had at least six hundred next-door neighbors, and the only one I ever knew was an old wino named McHenry who wandered into my apartment one night to borrow a cup of grog. But in Reckless Rockland you were *supposed* to love thy neighbors as thyself and simply because they had bought the house next door to you. They could be horse thieves, they could be dullards, they could be syphilitics—this did not matter. You knew them, dammit. You had to.

The Sheggittses lived next door to us. Harry Sheggitts was an engineer with a crew and a slide rule tie-clasp (does that not sum him up?)

and Bonnie Sheggitts was a lithe and limber copperhead. That is, she had copper-colored hair. She wasn't a snake, exactly.

We played bridge with the Sheggittses, and if anyone knows a better way to destroy an evening, I'll have to hear about it sometime. We played ping pong with the Sheggittses, and there's a better way than bridge, now that I think upon it. The high points came when Bonnie lurched across the table after a hard rebound, giving me a good look at her own high points. But a glance of breast-flesh covered with cotton is not enough to carry an insupportable evening.

We bowled with the Sheggittses, and we picnicked with the Sheggittses, and we drank with the Sheggittses, and if there was one thing I didn't want to see after a bitchy day at MGSR&S, it was Harry Sheggitts's pink face shining at me over his slide rule tie-clasp. I was so sick of the nuances of neighborliness that I almost missed out on my share in the Great American Dream, suburban division.

Then this Friday came around. It was one of those long lazy days in early autumn, and when I awoke with somebody else's head on my shoulders I knew at once that the bully boys at the ad farm would not see me that day. I buried face in pillow and listened to bombs going off in my head, dozing like a tired Londoner during the Blitz until nineish, whereupon I called my office and told them I had a small case of impetigo complicated by tertiary syphilis and that they wouldn't see me until Monday.

"I feel hellish," I told Helen. "I think I'll stick close to home today."

"They won't deduct from your pay, will they?"

The kind and considerate helpmate with her heart in the right place. "No," I said. "They don't exactly pay me by the hour anymore. You can relax now."

I had a slow leisurely breakfast, complicated by my inability to taste anything. I sat in the backyard and let the morning go to hell, and in mid-afternoon I was still in the backyard and Helen was out buying things. It was her favorite sport, running far ahead of guess-what, and she was good at it.

And there, Dear Reader, was Bonnie Sheggitts.

There doesn't quite narrow it down, does it? There, across the fence in her own backyard, was the copper-haired Bonnie. She was alone, stretched prone upon a terry cloth-covered chaise, wearing tight shorts and no bra. Her arms almost but not quite obscured her breasts. Her body'd been gloriously tanned—funny how you fail to notice such things while playing ping pong or bridge—and her hair was magnificent against the tanned skin, and I stood up and walked to the fence separating their yard from ours. I did this for a very simple reason. I wanted a better look at her.

And, slowly, her head turned. Her eyes opened, and looked at me, and her red mouth smiled. "Well, hello," she said.

"Hello."

"Helen home?"

"No."

"But you are, huh?"

"Didn't go to the office today." Inspired conversation, no. But we and Harry and Bonnie had somehow striven to *avoid* inspired conversation. Helen talked about shopping, and Harry mouthed platitude to the eternal glory of (1) the engineering profession (2) the Republican Party and (3) God. "Stayed home," I went on, brilliantly.

"Oh," she said. "Come on over here, Harvey, and talk to me."

I thought of climbing the fence. If I had, it would have buckled or I would have torn my slacks, or something. So I walked down our driveway and across in front of their colonial ranch—a specimen quite as absurd as our colonial split—and up their driveway, and there she was, by God, on the chaise.

"Harvey," she said, "rub my back, huh?"

The Great American Dream, suburban div. Love thy neighbor as thyself, and love thy neighbor's wife even more, and rub her back and kiss her in the kitchen and, when the opportunity arises, take her to bed. I rubbed Bonnie's back, and I felt how warmly smooth her skin was. And, like a kitten, she purred.

"I'm not a tramp," she said. "You know that, don't you?"

"Of course, Bonnie."

"But you can't imagine what it's like. Being married to Harry, I mean. It's not heaven."

"I can imagine."

"Harry the engineer. I thought it would be better than typing letters and taking dictation for the rest of my life, and I guess I was wrong. He's so dull, and in bed—you can't imagine."

My hands moved, gently, to her shoulders. They massaged, and she raised herself slightly on her elbows, and my hands moved to the tops of her breasts.

"Sex is a problem in logistics to him," she said. "Or something like that. Harry has a slide rule at his legs, Harvey."

Now there was an image with possibilities. But, muse upon it all you will, Bonnie offered too many possibilities of her own for me to think such a much of Harry. My hands had located those mammaries by now, and I held firm flesh in both hands, and nipples went stiff against my palms.

"Helen doesn't understand me," I said.

"I never thought she did."

"She doesn't. Not at all."

Now lest you think I was boyishly banal with that line, I must explain something. Remember when you laid little girls in the schoolyard, and they asked you if you loved them? You didn't, of course, but you said you did. They didn't believe it, of course, but it made things easier. Before you lay an unmarried girl, you tell her that you love her. It's a lie. She knows it's a lie. You tell her anyway because it's what she wants to hear.

My wife doesn't understand me is the *I love you* of adultery, the sine qua non of seducing your neighbor's wife. It may be true—it certainly was, in my precious case, for what it's worth—but true or false it must be whispered intensely before you pin the horns on the man next door. So we went through that sequence, and then Bouncy Bonnie rolled onto her back and I covered her breasts with my chest and kissed her for all I was worth.

"I need you," I said.

"I know. And I need you."

"Where?"

"Here."

"Too open. Too many people could drift around. Not here, Bonnie."

"Where?"

"Inside," I said. "Your house."

"Can't. The maid's cleaning the place."

So Harry Sheggitts had a maid for his wife. If the game were being played properly, the maid was young and willing and Harry was laying her from time to time. Another wrinkle in the Great American Dream.

"Your house, Harvey?"

"Sure. Fine. Helen's out, she's buying a store or two, we have plenty of time."

"Oh, good. Oh, let's hurry." This because my hands were busy, and her pulse was racing, and she was ready. And so was I.

We could have run around her colonial ranch and up my driveway, but somehow that would have spoiled things. So we leaped over the fence, and I didn't even tear my trousers, and we skipped into my split-level trap, she with her breasts bouncing and I with my tongue hanging out passionately.

Inside, I grabbed her and kissed her. Her breasts dug into my chest and her arms wound round me, and I very nearly threw her down on the floor. But there was poetry in my soul. I was married to a frigid Bridget if there ever was one, and I was about to bang the wife next door in my iceberg's security nest in the boondocks, and when you do something like that you have to do it right. So I headed Bonnie up two half-flights of stairs, since split-levels never have anything you can call a real staircase, and I steered her into the master bedroom and plunged her down on the king-size extra-length bed, and I jumped her.

Adultery can be fun. Now there's a campaign slogan, sweetie—and already I can hear the brainstorming sessions, with all of us sitting around an oaken table and talking up ways to sell adultery to the American public. Give 'em something they don't need, boyos. But adultery *can* be fun. Here I was, cheating on a wife I couldn't stand, and here Bonnie was cheating on a husband I couldn't stand, and what more could I have asked for?

Well, I'll tell you. I could have asked for privacy.

We got rid of Bonnie's shorts, and we got rid of all my clothes, and we pressed flesh against flesh and sighed together.

"Harry's dull," she moaned.

"My wife doesn't understand me," I grunted passionately.

And, with those rites out of the way, it was time. She let out a luxurious sigh and spread herself out upon her back, breasts rampant and thighs couchant. And, with the facility of an accomplished suburban do-it-yourselfer, I inserted Tenon A into Mortise B and grommeted industriously.

As we toiled together, it became obvious to me that one of two possibilities was true. Either Harry Sheggitts was neglecting this delightful female shamefully, or this delightful female was a card-carrying nymphomaniac. Because Bonnie rolled and swerved and buckled like a ship on the high seas, and moans tore from her red mouth, and she was having a high old time.

Remember an aside earlier? I mentioned, at the time, that I could have asked for privacy. This was true.

Because, just as we finished, just as a final groan tore from that throat and just as I filled her with the final evidence of my love and the last proof that, by George, my wife didn't understand me, there was a third person in the room.

Helen, natch.

"I just don't understand," Helen was saying. And I thought: See, Bonnie? I *told* you she didn't understand.

"Listen," she said. "Just tell me what it's all about. That's all."

I hadn't had an answer for Helen. We survived that domestic crisis, although the Sheggittses moved to Fairfield County not long afterward, but I had no answer at the time. But now, looking down at the bloody form of the troll, I did have an answer. God knows where it came from. Madison Avenue trains one well—I'd been thinking on my feet for years, and I knew how, by George.

"Sure," I said. "I'll tell you, you rotten bastard."

I dipped into my jacket pocket, yanked my wallet free, flipped it open and gave him a very brief peek at a card. The card entitled me to charge gasoline purchases at any Esso station in the world, but I didn't let him see all that much of it.

"Harvey Burns," I snapped. "Continental Detective Agency. You're trapped, buddy boy. You're coming back to the States and you're going to be in jail for ages. You'll die there, you bastard."

"You're crazy." blubbered the troll.

"Yeah?"

"I can't be extradited. I—"

"You can be snatched." I told him. "And that's what's happening. You can be marched out of here at gunpoint."

"That's illegal."

I gave him a lopsided grin. Not like Kirk Douglas now, but more like Bogart in *The Maltese Falcon*. "So's larceny," I drawled, sort of. "And I got a hunch that nobody's going to care how illegal the snatch is, Dixon boy. Once you're back in the States, nobody's going to ask how you got there, and nobody's going to listen when you try crying to them. You're going to die in jail, you bastard."

Ever see a man die inside right before your eyes? The troll did that. His whole face went as red as his bloody nose, and then it turned white, and I thought he was going to do the heart attack bit right before our very. But old Dixon was made of sterner stuff. He swallowed, and he gulped, and he drooled a little, and then his eyes grew crafty.

"Listen." he said, "we could make a deal."

"No deal."

"I've got a lot of money," he said, neatly baiting the trap he had already gotten caught in. "Do you know how much money I took from that corporation?"

"Seven hundred thou."

"That's right."

"So?"

He wet his lips with a nervous tongue. "That's a lot of money," he said.

"I know. That's why they want to toss you in the tank and throw the key away."

"A lot of money," said he, cringing. "I could…I could give you some of that money. You could go away, and I could stay here, and then—"

"No deal," I said. But I made it sound weak. And bit by bit I let him twist my arm until he had me right where I wanted him. No business crook in creation is ever the match of a larcenous ad man. It'sour forte.

"I could give you twenty thousand dollars," he said. He was standing up now, albeit shakily, and I replied to his offer with a punch in the nose. When he got up, fresh blood flowing through those nasal passages, he offered fifty thou. Instead of hitting him I told him to double it, and he was too nervous to haggle. He sent a servant for a suitcase full of money. One hundred thousand pretty dollars. A fat round sum.

"We got to take the kid," I said. "You know—I have to say you skipped and I couldn't find you, so I can hardly leave the kid. It won't work."

"Take the little bastard," the troll said.

"You don't mind?"

"Take him and shove him," the troll said. "I need him like a hole in the head. If it weren't for that little bastard I wouldn't be shelling out a hundred thousand dollars. Bury him someplace, the little bastard."

That almost got him another punch in the nose, but he would never have understood. So we left, with Jodi toting Rhett by the hand and with me toting the suitcase by the handle. I had Rhett's suitcase, too. And we loaded ourselves and Rhett and the suitcases into a passing hack, and back we went to the hotel.

It had been a lovely morning.

"Harvey," Jodi was saying, "I think you're the cleverest and most wonderful man in the world."

I told her that, in all probability, she was quite correct. We were in the hotel room, and Rhett was making a fist and pummeling me in the stomach. I had shown him how to keep his thumb outside his fingers and how to put all his strength into his punch, but he wasn't doing much damage.

"Bastard," he said, belting me. "Bastard."

He was cuter than a bedbug.

"Harvey?"

"Mmmmm."

"What do we do now?"

"We don't go back to the States," I said.

"Good."

"Because I'm sick of Helen, and of advertising."

"I'm sick of Al," she said. "And of whoring."

"I'm sick of New York," I said. "And Rockland."

"We could stay in Brazil—"

"I think I could learn to get sick of Brazil," I said. "The troll lives here, and that alone could do it. Besides, all these old Nazis. They get to me."

"What do we do then, Harvey?"

I moved Rhett gently out of the way and gripped her by her warm shoulders. "We have passports," I said. "Passports for Harvey Christopher and Jodi Christopher and Rhett Christopher, as fine a family group as I've ever imagined. We have a suitcase filled with money, and it will take us well nigh forever to spend all of it. I'm sure we'll manage."

"You've got blood on your knuckles," Jodi said.

"True."

"My poor hero," she said. "Harvey, are you in a terrible rush to get out of Brazil?"

"Well—"

"Rhett," she cooed, "go sit in the bathroom for a while like a good little boy. Your father and I have something to do."

"Is he my father?"

"Sure," I said. "I'm your father, and this beautiful woman is your mother."

"Then who was the old bastard?"

"Just an old bastard," I said. "Now go in the bathroom like a good boy."

He went into the bathroom like a good boy, and I went into Jodi like a good man, and the world went into a tailspin, like the good little world it was.

That night we caught a plane to Buenos Aires, and we tried Argentina for size, but there were even more old Nazis around and they depressed me. So we went to Chile next, and we found a nice city in Chile, and we're there now.

"Suppose they come looking for us," Jodi asked once. "Suppose they want to take us back."

"It'll never happen."

"No?"

"No. Bigamy isn't something they extradite you for, and neither is desertion."

"How about extortion and kidnapping?"

I told her the troll would never make much fuss on either count, and this pacified her. But just to make sure we've applied for Chilean citizenship. A nice country, Chile. Peaceful and quiet. You have to get used to the idea of snow in June and hot weather for Christmas but if the seasons are upside-down at least the rest of life is on more of an even keel than it ever was in New York.

So here we are, in Chile. We rented a cute little bungalooloo on the outskirts of town and I've been planting shrubbery around it and doing other things to make it a place to live in. Rhett's at school now and speaks Spanish like a native of modern-day Manhattan, and he's been teaching us. He scared one teacher a little, asking her how to say bastard in Spanish, but we weathered the crisis and all is well. Life is real and life is earnest, and it's a pleasant switch.

I won't tell you the name of the town, because you might be something of a troublemaker. I don't think you could make much trouble even if I did, but we Ulcer Gulch boys are a rough breed and I take no chances. It's a town, and we like it here. That's all you have to know.

I'm happy, Jodi's happy, and little Rhett is happy. A splendid little group. We watch 3½ hours of television every day, we use Breeno Toothpaste, and—regular as clockwork—our washing machine clogs up from too many suds.

You don't believe it? In *Chile?* Chile's the end of the *world,* fer Pete's sakes, right? Never even heard a' electricity, correct?

You better believe it, buddy, because if you *don't* believe it, maybe the way you live isn't so hotsy-totsereeny after all, right?

So keep your nose to the old grindstone, and run yourself up the flagpole and see who salutes you. I'd say it's been fun, but it hasn't, and it's fun now, and I'm happy.

And that is why I never did get back to the office.

But on Mad Ave we always did take long lunch hours.